TEMPTATION'S TOUCH

Calinda luxuriated in the over-sized tub before pulling the cord to rinse her hair. She leaned backward, eyes closed, as the water splashed over her long tresses.

"Need me to hold that rope for you?" Lynx asked.

"How dare you come in here!" she shrieked, releasing the cord to sink down into the water. "You're a devil, Lynx Cardone."

He chuckled softly and winked at her. His fingers grazed her flushed cheek as he moved wet curls from her upturned face. His fingers made disturbing contact with her moist shoulder, then slipped down her back as he asked, "Need any help scrubbing your back?"

He leaned toward her, closing his mouth over hers. Her lips eagerly surrendered to his as he pulled her closer. The kiss became demanding and urgent, as did his passion. His lips caressed her face and roamed over her silken flesh.

He groaned in mounting desire. "You're a dangerous temptation, Calinda Braxton," he murmured hoarsely.

"So are you, Lynx Cardone," she replied in a strained voice. "More than you'll ever know . . ."

Janelle Taylor

FIRST LOVE, WILD LOVE

ZEBRA BOOKS
KENSINGTON PUBLISHING CORP.

For:

Tony W. and Stanley W.,
my terrific brothers and best friends
who shared my "tomboy" days.

and for:

Peggy C. and Sylvia T.,
two very special friends for many years.

ZEBRA BOOKS

are published by

Kensington Publishing Corp.
475 Park Avenue South
New York, N.Y. 10015

Copyright © 1984 by Janelle Taylor

First printing: October 1984

Printed in the United States of America

I wish to express my gratitude to the staff of the Texas Ranger Museum in Waco and to the staffs of many Texas Tourists Bureaus across the Lone Star State for graciously and unselfishly sharing their time, knowledge, and research materials with me. I also wish to thank Debby Pitzer for sharing interesting facts about Texas and the famed Rangers, of whom her uncle was a past member. I'm indebted to Trace Taylor for supplying the Spanish dialogue. For their assistance on the history of Texas railroads and factual train robberies, I am beholden to Oliver Brown and Anne Jones.

"... The character of the Texas Ranger is now well-known by both friend and foe. As a mounted soldier he has had no counterpart in any age or country. Neither Cavalier nor Cossack, Mameluke nor Moss-trooper are like him; and yet, in some respects, he resembles them all. Chivalrous, bold, and impetuous in action, he is yet wary and calculating, always impatient of restraint, and sometimes unscrupulous and unmerciful. He is ununiformed, and undrilled, and performs his active duties thoroughly, but with little regard to order or system. He is an excellent rider and a dead shot. His arms are a rifle, Colt's revolving pistol, and a knife."

— Giddings, "Sketches"

"A Texas Ranger can ride like a Mexican, trail like an Indian, shoot like a Tennessean, and fight like a devil."

— observation of a noted Texas Ranger

SILVER SPURS AND RED SATIN

Adorned in Red Satin, part woman, part child;
Meeting by chance in a land raw and wild.
Without her red satin, she captured his heart;
Tall, golden stranger branding love's mark.
Stolen moments together, Duty tearing them apart;
Passion burning brightly, Flame of his heart.

The gunslinger, a loner, skilled in diversity;
A hero in an age of a half-savage country.
Symbol of Justice, so strong and so vital;
Averting violence with iron will and metal.
His ivory-handled Colts flashing a deadly glint of
steel;
A shiny star, his trademark on a silver heel.

Becoming a woman, both cautious and just;
With grit, trading chantilly for denim and dust.
Unaware of her bonds to a prosperous empire;
Breaking her spirit, tho' challenge her desire.
Drifting in and out of her life, this golden stranger;
By Fate or his purpose, there to rescue her from
danger.

Dark secrets of the past gradually unfold;
No more haunting memories ravish his soul.
Black magic Ranger, deft in his art;
Lady in Red Satin, Flame of his heart.
Fast rides the Ranger through an unsettled town;
To trade in Silver Spurs for her Red Satin gown . . .

— Penny M. Thomas and Janelle Taylor

Chapter One

May, 1878

Unusually warm and humid weather assailed the four people confined inside the jolting stagecoach for Fort Worth. The steady pounding of hooves mingled with the creaking of wood and the grinding of metal to noisily assault the passengers' ears. Deep ruts in the well-travelled road prevented all comfort, even if the hard wooden benches would allow any. The narrow, oblong windows refused to allow any refreshing breezes that might have soothed irritable minds and cooled damp bodies. Although the distance between Dallas and Fort Worth was only twenty miles, the bumpy journey seemed lengthy and monotonous. By now, muscles were stiff, bodies were bruised, and restless minds sought any source of distraction.

Hoping to improve her comfort, Calinda Braxton shifted against the torturous seat as she courteously pretended to listen to the droning voice of Cyrus Peabody as the boastful man spun his enlarged yarns of the West, Texas in particular. Seemingly endowed with endless vitality, the gregarious newspaperman embellished his accounts of many violent episodes in the area's past and present. Although Cyrus sounded as if he had personally staged and reported those deadly events, Calinda thought he was full of hot air. Without a doubt, at the first sign of trouble or peril, a bold yellow stripe would shine brightly down the back of the talkative owner of the *Austin Examiner.*

As Cyrus droned on and on, Calinda assumed a pleasant and attentive look as her mind wandered hundreds of miles from the bleak reality and loneliness before her. As much as she wished she could prevent their intrusion, the haunting memories came calling once more. Resigned to their relentless invasion, Calinda allowed her mind to retrace her puzzling and painful past.

Calinda vainly attempted to recall life with her father, Elliott Braxton, whom she hadn't seen since 1863 when he had demanded his wife and four-year-old child sail to relatives in England to avoid the war that was spreading viciously and rapidly toward their Georgia home. The following fifteen years had passed slowly, as she grew from a skinny and awkward child with carrot-colored braids to a graceful and bright young lady with golden red curls.

She wondered if her vague recollections of her father were a result of a poor memory or a defensive effort to protect herself from anguish. Without her locket, could she even envision his image? She touched the golden object beneath her dress. How cruel for a father to be only a face in a locket.

After the Civil War, her father had written to say he

was heading for Texas to buy land and build a new home; he would send for them when all was ready and safe. As the years passed, his letters grew more and more infrequent, until finally none came at all. Calinda's uncle had written to her father to reveal her mother's sudden death in 1870. Elliott's last response had been, "Since Calinda is only eleven and this area is too rough for a child, please keep her in school there until I am firmly established here and can come for her."

Calinda had borne her loneliness, disappointments, and grief and completed her schooling. But Elliott had not kept his promise; he had never come for her or sent for her. Now, Calinda was almost nineteen and school had been over since last summer. It was time to discover the reason for her father's five years of silence. Rankin Cardone was the only clue to her father. She had nothing to lose in England. To begin a new life, she must settle her old one. The first step along her daring journey was to seek out Rankin.

Whether or not Elliott Braxton admitted it or desired it, she was his responsibility, one ignored too long. How did she feel about this stranger who was her father? What if he didn't love her or want her? No, that was unthinkable, unacceptable.

When her uncle, verging on financial destitution, had sailed for America in April to settle some pressing business, he sought to relieve himself of one financial burden which he said he had covered long enough and brought Calinda along so she could join her father. Calinda had been only too happy to begin a search for her errant father and to be free of her relatives' guardianship. She was grateful to be away from the Simpsons' control and selfish demands. Her aunt and uncle would have been only too glad to keep her around if

11

she had agreed to wed one of the wealthy suitors who came courting, one who might be persuaded to divest the Simpsons of their careless money problems in exchange for Calinda's coveted hand in marriage.

The Simpson family had never approved of Elliott Braxton. To make matters worse, Miranda Braxton and her four-year-old child had been "dumped" on them during a terrible period of history, then practically "ignored and abandoned by that selfish, worthless rake." As long as Miranda was able to protect Calinda and Elliott sent money for their support, their existence in England had been tolerable. But after Miranda died and Elliott halted his support and letters, matters had slowly deteriorated.

After arranging Calinda's train passage to Dallas, Thomas Simpson had placed Calinda in charge of her own safety and fate. In Dallas, she purchased a stagecoach ticket to Fort Worth; from there she would send word to the Cardone Ranch. In her father's last letter, he had written that Rankin Cardone was his "closest friend and eventual partner in a cattle spread west of Fort Worth." In that letter he had promised Calinda that she would come to live on the Cardone Ranch in Texas just as soon as the partnership was finalized and she had completed her schooling in England. Why had her father ignored her since then? Soon she would have answers.

Despite her eagerness and suspense, the trip west had been uncomfortable and intimidating. Along the way, Calinda had purchased books and newspapers to acquaint herself with her imminent new surroundings. The gentle and impressionable girl had been alarmed and dismayed to read of a rugged, lawless land. The paper novels had recounted tales of infamous outlaws, vengeful Indian raids, greedy cattle-rustling, lynchings and riots, brazen gunfights on town streets, and bloody battles with Mexicans. But there were also stories of heroic men who fought against immense odds and under terrible conditions for "law and order."

Calinda halted her mental roamings to listen to Cyrus' versions of recent train-robberies conducted by a gang of unknown desperadoes. There had been four daring attacks around Dallas since February. Cyrus almost sounded disappointed that their train hadn't been attacked. Calinda smiled to herself. She had a feeling Cyrus would have fainted from fear if one of those bandits had stuck a gun to his hawkish nose and demanded his money or his life.

Calinda was delighted her stay in Dallas, the self-appointed headquarters for large groups of heavily-armed detectives and bounty hunters, had been brief. The town was bursting with Pinkerton detectives, railroad detectives, bounty hunters, a U.S. marshal with countless deputies, special agents from the express companies, and secret agents from the U.S. government. Strangely, she hadn't seen even one Texas Ranger.

To distract Cyrus from his monotonous narration, Calinda asked him about the Texas Rangers. Cyrus was only too willing to expose his opinions and knowledge, especially to a beautiful woman. He recognized fine breeding and intelligence when he met them. But never had he faced them in such a charming and beautiful package. He had furtively admired the arresting contrasts of Calinda's stunning appeal many times along this route. Her eyes were large and expressive, colored like velvety green leaves. The softness and

13

shading of her unmarred complexion enchanted him. She possessed a body destined to be envied by women and desired by men. Her tumbling curls were light auburn with highlights of brassy gold; when the sun danced over them, they glowed as if containing an inner fire. Surely it was a punishable crime to look like Calinda Braxton, a sinful temptation! He leaned forward as he spoke, anxious to impress her.

"The Rangers started back in '35; they were dissolved during the War. But when the military pulled out and things got real bad, the Rangers were reactivated in '74. They're a special unit of men, around four or five hundred for the entire state." He grinned.

"How large is Texas?" Calinda asked.

"Bigger than the country of France," Cyrus boasted.

"If you have marshals and sheriffs, why do you need special Rangers? Are things that awful here?" she inquired worriedly.

"This territory's big and wild. Sheriffs have to remain near their own towns. Marshals usually work the big towns or deal with the problems that affect the American government, like the theft of U.S. mail and money. Rangers can go anywhere. Rangers don't bow to anybody or anything. They're feared and hated by outlaws throughout the state. Whenever there's trouble, a Ranger isn't far behind," he said proudly.

"I haven't seen one yet," Calinda remarked.

"Probably wouldn't know if you did. They don't wear uniforms, just lots of weapons. Some say they make their own law, but they do their duty. Braver, more cunning men were never born."

"They sound like powerful and proud men," she commented, pleased to have gotten Cyrus talking

14

about something so interesting.

"The ones I've met are surprisingly modest and reserved. They are very intelligent, and most are well-educated men from the best families. A Ranger can stare death in the face and never bat an eye."

"You make them sound infallible," she pressed curiously.

"They're cool-headed and wary. Most of them work alone or in small groups. One Ranger can bluff or capture five to ten desperadoes just on his reputation as a Ranger. Sometimes they don't even have to fight or shoot; a Texas Ranger turns even a smug and desperate outlaw into a coward. They never give up on any mission, even into hell. I've printed true stories about one or more Rangers riding into a riotous mob or large band of marauding Indians or Mexican bandits and winning the fight. I've heard they would die before yielding to any threat. We westerners are known for our courage and daring," he bragged.

Calinda was about to ask Cyrus about Rankin Cardone when shots rang out behind the stagecoach. The driver whipped the team of horses into a swift run, his shouts encouraging the animals to move faster. The two male passengers were nearly tossed into the laps of the two females as the stage thundered precariously down the road. The guard and outlaws exchanged ominous gunfire as the bandits closed in on their target. The combined din of metal, wood, gunfire, and hooves nearly drowned out the driver's commands to the six-horse team. The landscape flashed by so rapidly that it became a blur of abundant ecru and scanty green.

As Calinda turned to glance out the window, Cyrus grabbed her shoulder and shouted to keep her hands off the windows or she might lose a finger or two. Calinda's dark emerald eyes widened. "They're shooting at us?" she asked incredulously.

"Keep your head down; don't give them an easy target!" Bill Farns, a Fort Worth merchant, yelled at her as he slumped in the wooden seat, silently praying the baggage bound to the rear would prevent a lethal bullet from entering his back.

As if this were a common occurrence, the two men began looking for hiding places for their money and valuables. Neither man drew his weapon. Apparently, they had no desire to fight. Everything seemed predestined: the exchange of gunfire, the futile and mandatory flight of the stagecoach, and the inevitable surrender.

The other female passenger didn't panic — she had nothing worth stealing. Calinda had even given her money for food at their last stop. Twenty-year-old Callie O'Hara was heading for her new job at the Red Satin Saloon in Fort Worth. Calinda had tried to converse with the remote and haughty Irish lass several times during their trip, but Callie was decidedly cold. Now she just stared straight ahead, seemingly unfazed by the danger they all faced.

Several bullets smashed into the fleeing stagecoach. The mingled noises of horses' hooves and gunfire drew closer. Above the clamor, the guard shouted, "I'm hit!," then his Winchester was silent.

But the stubborn driver continued his hasty fight toward town. As the perilous drama raged on, Calinda stared at the two men inside the coach. "Why aren't you shooting at them?" she demanded.

"Won't do any good," Bill vowed fearfully. He had stuffed his money into his boot and covered it with his

16

pants leg. Pale and shaky, he was clinging to the seat for dear life.

Calinda tried once more. "They're shooting at us; we could get killed! Why won't you defend us? You heard the guard—he's wounded. This stage can't out-run their horses. We'll be robbed!"

"Robbed is better than murdered," Cyrus informed the naive Calinda. "If we fire at them, they'll make us pay when we're stopped. It's best to give in and let them take what they want."

"Give me your gun. I'm not afraid to defend myself. I'm not a coward. They won't rob me without a fight," she bravely shouted.

"You gonna kill 'em?" Bill Farns sneered. "That's the only way to stop 'em. All you have to do is wound one of them and they'll fight like crazed cocks. You ain't gonna get us killed playing heroine."

Before Calinda could voice her outrage, the stage slowed to a halt. The exhausted team was lathered and wheezing; it was time to surrender. The stage was in-stantly surrounded by a masked gang of eight men. Each bandit had two pistols pointing at the driver and his anxious charges. When one outlaw demanded that their guns be tossed to the ground, all four men com-plied.

Next, the stage occupants were ordered to step out-side. The driver and wounded guard remained on their lofty perch. The two male passengers descended to the dusty ground, then helped the two women out. One outlaw, probably their leader, prodded his horse for-ward to within a few feet of the small group. Above his black bandanna, his eyes showed cold amusement as they viewed the terror of the two men, mild indif-ference as they drifted over Callie, and visible pleasure as they slowly raked over the auburn-haired treasure.

Calinda trembled, but her face appeared impassive and her poise unruffled. She didn't like the way the bandit leader was staring at her. For an instant, she was relieved she hadn't shot at them and drawn their anger. Then she decided that armed resistance might have driven them away.

Two outlaws remained on their horses as guards while the others dismounted to carry out their plans. The driver was ordered to hand down the U.S. mail and a strongbox with money. The male passengers were searched and relieved of their money and watches. Callie convinced the bandit before her that she was penniless and jewel-free. The self-assured leader then approached Calinda, holding out his hand for her drawstring purse and jewelry.

There was still a glow in his eyes which Calinda noticed and dreaded. Still, she moved her purse behind her slender back and obstinately shook her head, tawny red curls shimmering over her shoulders with her defiant movement. The leader's eyes registered surprise, then humor.

"The money, Ma'am," he demanded as he holstered his weapon, placed his hands on his hips and assumed a confident stance.

"No," Calinda refused. "It's mine."

"You'll have your life if you obey before my patience wears out," he retorted mirthfully.

He was playing with her. She was sure he was grinning beneath that triangular mask and her chin jutted out in continued rebellion. "I've never heard of outlaws murdering innocent women over a small amount of money," she boldly bluffed.

"Give it to him, Miss Braxton," Cyrus anxiously encouraged.

"No," Calinda recklessly stood her shaky ground. Violence was an unknown force to her, one she failed to recognize or wisely respect.

"Need some help with that little filly?" another bandit offered, laughing. A chorus of chuckles filled the stuffy air, altering the mood of the leader.

"I'm in a hurry, Miss B. I don't normally go around roughing up beautiful women, but I can if you force me. The jewelry and money," he demanded imperiously, his voice and gaze now chilly.

Calinda took a few steps backward and shook her head. If she were going to be robbed, it wouldn't be with her cooperation! Besides, she needed what little money there was in the purse. She would be in a terrible state if her father had left this area. She tried to reason with him. "Please, it's all I have until I can locate my father. I don't have any friends or relatives here. If you take the money, how will I survive? Surely my meager cash cannot be that vital to you?"

A curious look filled the insolent stranger's eyes. He almost appeared tempted not to rob her. "Sorry, Miss B," he finally said, then reached for the purse she clutched tightly behind her.

Calinda struggled for possession of the purse. Within moments, she found herself breathless, her dress torn, and her purse in the hands of the leader. One man held her securely while the leader removed a sapphire ring and an inexpensive cameo brooch.

Finally realizing she was helpless, Calinda ceased her resistance. But her torn dress had revealed a hidden treasure, more precious to Calinda than the money or other jewelry — a locket with her parents' picture. The bandit snatched it, leaving a gradually

19

reddening streak on her ivory neck. Calinda fought with renewed determination and strength.

"Take the money and jewels, but not the locket. Please . . ."

The outlaw eyed the gold locket in his sweaty palm, then the beseeching look on the girl's face. He flipped it open, and saw the reason for her battle. "Your folks dead?" he unexpectedly asked.

Hoping her answer would convince him to return the prized locket, she nodded, her entrancing eyes misty. "Please don't steal it," she pleaded softly.

"If you hadn't cost me so much time and trouble, I wouldn't." After checking her purse, he glanced at her and asked, "This all the money you have? Any hidden? Maybe I should search you."

His words sent shivers of alarm over Calinda. She went rigid and silent, wondering if he would carry out his petrifying threat. "No," he said then. "You wouldn't have fought for this measly bit of money if you had more." He chuckled when she exhaled loudly in relief. "Let 'er go."

As she was released, Calinda surged forward to snatch the locket. When the outlaw instinctively reacted to her unexpected attack, she was shoved backwards and landed with a loud thud against the stage. This harsh treatment instantly spurred the injured guard into action; he reached for a concealed rifle. One of the outlaws shot him before he could take aim.

Calinda screamed and ran to kneel over the fallen man. The locket hadn't been worth a man's life. She looked up at the masked leader in disbelief, her face white and her expression frozen. For a moment, no one spoke or moved as Calinda Braxton stared at the notorious Sam Bass. What shocked her most was the outlaw's total lack of remorse or concern, which he flaunted with a cocky stance and laughing eyes. Clearly and belatedly, she knew this man was lethal and ruthless.

Driven beyond all caution and wisdom, Calinda stood up and squared her shoulders proudly. Glaring coldly at the bandit, she held our her hand. "Give me the locket; he paid for it with his life."

"You're a stupid girl, Miss B. I've killed more men than you have fingers and toes. Don't tempt me to add a female notch to my gun," he warned.

"You murder men, then boast about it? You're an animal," she sneered.

Sam's eyes appraised this girl who was as stubborn and brave as any of his men. He respected courage, except when it was a hindrance. To end this crazy stand-off, he shoved Calinda aside. She fell backward and struck her head against the stage wheel, then slid unconscious to the ground. Sam resisted the urge to check her injury and ordered his gang to search the baggage.

More money and valuables were added to the gang's pile as they looted the men's luggage. When they opened Calinda's, the thieves were delighted with the expensive gowns and frilly lingerie and took Calinda's baggage as gifts for their women.

When Calinda awoke, all she had was the dirty, torn dress she wore. Unable to stem her anger, she berated the two men for their cowardice, but was told she had only herself to blame for her injuries and losses. Callie O'Hara remained silent and watchful. She was glad to see the gently-reared beauty defeated, but didn't dare show her viciousness before the men who might be her customers. The driver carried the guard's body on the stage, shaking his head at the rash loss of life; still he felt a begrudging respect for Calinda's courage. Bill, however felt no such admiration.

"If you hadn't fought them, they probably wouldn't have searched our baggage. Or stolen yours for spite. If that guard hadn't tried to help you, he wouldn't be dead," Bill angrily heaped his charges on Calinda to ease his own humiliation. It galled any man to play a coward, even if he was one.

"If you two had helped the guard shoot at them, we might have scared them off!" she shouted back at him. "Those outlaws wouldn't be so bold if they weren't allowed to rob people like us so easily!"

"You fought 'em, and what did it get you?" Bill scoffed.

"One person couldn't battle eight, but four could have. Besides, at least I have some pride."

"That's all you have left, girly," the driver added sullenly.

"Stop this bickering. We've got to get to town and tell the sheriff," Cyrus interrupted their quarrel. "Maybe the posse can help us."

Calinda sat in the corner as they made their pensive trip into Fort Worth. At least she could get that much closer to her father and the Cardone Ranch. She would contact the sheriff and have him send word to Rankin Cordone of her arrival, if her letters hadn't already reached him. But what would she do until help reached her? She felt vulnerable, doubtful, and afraid. She certainly couldn't ask Bill or Cyrus for assistance, not after her brazen tirades and insults. Perhaps they had been wiser after all. Perhaps it was best to swallow pride and allow the bandits their way until the law could pursue them. It was clear her resistance had been futile and costly.

After their late arrival in Fort Worth, Calinda's problems mounted by the hour. The town was rough and the men rowdy, just like the descriptions in the paper novels. She didn't know anyone, except the passengers, who had all disappeared. Even the stage office was closed by the time she discovered that the sheriff and his deputies had been out pursuing bank robbers since that morning. Most of the stores were closed.

Dusk was gradually enveloping the town, and the streets were slowly filling with noisy men and horses. She could hear music, but it was coming from run-down saloons. Calinda had approached two boarding houses and one hotel, to learn none of them would accept her presence with only the promise of repayment when her father arrived. To her further alarm, Calinda discovered that her father's name was unknown in town. And when she mentioned Rankin Cordone, she was met with skepticism. It was apparent her father was not that powerful man's partner. Her claims only inspired mistrust and her apprehensions and doubts increased with the shadows.

Calinda stood on the wooden walkway pondering her next move. Angry and frightened, she had no place to go. Several men paused to offer crude solutions to her predicament. What kind of place was this? Would no one help a young woman in terrible straits, a woman robbed near their town, a woman without family or money? Did they feel no concern or responsibility toward her? Soon, any hope for assistance vanished as family people went home for their evening meal. Only saloon girls and cowpokes were on the street. Calinda honestly didn't know what to do or where to turn. She berated herself for her dwindling courage, independence, and resourcefulness.

"You be Miss Braxton?" a gruff voice inquired from behind.

Calinda turned and nodded, tears misting her eyes. A hefty woman with faded blonde hair and a painted face stepped forward. Her scarlet dress was snug-fitting over her round body. Yet there was a gentleness in her expression as she smiled at Calinda.

"I be Nelle O'Hara, Callie's cousin. Callie told me 'bout yore troubles on the stage and the money you give her. Women like us don't git such kindness from ladies like you. I owns the Red Satin Saloon down the street. You be welcomed ta stay there till you kin locate yore kinfolk. The place's noisy, but she's clean and safe. Won't nobody harm you whilst you're under my roof." Nelle kept it to herself that the ungrateful and cold-hearted Callie had laughed at Calinda's predicament.

"I . . ." Calinda started to refuse her generous invitation, but fell silent. How could she stay in such a place. How could she not? It was the only help she had been offered. She couldn't stand here all night in this dangerous cowtown. "I don't have any money to pay you." Calinda was beginning to understand the full extent of the danger she was in today. Still, she had to stay until she could locate Rankin.

"Don't you be worryin' yore pretty head none. You kin stay with us till the sheriff gits back, then he kin help you. I knows it ain't the kind of place you're used to, but you'll be safe. I seed you standin' here alone and scared; folks 'round these parts don't take ta strangers, not without some price I doubts you'd be wantin' ta pay. Decent folks, me big toe. Can't even help a lady in trouble," Nelle muttered. As she awaited the girl's answer, Nelle shifted uneasily. Maybe this girl reminded her too much of her own daughter who was back East in school, away from the crude life in a saloon.

"But how can I repay your kindness?" Calinda fretted anxiously.

"No need. Jus' come along. We'll git you a hot bath and some warm victuals. I'll have Maggie stitch yore dress fur you. By mornin' you'll be feelin' sunny," she said confidently, taking Calinda in tow.

Nelle and Calinda made their way to the Red Satin Saloon and went inside. They walked through the noisy crowd of working girls, appropriately attired in red satin dresses trimmed in black lace, and rough-looking men. Calinda's face flamed as men approached them to check on Darlin' Nelle's newest girl. Nelle quickly and cheerfully corrected the bewitched cowboys and fancy gamblers. Embarrassed and vexed, Calinda cautiously held her tongue and temper, not daring to offend her only source of help.

Calinda tightly gripped her torn dress as the two women wove through tables and chairs in the cluttered room, then climbed the stairs and walked down a long hallway. Nelle halted before a door and unlocked it. She went inside and motioned for Calinda to follow her. Nelle lit two lanterns and turned to smile genially at the exhausted girl. Calinda was glancing around, pleased and surprised to find the room was nicely furnished and exceptionally clean.

"See, tain't so bad," the older woman encouraged.

Calinda smiled at her and nodded.

"You makes yoreself at home, Miss Braxton," Nelle said. "I'll fetch you some hot food and a bath. Jus' rest

25

and calm yourself. You've had a rough day."

As Nelle was leaving, Calinda said, "Thank you, Nelle, and please thank Callie for me."

Nelle chuckled and smiled again. After she'd gone, Calinda dropped into a plush chair and stared into space, trying to relax her tense mind and body. She hadn't moved when Nelle and a black man appeared with her food and a wooden tub. Nelle chatted freely while Calinda ate and the man hauled in hot water for the tub. Nelle actually blushed when she handed Calinda a red satin dancehall dress like ones they'd seen below and a fiery-colored flimsy nightgown edged with what looked like wicked ebony lace.

"I'm sorry, Miss Braxton, but that's all the clothes I has ta offer here at the saloon. I'll have yours repaired and washed and I'll return 'em in the mornin'." They talked a while longer and Calinda told her about the robbery and her motives for coming West alone, touching the tender-hearted Nelle with her plight and courage.

Calinda thanked her again before Nelle left her. After the bath, Calinda slipped into the seductive dress that exposed the upper portion of her creamy bosom, unable to put on the revealing nightgown. Soon, a knock sounded at her door. Apprehensive, she asked who was there. It was a drunken customer at the wrong room. For a time, he was determined to come inside and he rattled the doorknob and bumped the door with his shoulder. As he spouted curses at the delay, the besieged girl cringed against the wall, trying to shut out his vulgar words. For a horrifying moment, she feared he was going to break down the door and assault her, but Nelle came along and pointed him in the right direction, then entered to calm Calinda's distraught nerves.

After the tub and water were removed by the lanky black man, Nelle stayed with Calinda, who was suddenly overcome by all that had happened. She began to shake and cry softly, and her distress tugged at Nelle's heart. Although she could be a tough businesswoman, and was stern with her working girls, Nelle was also a gentle and caring person. She just couldn't afford to show it most of the time.

"You poor child," Nelle softly encouraged. "That noise'll go on far into the nite. I brung some medicine to calm yore nerves and help you sleep. I knows you must be bone-tired and scared stiff."

At Nelle's order, Calinda managed to force down a teaspoon of laudanum. "Now, you git ready fur bed. This here's a private room; my friend won't mind you using it while he's away. Don't you fret none; you'll be fine when the sun shows its face. I'll take you ta see the sheriff. Afore you kin think, you'll be home safe agin."

Nelle left Calinda alone. As she lumbered down the hallway, she worried over the fact that she had placed Calinda in the privately rented room of a special customer, an irresistibly handsome loner who wasn't supposed to show up for weeks. But it was the only room fit for such a charming lady. And the mysterious cowboy would never know.

Nelle sighed as she thought about him. That golden stallion was a complex and private man, one who thrived on his freedom and daring adventures. Although she had known him for years, she really didn't know him at all. He was a natural-born charmer when the mood struck him, but was very selective with his female companions. Nelle doubted there was a woman alive who wouldn't give her soul to corral that untamed creature. If she were younger and prettier . . . She chided her foolishness; that Texan would never wed a tainted woman, if he ever wed. Not that he was arrogant or cynical, he just appeared unsusceptible to love, a man content to feed his passions when they demanded appeasement. He was a perfect specimen of a man. His appeal to women was a vivid fact, a fact he nonchalantly accepted. He was quick to reveal he made no promises to any female, nor did he take kindly to those who tried to force their attentions on him.

It was known the cunning and clear-headed rebel feared nothing and no one. He was an expert horseman and crack shot. Few men challenged him or his ivory-handed Colts. But he was wary and mysterious, and kept to himself a great deal. Alert and agile, he had never lost a fist or gun fight. He was feared, respected, or envied by most men and desired by all women whose eyes feasted on him. He was a self-assured and easy-going devil, but the cowboy could be tough and cold when a situation demanded it. He had the money and power to come and go as he pleased. He could be a coveted friend or a deadly enemy.

Nelle fretted over facts she wished she didn't know, but a woman in her position often learned closely guarded secrets. Miss Braxton was here to seek her father through Rankin Cardone. What would Calinda do and say when she discovered the last man who would aid her was Rankin Cardone? Rankin was a wealthy and powerful man, a man who dealt fairly with friends and ruthlessly with enemies.

It was obvious from Calinda's earlier confession that there were many things the girl didn't know. She

was so naive about the perils before her. Nelle wondered if she should enlighten Calinda. She quickly decided no, since Rankin wasn't a man she'd like to have
as an enemy. If that girl knew what was hovering over
her lovely head, she would run like the wind!

Nelle also had Callie O'Hara to worry her. Callie
was refusing to work! That hateful cousin of hers had
a temper to match her fiery hair. But tonight, Nelle
had an even more pressing matter on her mind. Her
beloved trail-boss had arrived and was waiting in her
room. Giggling with joy, Nelle dismissed both girls
from her mind.

The loud music and raucous laughter from downstairs drifted into Calinda's borrowed room. Her head
was spinning from the potent drug and she was tormented by thoughts of her harrowing episode. She reluctantly changed into the flimsy nightgown, tossing
the red satin gown over a chair. She stumbled to the
bed and slipped between the clean sheets. Crying
softly, Calinda soon fell asleep.

Downstairs, a man attired in jet black entered the
saloon and casually tossed down two whiskies. He had
removed his dark hat to run lean, deft fingers through
a tousled mane of amber hair which blazed like ripened wheat beneath the sun. He exuded an undeniable
contempt for danger and a matchless confidence. He
was over six feet tall and his body rippled with well-
toned, flexible muscles. His flesh had been lovingly
and deeply kissed by the sun. A tangible air of brute
strength and keen alertness clung to him. His violent
and demanding lifestyle had honed his stalwart body
and sharp mind to an impressive degree—his sole

goals were success and survival. His physical prowess
and intelligence made him a formidable opponent.
Not even a minuscule glimmer of self-doubt could be
sighted in that tawny gaze; his eyes were as perceptive
and intimidating as a crafty lion's. And to the women
present, it seemed that beneath that black outfit was
the form of a bronzed god.

Several saloon girls rushed over, eagerly vying for
his attention; but the distracted man wasn't in such a
mood tonight. Flashing them a beguiling and falsely
rueful grin, he pleasantly refused their company.
After a few words with the bartender, he took a bottle
and headed to his room. As he agilely mounted the
steps, he admitted he was growing weary of this secret
work with the Texas Rangers with its countless sacrifices and demands. He had had enough of battling
renegade Indians, Mexican bandits, and an abundance of outlaws and cutthroats. He was bored with
foiling fence-cutters and rustlers, tracking train and
stage robbers, dogging wanted men, living among disgusting outlaws to learn their plans and identities. If
he couldn't openly and proudly be a Ranger, why keep
endangering his life? He didn't like the reputation he
was attaining as a superior gunslinger and arrogant
rebel. Since he couldn't deny his deed or give the reasons behind them, he was rapidly becoming an unsa-
vory legend. And glory-hungry, gun-toting fools loved
nothing more than unseating legends.

After roaming around for two years, he had gone
into secret service for the railroad and U.S. government at the age of twenty. When his job began to send
him across the West in '76, he had joined up with the
Rangers. He usually liked being on the move, but here
in Texas certain personal matters controlled his

thoughts and needs, even after so many years. He had craved the excitement and distractions which his work had offered; he had needed them, still needed them. But something was going crazy inside his head these days. He was becoming dissatisfied, moody, and tense. What was this loneliness or emptiness that plagued him? What was this wild and urgent desire to find the missing element in his life? He possessed so much, had the means and talents to obtain anything he desired; what was left to win or to gain? Yet, how could even a clever and fearless man vanquish an intangible desire?

Maybe it was time to end this work and settle down at home to face other responsibilities. Just as soon as he solved the Sam Bass question, perhaps he would. But so far every attempt to hook up with the Bass gang had failed, and he couldn't accept that. It was clear Bass was working these parts, but the outlaw was sly and deadly. With Major John Jones arriving nearby, perhaps together they could end Bass's career quickly and efficiently. For now, he would rest himself and his horse, then head for Dallas at first light.

He grinned as he climbed the last few steps. Only two men were aware of his identity, but many criminals knew of a daring and unknown Ranger who left his mark of victory on their saddles or holsters: a tiny star that symbolized law and revealed a deadly warning. But this man wanted what other Rangers possessed, respect. The mere mention of a Ranger's name could inspire fear and reluctance in foes. Since he kept his identity concealed, he always had to battle to prove himself or to survive.

The lithe cowboy unlocked his door and walked inside. Noting the softened glow of a burning lantern, he was instantly on alert, his left hand lightly grazing the butt of his pistol. Soundlessly laying his saddle-bag and hat in a chair, he headed for the bed and stared down at the enchanting bundle asleep there. His gaze flickered from the discarded red satin dress to the beautiful creature clad in a revealing nightgown; the sheet had been shoved aside in the stuffy room and all of the vixen's treasures were revealed to his surprised eyes.

With fluid movements, he headed to the window and opened it to invite fresh air inside. He unfastened his hand-tooled double-holstered leather belt and hung it over the chair. He bent down to remove his spurs, and added them to his pile of discarded possessions. The girl hadn't moved yet. Going over to the bed, he sat down, the mattress sinking under his weight. Still, no response to his arrival.

He stared at the unfamiliar girl for a time. His loins instinctively and vexingly tightened, but he restrained his physical urge. He was too fatigued to play games with an audacious saloon girl — one as beautiful as this must have had numberless men in her life. All he wanted was her absence and a good night's sleep. He reached over and shook her, but she didn't respond. She was stupid and brazen to invade his privacy, but her lesson could be taught later when he was revived.

"Up, pretty lady, I'm too tired tonight," he said in a mellow voice, thinking it easier to use fatigue as an excuse for his lack of interest.

Deeply entrapped by drugged slumber, Calinda didn't react to his presence or his voice. His gaze eased over her fiery chestnut curls and breath-taking form. Her flesh was smooth and creamy. She was slim, but shapely. Her transparent gown left nothing to his imagination. She was the most beautiful woman he had ever seen. As he pondered how many men had caused her exhaustion tonight, he was irrationally provoked by how she was affecting him. She was a whore, probably a very busy one! He shook her, roughly and firmly. "Get your eyes open and your feet moving, Ma'am." He desired her, but would never stand in a lengthy line for the attentions that paid for her crude survival.

Calinda stirred and fluttered her green eyes, hazily taking in this image of irresistible manhood.

"What's your name?" he asked.

"Ca . . ." she dreamily attempted to answer, but couldn't force her name past her dry tongue. She tried to focus on the arresting illusion clad in devilish ebony hovering over her.

"Callie?" he assisted here, recalling the bartender's words about a lovely newcomer with that name. Fuzzily hearing the name her mother had called her as a child, she nodded. "What are you doing in here, Callie? This is a private room."

"No other place to go," she murmured hazily.

"Why did you come to my room?" he persisted, intrigued.

"Only safe place . . . Had to get away . . ."

"Did Nelle send you here?" he continued in a lazy drawl.

"Yes. Said stay here until I work out these . . ."

"Where did you live?" he asked. "Safe . . . Get away . . ." his keen mind echoed. Probably from customers and their abundant demands!

"No home . . . Mama dead . . . Papa . . . Lost everything . . . Must stay . . ." The unfinished, hazy words tumbled out to form mistaken conclusions in

33

his befuddled mind and inflamed body.

"Ever work in a saloon before?" he demanded casually, sensing something different and haunting about this delicate girl.

"Never," she mumbled in answer to the strange question.

"I see," he thoughtfully murmured. His investigative mind went to spinning with questions and doubts. Had she completed her first day in this kind of job? Or would she begin tomorrow? Was she here of her own free will? Had that mischievous Nelle sent her for his enjoyment? For certain, this would be his only chance to enjoy this unselfish gift, before she was tarnished from months of visits to countless beds of any male who could afford her price. Common whores didn't appeal to him, but there was nothing common about his girl. From her looks, she would be in popular demand. How could any female condemn herself to such an existence? Surely one such as Callie could have her choice of husbands. Was she a penniless widow? A runaway from a terrible home? Why would she choose such a degrading life over a respectable one? Despite the temptation this proud Ranger was reluctant to take advantage of this enticing set-up.

"I'm thirsty," Calinda managed to say, feeling the room spin around her.

All he had was a bottle of superior whiskey. He poured her a glass and helped her sit up to drink it, supporting her lax body against his strong one. The biting liquid was strong, but wet. Calinda automatically thanked him, before her senses went rushing around again.

He placed the empty glass on the table, then eased Calinda down on the bed. He grinned in amusement;

she clearly wasn't used to potent drinks and she possessed good manners. When she smiled up at him, he lazily stretched out beside her, hesitating to end this pleasing contact. He reclined on his left side, his jaw cupped in his hand. He absently shoved a straying vibrant curl from her ivory face. His finger made a compelling trek over her forehead, down her cheek, across her pert nose, past her dainty chin, and to her inviting lips. At the tickling sensations, she smiled and shifted, those verdant green eyes pulling his gaze to hers.

"Do you want to be here with me, Callie?" he inquired tensely, despite the thunderous warning inside his head that screamed of the danger she presented, a warning he helplessly denied.

"Yes," the spoken word escaped her lips softly, as she tried to clear her somnolent wits, too late . . .

Chapter Two

This special Ranger was adept at handling emergencies or hazards; he usually knew how to prepare for them and master them with unerring accuracy, speed, and courage. But this situation was uncommon. Even his many skills couldn't tell him what to do with this particular crisis. He suspected this new saloon girl had heard of his daring exploits and good looks, and perhaps found him desirable on reputation alone. Was she lurking here to guilefully cast her spell over him? As he eyed her compelling beauty, he grew inexplicably angry. Maybe it was because she looked so innocent and vulnerable. Unlike like the other saloon girls she was unpainted and presented a soft seductiveness which was overwhelming. She looked as if she belonged in elegant silk gowns rather than in the garish red satin one, and he was struck by the dangerous appeal of the sheer nightgown in bright crimson which made a startling contrast to her creamy flesh. Callie was as bewitching and devious as his mother. No, he wouldn't permit that selfish bitch to torment him tonight.

Still, that tiny comparison sparked more anger within him, adding dashes of fierce spite. Damn any *puta* who could retain such a look of purity and charm while she coldly trampled on lonely and unsuspecting male hearts, especially his! How dare this creature set a provocative trap for him! How dare she steal inside his head!

Even as she slept, her lips curled up in an inviting smile that played havoc on a man's senses. Evidently she wanted to begin her new career in Fort Worth with him as her first prize. She had probably brazenly entered his hide-away to seduce him, perhaps to prove she possessed the power to captivate even the cynical and elusive Unknown Ranger.

A beguiling and devilish grin tugged at the corners of his wide and full lips. His tawny eyes glowed with mischievous lights. He ran his strong fingers through his curling mane of dark blond hair. Strangely, he was no longer tired and bored; his senses were alive and alert. It had been a long time since he had taken a woman in bed, and he found Calinda utterly arresting. A soft chuckle escaped his lips as he decided to accept her implied invitation.

The intrigued Ranger stood up and stripped off his clothes and boots. Filling the wash-basin, he removed the trail-dust from his face and hands, leisurely taking the time to shave. He removed the covers and drank in the invigorating sight, then joined her. Drugged with Nelle's laudanum, the Ranger's whiskey, and her own exhaustion, Calinda didn't react as the impulsive stranger undressed her to admire her beauty. He bent over and captured the lips which seemed to beg for his.

With expertise, he skillfully stormed her body with deft hands and bedeviling lips, exploring curvy regions and flat planes.

Calinda lacked the strength, awareness, or logic to resist him as she surrendered to the intoxicating kisses and stirring caresses of the golden man of her dreams.

As Calinda's arms unknowingly encircled the man's iron-muscled body and her lips answered the call from his, his resentment melted away. All he wanted was to make tender and passionate love to this mysterious siren. If Calinda's mind had any intention of freeing her from its torpid state, the thought was quickly dismissed as she revelled in the warmth, protection, and heated desire of this enchanting stranger. Nature took over her blurry senses and demanded she respond to his urgent messages and unleash her unbridled passion to match his.

The now enraptured Ranger eased between her thighs and tenderly, yet persistently, probed at her maidenhead, ignoring its meaningful presence. Ensnared by potent desire and her eager encouragement, he was hurled beyond control or reason. She smelled as fresh as a field of wildflowers and her loving was as sultry as the hottest summer day. As the barrier against his possession gave way, her small cry of discomfort reached his fuzzy brain. Virgin! The word ricocheted through his confused mind like a perilous gunshot, then gradually receded in a fading echo.

Governed by the insistent throbbing within his manhood, he entered and withdrew gently until her brief struggle halted. Her skin was as soft and white as the petals on a loquat flower. The peaks on her taut breasts were firm and sweet. As Calinda's arms eased around his tantalizing body and her lips yielded to his kisses, logic escaped him for a time as his hungry body urged him to feast on the fruits of his labor and to submit to her bewitching pervasion of his senses.

Blissfully appeased, the sated rogue eased to her side, retaining his possessive hold on her. He shifted his head to gaze down at her; she was snuggled peacefully into his embrace. A curiously warm and happy feeling flowed over him. Bemused by the odd sensations and thoughts which assailed his mind and body, he couldn't seem to pull his eyes from her serene face. Watching and touching her gave him intense pleasure. Normally one sexual union was sufficient to satisfy his needs. But he fiercely desired this girl again this moment! He bent over to nibble at her lips, then passed his tongue over them. His body was simmering with desire, preparing to boil with molten passion. There was no way he could go to sleep yet. With renewed vigor, he enticed her once more, whispering, "Love me again, my fiery vixen."

Calinda stirred, her green eyes dreamily focused on his tawny gaze. She caressed his tanned cheek and nestled against his coppery frame, sighing contentedly. In Calinda's whiskey- and laudanum-dulled mind, all she heard was the mingled pounding of passion's fiery blood and the muffled instructions of her bronzed lover. As his lips and hands worked magic upon her quivering body, his voice and face vanquished all but this undeniable craving to forge their bodies and hearts. What knowledge instinct didn't supply, he did.

Calinda relaxed into the softness of the bed, allowing him full control of the situation and abandoning her will to his. When the wildly wonderful invasion became too bittersweet to simply enjoy, Calinda feverishly matched his movements. Their bodies and spirits

39

blended into one driving force, one commitment to shared pleasure.

Calinda's senses reeled with the exquisite entice-ments. In the pit of her womanhood, an aching need fused with ecstatic delight. She was striving urgently for a goal she didn't comprehend until she was force-fully rocked by the stunning climax to her sensual drama. Her body stiffened momentarily, then tingled and warmed. Her hold on her dream lover tightened; her lips meshed with his as entreating moans slipped from her throat. Her body writhed and pressed up-ward to glue her moist flesh to his until each rapturous spasm ceased. After willingly sharing this intoxicating and enlightening experience, she settled down to savor the tranquil aftermath.

Calinda's cheek lay against his chest, her eyes closed dreamily. His strong fingers wandered through her silky hair and over her naked shoulders as his lips dropped tiny kisses over her temple. Her head moved slightly as she relished the feel of his damp and firm shoulder against her satiny cheek; she inhaled the manly fragrance which filled her nostrils. She felt so warm, safe, and happy in his arms, so empty of cares and doubts. Like a newly bloomed flower in a field of ripened wheat, she was totally content to be a part of his golden domain.

As her fingers played with dampened curls on his muscled chest, a mellow voice rent the romantic si-lence when it murmured, "I've never met a woman so beautiful and innocent, yet so skillful she steals your mind. I'm afraid you're going to be unforgettable. I surely wish I didn't have to ride out at dawn."

The Ranger inhaled deeply, then allowed the air to escape his lungs quietly. He hugged her tightly, then chuckled as he questioned his good fortune, "Why me, love? You could have any male around." He knew now that he had never experienced real passion until tonight, until this female. Never had he been so aware of each instant of lovemaking. It was so different with her, so stimulating, so consuming, so utterly satisfying. Yep, there was plenty to learn from this unique treasure.

Even as he spoke these words, the laudanum and whiskey were gradually losing their potent and witdulling effects. The reality of the naked body cuddled next to hers registered in her whirling brain, as did the implication of their intimate position. She swallowed with difficulty, gaping at the brawny chest within inches of her wide eyes, fearing to lift her head to view the face of her mysterious lover.

Her movements caught his attention. He opened amber eyes to discover startled green ones locked on him. He smiled, causing her stupefied gaze to rivet to his sensual lips, then back to his beguiling gaze. Instantly, he knew something was amiss.

Calinda blinked her eyes and shook her head to test this shocking reality. She knew this man—didn't she? From where? When? How had she come to be in bed with this handsome devil, naked in his strong arms? Why was she boldly fondling his chest! How could she recognize his face and voice, and yet not know his name or when they met? Remember . . . Her fantasy . . . The mental pictures which flashed across her warring brain stunned her. It hadn't been a dream?

When she tried to free herself, the golden stranger refused to release her. "Let go of me, you beast," she ordered hoarsely, shoving at the immovable chest. "If I had a gun, I'd kill you," she warned as her voice strengthened. What black magic had lured her into this compelling demon's bed? He was behaving as if he owned her body and soul! "Take your filthy hands off me!" she panted when he retained his painlessly firm embrace as his piercing eyes observed her.

When the girl began to thrash angrily like a frenzied badger in a steel trap, he captured her wrists and pinned her nude body beneath his. "What the hell!" he stormed at her unexpected behavior. "What's wrong with you, woman? You make love to me, then attack me like a wildcat! Calm down and explain yourself!"

"You break into my room and ravish me, then act the victim? Release me this instant, you vile brute! I'll have you arrested for this wicked crime against me. I'll scream," she warned as his tawny eyes frosted visibly at her threat. Calinda had been about to fight him tooth and nail for her freedom, but his glacial stare inspired trepidation and warned her to use caution and defensive guile. She must get free.

"Your room? Ravish you?" he repeated the unexpected charges, then chuckled at their absurdity. "I don't know what trick you're trying to pull on me, but it won't work. Sorry if I hurt you, green eyes, but you should have warned me you'd never made love before. Still it doesn't justify you accusing me of rape. As for breaking into *your room*, that's another mistake in this scheme of yours," he mockingly scolded. "Didn't Nelle warn you to stay out of my private quarters? I know you're new here, but it's dangerous to sneak into a fellow's room and bed." He didn't smile as he watched the curious array of emotions which came and went on her ashen face.

"Your room and bed?" she echoed in sarcastic fury, instantly recalling Nelle's allusion to this being a privately owned room. *His?*

"Yep. You were lying in wait for me tonight, weren't you? How'd you know I'd be arriving so soon after you hired on? Besides what made you believe I wouldn't toss you out on your pretty tail? I must confess, you were a nice surprise." Having been the first man in her life, he felt great relief, excitement, and heady power. Could she be persuaded to become his private property? She was too lovely and unique to endure a whorish life.

His mocking words were frightfully enlightening. "I wasn't waiting here for you or anyone! If this is your private room, then Nelle made a terrible mistake. I'm not a saloon girl; I'd never work in a horrible place like this. Even if what you claim is true, you still assaulted me!" she hotly accused. "Get off me!"

"Not until you explain what you're doing naked in my bed," he flatly refused. "Either speak up, or we'll be here like this all night."

Calinda was panicked by his determination. She tried to forget her innocent part in his wild charade. Was he the owner of this room? Had he mistaken her identity and reason for being here? What harm could the truth do? "Nelle let me stay here tonight because I didn't have anywhere else to go. I was robbed today outside town on the stagecoach."

"Then why didn't you say something or stop me?" he asked, an uneasy feeling washing over him, one oddly mingled with elation.

"I was too dazed. It must have been the sleeping drug Nelle gave me." As she eyed his bare chest, she swallowed loudly. Tears welled in her limpid eyes as she fought to move away from his warm touch, his flesh like a soft coppery blanket stretched tightly over a sturdy and

43

exquisitely molded frame of iron.

The Ranger was just as disquieted and confounded as she was. To his acute dismay, he discovered himself in the novel position of feeling ashamed and thoroughly unsettled. He needed to get to the bottom of this dark well of mystery.

If she was telling the truth about being in his room and being drugged, that meant . . . Those arresting green eyes bright with unshed tears plagued him. "When I found you sprawled in my bed with little but your skin on, what was I supposed to think? You told me Nelle sent you, and you said you wanted to be here with me! Darnit, woman, you kept smiling at me and encouraging me! You did respond to me, green eyes, like no other female I've known," he defensively asserted. "The bartender told be about a new girl with fiery locks."

Those shocking remarks caused her to miss his last statement which would have clarified the misunderstanding. "What kind of beast ravishes a woman while she's senseless!" she charged angrily. "Even if Nelle made a mistake letting me sleep here, you didn't have to take advantage of me! Would you rape any woman found in your bed?" she berated him, as hazy memories of their lovemaking, alarming memories which she pushed aside, unclouded in her steadily clearing mind. "You're no better than those outlaws who attacked and robbed me, or those selfish people in this town who wouldn't even help me! How dare you mistake me for a wh . . . saloon girl."

"You can't put all the blame for this mistake on me. What kind of father would turn loose an innocent beauty like you to go roaming around in a dangerous territory? Nelle was crazy to put you in my bed dressed like that. Nobody uses this room but me. Any man would have lost his head in a set-up like this!"

"Evidently Nelle wasn't expecting you, but she could have warned me. And I wasn't 'roaming around'! I was riding a stage under guard. How do you people live under such violent conditions? Who are you?" she abruptly asked the rigid stranger with eyes entreating and piercing.

"Tex," he offered, not wanting her to learn his identity and risk complications. With luck, she would be gone tomorrow. At least, he would be. Instantly that knowledge piqued him. How could he leave her in trouble and danger, without money or protection? He knew nothing about virgins—had he hurt her on this first sexual encounter?

"Considering I'm partly to blame for this . . . mix-up, I'll give you some money to get home," he offered sullenly, failing to comprehend why he was speaking and acting in this insensitive way. He was having a terrible time holding his tough exterior in place.

Humiliated and angered, Calinda inhaled sharply. "You vile scoundrel! Your money can't pay for this outrage! Get out of here!" she ordered coldly, pounding on the sturdy chest. She needed solitude to decide how to deal with this staggering episode.

"Aren't you forgetting this is my room? If you don't like my company, dress and leave," he playfully suggested, waiting for her next move in this stimulating contest of wills. "I want to help you."

"What?" she blurted, staring at him. He had casually stolen her purity and was now tossing her out of this questionable room? She had no clothes or money! He wouldn't dare! He was the villain here!

"Get a room at the hotel," he added, grinning roguishly. "I apologized for my error, but I could lose con-

45

trol of myself again," he hinted, rolling to his side and propping on his left elbow to observe her.

"Error? You call what you did a simple error?" she demanded sarcastically, emerald eyes narrowed in outrage and distress.

"My first one," he informed her, as if shocked himself, then chuckled at her expression. "I guess I'm not perfect after all," he added.

Incensed, Calinda snapped. "You're despicable!"

"I've been called worse," he casually parried her insult.

"You are," she added, gritting her teeth at her helpless position. She had believed it could be no worse, but it was. She had no possessions or a weapon. Even her sharp wits were betraying her! She hated her scant choices. Either she could summon the sheriff and let everyone know she had been ravished by this carefree devil, or she could dress and leave as he so insensitively suggested. If she didn't accept his money, the hotel wouldn't accept her. If she did, she would be no better than the girls here who sold their bodies! Damn him!

"You're right, Callie," he agreed contritely as he witnessed her dilemma. She was so beautiful and vulnerable. "Callie what?"

"None of your business," she said frostily. When she found her father, she would have him discover this man's name and punish him! But punish him without permanently staining her reputation!

"Go to sleep, Callie. I'm exhausted. I promise you'll be safe tonight," he suddenly coaxed her, sounding serious and looking sincere. To steady his own nerves, the cowboy sat up and turned his back for a drink. Calinda couldn't help but see that the twisted sheet didn't conceal his firm buttocks. After the whiskey was poured and downed, he sat quietly for a time.

46

Calinda was about to spew forth another stinging tirade. When she turned in that direction, she couldn't
speak. Caught unaware by the sight which greeted her
gaze, she helplessly allowed her entranced eyes to wander over his coppery body of rippling muscles. He was
lean and tall, his skin was smooth and unscarred. His
tawny hair curled under at his nape and was full and
wavy. Calinda found herself wondering who and what
he was, this cunning seducer. When his hand went up to
ruffle his hair, she stared at it, recalling how sensuously it
had tormented and stimulated her body. The white
statues of Apollo and Adonis couldn't match the perfec-
tion of his golden body. Growing warm and tense, she
hurriedly pulled her eyes away from him.

"Well?" he split the silence, bemused by her lack of
vengeful threats from her family and the law. He
abruptly recalled her mumblings about no home and
family. Maybe she had been dreaming. He was instinctively aware of her previous scrutiny. "Staying or leaving?" he clarified unnecessarily. "You know how it'll look
if you traipse over to the hotel at this hour in that outfit?
You can go to the law if you wish, but I wouldn't advise
it. I didn't rape you, love. You know I'll have to tell my
side of this mix-up. We're trapped together, Callie. Admit it and turn in. I know this has been a frightening day
for you, a crazy experience for both of us. But I swear I
won't hurt you or touch you again." His voice was as soft
and warm as a summer day.

"Stay here with you?" she furiously scoffed, vexed by
the way his words and voice affected her. "You're mad!"
To gain thinking distance, she snatched the discarded
coverlet and wound it about her trembling body. Being
naked made her feel even more defenseless and hazy-
headed! She wanted to pounce on him and beat him

47

soundly; but she knew she hadn't the strength to hurt him. She couldn't allow him to go free, unpunished. But it was foolish to provoke him tonight; her revenge must be postponed until she had favorable odds.

"Why not? You have my word I won't . . ." he began.

"Don't you dare turn around!" she shrieked, adjusting the protective covering as humorous chuckles escaped him.

To appease her distraught senses, he relented to her panicky request. "It's easy to see you're a lady who's found herself in a perilous and embarrassing position. In spite of what happened earlier, I'm not a heartless animal. I don't force myself on any woman, especially not on a defenseless creature as beautiful and delicate as you. I can't erase tonight, but I can offer you my protection and hospitality."

"How chivalrous," she sneered, eyeing him suspiciously. Somehow she sensed she could trust him. Why, she couldn't explain or comprehend, unless it was the look in his mesmeric eyes or the tone to his stirring voice. Small rays of gentleness filtered through the tiny holes she had pierced in his hard facade, illuminating traits she found strange and pleasing. "I'll find Nelle and see if she has another place I can sleep."

"I wouldn't disturb here, she's busy with her sweetheart. Besides, this is the safest room here, even with me in it. I doubt the customers and working girls will take kindly to you tapping on their doors this time of night. Where were you heading?" he inquired.

Calinda cautiously lied, "To a town called Austin. My father's there and I was heading to join him. I've been in school back East." It was absurd to be carrying on a conversation with this rake.

Perceptive, the man knew she had spoken only half-truths, but he didn't want to reveal excessive interest by pressing her or contradicting her. She should have known those lucid green eyes read as easily as a marked trail. Too bad he didn't have time to study this exquisite girl more closely. He could sense her uncertainty and fear. She reminded him of a trapped rabbit, and twinges of remorse and tenderness pulled at his heart and mind. He was about to tell her she could stay in his room as long as necessary, but ruefully changed his mind. Once she contacted her father and revealed tonight's events, he didn't need an irate father tampering with his tight schedule or endangering his secret identity. They would meet again — Callie couldn't be difficult to trace . . .

"Evidently you have no intention of leaving, so I will. Would you please wait outside while I dress?" she said in an acid tone. "After what you did, you would leave me alone if you were any kind of gentleman." When the trailing coverlet tangled her bare feet, the top portion nearly escaped her tight grip as she reached for the bed-post to steady her balance. He wouldn't be grinning if she could reach one of his guns! But if she made a try for it, he would be on her in a moment. Besides, she didn't know how to use it!

He laughed as her cheeks burned a vivid red, aware of her longing gaze on his Colts. Her dismissal of that idea revealed her intelligence, not cowardice. When she glared at him, he playfully crossed his heart and huskily vowed, "I promise I'll be a perfect gentleman, Callie. If I hadn't been sleeping on the hard ground for weeks, I'd sleep on the floor. Been looking forward to my soft bed and there isn't enough cover to make a comfortable pal-let. I'm afraid that sofa's too short for a man six-four," he added before she could suggest it. "This bed's big enough to share. If I was truly a dangerous brute, Callie,

I could hold you here by force or just as easily toss you out. Come to bed. We're both tired and confused."

"I can't sleep like this," she argued his ridiculous solution. He was a smug and beguiling devil! Was he crazy as well as daring!

The flustered man assumed she meant sleep naked as he watched her clutch the cover to her bare body, as if fearing it would dislodge during the night or their bodies would make perilous contact. He reached for the nightgown, then changed his mind. "You might as well wear nothing as that see-through garb," he stated, looking about anxiously. If he was going to keep his vow, he couldn't be overly tempted! Then again, just looking at her accomplished that feat. Never had his control been so sorely strained!

He flung her his shirt and laughingly said, "This should protect you from my lecherous eyes, my wild vixen." Their gazes locked on the black shirt, both knowing how easily it could yield to his strength.

"You make this sound like some kind of mischievous game," she sneered at him, taking it and slipping it on. "If you lack the decency to let me stay here tonight, I insist you give me privacy to change," she ordered, chafed by his playful manner.

"I know it isn't a game, Callie. I've asked you to stay." He softened his words and gaze. How could he leave her so soon?

"To stay here with you! I'm not some whore, Tex! One of us has to leave," she persisted, a note of pleading edging her voice.

The Ranger suspected she might visit the sheriff's office if he forced her out tonight. He couldn't afford trouble. Besides, he was riding out early in the morning. He might as well sleep in the stable loft. Who knew what his generosity could earn him on a future day . . .

"All right, Callie, have it your way," he yielded. "Do you want to turn your back or wait outside while I dress?" he teased.

"You'll leave?" She couldn't believe she'd won.

"I can't have you traipsing around looking for a place to sleep. I will need my shirt," he hinted, laughing at her skeptical expression. "If you want that modesty to remain intact, best turn around, love."

Calinda slipped off his shirt and tossed it on the rumpled bed, then turned away. She waited anxiously as she heard the bed squeak. She closed her eyes tightly and leaned against the bedpost, praying he was being honest.

As he dressed to depart, the puzzled man was trapped in pensive reflections. Clearly he had misjudged her and this situation, but it wasn't entirely his fault. He was almost annoyed Callie hadn't laid a trap for him. At least he wouldn't feel so strange and remorseful if it had been a pre-planned deed. Her fiery passion couldn't be forgotten. Question was, had it been spontaneous or involuntary, a result of drugged senses? Would he ever see her again? These emotions were new and potent and he didn't know how to resist or accept them. Why did this slip of a girl offer such an alarming threat? What made her so different from other women? He didn't even know her! Yet he was actually giving up his comfortable room and bed for a stranger, one who viewed him the blackguard of all time! *Caramba!* He must be bored and fatigued to be thinking and feeling such contradictory emotions!

He pulled on his snug ebony pants and boots, then reached for the shirt she had been wearing. He strapped on his holsters and dropped the two Colts into place, ignoring the tightening in his pants as he viewed her slender back and inhaled her fragrance on his shirt. He berated his crazy indecision, this impulse to refuse to leave, this impulse to storm her with passionate kisses and stirring caresses. He flexed his strong hands as they itched to wander over her stimulating territory, upon which he had mentally staked a claim.

"Sure you want me to leave you alone in this dangerous place?" he inquired so close to her face she could feel the warmth of his breath.

She jumped, her eyes opening. "I'll be fine after you're gone," she sassily informed him before their gazes met to fluster her.

His eyes roved her face, the simple action pleasing to him. "Perhaps we'll meet again, Callie, under better circumstances."

"I pray I never set eyes on you again," she panted, her anger curiously returning as he made ready to leave.

The Ranger studied her flushed face and guilt-riddled look for a time. He was tempted to sweep her into his arms and prove her words a desperate lie. "If a certain gunslinger has his way, you might get your prayer answered before this week's out," he stated, watching for a reaction.

Calinda briefly fell for his ruse, but quickly controlled herself. She watched him place the dark hat on his tawny head before swaggering to the door. Tossing his saddlebags over his shoulder, he grinned and winked. "Nite, Callie, See you around," he murmured, then left. Calinda rushed forward to lock the door, forgetting he had a key.

She paced the floor for a lengthy time. It was hard to believe such things had taken place in one short day. She had another demanding day tomorrow; her head was throbbing and she needed sleep. She noticed the bottle left behind; she poured a drink and forced it down. This time, she removed the cover from her body and slipped nude between the mussed sheets. She sighed loudly and relaxed into the softness of the bed, inhaling his lingering fragrance on the pillow. Incredibly, she was soon sleeping peacefully. Maybe it was the dangers and violence she had witnessed and endured this day that made her feel safe in this particular room. Or perhaps it was the incredible nature of this day's events and emotions that made what happened this night seem unreal. Suddenly, it all seemed only a dream again . . .

The Ranger made his way toward the stable just as a heavy rain began. Before he could reach the entrance, he was soaked. As he stepped inside the enclosure, he cursed this strange day. The air was crisp at this late hour. He shivered and chided his sacrifice. He was tired, chilly, and miserable: all for a stubborn female! What did it matter if he had endured worse conditions? Tonight, his discomfort was self-imposed. He paced the dirt floor, berating himself and the girl sleeping warm and secure in his bed.

His whiskey should warm him. But he had left it behind. She would be panicked by his return, but what the hell! He could suffer only so much for an innocent mistake. He headed for the saloon, not bothering to run since he was already thoroughly saturated.

He quietly unlocked the door and peeked inside. She appeared to be sleeping. As if for a frightened child, the lantern had been left burning. As Calinda rolled to her side, the sheet slipped away to reveal most of her slender back. His white teeth gleamed as he grimaced, his arms aching to ease around her. Calinda sighed tranquilly and curled into a tight ball, fiery curls spreading over the white pillow.

The Ranger couldn't find the willpower to move, remembering how it had felt with the girl nestled against him. He irrationally cursed himself for giving his word not to touch her again; his loins ached for her. He yearned to feel those soft hands wandering over his body again, to bury his nose in that fragrant hair, to ride over the stirring hills and peaceful plains with a first love, a wild love. He had never broken his word, and he wouldn't start with this tempting treat. But watching her was as painful as falling into a thistle of bull nettles. He fretted over the novel emotions he was experiencing. The instinctive hair on the back of his neck seemed to bristle in warning. It was past time to get the hell out of this room!

Feeling slightly ridiculous, but trained to be wary and careful, the lawman soundlessly searched the room and under the edge of the mattress for a weapon or concealed clue to this delightful creature. Finding none, he sighed gratefully for that good luck. After all, some women were known to be vengeful and selfish . . .

Calinda stirred again, as if restless. Before she turned to her stomach and snuggled into his deserted place, he studied her intently, as if he could ever forget a line or curve on her ravishing face and body. He went to the corner table. He took a piece of paper and scribbled a note, then placed it and some money on her pillow. If Nelle was up before he rode off, he would question her about this mysterious girl. If not, then he would do so the next time he came to Fort Worth. He glanced at her a final time, wondering why he was having such a difficult time breathing, and departing. It wasn't like him to allow any distractions to his duty. Having never before avoided a threat or a challenge, he scurried from both in her.

He returned to the stable and stripped off the wet clothes, pulling on a pair of lightweight longjohns to ward off a chill. He took several large gulps of whiskey and snuggled into the wiry hay and scratchy blanket. As the Ranger continued to lie there awake and restless, defensive doubts badgered his keen mind. Was it possible two redheads would show up at the same saloon, the same day, with the same first name? Would Nelle loan his private room to a total stranger? If Nelle had been swayed by this girl's troubles, why didn't she loan her two dollars for a hotel room? If Callie was playing some game, she had selected the wrong man to dupe. It didn't seem logical for a "lady" to be travelling alone in the wild West. Surely this girl wasn't a female detective, out to use him for information? Several cattle barons, one in particular, was under investigation; but would they hire a beautiful vixen to waylay him? Perhaps his undercover job made him too leery, but there was one powerful *haciendado* he couldn't ignore . . .

The wily Texan had slain many men, some in the line of duty and some from challenges that couldn't be handled any other way. Could she be a vengeful sweetheart, daughter, or sister? Improbable, he concluded, but not impossible. Her prior innocence ruled out vindictive widow. He was relieved that Nelle had been warned never to reveal his name or location to any curious person. It was a difficult search, but the persistent drifter finally located dreamland and entered its enticing gates. It was only a few hours before he was up and dressed, riding off to Dallas to meet with Major Jones, not daring to check on Callie again.

Hours later, Calinda stirred. Slowly her hazy mind and heavy eyes cleared. She bolted up in the bed and looked around; something was different. The window was closed; the lantern was out; the bottle was gone. Staring at her naked body, she fumed at his unforgivable action. He had returned while she was sleeping! She hurried to make certain the door was locked, sighing when it was though she knew he had a key. Her gaze touched on the money on the pillow, bringing a flush to her face and anger to her mind. Was he paying her like some harlot? She stalked to the bed and seized the unsigned note. Stunned, she read it a second time:

Callie,

Sorry about our delightful mistake last night. Buy some clothes and a gun. Get to the hotel and stay put until you can get on your way home. Next time we meet, my flame-haired beauty, my chivalrous promise will be worthless. Rest assured, we will meet again. Keep a sharp eye over your lovely shoulder. One day I'll ride up behind you when you least expect it.

Calinda was addled, but annoyingly warmed. How dare that arrogant rebel order her around! "Our mistake," she scoffed. But he had kept his word, and he had left her some money. "No doubt you'll expect payment for it if we do ever meet again," she whispered apprehensively, then scolded herself for the surge of eager suspense that followed. Even if it had been a misunderstanding, she had a right to this money in view of what he had taken from her. As soon as her dress was repaired, she would take his suggestions. She would shop for clothes and buy a gun, then register at the hotel and wait for the sheriff to assist her. If Tex came around again before her departure, he would find himself on the barrel end of the gun he had generously purchased!

Yet as Calinda waited for Nelle to appear, she found herself thinking about the trespasser who had abruptly invaded her world and selfishly changed it, then just as mysteriously departed. Was his note a promise, a threat, or a joke? As she reflected on his touch and kisses, she trembled. How could a beguiling stranger cause her body to sing such forbidden and romantic songs and entice her traitorous heart to dream of meeting him again. She must be going daft!

When Nelle came to bring her garments and breakfast, Calinda didn't mention Tex's noctural visit. Nelle appeared flustered and rushed this morning, quickly leaving with the promise to return later. Recalling the stranger's words about Nelle's sweetheart, Calinda decided Nelle was either spending every available minute with him or was bidding him a sad farewell. Calinda ate slowly, then dressed, After which, she impatiently sat waiting for Nelle's return.

Just before noon, the hefty and genial woman returned. When Calinda casually inquired about the owner of her room, Nelle told her not to worry, that he wouldn't mind her staying here one night. When Calinda pressed for more information about him, Nelle reluctantly told Calinda he was Cody Richards, a wealthy rancher's son from down Laredo way. When Calinda asked how often he came to town, Nelle said he only showed up about every six weeks to relax and have some fun.

It would be dusk, when Jake Tarply the bartender came to work, before Nelle would learn of the cowboy's unexpected visit. A new mystery would be added to Nelle's immense collection. She would wonder why Calinda had kept silent. And again today, Nelle had her guileful cousin to fret over, for the audacious Callie had stolen money and vanished at dawn, After having been seen in the company of a notorious gunslinger!

Calinda was shown to the sheriff's office, then Nelle went about her flurry of business. Calinda related her story to the sympathetic man, who promptly informed her there was little chance of getting back her possessions. Calinda was distraught. She told the sheriff he could keep everything as a reward if he only recovered the locket. After promising to do all he could, Calinda went to the hotel to register. The owner was surprised to see her again this morning. If she had any other choice, she wouldn't stay in his hotel.

Later, she went to the telegraph office to hire a messenger to deliver two letters to the Cardone Ranch, one to her father and one to Rankin Cardone in case her father was absent. When that task was finished, she headed for the mercantile store to purchase the needed garments. There was little to choose from in her size, so Calinda purchased two simple dresses, cotton underwear, toiletries, and a plain nightgown. Having nothing to occupy her time until her father or Mister Cardone appeared, she purchased another book to while away the hours and to distract her from thoughts of Cody.

Knowing Nelle deserved a brief explanation, Calinda went to see her later that afternoon. Nelle sensed her embarrassment, tension, and reluctance as Calinda told her false story. Calinda said the banker had loaned her money until her father or Mister Cardone arrived. She tried to pay Nelle for her kindness, but Nelle refused. When Calinda asked about Callie, Nelle dropped several enlightening clues to the event of last night. Nelle was surprised when the young woman hugged her fondly and thanked her before leaving.

As Calinda returned to the hotel, she realized how the

beguiling stranger had made such a tormenting error; he had been told about the arrival of Callie and had mistaken Calinda for the new girl. In light of the crazy set of coincidences, the outcome was logical. Yet, he had made love to the wrong woman, if only she hadn't been dazed! Had Cody learned of his error? Was that why he had returned to leave the money and note? Or did he still think she was Callie O'Hara . . .

Calinda slept fitfully that night, but dreamed about the bronzed stranger with tawny eyes. For two days, she paced the wooden floor of her room, waiting and praying. The tall stranger didn't return to town; or if he did, Calinda never saw him from her window which faced the main street. The sheriff called once, to tell Calinda there was no news on the robbery. In the raw cowtown, Calinda dared not go out alone, especially not after her initial experiences here in Texas. After each meal, she would return to her room to wait.

By the third day, she was growing anxious. If she didn't hear something today, she would send another message and speak bluntly with the sheriff. Surely it couldn't take much longer for her message to arrive and to get a response. Calinda dreaded to think about her future if her father was gone. Her only friend was a tender-hearted saloon madam. If only Cody . . . he had probably dismissed her from his mind the instant the door closed behind his towering and virile frame. She cursed Cody for his hold over her mind and body.

To her dismay, she suddenly wondered how to deal with another problem—what if Rankin Cardone didn't live around here anymore? He was the only clue to her father! She hastily dismissed that fear, for the messenger had taken her money and agreed to deliver her letters.

Mid-morning, a loud knock sounded on her door.

When she asked who was there, a masculine voice replied, "Rankin Cardone, *Senorita*. May I come in and speak with you?"

Relieved and excited, Calinda unlocked the door and opened it. Her smile froze in place when she saw he was alone. She dreaded to hear the meaning behind her father's absence.

"You wanted to see me?" Rankin asked crisply, eyeing her intently. He obviously held an inner strength which matched his supple frame.

"Yes. Please come in," she offered politely, then stepped aside.

Chapter Three

The formidable *haciendado* entered her room and sat down in a chair, his movements fluid and controlled. It was impossible to miss his aura of wealth, power, and self-assurance. As if a man at ease anywhere, he crossed his right ankle over his left thigh. Rankin Cardone presented a most distinguished figure, tall and muscular. Though he must have been nearly fifty, he certainly did not look his age. Impeccably dressed, he wore garments that suggested a Spanish flair. Except for a white shirt, he was clad in black. A narrow length of black silk was tied around his collar, its tails dangling down the front of his ruffled shirt. He casually removed his hat and placed it on his lap, his fingers caressing the braided band as a child would stroke a furry kitten. His boots were highly polished; for a moment Calinda wondered if she could see her face reflected there.

His sable hair was peppered lightly with silver at the temples. He wore a thin mustache which curled slightly on both ends and a neatly trimmed Vandyke beard. His features bore an aristocratic mien. Suddenly his last name struck a note, Spanish or Mexican? His forceful gaze seemed to penetrate Calinda's flesh, making her uneasy. The expression on Rankin's face was resolute, his thoughts and feelings unreadable. He gazed at her as if assessing a new breed of stock. Although Calinda was accustomed to meeting people of wealth and prestige, this man tampered with her poise and confidence.

Calinda walked forward and sat down on the edge of the bed. "I'm sorry if I'm inconveniencing you, Mister Cardone. Why didn't my father come? Why did he send you? Is he busy or away?" she asked, hardly knowing where to begin.

One brow lifted inquisitively and his dark eyes intentionally clouded with confusion. "Your arrival and frantic summons came as a complete surprise to me. Since your message sounded so urgent, I felt I should respond personally. I am greatly puzzled, *Senorita*. Why are you seeking Elliott Braxton at the Cardone Ranch?"

"You're saying my father doesn't work or live at your ranch?" she questioned apprehensively, her eyes pleading for a negative reply.

"Where would you get such ideas, *Senorita?*"

"His last letter told me about you and the ranch. I was supposed to join him when I finished school in England," she replied hoarsely.

To test her depth of knowledge or questionable intentions, Rankin probingly disputed, "Impossible. Brax has been gone for years. Who are you, *Senorita?* Why did you really come?" he asked unflinchingly.

Bemused, Calinda arose quickly and gaped at him,

her face paling. "He's gone?" she asked in a strained voice.

"Probably dead," Rankin declared to test her reaction.

The room spun dizzily, then went black as Calinda slipped to the floor in a faint. Rankin was spurred into motion, coming to her side. He lifted her limp body and placed her on the bed. Taking a wet cloth, he mopped her ashen face until she stirred. In spite of his calm facade, Rankin's mind was whirling with wild speculations. What did this girl expect from him? Was she really Calinda Braxton? She didn't favor Brax at all. Bitterness and hatred smoldered within Rankin. Aware of the stakes, he quickly warned himself to be cautious and alert.

When Calinda began to sob, Rankin quietly said, "I'm sorry, *Senorita* Braxton: I should not have been so blunt. We only assume your father is dead; he vanished years ago. All of your letters to him were returned. Why did you come here?"

Her voice trembling with emotion, but edged with new hope, she told Rankin what had brought her to this moment. "I'm just as confused as you, sir. If you returned my letters, they never reached me. Why would he leave without telling me? I never imagined you wouldn't be able to help me." She tried to master her tears and grief.

Rankin didn't know what to think. Perhaps this girl was ignorant of the turbulent past. But did he owe anything to the daughter of his treacherous enemy? Still, her fear and sadness, if they were real, touched and disarmed him.

"Why would you come this far without hearing from Brax for years? I cannot understand why Brax didn't inform you of his departure."

Calinda explained her reasons and predicament, adding details of the recent robbery. Rankin concluded either she was an excellent deceiver or she didn't know the truth. This girl and curious situation could be dangerous. She could accidentally or rashly uncover the buried past . . . He needed time to observe her, to glean more facts.

A genial smile flickered on Rankin's lips as a plan formulated in his keen mind. "There is but one action to take. You'll come to the Cardone Ranch until we can decide what to do with you."

"I couldn't impose on you, Mister Cardone," she weakly argued.

"Don't be foolish, *Senorita* Braxton. Of course you'll come. You can hardly remain here accepting charity. Besides, this is no place for a young lady alone. You'll be my guest for as long as you wish." No matter what her motive, she must go with him.

A sunny and trusting smile brightened Calinda's face, softening her eyes. "You're very kind, Mister Cardone. Do you think there's any possibility my father's alive? Did anyone search for him?"

"Yes, *Senorita* Braxton. I personally conducted a lengthy search, then hired a Pinkerton detective. Nothing. When so much time passed without word or a clue, we gave up all hope. Brax was always craving new adventures and chasing dreams. Perhaps he'll return one day."

In her distracted state, Calinda missed the coldness in Rankin's voice and eyes and the intensity of his observation. Within the hour, she was packed and on her way to the Cardone Ranch, under the eagle eye of Rankin and several of his men.

To prevent her from asking too many questions, Rankin conversed on Texas, cattle, local events, and the landscape. Calinda was amazed by the scenery. She had never seen such openness, such seemingly endless grasslands and pale blue skies. Mountains could be viewed in the distance. In some areas, no trees or bushes existed. In others, they sparsely dotted the land in scattered clusters or stood singularly like a lonely person. Wild cactus and white yuccas were abundant, as were a variety of colorful wildflowers. Some fields appeared sown in thousands of golden-rods, Indian paintbrush, or blue bonnets. To take her mind off her dilemma, Calinda turned this way and that to take in the panorama, a ruggedly beautiful setting.

As they passed fenced areas, she watched healthy cattle and sleek horses as they grazed or moved about aimlessly. Sometimes mounted cowboys could be seen herding them or kneeling beside fires with branding irons. When Calinda asked if branding hurt the animals, Rankin eagerly launched into an explanation of the necessary task.

"A brand is like your name. Any man can capture and sell mavericks, unbranded cattle that roam free. It's important to use a mark that can't be changed by rustlers or be read in another way by some dishonest rancher. Branding might sting for a minute, but it's quickly forgotten. We try to do horses and cattle while they're young. There's a certain way to read a brand. It starts from top to bottom, then from left to right. If a letter is in a slanted position, it's called tumbling. If it's lying on its side, it's called lazy. Naturally a rocker on its base means rocking something, or wings on its sides means flying something. I'll show you all about them on the ranch."

"That sounds most intriguing," she said, eyes aglow.

"Do you know how to ride and shoot?" he asked curiously, glancing at the exquisite lady in the cheap, cotton dress.

"I'm a good rider, and I can handle a rifle. From what I've observed so far, both traits appear vital out here."

"Most assuredly, *Senorita* Braxton. I'll have one of my men teach you how to fire a pistol. One never knows when one's life might be in jeopardy." He chuckled at her hasty agreement.

"Do you have any family, Mister Cardone?' she inquired.

"One son. My wife . . . is no more."

Calinda graciously dismissed the grim mention of his deceased wife. "I look forward to meeting your son. I hope he won't mind my intrusion." Calinda was charmed by his easy manner and stimulating personality, taking an instant liking to this man. Despite their unlikely meeting, they had discovered an easy rapport.

"Lynx is rarely home. He prefers to roam. This area often inspires wildness in young bucks. I'm hoping he'll be ready to settle down soon." Calinda's arrival had been a shock to Rankin, and he was feeling more talkative than usual in his troubled state. It was uncanny, but she possessed a rare talent for liberating him of doubts and restraints.

Calinda noted the trace of sadness in Rankin's expression as he unknowingly allowed it to surface. Her heart went out to him; he must be terribly lonely with his wife dead and his son off sowing wild oats. If Lynx favored his father, he must be a handsome man. "How did he get such an unusual name?" she asked politely.

Rankin gazed off as he told her the fascinating story of his son's birth. "That was before the ranch was settled and our house was ready. Laura and I were living in a cabin in the edge of the mountains, waiting for winter to let up. I was trapping and hunting. One day I returned to find my only son arriving early. When he made his howling entrance, the first thing I grabbed to wrap him in was a lynx hide. Might add, he seems to have grown up as wild and cunning as one."

Traveling a road from his past and exploring Calinda's reactions, Rankin talked on. "Lynx was terribly upset when Laura was taken from us. He couldn't seem to sit still a minute. He became moody and reckless. Every time he rides off, I wonder if he'll get home alive. He's been in more gunfights and fistfights than I care to recall. I think that reputation of his has him bewitched; sometimes he acts like he can challenge and defeat Satan himself. In fact, I wouldn't be at all surprised if he did. I've scolded and reasoned for years. Hasn't done any good. God help any fool who crosses him." From the corner of his dark eyes, Rankin watched the girl sitting next to him. If any of those facts were familiar to her, it didn't show; nor did she seem to doubt or fear him. Rankin couldn't allow Calinda to discover what had happened with Brax, nor to become mistrustful of the Cardones.

Calinda felt Rankin had been speaking about himself as much as his carefree son. This Lynx should be ashamed of his selfishness; it was clear his father needed and loved him. She wanted to ask more questions, but didn't want to be impolite. When she tried to probe into her father's departure and past life on the ranch, Rankin asked her to wait until later when they could speak in private.

By dusk, the Cardone Ranch was in sight. They travelled for miles after Rankin told her they were on his land, then for many more miles after passing under the gatepost with the "C" over the "R". Evidently the Cardone Ranch was massive. The landscape was peaceful and lovely. Large herds of cattle and groups of horses could be seen at intervals. She was filled with awe and excitement.

When they approached the house, Calinda's eyes widened in astonishment. It was a two-story, oblong structure which hinted at a *hacienda* facade. The exterior was adobe, sheathed in sandy-colored stucco. The roofs on the house and the verandas were covered with mission tile, dull red terra cotta. The front portico spanned the full length of the house, displaying five large arches through which the downstairs doors and windows were visible. The curved arches were edged with muddy red adobe blocks, as were all windows on the first and second floors. Two private balconies were set on either end of the top floor, each with a front and side arch for views. The house and private yards were enclosed by an irregular stone wall. With cactus gardens scattered around, the scene was enchanting and heart-warming.

A short distance away, there were other structures, well-kept and solid. She noticed three stone bunkhouses with a separate cookhouse, two lofty barns, several supply sheds, a windmill and watertower, sturdy corrals, and miles of fencing. She couldn't help but wonder why her father would desert such a lovely locale and good man.

When the carriage halted, Rankin helped Calinda

down. A dark-haired, dark-eyed young woman left the house to join them, halting near Rankin to glower at Calinda with visible displeasure. She was introduced as Salina Mendoza, housekeeper and cook. Salina's colorful skirt swayed as her shapely body moved. She was wearing a white peasant blouse that hinted at a large bosom. Her mouth was painted red; her skin was olive and smooth. Midnight hair tumbled over her dark shoulders; her nearly black eyes were chilly and mocking. She merely nodded when Calinda spoke to her. Tossing a *"Disculpa,"* excuse me, over her shoulder, Salina turned and strutted inside with Calinda's small bundle clutched beneath one arm.

As they stepped into the entry hall, Rankin was telling Calinda she would need clothes made very soon. He suggested a party in the near future to introduce her to his neighbors, implying a lengthy stay. He could hardly keep his past friendship with her father a secret, so he used it as the motive for helping her. For now, he simply needed to discover how much she knew and why she had appeared suddenly.

Rankin doubted that Brax had confided in a distant family which he had abandoned and betrayed. The question remained, was Calinda Braxton as genuine and naive as she claimed and appeared? The best solution was to wait until Lynx came home. With Lynx's intuition, intelligence, and charming prowess, he would extract the truth and deal with it. If she was guilty, *Que lastima . . .*

Just inside the doorway, Calinda visually explored her new surroundings. To the left, a bowed arch revealed a striking dining room. An open door beyond it exposed the kitchen. Straight ahead, there were steps leading upstairs. Beside the stairs, she could partially view the bedroom used by Rankin. To her right, double wooden doors opened into an immense living area. To the rear of that room was Rankin's office, with doors opening into it and his bedroom.

Salina returned to show Calinda to a guest room on the second floor, a spacious and feminine room with a small front balcony and a large veranda to the rear. Salina spoke little and seemed to enjoy revealing her dislike of the beautiful stranger. Salina left her alone.

The moment the nasty girl left, Calinda examined her room. The furnishings were Spanish; the color scheme was in shades of blue, gold, and ivory. There was a sitting area to the front which opened onto the private balcony. She peered out the double glassed doors to the rear. A roofed veranda went from one end of the house to the other, again with three large arches before three sets of double doors. After freshening herself, Calinda donned a plain dress and went downstairs for dinner.

Rankin was relaxed in this controlled setting. Tonight, he chatted easily and smiled freely. The roast and fresh vegetables were delicious, a rare treat after her recent meals. Salina cleared the table as Rankin and Calinda went into a very masculine living room for a glass of sherry.

Calinda wandered around the spacious area as she sipped her sherry. As they sat, they conversed on the heavy and skillfully carved furniture, the chair made of horns from steers, the swords and guns displayed on one wall, the large buffalo head mounted over an enormous fireplace, various objects of Spanish art exhibited, and tapestries which added color and enchantment to the rectangular room, as did several multi-colored rugs placed on the highly polished wooden floor. Rankin pointed out the *"vegas,"* ceiling beams in cottonwood, and *"rajas,"* split cottonwood molding vertically attached to the walls every three feet. As with the exterior, the interior adobe walls were sheathed in beige stucco. There were two sets of double glass-doors, one leading to a side portico and one leading to the front veranda. Even though it lacked a feminine touch, Calinda found it appealing. To one end, there was a billiard table. Rankin said he would teach her that game.

The hour grew late as Rankin told Calinda carefully selected tales of how he and her father had spent earlier days. There were only a few hired hands still around from those years; they had been warned not to mention Brax or those past times. Calinda heard how her father had fought Indians and nature side-by-side with Rankin while he was carving out this empire which rivaled the King Ranch to the south near Laredo and the XIT to the northeast. Rankin disclosed many colorful past adventures, all of which Calinda found stimulating. She warmed at the slight mention of Laredo . . .

Rankin told Cal that Brax "just up and left one day", never to return or send a message of his whereabouts. "Brax made a terrible mistake, Calinda. We would have been great partners. If things had been different, both you and Lynx would be living here." Once again, Rankin gingerly questioned Brax's letters to her in England.

Calinda felt embarrassed about her father's actions toward her and her mother and to this generous man. Evidently her father had become greedy, selfish, and ungrateful. Rankin was surprised when Calinda apologized for her father's conduct. "I don't know what I would have done if you hadn't shown up, Mister Cardone. Considering how my father repaid your kindness, I'm amazed you did. Why would he leave here? Why didn't he confide in you or contact me?"

"In those early days, Brax and I were best friends, Calinda. I could hardly allow his daughter to fend for herself. Brax was like a man driven by some inexplicable force; maybe he found life here dull after the danger was past and the challenges were fewer. But I am sorry for what he put you through. You can stay here as long as you wish. I've missed laughter and beauty in this house. Come and go as you wish. Ask for anything you want or need. I owe Brax plenty. You have no place to go. I doubt you wish to return to England, and you have no other kin." He felt those reasons should hold her here until this precarious mystery could be solved. Besides, he desired her to remain.

His hospitality and friendship were godsends, and Calinda was drawn to them. "I insist on helping out, Mister Cardone. I can cook and clean. This is a large house for Salina to manage alone."

"A special guest doesn't work, *Senorita*," he teased mirthfully before they went their separate ways.

When Calinda awoke the next morning and went downstairs, she found Rankin gone and Salina busy with chores. When she offered to help, she quickly discovered Salina wasn't receptive to that idea. In fact, Salina waited on her as an honored guest in this house, as Rankin had ordered with the hope of disarming Calinda.

Calinda walked around the house and yards, trying to avoid Salina's glacial path and sharp tongue. She couldn't decide why the Mexican girl was so hostile. It seemed best to ignore Salina and evade her. If she stayed very long, she would find a way to halt this silly conflict with that tempestuous girl. Calinda wasn't one to accept charity or to laze around. But she had suffered several defeats and needed time to regroup her thoughts and to make future plans. Although she had never thought of getting a job, it seemed the only course for survival. The idea of teaching or sewing for the rest of her life sounded repulsive and boring. But what else could a woman do?

Calinda ate lunch in the quiet dining room, feeling very small at the lengthy table. Afterwards, she boldly explored the upstairs while Salina was occupied with laundry. At the top of the stairs, a hallway ran in either direction. She went to her left, to locate a room on the end which matched hers in size and shape. Obviously, from the manly decor, it was Lynx's room. On both sides of the stairway, she found two smaller rooms; one hinted at a previous nursery and the other was a storage room for linens and so forth. Between her room and Lynx's was another, but smaller, guestroom.

She walked to the veranda, promptly aware all three bedrooms opened onto it. As with the front two balconies, it had a waist-high adobe railing for safety. She strolled to each of the three back arches and two side ones to scan the picturesque setting. From her lofty position, she could see a distance in many directions. She leaned over the edge, mildly surprised to see the bottom floor revealed only windows. She did notice two other entrances, one for the kitchen and one she would learn was Salina's room. She sat in one of the chairs and allowed her placid senses to be engulfed by the splendor of nature before her gaze.

When Rankin hadn't returned by evening, Calinda questioned the sullen Salina about him and his return.

73

The girl's eyes flung daggers at Calinda as Salina informed her Rankin wouldn't be home until tomorrow night, that he had gone to purchase her some clothes in several nearby towns. The Mexican girl bade Calinda goodnight and went to her room in the rear of the house, with only an outside entrance.

Calinda went to the sitting room and selected a book from the shelves. She read for a while, then went to bed. Why hadn't Rankin told her his plans? A surprise? But why take such pains and expense with her? Evidently he was very lonely and wanted to keep her around.

Lying in bed, Calinda's mind rebelliously chased a sunny-haired man with mocking tawny eyes. How she wished she could forget Cody and his bedeviling touch. Why did little twinges pain her when she realized she would never see him again? His smiling face with its twinkling eyes loomed before her dreamy vision. She snuggled into the bed, recalling how his embrace had felt, how he had smelled, how his shirt had felt clinging to her nude body. Her fingers trailed over her lips as they craved to taste his again.

She felt warm and edgy, but didn't know why. She shifted this way and that, trying to find a comfortable position. He was like a pesty insect, buzzing around inside her head, refusing to leave her in peace. *Cody Richards,* her mind murmured softly, *damn you for haunting me.* Did she dare ask Rankin about this mysterious Cody?

Suspense filled Calinda's heart as dreams of what she would say and do if Cody discovered her identity and pursued her flashed through her mind. Would he check on her when he returned to Fort Worth and the Red Satin Saloon? Had he only been looking for a good time that night? Nelle had said that was the reason for his room and trips there. What if he was married? She hadn't even asked Nelle about that possibility. What was Cody really like? How far away was this Laredo? Would he bother to look her up one day? Probably not. A man with Cody's looks and wealth could have any woman, many women. Even though he had cunningly seduced her, he no doubt felt he didn't owe her anything since he had left her money and a crafty apology! But he did owe her something. He had forced himself into her life and heart and made an unforgettable impression there. By now, Cody had probably forgotten all about her and their night together . . .

To the east of Dallas, Major John Jones was having a meeting with his undercover Ranger, the mysterious and irresistible man who filled Calinda's dreams. Major Jones possessed all the traits demanded for a successful leader: he was a man with superior intelligence, a man feared and respected for his courage and daring, a man with a cool head and unerring judgment, a man who would give quarter and never ask for it. Jones was short and slender for such a powerful force, standing under five-nine and weighing less than one hundred and forty. Yet, he exuded strength and confidence.

Lynx Cardone listened as his superior told him General Steele had ordered Jones to Denton County to study the violence and crimes there. When Lynx remarked he was growing weary of his secret service, Major Jones reminded him of the importance of his undercover work. He listed several examples, two of which included getting into tight places and giving advanced warning of planned Ranger assassinations like he did in June of '77. A man in Lynx's stealthy position could ride into a troubled area, study it, then report to the arriving Rangers. Lynx's clues often aided their work and safety. But the perceptive Jones sensed a novel tension in his friend and fellow Ranger. As Jones watched Lynx, his penetrating eyes saw a noticeable glow of vitality and gentleness, a sensitivity and alertness which were rare.

A quiet and deliberate man, Major Jones laughed softly and said, "Maybe we'll have help on this problem. The Pinkerton men are holed up at LeGrand, and Marshal Russell and his deputies are over at the Windsor Hotel. We've got more bounty hunters, special agents, and detectives in town than Texas has cattle." He lightly stroked a thick mustache which almost concealed his upper lip. He was the perfect image of the aristocratic Southern gentleman.

"Is Armstrong coming in on this mission?" Lynx asked, watching Jones's dark eyes twinkle.

"He's working the southern area, down Kerrville and San Antonio way. Here's your crime book, Lynx. Don't lose it," he jested.

Lynx scanned the vital book which listed the names and descriptions of wanted men. Lynx sipped his coffee as Major Jones tossed his gear on the bed. Lynx's gaze eased over the supplies which all Rangers carried: Winchester rifle, Colt pistols with their eagles carved on ivory handles, Bowie knife, blanket, gum coat, riata, ammo, salt, and sweetened and dried corn for relieving thirst.

"It won't be much longer before you can wear your badge, Lynx. Be patient, son, you're doing us a valuable service. You've figured out it's the Bass gang that's operating around here?"

Lynx nodded his head. Jones continued, "I'm setting Peak on his trail. See if you can latch on to any of Sam's men. Here's a list of their names; memorize it and burn it."

Lynx read the seven names listed under Sam Bass's. There was an eighth name with a question mark beside it. Jones explained, "We're not sure about Murphy. Just be aware of him. Bass seems to be favoring the Texas Central and the Texas & Pacific Railroads. I'm checking their schedules now. I'll fill you in later. I sent for Lieutenant Reynolds, but don't know when he'll arrive. Quick as I get this matter studied, I'll decide how many Rangers we'll be needing."

"Where's McNelly?" Lynx asked, leaning back in the chair.

"Down Palo Alto way. He's needed there right now."

"I'll hang around the Split Horn Saloon a few days."

Jones halted his work to glance at his friend. "That's a rough place, Lynx. Be careful. Been home lately?"

Lynx sighed heavily and stroked his bristly chin. "Not in months. For the time being, that seems best." He chuckled wryly.

"Rankin still flaying your hide?" Jones teased knowingly.

"He will until he learns the truth."

"Won't be much longer," John Jones encouraged once more.

"I hope not, sir." Lynx didn't tell Jones about the flame-haired girl who continued to haunt him, even though he struggled to erase her from his mind.

Maybe he should ride over to Fort Worth tomorrow and see if Callie was still around and if she was all right. He wasn't sure if he dared see her this soon, but this ignorance was sheer torture.

When Lynx rode to the Red Satin Saloon that following night, only Jake Tarply knew of his coming or going. When he discovered Jake out back taking a break for fresh air, Lynx questioned him about the redhead who had arrived by stage a few days past. After learning what he had come for, Lynx mounted and raced the wind to Dallas, cursing Callie O'Hara all the way and berating himself for even caring about her.

The little vixen had fooled him completely, an uncommon mistake on his part, one which rankled for several reasons. When Callie's outlaw sweetheart discovered Lynx Cardone had bedded his stunning *zorra* first, perhaps a future showdown would result from his reckless night of passion. Lynx chuckled coldly. He might enjoy this one!

Anger and revenge gnawed at Lynx. He shouldn't have given Callie another thought. Why had he allowed that conniving bitch to burn through his tough hide? Apparently the only truth to leave her soft lips concerned the stage hold-up and her losses, which she deviously recovered at his and Nelle's expenses. But the traitorous Callie would pay dearly if and when their paths crossed again! Cousin or not, how dare Callie betray darlin' Nelle! Tonight, the flame in his heart smoldered brightly with fury, not passion . . .

Like a child at birthday or Christmas time, Calinda squealed with excitement and pleasure as she opened

78

the boxes Rankin had placed on her bed. His taste was excellent and his generosity extravagant. Everything Calinda could need or want was there. Rankin had taken one of her dresses and an outline of her shoe for appropriate sizes. He had even purchased jeans and boots for riding, as western women could dress and ride like men. There were dresses, nightgowns, underwear, shirts, pants, skirts, blouses, shoes, boots, and a gun with a leather holster.

Calinda argued against the expense but Rankin said, "While I was in town on business, I remembered the robbery and your losses. Your father left before I paid him for the last cattle drive. I only spent the money due him; he shouldn't mind."

That last lie eased Calinda's conscience. But she knew from Salina that Rankin had gone specifically to shop for her. Evidently he was proud and didn't want her to guess his kind motives. Rankin was slightly flustered when the young girl hugged him and thanked him over and over. "A lovely young lady should be dressed in silks and satins, but that's the best they had to offer nearby. Next time I go to Wichita Falls or San Antonio, you can tag along and choose some more clothes. When I show you off to my friends and neighbors, I want you to be the prettiest girl in Texas."

As Calinda admired the clothes, Rankin watched her closely. She possessed many fine qualities. Even if she had originally come here to cause trouble, Rankin would soon have her too indebted and charmed to do so. If she was anything like she seemed, she wouldn't have the stomach or desire to deceive or betray the Cardones.

Impressionable and susceptible, Calinda was overwhelmed by Rankin's plans and actions. The next few weeks saw her adjusting easily and quickly to life on the Cardone Ranch. As she eased into the ranch routine, she showed a freshness and warmth which appealed to Rankin. During these past years, Rankin hadn't realized how lonely and barren his life had become. Rankin found himself enjoying Calinda's wit, charm, and intelligence. She sparkled with life and made him feel vital and young again. A budding fondness and delight in her companionship came to pass during those following weeks after her arrival, deepening in spite of his lingering doubts and resistance.

Frequently they were seen riding together, laughing freely and getting to know each other as Rankin introduced Calinda to his cattle spread and way of life. During meals, they would engage in stimulating conversation. Calinda's eyes would shine with enthusiasm as Rankin told her the history of the west and his ranch. She came to respect and admire him and to love the ranch and her new existence. Helpless to alter her situation, she eagerly accepted it. Each task learned or observed was done with carefree adventure and gay spirit.

True to his word, Rankin taught Calinda how to play billiards, then cards. Many nights their laughter and wagers could be heard above the stillness of the night. Calinda learned to ride a horse western style. She watched calves and colts being branded. She perched on the corral fence in her jeans, boots, and colorful shirt as cowboys broke wild horses. She rode beside Rankin as he checked on herds or fences. Each passing day drew them closer, a respect and admiration for each blooming steadily. Neither mentioned Calinda's departure, as if it were unthinkable.

At times, Calinda thought she noted strange looks

in Rankin's eyes, but dismissed them as tricks of light or attributed them to fatigue. It almost seemed Rankin wanted to fully accept her permanent residence and affections, but was afraid to do so. Sometimes, Calinda sensed he was withholding facts from her, that he was telling her only what he wanted her to know. She scolded herself for harboring such unkind suspicions. When Rankin was distant or moody, she concluded it was from loneliness for his son or perhaps painful memories which her feminine presence inspired. Calinda decided that Rankin was a wary man, a man afraid to share too much of himself, a man afraid of being hurt or deserted. To Calinda, Rankin was a special and uncommon man, a private man who defended his home and feelings. It didn't take long for the ranch to seem like home and Rankin like family.

Rankin dreaded the facts this girl might uncover, facts he wanted to remain buried. He knew he was becoming extremely fond of Calinda; he was beginning to trust her. He was torn between two warring emotions. It was difficult to see Calinda as Brax's child, but she was. Was it dangerous or insane to keep her around? Should he give her money and send her away? How could a sweet, artless child survive alone? Calinda hadn't said or done anything unusual. Rankin fretted over this affection which was destroying his clear head and lessening his desire for revenge. But Rankin selfishly ignored his qualms, deciding to deal with Calinda's reality and future some distant day.

One night, Calinda was asking Rankin if there was anything they could do to try to locate her father. Rankin stiffened and grew silent, taken off guard by her unexpected question. His voice was bitter and sullen as he advised her to accept her loss. When she rejected that harsh suggestion, she was stunned when Rankin reminded her of her father's abandonment, and told her Brax had been selfish and insensitive.

"How can you speak of him this way?" she asked sadly.

"You forget, Cal," he stated, calling her by his chosen nickname, "I knew him for years, but you haven't seen him since you were a baby. A man can change greatly in that length of time. Looking back, I doubt I knew him at all. I'm sorry if you find the truth painful and upsetting, but you persist in learning it. Do not press for facts which will hurt you. Brax helped me carve this ranch out of a dangerous wilderness, then deserted it before we could enjoy our success. He was like my brother; Lynx loved him and looked up to him. I think that's part of Lynx's problem. My son has never gotten over what happened that day." Angered, he had made a careless slip.

"I don't understand," she murmured, observing him closely, hearing an odd inflection in his words.

To gain Calinda's sympathy and to prevent more discussion, Rankin said, "I've told you all I can; the past is a painful subject, Cal. You see, we . . . lost Laura that same day. It was hard for a teenager to lose two people in one blow. Sometimes I think Lynx loved and respected Brax more than me."

A twinge nipped at Calinda. What had destroyed the closeness between Rankin and her father? Why would Brax abruptly disappear? There was a mystery here which Calinda felt she shouldn't question now, but would study later. Rankin had shown some strong feelings which alarmed Calinda: resentment, anger, and coldness. She recalled their first meeting with rising curiosity. Rankin had surely mistrusted and disliked her. Why? Very strange . . .

As if ignorant of his slips, Rankin stood up and stretched. He suggested they turn in for the night. Calinda went to her room with mounting intrigue to keep her company. Clearly, Rankin Cardone didn't want to discuss her father or the muddy past. Did Rankin blame her father for adding to their misery and grief, for Lynx's departure and continued absence? Did he also blame her? Apparently her father and Lynx had left at a painful moment in time, left Rankin to suffer and to recover on his own. If such talks made him edgy and unhappy, Calinda, as his guest, shouldn't broach them, for now.

Another storm was brewing in the Cardone house. Witnessing the growing bond between Rankin and Calinda, Salina did everything she could to prove Calinda didn't belong in Texas and that she was taking advantage of Rankin's charity. Salina tried to inspire resentment toward Calinda, to make Calinda appear a haughty and soft lady who should be asked to leave. The fiery tempered and envious Salina wanted Calinda gone before Lynx's return. She was determined to do anything to become the mistress of this ranch, the wife of Lynx Cardone. Her snide remarks and jealousy soon grew visible to the men and to Rankin, all of whom dismissed it as harmless feminine rivalry.

When Salina continued her hatefulness toward Calinda, Rankin warned the feisty girl to behave, but that only increased Salina's envy and malice. It didn't help matters when Calinda insisted on doing her own chores: washing and ironing her clothes, helping to set and clear the table, and cleaning her own room. Such tasks only proved Calinda wasn't soft and vain, much to Salina's chagrin.

Calinda was well-liked and received by the ranch-hands. She was a breath of fresh air on a stifling day. She was taught to shoot and ride as well as the men. Each day her knowledge and skills increased.

On Saturday, Rankin took Calinda along to a neighbor's barbecue and dance. Her winning charm and freshness helped her make friends quickly and easily. As Rankin watched her talking and learning to square-dance, a new idea came to mind . . .

Rankin reassessed his situation. Calinda was resilient and well-bred. She was beautiful and friendly. If his plans could be carried out, Calinda would be the ideal choice for a Cardone, a perfect wife for his wayward son. An heir would solve all of his problems. Was it possible to entice Lynx to marry her? A striking wife and child might persuade Lynx to remain home. With so much at stake, could Lynx be compelled to respond to his duties just once? Surely one look at Cal and Lynx would accept his vital role as husband and father . . . Too, Lynx was a man to turn a woman's head. If Lynx agreed to his scheme, Calinda shouldn't be able to resist his charms and prowess. After all, if Cal made trouble, Lynx would be the eventual loser. After a marriage between them, it wouldn't matter what Calinda discovered . . . Besides, Rankin trusted and adored her.

When Salina noticed Rankin elaborating on Lynx's good looks and strong character and hinting at how he needed to settle down, she sensed what the older man was plotting. She fumed and ranted in her room at night. Calinda Braxton would never get Lynx Cardone!

That next day, Salina initiated her own scheme. When Calinda entered the kitchen for the dishes, Salina glanced at her. *"Mi amor* will be home soon," she stated casually. *"Tengo muchos ansioso.* He is so *caronil,* so *intrepido. Tanto guapo, un ardiente pasion,"* she stated dramatically, sighing as if caught in the throes of fiery passion.

Calinda turned to look at her. "I beg your pardon?" she said, doubting her ears. Had the girl actually spoken to her? The Spanish words were unknown to Calinda, but she'd recognized that sensual tone.

"Cobre piel . . . Dorado ojo . . . Rubio cabello," she sighed passionately as she described Lynx's golden appearance.

"I don't understand Spanish, Salina," she told the dreamy girl.

"I said, my love is coming soon. He is so virile, so handsome, so intrepid, and so passionate. I quiver with eagerness. When you see him, *Senorita* Braxton, remember, he is taken," she seductively warned, continuing calmly with her chore.

"Taken? By whom?" Calinda asked. Rankin hadn't mentioned a sweetheart. What was Salina up to now?

"By me," the girl smugly claimed, tapping her chest. "Lynx has eyes for me alone. We are *mucho* close," she alleged, crossing her fingers as an example. "When he is home, I have no time for chores. You wish to help? Work while I am with him. He is *mucho* tempting, so remember you are a *dama,* a lady," she stressed sarcastically. "Do not charm him or sneak into his room. I do not carry this knife without reason," she brazenly threatened, pulling up her skirt to expose the shiny blade strapped to her inner thigh. "Lynx Cardone is mine. You have the *hidalgo encantado . . . Senor* Cardone bewitched, but do not toss your charms on Lynx. A real lady would not be living off a *caballero*. Return to where you belong."

"I belong here as long as Rankin wants me to stay," Calinda calmly stated. "As to Lynx, you have no worries about me. If he was a real man, he would be home where he belongs."

"I would not speak so to Lynx. He has a short fuse and quick gun. No one, including his papa, tells him what to do. He is like a blue norther: powerful, cold, destructive. You should hide in fear while he is home. *Senoritas* like you he chews up and spits out like old tobacco. Be on guard, *Senorita* Braxton, Lynx is a *hombre* as you have never met before. But do not be fooled by his charms and good looks; he uses them as weapons, always with a purpose. I will slit the throat of any girl who forgets he is mine."

Calinda realized the Mexican girl was doing her best to intimidate her, to speak understandable English in that thick accent of hers. She smiled sweetly and inquired, "What does *Llama de mi corazon* mean?"

Salina gaped at her for the silly question, then sneered, "Flame of my heart; why? Did you not hear my warnings?" she demanded.

"No warning is necessary; I don't chase men, any man." She left the kitchen without explaining herself, mentally savoring the endearment Cody had murmured that fateful night, wondering why it had flashed across her mind.

Naturally Calinda didn't relate that ridiculous conversation to Rankin. In fact, she and Rankin spoke little that night at supper. His mind seemed on a matter far removed from her. Shortly after their meal, Rankin entered his office to do bookwork.

Calinda went to her room to read before bedtime. Salina's words and warnings chewed at her. Were Lynx and Salina in love? Did the Mexican girl fear Calinda could replace her? Would this wealthy and handsome son marry a servant? Evidently from the recent conversations, this mysterious Lynx was due for a visit soon. Calinda's ears had been flooded with stirring tales and descriptions of Lynx. As Salina's resentment had increased and she was now voicing a claim on Lynx, Calinda was sorely tempted to vex Salina by boldly flirting with Lynx when he came home. She couldn't behave like that.

Calinda wondered about Lynx. He was said to be a handsome and dauntless rogue. The wranglers and Salina made him sound larger than life, a compelling legend, a man of matchless prowess. Calinda laughed softly. What if this Lynx was actually clumsy and plain? What if he was only a boastful and insipid bumpkin? On the other hand, what if he was invincible, arrogant, cold, and deadly . . .

After the magnetic stranger in the Red Satin Saloon, could she ever desire another man? Could any man match Cody's prowess and looks? Calinda was plagued by memories of him and doubts of her future. She couldn't and wouldn't return to England. How could she search for Brax in this vast and wild territory? Should she leave and begin a new life? Where? How? Doing what?

Life was peaceful on the Cardone Ranch. She felt safe and happy. She couldn't bear the thought of leaving this security to face unknown dangers and fierce challenges. What to do? At times, Rankin was so odd. Yet, he seemed to care for her and about her. He claimed he wanted her to remain, but for how long?

As long as she complied to his terms, he enjoyed her company. But what was the truth about her father? Without money and protection, she was literally trapped here. Besides, she wanted to meet this Lynx just once . . .

The next afternoon, Calinda received another startling surprise. Several trunks were brought to her room, trunks filled with clothes and jewels which had belonged to Laura Cardone. Rankin insisted she take and use whatever fit and was still in good repair. Pressed, Calinda accepted this added act of kindness and generosity. She was astonished by the elegant gowns and costly jewels in the trunks. And each garment she tried on fit perfectly. She wished Rankin would show her a picture of Laura, but he didn't.

When Calinda questioned Rankin about her future, he smiled and told her not to worry, that she was welcome to live here forever. "But, Rankin," she reasoned, "I'm not even family. What will people think if I continue to live here? At least put me to work," she coaxed.

"Who cares about idle gossip? Who would dare to speak against Rankin Cardone? From this day on, you are as family. You don't want to leave, and I wish you to stay. Why must we be miserable to please others? No more silly talk about leaving," he ordered sternly, affectionately cuffing her chin.

The next afternoon, Calinda went to her private balcony to catch a breath of air. She looked out over the grassy terrain before her line of vision. She saw Rankin on horseback in the distance, talking with another man whose back was to her. She observed them for a time, then leaned against the solid corner portion between the two arches, concealed from view. Without spoiling the closeness between them, she needed to persuade Rankin to clarify the past, to learn more about her father, to decide if and how to locate Elliott Braxton. She needed to make a decision: to live here or to go look for Brax. It dismayed her to realize she was calling and viewing him more and more as Brax, a stranger, not as her father . . .

"So, you've finally come to visit," Rankin commented merrily.

"You don't look pleased to see me, father," Lynx teased, a broad grin making tiny creases near his amber eyes and full mouth. "Should I have requested a visit before surprising you?" he joshed.

"I'm always happy when you come home. But I'd be happier if you'd stay. I also have a surprise for you; we have a guest, a beautiful one," Rankin hinted, dreading his son's reaction.

Lynx wailed humorously, "Not another rancher's daughter to toss in my lap? I thought you'd grown tired of matching me up to fillies."

Lynx's smile was rapidly replaced by a frigid scowl as he listened to his father's startling news. "You're not serious, father? Do you realize the trouble she can make?"

Rankin explained what he had discovered about Calinda Braxton and his impressions of her. Lynx straightened in his saddle as he unwillingly absorbed the incredible story. He was astonished and vexed when Rankin alleged Calinda's innocence and ignorance, then expounded on her good virtues and beauty. "I can't believe you would allow a slithering viper to nest in our home," he scolded angrily. "What if she's playing you for a fool, father? If not, what if she discovers the truth?"

"Cal isn't like Brax, son. I doubt Brax told Miranda or Cal anything. I'm positive she is honest and vulnerable."

"You don't mind if I decide for myself? Let's go have a look at your Cal," Lynx said coldly, sitting rigid in his saddle.

As they were riding in, one of the men shouted to the others, "Lynx is home, boys. He's coming in with the boss."

That news caught Calinda's attention. She remained concealed behind the wide span on the balcony, peering out to see this legend for herself. As Rankin and Lynx halted and dismounted, Calinda's eyes blinked rapidly in disbelief, then stared at the tall figure of the man greeting his friends below. Cody Richards! Tex! Lynx Cardone . . .

As Lynx joked and talked with the cowpunchers who gathered around, Calinda listened to the mellow and stirring voice she would never forget. It was undeniably and terrifyingly clear the mysterious stranger and Lynx Cardone were the same man. Why had dear Nelle lied to her? It was impossible for Nelle not to know who this wealthy and irresistibly handsome man was. Had Lynx discovered who she was after leaving her that night? Was that why he had left the money? Was this the meaning of the last words of that note . . .

Cal wouldn't humiliate herself and her gracious host by confronting his son with his wicked conduct in Fort Worth. Yet, how could she calmly stroll downstairs and act as if they had never met? How would Lynx react to seeing her again, in his home? Maybe

Salina was right, she should hide in her room! No, she couldn't do that.

Resentment and spite filled Calinda as she watched him laugh happily as if he were without a care in the world. Surely the note had been a jest! Doubtlessly he had assumed their paths would never cross again. Calinda suddenly realized she possessed the delightful element of surprise; Lynx would be shocked and distressed by their unexpected meeting, especially under these circumstances. He wouldn't dare do or say anything wrong before his father. Dreams of revenge challenged her to repay him, to teach the arrogant rogue a lesson. She would see him squirm in dread of her devastating revelation of his vile behavior, squirm and worry. It vexed Calinda to admit perhaps Salina's description of him hadn't been exaggerated at all. No doubt they made a fine pair!

Calinda remained out of sight until the two men entered the house, then she hurried into her room. She rushed to her closet and searched it for a particular dress which had belonged to Laura, one in elegant red satin and trimmed in expensive black lace. This outfit should certainly jog his memory. When she was ready for the evening meal, she brushed her fiery chestnut locks until they bounced and shone with golden lights. Even if the dress clashed with her hair, no matter.

She answered the knock at her door; it was Salina coming to tell her of Lynx's arrival and the dinner hour. The girl's dark eyes narrowed in rage as they slipped over the exquisite Calinda.

"Have you forgotten my warning, *bruja?*" she purred venomously.

"Perhaps if we go downstairs and you repeat it before both men, then I shall always recall it," Calinda warned in return, rankled by the girl's antagonistic manner and taut with apprehension. "I could care less about you or Lynx Cardone. Threaten me once more, and I will make certain Rankin learns of it instantly. Is that clear, Salina?"

Salina was shocked by Calinda's sudden display of mettle and daring. She nodded, then disappeared. Calinda gracefully walked down the stairs, her legs shaky. As she was about to knock on the closed door, Rankin opened it and came out into the entry hall.

Since it had become their habit to dress for dinner, Rankin never suspected Calinda's mischievous and dangerous ploy. He looked her over and smiled in pleasure, imagining his son's reaction to this lovely creature. He glanced inside and said, "Lynx, this is Calinda Braxton. Cal, my son Lynx." As Rankin made the introductions, he failed to witness Calinda's feigned look of surprise and following glare of fury which she cunningly dismissed before he turned to her again. But Rankin alertly caught the astonishment and another unknown emotion which flashed over his son's face. He hastily decided his son was pleasantly surprised to find Calinda Braxton so entrancing. "You two get acquainted while I go tell Salina we're ready for dinner to be served." With that, Rankin left them alone, pulling the door shut.

Neither Calinda nor Lynx moved or spoke for a short time, each deliberating how to handle this precarious situation. His gaze mocking, Lynx scoffed sarcastically, "You're Calinda Braxton?"

"Yes, but you aren't Tex, or Cody Richards," she sneered.

"Cody Richards?" he repeated in confusion.

"When I asked Nelle about the room's owner that

next morning, she told me your name was Cody Richards," Cal said.

Lynx stared at her skeptically. "How could you ask anything about me when you skipped out at dawn with Cousin Nelle's earnings? Didn't I leave enough money? I must have been dazed with fatigue; I never pegged you as a thief and a liar. What did your lover say about your night with me? Or didn't anyone tell you he's a deadly killer? Just what are you two trying to pull on the Cardones, Miss Callie O'Hara?" Lynx sarcastically responded. Was this girl more cunning and daring than he could imagine? Whatever she was trying to pull, he would enjoy defeating her!

It was Calinda's turn to look puzzled, then all at once she understood. She laughed coldly, relishing his dismay as she corrected his mistaken impressions. "My mother was the only one to call me Callie; she's dead now. In my stupor that night, I answered to it. To my misfortune, you persist in confusing me with Callie O'Hara, Nelle's cousin. Unfortunately, we arrived on the same stage, and we're both redheads. I have never been a thief or a harlot. As to being a liar, surely you know why I misled you about my destination, to prevent any future contact with a lecherous beast. As you can see, Mister Cardone, you have the wrong Callie again, as you did that night. If you doubt me or my word, go ask Nelle," she frostily suggested.

Lynx's keen mind seized these facts, quickly sorting and storing them. Had he been set up by Elliott Braxton's treacherous and beautiful daughter? What were the odds against Calinda Braxton accidentally landing in his bed and arms? *Two Callies?* He strolled forward and halted before her. His hand came up to stroke her fiery cheek as he huskily remarked, "From where I'm standing, I'd say I have the right one, for a change, Miss Callie Braxton. Red satin suits you after all. But you certainly go to rash lengths to meet and charm a cowpoke."

Calinda drew back her hand to slap the smug look off his mocking face. Lynx painlessly captured it before it could complete its task. He chuckled. "At least you're wide awake tonight. I'd like some straight answers later. I didn't realize you'd use my money to settle yourself in my home," he teased, oddly delighted to see her tonight.

"Considering how we met, Mister Cardone, I'd say I earned your monetary assistance. But if I had known who you were, I wouldn't be here right now. It appears lying about your name was another error."

His tawny eyes travelled over her furious expression. "What else do you think you've earned, Callie?" he asked, his voice deceptively soft.

"I don't understand," she replied, trying to pull free. "If you think I'm here because of you or what happened, you're vastly mistaken."

"We'll see, won't we?" he hinted mysteriously, then released his hold and stepped away from her. He turned his back to retrieve his brandy, his senses whirling madly at her nearness.

Calinda's hand impulsively reached out as if to snatch his gun. "I wouldn't if I were you, Callie," he warned coldly without moving or turning. "I have a reputation for dealing harshly with people who pull guns on me."

"You have eyes in the back of your head?" she snapped nervously.

"A man in my position must to survive." As he turned and faced her, he said, "Don't ever draw a gun on anyone unless you intend to use it. They might not be as even-tempered or forgiving as I am."

"What if I intended to use it?" she challenged.

Lynx didn't flinch when he stated seriously, "If you dare to challenge me, be prepared to pay the price for defeat." Calinda couldn't tell what challenge he was referring to at that moment.

"If you dare to ravish a female in her sleep, you should be prepared to pay the price for your crime," she warned in return.

Abruptly Lynx filled the room with lusty laughter. "I must admit, you're one brave and reckless gal, Calinda Braxton. It seems we've gotten off on the wrong foot again. Would another apology settle those ruffled feathers?" He leaned against the billiard table and crossed one booted foot over the other, observing her with a roguish smile. Maybe his father was accurate in his assessments. Even so, she would be a stimulating riddle to solve.

"An apology is insignificant for what you did, Mister Cardone."

"Tonight, or back in Fort Worth?" he playfully jested, as they both recalled the implication in his note. "I did plan to seek you out one day soon, but I never expected to find you waiting here for my return. This looks to be a most interesting reunion. Just imagine, you and me living under the same roof. Think we should let Father in on our little secret?" He chuckled when she blushed and stiffened.

"You wouldn't dare confess what you did to me! But if you come near me again, I'll tell him! If you think your money absolves you of guilt, you're wrong. I'm not afraid of you, but I wouldn't want to hurt your father by telling him what a villain you are. From what

95

I hear, your visits are short and rare; thankfully," she scoffed to nettle him. His smoldering eyes seemed to scorch her.

He laughed heartily. "Maybe I should make some exceptions and changes this trip. What do you think, Callie, *mi bello flor?*"

Before Calinda could reply, Rankin returned to tell them dinner was ready, cognizant of the fiery sparks between them. Setting down his glass and straightening, Lynx smiled sensuously at her and waved her forward. "After you, Callie. It sure is nice to be home, Father."

Calinda shot him a look of warning before she turned to follow Rankin into the dining room with Lynx closely behind her.

Chapter Four

As the meal was served and eaten, Calinda was hard pressed to remain poised enough to prevent curiosity or suspicion in Rankin or Salina. She wondered how a lady was supposed to act under such trying circumstances. Here she sat having dinner and sharing the company of the man with whom she had slept, the man who had claimed her purity, the man who inflamed her senses with his very presence, the man who seemed to comprehend his provocative effect upon her and was playfully taking advantage of her discomfiture and necessary silence. She wanted to hate him and to punish him, but could do neither.

Rankin sat at the end of the long table, with Calinda on the right side and Lynx on the left, facing each other. Calinda politely dined and listened while the two men did most of the talking. Never had she seen Rankin's eyes glow with such warmth and pleasure, proclaiming his love and need for his son. Calinda was fascinated with the easy rapport and genial manner between the two men. Not a single cross word or surly expression had passed between them. They appeared overjoyed with this visit, delighting in every moment and word.

The conversation waxed between the ranch and Texas happenings. Calinda watched the variety of emotional reactions come and go on the beguiling face of a man who was no longer a stranger. Except in character, he was perfect, a fact which disturbed her. His features were strong and well-blended to promote a facade of strength, looks, and self-assurance. She could mentally envision the tall, steely-muscled body in smooth bronze beneath his snug black pants, baby blue shirt, and black leather vest. She shifted in her chair and tore her probing eyes from the magnetic Lynx. She found herself wanting to run her fingers through that enticing head of brandy-colored hair and to gaze longingly into those amber eyes. What had gotten into her? She was as nervous as a yearling around a hot branding iron.

A man keenly versed in making many observations simultaneously without appearing to have but one object of interest, Lynx was all too aware of the fetching girl before him and her furtive study of him as he attempted to focus his full attention on his father and their talk. Lynx was utterly intrigued by this stimulating turn of events. Later, he would make some inquiries in town, just to be certain there were two Callies indeed.

There was something about Callie and her abrupt arrival which troubled him. Since Lynx had never found any woman irresistible or unforgettable, he didn't realize it was the powerful attraction between them which plagued him. He attributed his uneasiness to suspicions. There were several unacceptable answers to this stunning mystery: she could be a clever spy or a money-grubbing imposter; she could be a malicious and sly conspirator; or she could be real . . .

The perceptive Rankin witnessed the undercurrents passing between Lynx and Calinda, swift currents which both were trying to dam and control. His heart soared with satisfaction. By mutual attraction or wily coercion, he would come out the winner if those two got together. Lynx and Calinda were both intelligent and stubborn. To avoid suspicions and rebellion, Rankin decided to allow Mother Nature to take her course first, and she seemed mighty busy already.

To draw Calinda into the conversation, Rankin spoke of her harrowing experience on the way to Fort Worth and dilemma after her arrival. Amusement sparkled in Lynx's eyes and he grinned raffishly. Calinda demurely lowered her lashes as if embarrassed about something, her cheeks glowing strangely. Rankin studied these reactions and wondered about them. It appeared those two shared a compelling secret. How was that possible since they had just met? Why was Calinda being so quiet and nervous? Why was Lynx so devilishly playful and attentive?

"I hope you learned a valuable lesson, Cal; don't fight odds greater than you. Some men are very dangerous and impulsive," Lynx beguilingly remarked. "You were lucky to come out unscathed. You're fortunate to have lost nothing more than clothes and jewels."

Calinda stared at him, then stated, "They had no right to steal my possessions or to threaten my life. In the same circumstances, I'll react the same way. I doubt you would give in willingly, even with overpowering odds against you," she added calmly, fuming inside, her words carrying dual meanings which he astutely understood. How dare he so boldly and rashly hint at their intimate misadventure! Did the unflappable rogue lack all manners, caution, and wits?

"But I'm a man; I carry a set of Colts which itch to speak for me. Perhaps I should teach you how to protect yourself while I'm home," he audaciously suggested. "I'm good at self-defense, and a *bello mariposa* is a tempting treasure." Yes, with her vivid beauty and delicate air, she presented the illusion of an exquisite butterfly.

"Rankin gave me a gun, and he taught me how to fire it. Next time, if there is a next time, the odds won't be so one-sided."

"I'll give you a piece of advice, Cal; men like those are deadly. They'd kill even a woman if she caused them trouble, shoot her and never glance back or think twice about it."

"Those are nearly the same words that bandit leader used to frighten me. I hope your knowledge and advice don't come from excessive experience," she remarked accusingly, wanting to ask for a translation of the softly spoken Spanish words. "You do have quite a reputation."

"Where females are concerned, from observations only. I've had my share of gunfights with men who simply want to see if they can out-draw me. Since I'm sitting here tonight, that should tell you who was the fastest and smartest," he said, without arrogance and with a subtle hint of dissatisfaction with his uncontrollable reputation.

"The hazard of being a famous gunslinger?" she probed.

Through clenched teeth, Lynx informed her, "I've never shot any man who didn't demand it, one way or another."

"What about your famed Texas Rangers? Why can't they clean up this lawlessness and keep the peace here?"

"They're trying their damnedest. Texas is a huge territory, too many warring factions, too many people looking out for themselves."

"What warring factions?" she inquired, listening intently.

"The Comanche and Apache Indians, Mexican bandits, and a wide assortment of American criminals. We're flooded with escaping convicts, rustlers, outlaws, gunmen, and such. Down South, Mexican bandits cross the border to rob and raid, then return to safety. The Rangers have pursued them many times, but the government doesn't like them encroaching on Mexican soil." Lynx couldn't bring himself to tell about the Alamo, where too many Rangers had died in defeat.

"To make matters worse for the Rangers, even supposedly law-abiding men cause trouble. We've had range feuds, fence-cuttings, riots, lynchings, and bouts of revenge. The Rangers spend as much time on battling ranchers and farmers as they do fighting crime."

"It sounds like an awful place to live. Why don't the ranchers and town people help the Rangers keep peace?"

"Texas was practically lawless after the War ended in '65. The soldiers who returned here or remained here afterwards were too used to the killing and violence. When anyone challenged them or harmed them, it was natural to fight back with bloodshed and strength. The South was bound together during the War. After it, everyone was out for himself. When the railroads pushed into Texas to haul cattle and sheep, train-robbers followed their progress to get rich. The biggest conflicts came with fencing. Grasslands and water-holes were claimed and protected by cattlemen. The farmers and squatters didn't care for barriers against them; neither did the sheep-herders. Many a killing and feud's been over those barbed strips."

Calinda and Rankin were most impressed by Lynx's span of knowledge. Calinda found herself mesmerized by his mellow drawl. The tone of Lynx's voice thrilled Rankin, for it told him there was much he didn't know about his grown son. Rankin found the emotions exposed there pleasing and enlightening. He smiled at Lynx, who didn't notice it as he and Calinda gazed enraptured at each other across the table. For a time, Rankin felt they didn't even acknowledge his presence.

"Lynx, why don't you take Cal for a stroll," Rankin suggested to give them time to be alone. "I promised to ride over to Rafe's to discuss his water problems," he added to remove himself graciously.

Lynx stood up, his agile frame drawing Calinda's eyes to it. Salina entered the room, heading for Lynx, smiling provocatively. As if she hadn't heard Rankin's words, Salina asked coyly, "When I finish my chores, can we take a walk, Lynx?"

Lynx tugged a dark curl and chuckled, his eyes glowing with a response which piqued Calinda, as he had intended it to do. "*Mañana,* Salina. I'm taking Cal for a stroll. Been good since I left?" he teased lazily.

"Claro esta, mi famoso vaquero," Salina promptly replied, eyes sending messages which even a dull-visioned man could read.

"You get your chores done, and I'll see you later," Lynx advised, as if planning some romantic rendezvous.

Calinda masked her warring emotions, hands clenched tightly on the edge of the table, as she arose. She must avoid this cunning devil. "I'm very tired, Mister Cardone. Perhaps Salina would accept the stroll in my place. I'll go to my room, then you can visit privately."

Neither man missed her inflection on the last two words. Rankin was relieved when he didn't have to insist their guest come first, since Lynx quickly took her unintentional bait. "It appears we're becoming sister and brother, Cal. We should get acquainted before I ride off again. No telling when I'll be home again."

Not wishing to cause more resentment in the Mexican girl, Calinda tried once more to dissuade him, inwardly afraid of being alone with him. "I'm sure there will be plenty of time tomorrow for us to talk, Mister Cardone. Salina has been looking forward to your homecoming. You don't want to disappoint her. Goodnight."

As Calinda turned to make a floating exit, Lynx was at her side, gripping her elbow. She was shocked when he teased, "Afraid to stroll in the dark with your new brother? I'm perfectly harmless; ask my father. Cardones are famous for their hospitality and manners."

Calinda reluctantly accepted the enforced invitation. "I'm well acquainted with the Cardone traits. If you insist," she casually yielded.

"I insist, Callie; and the name is Lynx."

After they left the room, Rankin turned to the furious Salina and stated coldly, "Need I remind you, Salina, you are my servant? Cal is a guest, and I will not tolerate such rude and brassy behavior. I should also remind you, Lynx is a Cardone. Don't interfere in his life. I will not speak further on these issues," he tersely warned.

Salina acknowledged his warnings, but dismissed them. Besides, the night was young and Lynx was within her reach once more. This time, he would discover she had become very much a woman. This time, she wouldn't accept another rejection from him.

Calinda and Lynx silently walked toward the corral, to halt there and to watch the moonlight dance off the shiny hides of the sleek horses. An Appaloosa stallion came trotting over for Lynx to nuzzle him affectionately. She witnessed the strong attachment between the mottled steed and his bronzed master. As Lynx fluffed Star's mane, Cal noted the stirring gentleness in his mood and expression. This man was capable of feeling and displaying a wide range of complex emotions.

"He's very beautiful," Calinda said softly.

"Out here, a man needs a tough and smart horse. If his mount isn't quick and alert, he can find himself in great danger. Go, Star, visit with your friends," he told the animal, who seemed to understand his words and returned to a small group on the far side of the corral.

As Rankin rode off, they both smiled and waved. After a few moments, Lynx asked, "You want to stroll or sit over there and talk?" pointing to a swing beneath an arched trellis which was covered with fragrant yellow roses, a highly romantic setting in the moonlight.

"Neither," she replied, tense and alert. "We have nothing to discuss. I only agreed to a walk to avoid a scene. Just stay clear of me."

When he took her hand to lead her to the swing, she yanked it away and glared at him. He laughed and taunted, "I don't bite, Cal."

"I think you do," she too quickly snapped, then flushed.

"Por Dios, you are afraid of me," he teased as if surprised.

Calinda ignored his taunt to sit down on the stone enclosure, instead of the swing which would allow him to be too close for comfort or attention. She might as well settle this trying matter. The uneven, adobe wall encircled the house, except for gates at intervals. Although it wouldn't deny entrance to wild animals, it offered a striking appearance and allowed privacy from the other structures. Without thinking about the stones snagging the red satin gown, Calinda defensively sat on a two-foot-high ledge, nestled safely between the four-foot-high posts.

Lynx pretended not to notice her action, one which exposed her anxiety. He negligently leaned against the pier to her right. "Tell me about yourself, Cal," he encouraged, gazing ahead.

"What?" she asked, as if her attention had strayed.

"I'm at a disadvantage. If I know Rankin, you're well-informed about me; but I know little about you."

"Well-informed? I only know you're a nasty villain. Dare I ask, are the rumors true? Is your reputation justified or exaggerated?"

Lynx turned to rest his left shoulder on the post and looked into her upturned face. "I'd be lying if I said no. Westerners demand legends and love creating

105

them. I just happen to be their target right now. Like I said, I've never killed an innocent man."

"Innocent in your eyes or the law's? How can you calmly take another man's life? Those bandits who attacked my stage murdered the guard. It didn't seem to bother any of them."

"If I didn't keep a cool head, I wouldn't be able to hesitate until the last minute before firing. If a man has a gun pointed at you and won't listen to reason, it's you or him. Frankly I don't care to have the thirsty ground drinking my blood."

"But what about the law? Can't they arrest such men?" she continued the grim talk, but wanted to ask much different questions.

"The law is rarely in the same place at the same time. Somehow it's impossible to stall a determined man until a Ranger or marshal can appear. This isn't England or the East, Cal; don't ever forget it."

"If you refused a challenge, would he kill you anyway?"

"Most would. To turn tail and run brands a man a coward. Cowards have a tough time out here. Men keep pushing them until they either leave or they fight. Since I live here, I'm forced to fight."

"Does killing become easier, as natural as a reflex?" she pressed.

"Not to me. I've set out to intentionally take only one man's life." He flattened his back against the cool stones, bending his knee and placing the bottom of his boot on the post near his other knee. He remained impassive as he chewed on a blade of sweetgrass.

"Who? Why?" she asked when he didn't expound.

106

"Perhaps I'll tell you one day, if you hang around." He glanced at her, a half-grin curling up one side of his inviting mouth.

"Did you kill him?" she persisted, having a need to know.

"Nope." He inhaled deeply, then slowly released it, as if mentally soothing a raw nerve which she was exposing.

"You changed your mind?" she continued softly.

"Never found him. Finally stopped wasting my time and energy," he murmured in a tone which mutely implored her to cease this topic.

She didn't. "If you located him today, would you kill him?"

There was a long and somber silence before Lynx said, "I honestly don't know. I'd have to see him again to learn if his crimes still matter to me. Isn't this a gloomy subject?" he hinted clearly.

"I'm sorry," she murmured to placate him.

He turned and gazed down at her. "Why?" he almost demanded.

Calinda's eyes were soft and her lips compelling as she replied, "Because he must have done something terrible to you to earn such hatred. Is he the reason you've stayed away from home so long, why you've grown so hard and cynical?"

"Am I cold and ruthless, Cal?" he asked unflinchingly.

To elude the snare which she had unwittingly set, she continued, "I don't know what you are, Lynx. I've never met anyone like you before. Sometimes I see the same pain and loneliness in your eyes and in Rankin's. You're both very good at covering your feelings. Why don't you come home, Lynx? Rankin misses you and

107

needs you here."

"What about you, Cal? Do you miss me and want me around?"

Calinda blushed and looked away. "Why should I? We're strangers. Besides, I won't be living here much longer," she added for some absurd reason. Thoroughly unsettled, she couldn't think clearly.

Lynx grasped her chin and lifted her head. "Why not?"

"I can't go on accepting your father's charity indefinitely; it isn't right. He's been wonderful to me, and I'm very fond of him."

"Where will you go? How will you live?" he asked curtly.

"I don't know." For a moment, she looked very young and vulnerable and afraid. "Do you mind if I stay here until I decide?"

"Why should I?" he inquired, drilling his gaze into hers.

"It is your home, and we . . ." She hastily fell silent.

"We, what, Cal?" he probed, searching her rosy face.

"Nothing," she verbally denied him an answer which her expression boldly supplied. She had rashly stepped into her own trap!

Lynx captured her face between his hands and lowered his head. His intention clear, she whispered fearfully, "Don't, Lynx."

Trapped between him and the confining posts, Calinda couldn't halt his action. His lips came down on hers in a tantalizing kiss. When she tried to turn her head, he held it securely, his lips parting hers and forging their mouths together. His strength superior and his desire great, he pulled her to her feet and imprisoned her in his embrace.

As his mouth seared over hers, Calinda struggled to retain her wits and control. She quivered as a dangerous wildfire licked at her body, wanting to burn away her resistance. As his lips moved from hers, she hoarsely demanded, "Stop it, Lynx."

The tall Texan leaned back and gazed into her panicky face. This wasn't the time or place to force the reality of their shared passion on her. "Sorry, Callie," he mumbled huskily, loosening his grip. "You are too damn beautiful and bewitching for your own good. We'd better go inside before I forget myself again."

Shaken, Calinda didn't respond. Lynx slipped his arm around her waist to escort her back to the house, aware of the tremors in her body. They said goodnight inside the door and Cal ascended the stairs on trembly legs. After watching which room she entered, Lynx grinned. He doubted his father would have given them such provocative solitude if he had known about their prior meeting and its results. Whatever happened from this point on with Cal, Lynx would never expose that night. Did he dare take advantage of their adjoining balcony . . .

An hour later, Calinda sat up in bed and strained to detect an unusual noise. Unable to fall asleep, she was lying there with her eyes shut and her mind open. Again a sharp "ping" was heard, then another. Knowing Rankin hadn't returned, she wondered if that devilish son of his was up to daring mischief. Cal eased out of her bed and cautiously went to peer out the rear door. Moonlight invaded the open spans between the arches, softly illuminating the shadowy veranda.

As Lynx walked to the railing to answer Salina's persistent summons, he was cognizant of the slit which appeared in Cal's door. No doubt Salina's less-than-quiet messages had alerted Cal. He was tempted to inspire jealousy in Calinda, but realized she wasn't the kind of woman who would accept a midnight rendezvous with a sultry Mexican servant. If Callie presumed there was something between him and Salina, she wouldn't look at him twice after tonight. If he was going to get any answers for himself and his father, he needed to polish his tarnished image. Anyway, he was annoyed with Salina's hot pursuit every time he came home. It was clear Salina desired him, but she craved a position as his wife even more. Lynx rebelled at such greedy deceit. It was time to make himself clear to the wanton Salina. This was the perfect set-up to get Salina off his back and to enchant Calinda into trusting him. "What gives?" Lynx asked crisply.

At his brusque tone, she petulantly said, "I missed you, Lynx. Why not come to my room? We can have a drink and . . . talk."

"I'm exhausted, Salina; it was a long and dusty ride."

"I could fix you a hot bath and scrub your back," she tempted.

"I just had one, but *gracias,*" he stated, running fingers through blond hair which was nearly dry, then over his clean-shaven face.

"A drink and massage might loosen those stiff muscles . . ."

"I've had my limit. A good night's sleep will do more for me tonight," he responded. Although they were passing words back and forth in muffled voices, Lynx knew they could be heard. He plotted what he wanted Cal to learn, without alerting Salina. Lynx realized Salina was purposely using English. Was this more than a

110

seduction attempt? A sly game to irk Cal? If not, why hadn't the Mexican tart stolen into his bedroom?

"I doubt your bed or sleep could relax you as quickly and enjoyably as my hands," she wickedly pressed, easing the neckline of her white blouse down to expose olive shoulders and the cleft of her bosom.

"You're a brazen hussy, Salina. *Vaya a la cama,*" he tested her.

"I go to bed, if you join me," she entreated seriously, wetting her lips and swaying erotically. "What do you say?" she coaxed.

"Don't you ever get tired of flirting with me? You should know by now the boss's son is off-limits," he made himself clearer, now that he was on to her sport. He didn't like to be duped for any reason.

"Whose rule is that? *El patron's?*" she challenged, undaunted.

"Mine," he stated casually, watching her twitch as if she had hot embers or chiggers in her drawers.

"Afraid I might be too demanding?" she teased.

"I just like to choose my own woman, Salina."

"Perhaps I am too much woman for you to handle," she mocked his male ego. "Perhaps you have lost your magic touch?"

"Perhaps not enough woman," he insultingly came back.

"*Inquieto? Pollo?*" She mockingly called him a frightened chicken. She cursed this foolish trick as she hoped Cal was asleep.

"I'm not afraid of anything; and you know it."

"You *encantado* with the little *senorita* your papa brought home? *Es barato puta* is trouble, Lynx," she angrily suggested, trying to inspire a spewing forth of stinging insults about Cal, if she were awake.

"I'll have to admit, she's a most enchanting lady. A mighty tempting treat for any man. But you could hardly call her a tart," he confessed slyly, then chuckled softly.

"A gunslinger and a *dama?* You don't stand a chance with her."

"Didn't say I wanted one. Don't have time for a woman right now, any kind. I'll be heading out again in a few days."

"Remember, *guapo diablo,* I am here if you change your mind."

Lynx watched her swaying movements until she disappeared from sight, no doubt heading to find someone else to douse her fiery passions, which was frequent from what he'd heard. One day those flames would engulf her. Lynx stretched and yawned, then returned to his room.

Calinda carefully closed the door, afraid to turn the lock for fear of his hearing it. It was impossible for anyone to climb to the balcony, so she decided to bolt it later. She didn't want Lynx to discover her furtive action. She smiled to herself, knowing Salina had lied about them. But why was she so ecstatic about that news? Funny, she was finding herself drawn to Lynx Cardone, even to his roguish manner. Maybe she should despise him for his seduction and spurn his nonchalant manner, but she didn't. He possessed such potent magic.

She stared at the wall, imagining that virile body stretched out on a bed next door. She knew too well what his lips and hands did to her body and mind. Was it possible to change a man like Lynx?

She paced the floor for a time, then halted with her back to the veranda doors. She whirled suddenly to head for her bed, nearly bumping into Lynx. Before she could shriek in alarm, his hand closed over her mouth and he shushed her. "Rankin's home, love."

When she regained her poise, he removed his hand. "What are you doing here? How did you sneak in?" she whispered.

"The door was unlocked. You were so deep in thought, you didn't hear me. Can we talk for a while?"

"Get out of my room. It's late, and I'm not dressed for company." She knew she should put on her robe, but she didn't move.

"I'm not company, and you're wearing more tonight than the last time I saw you. We need to talk, Callie."

"You arrogant, sneaky rogue. If we have anything else to say, it can be done tomorrow, downstairs," she told him.

"I doubt we'd want anyone to hear this discussion. I want to know what happened in Fort Worth after I left," he softly demanded.

"You dare to come here to question me about anything?"

"I want to know everything you said and did," he stressed, gripping her elbows and pulling her closer to him.

"You don't have any right to interrogate me," she panted.

"I'm not leaving until I have the truth, all of it."

"I'll scream," she threatened, noticing his look of determination.

"Be my guest," he invited, not the least concerned.

She gaped at him as he hastily slipped out of his shirt and boots. "What are you doing? Are you daft?" she asked in panic.

"If you're going to scream, I might as well help you

look the injured party. Wonder what Father will say when he knocks on the door to find his only son half-naked in your room . . ."

"You wouldn't dare humiliate and hurt him like that." She snatched up the discarded shirt and slammed it against his hard chest.

"I'm too intrigued to consider anybody's feelings but mine."

"I don't understand you, Lynx. Aren't you afraid I'll tell Rankin what happened in town? Why wait until now to come here? Why are you interested in what I said and did after you left?"

"I have my reasons," he stated flippantly, trailing a finger over her bare shoulder, then lifting her chin when she lowered her head. He had noticed the sullen inflection on her last few words.

"Such as?" she scoffed, shoving at the disturbing hand.

"I'm not here to answer questions, Callie, just to ask them."

Calinda fretted briefly. Her silence wasn't important. She just hated to yield to his insufferable demands. She related the account of her time in Fort Worth, then answered any remaining questions. He then insisted on practically hearing her life's story. Calinda was rankled, but complied, "Is that all, Mister Cardone? Do I pass inspection?"

"Father is becoming quite attached to you, Cal. I just wanted to make certain you deserve his help and affections. You pass all of my inspections," he ventured in a mysterious tone.

"If you're so concerned about Rankin, why don't you hang around and make sure I don't take advantage of him," she sneered.

114

"I just might do that, in a few months. Right now, I've got some vital matters to settle elsewhere."

"If you don't get killed first," she stated.

"If I don't get killed first," he infuriatingly mocked her. "Don't forget to lock your door this time," he taunted, grinning at her. "But you needn't worry; I won't be back, unless invited."

"That day will never dawn," she informed him.

"Don't be so positive. I seem to recall a fiery nature concealed beneath that lady-like exterior. One day, you'll realize you desire me as much as I desire you, even if you keep it a secret." Before Calinda could vent her anger on him, he seized her and kissed her soundly. When Calinda tried to break free of his powerful embrace, he tightened it. His lips seared over hers as he pressed her trembling body to his. As his lips teased over her eyes and ears, she pleaded for him to halt.

What was the matter with her? Even as she threatened to scream, all she wanted was to respond to him! In spite of their first meeting, she was weakening. If only he wasn't so magically overwhelming. His body was sending hers sweet and forbidden messages, which she must refuse. Drawing on what little strength and will she possessed, she struggled to halt this enticing madness.

Lynx yielded to her panic. He leaned back and smiled. "You say no, Callie, but you want to say yes." he murmured as his thumb passed over her throbbing lips. "I know you have reason to fear me and doubt me, maybe even despise me; but I hope you'll change your mind. You're the most desirable and refreshing vixen I've ever met." He left quickly while she was still stunned. "Goodnight, *Llama de mi corazon*," he lazily tossed over his shoulder at the last moment.

115

Calinda rushed to the door and bolted it, quivering. She fumed as she heard him chuckle merrily. She leaned against the door and sighed. This arrangement would never work. How could she remain here if Lynx decided to come home permanently? How would she ever resist him if he pressed her? She would die of embarrassment and shame if Rankin learned about them. She prayed he would leave quickly, then scolded herself for wishing he wouldn't. His parting words flowed over her as a gentle wave, "Flame of my heart." Why did he call her that in such a seductive tone? Why did he have such power over her?

Chapter Five

Calinda awoke sluggish and edgy, for she hadn't slept well after her confrontation with Lynx. Calinda didn't trust this mercurial man whose appeal was much too powerful and tempting. She was as much afraid of his contradictory behavior as she was of her own crazy emotions. As implausible as it was, she wanted to yield to him as much as she needed to resist. She frowned as she realized she was being just as contradictory as he was.

She found it hard to deal with the fact that Cody Richards was Lynx Cardone, a man whom she presumed she would never see again. What did Lynx want from her? Other than physical desire, did she have any effect upon him? Did he merely view her as an entertaining diversion, a convenient object upon which to sate his carnal urges? She couldn't get involved with that carefree rogue.

How would she feel and act if they had actually met

for the first time last night? But they hadn't; there was
a stolen night of passion between them. Too, Lynx's
smug attitude dismayed her. Last night, he had boldly
insinuated her eventual and uncontrollable surrender.
Surely her gaze and tremors had exposed her feelings
to a man of Lynx's experience. To deny his effect
would be absurd.

She dressed in pants, boots, and a cotton shirt before going downstairs. She had brushed her hair and
caught it back with a yellow ribbon. It was mid-morning, and the men were riding the range. Salina was
outside, hanging up freshly scrubbed laundry. Calinda
made her breakfast and sat down at the kitchen table
to eat it.

When Salina returned, she was just taking the last
bite. "What is this? I allow no one to mess up my
kitchen."

"Don't start on me this morning, Salina. I'll clean
up any mess I make. Find someone else to aggravate.
Just leave me alone today."

"Too hot to sleep after your stroll?" she hinted suggestively.

Calinda was fed up with Salina. This morning in
particular she didn't feel like matching words and wits
with this malicious female. "I take it you were. Next
time you make a late call on Mister Lynx Cardone,
would you be a little quieter?"

"You were spying on us?" she hotly accused.

"I didn't have to. You made no attempt to conceal
your plans. I'm sure you staged that little charade for
my benefit. Too bad Lynx wasn't forewarned to comply with the proper role. If he's yours as you claimed,
he seems ignorant of your close relationship."

"*Bruja!*" Salina sneered. "Stay away from Lynx;

he is mine."

"You don't say?" Calinda purred like a feisty cat. "He gave me the impression he was free for the taking," she boldly hinted.

"Don't you two think it a bit early in the day to be arguing over me?" Lynx's lazy drawl chided them from the doorway. Both women turned to watch him swagger into the room, chuckling. "Salina, I think it would be wise for you to watch your naughty tongue to our guest. As for you, Callie, please don't go harassing the hired help; it's hard to find good servants this far out."

Embarrassed, Calinda rebelled at his scolding, "She started it."

"You did," Salina quickly injected. "Stay out of my kitchen, and stop treating me like the dirt you walk on. I was here first."

"Calm down, Salina. Callie is free to come and go anywhere in this house, at any time," he stated, casting Calinda a mocking look.

"But, Lynx, she has been under foot for weeks. Is time for her visit to end, *si?*" Salina pouted, coming over to him to caress his muscled arm. *"Que me cuenta?"* she anxiously entreated.

"I say, you're acting like a spoiled child, Salina. I know you've had free run for a long time, but Callie isn't leaving any time soon, if at all," Lynx said clearly and firmly as Salina stared at him.

Calinda surged with anger; they were discussing her as if she were not present. "I'll leave when I please, Lynx," she stated tersely.

Lynx walked over and took her arm. "Let's go for a ride, Callie."

"I don't want to go riding with you," Calinda

refused flatly.

"I didn't ask. I'm telling you. Let's go," he ordered, nearly dragging her out of the house. "Stop being so childish and hateful."

"Let go of me, you brute," Cal panted, trying to pull free.

Out of Salina's hearing, he released her and scolded her again. "Don't ever lower yourself to cat-fight with a hired servant. She works here and takes orders, if you're strong enough to give them. Salina's a good worker, just bull-headed. If you let her, she'll walk all over you. Put her in her place, and she won't give you any more trouble or backtalk. Otherwise, we're going to have a war on our hands. Once it's out of control, either you'll leave or she'll quit. Where's some of that pluck and spirit you rain on me? You trying to run her off and take her place? You bucking for an excuse to remain here without charity?" he slyly taunted and unsettled her.

"Of course not! She's been like that ever since I arrived. I've tried to be nice, but it isn't my place or right to correct her. This morning I was tense. I'm sorry if I caused trouble."

"I'm glad to see you didn't get any more sleep than I did. What was Salina's thorn today?" he inquired in a lazy tone.

"The same as the other day, you. She's afraid . . ."

When Calinda stalled, he asked, "Afraid of what? You have this annoying habit of halting in mid-sentence. Say what you mean."

"Nothing," she snipped defiantly, turning her back to him.

He walked around her stiff body and bent forward, cocking his head to look up into her lowered face.

"Afraid you'll steal me from her?" he jested as their gazes locked.

"Yes," she replied icily. "But I told her she needn't worry."

"You're a bright girl, Callie. Surely you realize there's nothing between me and Salina, never has been. She can stake a claim, but it doesn't make it legal or true. Jealous?" he teased.

"Of course not. She thinks she has a claim on you. She even threatened me with a knife to stay clear of you." Calinda flushed in irritation. She hadn't meant to tell Lynx that.

Lynx filled with fury. He straightened, capturing her jawline between his fingers and thumb. "She what?" he stormed.

"She didn't exactly pull it on me. She just showed it to me and gave me several warnings about you. It's strapped to her thigh."

"If she ever draws a weapon on you, I'll break her hand," he threatened, totally serious.

"She wouldn't really, Lynx; she was just trying to scare me. I promise to behave from now on," she stated sarcastically.

"Salina has a temper, but she isn't stupid. I'll have a talk with her." His hold on her softened, as did his expression.

"Please don't. I'll take your advice and make my own stand."

"If you don't, I will. I won't allow her to terrorize you." His forefinger left her jawline to caress her cheek. For a brief and wild moment, it seemed as if he was about to kiss her right there in the open.

"You do enough of that," she vowed, glaring at him as she came to her senses. Why did he have his hypnotic effect over her?

"I don't mean to, Cal. You just have a way of provoking me to mischief. It isn't smart for us to quarrel in front of her. I know we met in a crazy way; but if you'll give yourself a chance to get to know me, I'm not as terrible as you think. How about a pardon?"

"What about our ride?" she reminded him, dropping the subject.

"Let's go," he took her defensive hint.

Lynx was amused when she insisted on saddling her own horse. They mounted up and rode off, heading toward some nearby foothills. Lynx waited near a bluff for Calinda to catch up with him. "It's lovely, Lynx; how can you bear to leave it so often?" For a girl who had been drilled in the social graces, she felt so unsure with him. She didn't know how to behave or how to converse with this unpredictable man.

She observed his warm gaze as it seemed to proudly caress the landscape. "The Cardone Ranch stretches as far as you can see in all directions, Cal. It's one of the largest and most successful spreads in the state. One day, it will all be mine," he added absently.

"You love this place, don't you?" she inquired.

"I helped steal it from the wilderness. I've got sweat, blood, and tears on nearly every acre. Look over there," he pointed to a dark splotch on the grassland. "That's some of the best cattle anywhere."

For the next few hours, they trotted or raced over the countryside. Lynx showed her lovely meadows, peaceful streams, cool clusters of trees, line-shacks, rolling hills, deep gullies, arroyos, and large spans of grasses and wildflowers which she had all seen before. But she viewed it differently under his guiding hand and descriptions. As they watered their horses in a sparkling pond, Lynx directed her attention to a lofty hill. "If I had been the first owner of this spread, I would have built the ranch-house there. You can see the sunrise and sunset, and you could look down on what you built and lived for."

He sat down and reclined, propping on his elbows and crossing his ankles. He removed his hat and fluffed his damp hair. He inhaled the freshness and sweet odors wafting on the breeze. He lay down and closed his eyes, relaxing. Lynx had never been more aware of how much he loved this ranch, of how ready and eager he was to come home.

Calinda assumed he was permitting the horses to cool and rest. She sat down near Lynx on the plush grass. It was very warm, so she removed her boots, planting her bare feet near her buttocks. She crossed her arms, rested them on her knees, then placed her chin on them. She watched the horses drink, then munch on grass near their hooves. She also inhaled the sweet aromas of blended nature. She was pleasantly fatigued and calmed. In this serene setting, she didn't feel threatened by anything or anyone, including her fiery passion for Lynx.

"Why don't you lie back and relax, Cal?" he suggested.

Without even thinking twice, she did. Closing her eyes, Calinda felt like a cloud drifting peacefully. When she opened her eyes later, Lynx was propped on his side, watching her. Their gazes fused. It seemed an eternity before Lynx bent over and kissed her.

After the heady kiss, Lynx caught her shoulders as he asked, "Why did you really come here, Cal? What do you want from us?"

Calinda assumed he was referring to their first

123

meeting. "I told you everything, Lynx. What happened between us at the saloon wasn't entirely your fault. I'm not here seeking vengeance or chasing after you. I swear I didn't know about you. Why don't you trust me?"

"You and your story are too good to be true," he confessed.

"But they are true, Lynx," she argued, missing his real point.

Lynx's grip tightened unknowingly as he pressed, "Swear you're telling the truth, Callie. Swear our meeting was only a coincidence."

"You're hurting me," she cried out, wincing in discomfort.

"Swear it," he insisted, loosening his hold. "You know the odds against Calinda Braxton winding up senseless in Lynx Cardone's bed."

"I swear it," she vowed, although she felt he wouldn't harm her if she refused. Was it his male pride, that survival instinct? He was afraid it was all a trick? "What happened with my father, Lynx?"

Lynx moved to get up. "Let's go; it's getting late."

Calinda grabbed his shoulder, causing him to topple against her. "Tell me the truth. Why did he leave the Cardone Ranch?"

"I can't say. You'll have to ask him, if you ever find him."

"Do you know where he went? Where he is?"

"No," he replied, a strange coldness filling his eyes.

"Swear it," she used his previous demand.

"I swear it," he replied honestly. "Brax and I were close friends. He didn't tell me he was leaving and I don't know where he went. He never wrote and told you anything about his plans?"

"For the last five years, I didn't receive any word from him. His letters were always few and sketchy until mother died. He told my relatives it was too wild and dangerous for a child out here. He persuaded them to keep me in school there. He promised he would send for me after it was over. He never came. I know very little about him. What was he like?"

"Then why did you come this far searching for him?"

Calinda explained about the Simpsons again. "I just don't understand him or what happened, Lynx. Isn't there anything you can tell me?" she pleaded. "Is my father the reason you don't trust me?"

"Do you trust the Simpsons? Do you think they might have kept some letters from you?" he speculated, dodging her questions.

"It's possible. But if they knew he wasn't here, why would they send me to join him? If they knew where he had moved to, wouldn't they tell me? Unless . . ." She became pensive.

"There you go halting again. Unless, what?" he probed.

"Unless he was sending money all along. If they were keeping the money, they couldn't tell me about his letters. If he mentioned he was leaving here without telling anyone, they might assume I'd never locate him to discover their deceptions."

"Were they capable of such plots?" he asked, needing to know if there was a letter telling about the past, or just as importantly Brax's new location. Perhaps the Simpsons allowed her to come here because they knew the truth. Perhaps they intended to let her settle in and then make demands on her new wealth as repayment for their care and support. He would warn his father to watch for any mail to Calinda from the Simpsons, or a visit by any English strangers.

"I hate to admit it, but I wouldn't doubt it. They were awful people. I'm glad to be free. But I never expected to walk into a den of cutthroats and thieves. I honestly thought my father was here."

"Were they cruel to you?" he demanded, annoyed at that idea.

"Not physically. They were pressuring me to marry some rich man so they could entice money from him to pay their debts. They lost all feeling and concern for me when I refused. I might have been raised like the English, but I deplore arranged marriages. Why should I ruin my life to help them out of a dilemma which they created?"

That told Lynx they probably didn't know anything. Her explanation also told him why she was so eager and desperate to flee them. "I'm sorry you came all this way for nothing, Cal. I wish I knew where Brax is; I honestly don't."

She smiled unexpectedly and confessed, "I'm not sorry. I've been freer and happier here these last few weeks than I was there for years. I have Rankin to thank."

"You're very fond of him, aren't you?"

"Yes, he's a very special man. You're lucky to have such a father, Lynx. I hope you realize it and appreciate him."

"You've missed having your parents and a home, haven't you?"

"Yes, especially on holidays. After Mama died, the Simpsons always made me feel so left out. They constantly harped on my father's foul deeds. I wanted to prove them wrong, but I guess I can't. You're fortunate to belong in a special place; I'm envious."

Lynx turned his head to listen to a muffled noise in the distance. "What is it?" Calinda asked, noting the echoing sound of a bell.

"Dinner time. Father is calling us home. We rarely use that bell anymore. My mother used to . . ."

He jumped up and bent over to take her hand to pull her to her feet. "Supper's getting cold, Miss Braxton."

He guided her to her horse and was about to give her a hand up. Warmed by his charming and sensitive face, she flashed him a smile and said, "I can manage. Thanks."

"I'm sure you can," he jested, then agilely mounted.

He leaned over and gripped her saddle-horn, grinning into her face. "Want to race me home? Winner chooses a prize?"

"No way, Lynx Cardone. I doubt any horse can beat yours. In fact, I doubt you would make any wager you weren't certain of winning. Now if I can race Star, you're on," she counter-challenged.

"Sorry, love, but Star doesn't allow anyone but me on his back."

His hand went behind her head and pulled it to his, sealing their lips for a breath-stealing kiss. When he straightened in his saddle, he laughed and said, "I reckon I deserve a reward for being good."

He flicked his reins and his horse galloped for home. Calinda laughed softly before speeding off after him. Lynx Cardone was proving to be a complex man, a man of many pleasing facets and emotions.

After dinner, Lynx took Calinda for another walk. They headed toward the bunkhouse where some of the men were sitting on the porch playing music. Calinda listened to the joyful sounds while Lynx joked and chatted with several men, allowing her another insight to him.

"Want to dance?" he asked, grinning and taking her hand.

"Here?" she debated, fearing contact with that hard frame.

"Why not?" he playfully reasoned, eyes glowing appreciatively.

"I'd feel silly," she argued, but he swept her into his arms and whirled her around, his merry laughter stirring her blood. He was an excellent dancer, but she should have known Lynx could do anything.

After the lengthy song ended, the cowhands clapped and howled. Lynx thanked them and led Calinda back toward the house, winded and unsettled. As they neared the stone fence, he plucked a wild yellow rose and handed it to her. He left her at the door, saying he was going for a late ride, sounding as if he needed solitude.

Calinda went inside, miffed he hadn't asked her to go along. Surely he wasn't going to call on some rancher's daughter? Instead of heading for her room, Calinda changed her mind and went to the water shed to take a cool bath. The shed was a wooden structure about eight by eight square, located near the back fence. There were tubs for washing and rinsing clothes, and a very large one for bathing dusty bodies. Soap and linens were always there, and it was simpler to bathe here than to carry endless buckets of water to one's room. The water tower was nearby, supplying all the fresh water one needed, warmed by the day's sun. If it was winter, there was a wood stove for heating it.

Calinda latched the door. She walked to the oversized tub which reminded her of an immense keg without a cover. She took the huge cork and plugged the hole which allowed the tub to empty itself through a small trough behind it. She enjoyed this cask-like tub which was roomy enough for two people and even had a seat on one side. She pulled the cord and allowed it to fill with tepid water. She stripped and immersed herself, relaxing carefree for a time. She took scented soap and lathered up from head to waist. She dipped over and over to rinse. She stood up and scrubbed her tingly flesh from the waist down. Afterwards she sat on the wooden seat and pulled the cord to thoroughly rinse her hair. Her head was leaning backwards and her eyes were closed as she allowed the water to splash over her long tresses.

"Need me to hold that rope for you?" Lynx asked.

Startled, her eyes and mouth flew open. Calinda hadn't released the cord, causing water to gush into them. She jerked aside, coughing and gagging, letting the cord free, wiping her eyes. "How dare you come in here!" she ranted at the chuckling man, folding her arms over her bare and wet chest, sinking to her neck in the water.

"I thought the latch was hung up, Cal. I didn't realize anyone would be in here this late. Did you need a cold bath?" he helplessly teased, his gaze taking in her face and upper body before she protectively sank behind the edge of the deep tub, leaving only her neck and head in view. Her cheeks were colorful and her eyes were stormy.

"Then why didn't you show some manners and leave when you found it occupied?" she panted in distress.

Lynx grinned, then negligently leaned against the wall. "Need any help? I'm good at scrubbing backs."

"I'm positive you've had plenty of practice, but no

thanks. I thought you were going riding," she reminded him nervously.

"Changed my mind. Thought I'd enjoy a relaxing bath more. Seems you had the same idea. Care if I join you?" he murmured huskily.

"Don't you dare, Lynx Cardone," she shrieked in panic. Lynx was a man who did as he pleased, and Calinda feared he might just take advantage of this heady situation. It was so difficult to think clearly when he was this close. At times, he was so magnetic, playful, attentive, and romantic. Other times, he was cool, insolent, and cynical. Calinda never knew what mood or behavior to expect from him.

Laughter came forth. "Be quiet," she warned, "Someone might hear you. What about that pardon you wanted?"

Lynx strolled forward. A few steps and a low platform had been constructed beside the tub to assist entrances and exits. Lynx sat down, the rim of the tub striking him at heart level. "Then I suggest we whisper. We certainly don't want anyone to learn our little secrets," he boldly teased, as if he had no intention of leaving soon. He propped his elbow on the edge of the tub, then rested his chin on his balled fist. He realized just how tempting, pleasing, and stirring she was.

To conceal her body, Calinda was given no choice but to snuggle against the edge of the tub, her chin resting on the rim to deny his softened gaze a clear view of anything, placing her in dangerously close proximity with him. "You're a devil, Lynx Cardone."

He chuckled softly and winked at her. His fingers grazed her scarlet cheek as he moved wet curls from her upturned face. As he shifted the heavy tresses to her back, his fingers made disturbing contact with her moist shoulder, then slipped down her back as he asked, "Sure you don't need any help? You can return the favor."

He was leaning forward, his face much too close to hers. "Please leave so I can dress," she entreated, her gaze locked on his face.

The cuff of his shirt was soaked as his fingers traced her spine. "You really know how to spoil a lonesome cowboy's fun. I'm enjoying the view. Never had a chance to share a lady's bath."

"Well, you're not sharing this lady's," she informed him. His touch and nearness were intimidating, but she dared not move.

"You're much too modest, Cal. After all, we have slept together. You don't have anything to hide from me."

"I didn't sleep with you; you slept with me," she disputed.

"Is there a difference?" he taunted, tracing her collarbone.

"Yes, a big one," she declared, nettled by his smug poise. He was thoroughly enjoying himself.

"How so, Callie?" he pressed mirthfully, covering her cold hands with his warm ones, leaning so close his breath touched her face.

"The end result was just as delightful."

"Please go away," she rashly cried. "I was distraught that night. I didn't know what I was saying or doing."

"You look rather distressed right now. Why?"

"You know why. You're embarrassing me," she accused.

"Surely you're not afraid I'm going to try to kiss you or seduce you? Why, Calinda Braxton, how could you think such insults?"

"Because you deserve them, Lynx Cardone. I don't trust you for a minute. You're always trying to disarm me. Stop teasing me, you rake. Didn't your father teach you any manners?"

"Guess I wasn't around long enough. You interested in giving me some lessons?" he mischievously inquired.

"You don't need lessons in anything. It must be nice to be perfect. But it certainly gives one a swollen head and vexing personality. Evidently I'm your only mistake."

"I didn't realize you possessed such a high opinion of me. I guess that means I'll have to live up to it, much as I'll hate myself for doing it. Chivalry is damned expensive." He stood up and shrugged. "Shall I wait outside, or do you intend to play a while longer?"

"I won't be much longer," she said, watching his departure.

She eyed the closed door, then hesitated before leaving the water. She hurriedly dried off and struggled into her clothes, wrapping a thick cloth around her wet hair. When she couldn't dislodge the cork, she called Lynx to help her. "It's stuck."

"I'll take care of it. You go inside and work on that hair if you don't want to turn in with a wet head," he politely offered.

"Thanks, Lynx," she murmured softly.

"Callie?" he called out as she started to leave.

She turned and responded, "Yes, Lynx?"

"Don't I get a goodnight kiss for being so helpful and courteous?"

Feeling protected by her clothing, Calinda smiled and placed a brief kiss on his cheek. "Thanks, and goodnight."

"That wasn't a kiss," he mocked, pulling her into his arms.

"It wasn't?" she daringly taunted.

"This is a kiss," he said, closing his mouth over hers.

Calinda's arms were trapped between them. If not, they would have eased around his narrow waist. Yet, her lips eagerly surrendered to his exploratory ones. His embrace tightened; his mouth refused to leave hers. The kiss became demanding and urgent, as did his passion. He removed the covering on her hair as his lips covered her face and roamed to her ears and throat.

He groaned in mounting desire. "You're a dangerous temptation, Calinda Braxton," he murmured hoarsely.

"So are you, Lynx Cardone," she replied in a strained voice as she pushed away from him, fighting to regain control of herself.

He caught her face between his hands, drilling his smoldering gaze into her matching one. "I want you, Cal," he stated simply.

"We can't, Lynx; it isn't right," she argued weakly against something she fiercely wanted.

"We already have," he reminded her, dropping kisses on her nose and eyes. "I need you. You're driving me crazy."

"Please don't, Lynx. We can't. I can't. I know what happened between us before, but it was a mistake. I can't sleep with you again."

"Damnit, Callie, you want me as much as I want you."

"I know," she confessed. "But that still doesn't make it right."

"Then don't tease me," he rebuked her responses.

"I didn't. You kissed me first," she protested, hurt.

"Don't you feel this need between us?" he irritably asked.

"But we aren't married, Lynx. I can't sleep with you like some harlot. Please don't spoil our truce. I want us to be friends."

"I can't marry anyone, Callie. I'm not ready to settle down. I've got some important things to do first. I need you. I can't even think straight with you around."

"Would you rather I leave the ranch?" she asked, wondering if he was hinting in that direction.

"Hell, no. I want you right here where . . . where I know you'll be safe and happy. But I want you, Callie, all of you."

"You can have me, Lynx, except in bed. If we slept together every time you came home, I'd be nothing more than your mistress. I'm not like that, Lynx. I don't think you know me at all."

"I want to know everything about you, Callie." Lynx was dismayed by her mention of marriage, a nice resolution to her problems.

"Then give it time, Lynx. It's hard enough to relax around you after what happened at the saloon. We need to discover each other first."

"I don't have time, Callie; I'll be leaving in a few days."

"Then make time, Lynx. No one's forcing you to go. If you really care for me and want me, then stay here and show me."

"I can't. I've given my word to help out a friend with a problem. You should recall, I always keep my word, even when it's hard."

"Does this friend need your help, or the aid of your guns?"

"Both, if it comes to that. I'm hoping I can settle his problems without shedding blood. It could be weeks or months before I get home."

"Please don't go, Lynx," she suddenly begged him. Fear and desire battled to be the dominant emotion in her expression.

Lynx realized Calinda felt more than passion for him, but what? He was baffled by that discovery, intimidated by it. First, a bold hint at marriage; then, hints at love and possessiveness; and then, hints at blackmail to keep him home . . . Inflaming her body and feeding her affections were dangerous actions. Callie was a woman, and he couldn't allow any holds over him at present. Callie was bright; she could start to put her nose where it didn't belong if she became determined to have him. He backed off.

"Go to your room, Callie, before I say or do something I'll regret. Since our timing is wrong, perhaps we should steer clear of each other while I'm home. If you're still around next time, maybe we can study this attraction between us. If not . . ." He shrugged.

Calinda stared at him. He was calmly dismissing her! Was this a cunning trick to entice her into his bed? He was making her refusal appear a stinging rejection. He wasn't being fair to demand all or nothing. He was just too accustomed to having his way. If he wanted to pretend there was nothing between them, let him. "That's fine with me, Mister Cardone," she scoffed, turning to leave.

"Callie?" he murmured again.

"What?" she snapped as she whirled to face him.

He grinned and tossed her the discarded cloth. "You

forgot something," he teased as the cloth struck her in the chest.

She instinctively reacted and caught it. "So did you, Lynx," she stated mysteriously, then left in a huff.

Knowing Lynx would probably take a long time in the water shed, Calinda stood on the balcony to allow the warm breeze to help dry her hair. She muttered to herself as she worked the tangles free and fiercely brushed it. When her task was completed, she walked into her room and went to bed, to toss and turn for hours before slumber released her from her doubts and tension.

The next day was tormenting for both Lynx and Calinda. He rode out with the men at dawn to distract himself from that puzzling piece of fluff in his house. He worked the fence-line until he was weary and sweaty. He didn't return until nearly dinner time. He headed for the water shed to remove the traces of dirt, sweat, and leather from his firm body. Afterwards, he went to his room to dress in Spanish trousers and a blood red silk shirt, which was left open to his heart. He tossed his dirty clothes in a corner, then pulled on his boots. He picked up his silver spurs and tossed them on a chair. He left his room to join his father.

Calinda had spent much of her day alone. Nearing the dinner hour, she had changed into a lovely dress in muted shades of green, enhancing the color of her eyes. Lynx hadn't been home all day, and she dreaded to see him tonight. Would he still be angry and sullen? She collected her nerves and headed to join the men.

Lynx nodded at her when she entered the room, but didn't make conversation or even smile. He was lazily sprawled in a comfortable chair, sipping a whiskey. Calinda glanced at him and spoke guardedly. She walked over to Rankin and smiled warmly. They chatted for a few moments before Salina came to announce dinner.

Salina flashed Lynx a seductive smile, which he returned in like manner to annoy Calinda. Calinda pretended not to notice. Dinner was long and painful for her, as Lynx totally ignored her. He talked genially with his father, but left her out of the conversation. When Rankin would draw her into it by choosing a mutual topic, Lynx would promptly change the subject back to ranching and cattle, or some business or event of which she was uninformed.

Calinda sat quietly and politely, knowing Lynx was intentionally excluding her, making her feel unwelcomed and saddened. Clearly he was attempting to make a point, to unsettle her. To verbally spar with him at the table would only enlighten Rankin to a problem between them. Being well-trained and well-bred, Calinda suffered in silence. Her poise and pleasant expression didn't reveal the battle within her.

But Rankin witnessed clues which tugged at his imagination. It wasn't like Calinda to be so reserved, to keep her lashes lowered so frequently, to absently toy with the food on her plate. Neither was it like his son to be so talkative, nor was it like Lynx to be subtly rude or to dominate the conversation. Lynx appeared overly carefree and energetic tonight. Rankin knew his son was playing some game with Calinda. But why? What was going on between those two? After dinner, Rankin suggested the two young people take a walk.

Calinda stiffened noticeably, then forced herself to relax. She didn't have time to formulate an excuse before Lynx was saying, "Not tonight. Sorry, Callie. I think I'll stroll down to the bunkhouse and visit with the boys a while. I might head into the high country tomorrow to look around before I leave. See you two later." He was up and gone before either Calinda or Rankin could speak.

Rankin persuaded Calinda to play a few games of billiards. She was distracted, and allowed him to win easily. He teased, "You aren't yourself tonight, Cal. Something bothering you?"

"I guess I just feel out of place here. I'm not used to so much free time and luxury. I know I should have made a decision by now, but I haven't. What do you suggest, Rankin?" If Lynx wanted her gone, would Rankin comply? Would Lynx make unreasonable demands on her if she remained?

"Maybe I should put you to work as one of my ranch-hands and burn off some of that excess energy and boredom. There's no decision to be made, Cal; you'll live here as long as you please."

"But what about my father, Rankin?" she implored.

"There's nothing you can do about Brax, Cal. If he ever returns, you'll be here waiting for him. If he writes you in England, the Simpsons will let you or him know where to find you. Accept it, Cal, you're better off here than anywhere else."

"I suppose you're right," she concurred. "But I would feel better if I did something around here to earn my keep."

"Then I'll look around for an appropriate chore for you. Does that ease your worries?" he teased her.

She smiled and nodded. They played one last game before they turned in for the night. It was nearly eleven, and Lynx hadn't returned. Her nerves were as tight as a miser with his money.

Calinda entered her room and slipped into one of the sensual nightgowns which had belonged to Laura Cardone. She stroked the silky garment, admiring its cool softness and lovely shade of deep green. She decided that either Laura or Rankin had extravagant and excellent taste in clothing; the gown was exquisite and provocative, one to stir a man's blood and daze his senses. How she wished Laura was still alive. It would make things so much easier for her.

Too keyed up to sleep, Calinda paced the floor again tonight. She went to the fireplace and rested her forehead against the mantel, gazing into the dark hole which lightly smelled of past fires. Right now, her future was as obscure as the blackness behind the hearth.

Why were life and love so complicated, so demanding, so frightening? Why was it all right for a man to yield to his passions, while a woman was compelled to subdue and deny hers? Just thinking about Lynx rekindled those forbidden flames of desire. She wanted him and needed him. Did she dare play such a perilous and costly game? Was she falling in love with him? Did he feel anything other than carnal desire for her? Was he with another woman? How long could she resist this hunger for him, conquer these yearnings? At least it would be harder, rather impossible, to be tempted once he left. Left? That word tortured her. She sniffled as if weeping, inhaling raggedly.

Strong hands gently grasped her shoulders from behind. She jumped and turned to face Lynx. Had she left the door unlocked again? Intentionally? She couldn't make out his face in the darkness, but she could sense his gaze roaming over her body, seeming to brand it.

"You're up mighty late, Callie. Missing me already? Worried about my safety?" he teased, his face hidden from her probing gaze.

She wanted nothing more than to fling herself into his embrace. Instead, she responded in a quavering voice, "Don't be absurd."

He craftily provoked her, "You're just as attracted to me as I am to you. You just won't admit it. Frankly, it's a most inconvenient time to be troubled by such cravings. I'd be obliged if you'd hang around until I come home again; I'd like to find out why I find you haunting me all the time. When Jake gave me all that phony information, I was ready to strangle you. What is it about you, Callie, that makes my guts twist and the hair on my neck stand up in warning?"

"If these are compliments, Lynx, they're the most unusual ones I've ever received. I haven't made any attempts to catch your eye."

"I know. Why not? Am I too repulsive for a well-bred lady?" he speculated, his hands leisurely moving up and down her bare arms.

"I find you insufferable and exasperating, but not repulsive," she admitted cautiously. "I doubt you and I have anything in common."

"More than you imagine, Callie," he whispered hoarsely.

"You're mistaken, Lynx; we're nothing alike."

"Won't be my first mistake where you're concerned, will it?"

"Do you mind if we forget about that night?" She felt shaky, innocently resting her palms against his chest to steady herself. Warmth, firmness, and a heavily thudding heart tantalized her sensitive hands.

"I can't. Have you? Was it a fatal error, Callie?" he

asked, his hands halting their journey. He watched her in the scant light.

"Fatal error?" she repeated, losing his meaning, wishing she could see his expression. She didn't know her face was vaguely visible.

"Did it kill any hope of our becoming friends?"

"Us, friends?" she echoed, sadness flooding her eyes.

"Why not? Looks like we'll be living in the same home."

"Only until I can leave. And you don't live here."

"You have no family or money, Callie. Just where can you go and do what? Jobs for women are few, with lousy pay and harsh conditions. You're safer and happier here. Why leave?"

"It just doesn't seem right to live with two strange men, especially when one resents me and harries me all the time."

"You can hardly call me or Father a stranger. Besides, you . . ."

When he halted and dropped his hands to his sides, she asked, "I'm, what?" Her gaze filled with intrigue and attention. Her hands had detected the sudden increase in his heart-rate and his rigidity.

"You're welcomed by both of us," he said.

Calinda knew that wasn't what he had started to say. She wondered what new sport he was attempting now. "Thanks, but I still don't feel comfortable accepting extended charity."

"Would it help if I begged you to stay?" he tested a suspicion.

"Would you?" she challenged, straining to see him.

"Nope, but I would ask seriously. I never beg for anything."

"At least you're honest," she said too quickly. "It's late. You'd best leave now before we quarrel again. After the way we acted tonight, I'm sure Rankin wonders what's going on between us."

"Do I get a goodnight kiss from my new sister?"

"I doubt you view me as such, or ever would."

"You're right, Callie. I hope you don't mind if I call you that." Lynx cursed this visit home which seemed to be exposing the missing facets to his life, facets which he couldn't explore or claim at present.

"Do as you please," she stated unthinkingly.

"Right now, I please to kiss you," he murmured, then swept her into his arms. "I guess I was a little asinine last night and today. I don't meet many ladies. You give a man strange ideas, Callie."

Calinda's hands braced against his hard chest. "No."

"But you said I could do as I pleased," he mocked her resistance.

"Leave before Rankin learns you were in my room. We must be careful. There's no telling what he would do if he learned about us. Are you trying to get me thrown out? You've already seduced me. Now you're sneaking in here trying to . . ."

Without warning, Lynx released her. At the torturously familiar words, he rubbed his forehead as if it ached unmercifully. His expression changed drastically, his eyes chilling and narrowing as the past threatened to devour him. He glared at her for a moment, then asked, "Have you been wearing my mother's clothes? That's her gown, isn't it?"

"Yes, why?" She was startled by his harshness.

"How dare you presume to do something like that?" His voice was harsh with anger. My God, why hadn't

142

he warned his father? Why hadn't he seen Brax for the snake he was? Now Callie was in Laura's clothes and home, trying to take her place.

"Your father gave them to me and insisted I use them. If it upsets you, I won't wear any of them again." Calinda assumed his lingering grief had inspired his outburst, and the anguish in his eyes kept her from throwing angry words back at him. When he continued to glare at her, she touched his arm and promised, "It won't happen again, Lynx. I'm sorry."

He stared at the sensual gown, then her. "It doesn't matter. They should have been burned. It just shocked me. See you tomorrow." With that, he left quickly.

Both their doors had been left open during his hasty flight. Calinda could hear Lynx pacing his floor and mumbling to himself. Her tender and warring heart reached out to him. It had been years since Laura's death, and he was still resisting the healing process. Or so Calinda assumed. Evidently he had been too surprised by her presence to realize whose clothes she had been wearing. When it struck home, it had been devastating. There must be something she could say or do . . .

Calinda walked to Lynx's room and went inside, closing the door behind her out of habit. He was in bed now. He turned his head on the pillow and looked at her. Slowly Calinda went forward to stop and glance down at him. He looked so troubled. "Lynx, I'm truly sorry. If I had known how it would hurt you, I would never have worn them. Rankin told me about your mother's death. I know it hurts deeply, but you must let go, let the wounds heal. When my mother died, I was numb for a long time. You must accept it. Don't you see what it's doing to you?"

"It isn't that easy, Callie. You don't understand."

"Would you like to talk about her? Sometimes that helps. She wouldn't want you to suffer like this."

Lynx laughed coldly. If Laura had truly loved him, she would never have deserted him. Lynx could almost understand her falling out of love with her husband and falling in love with Brax, but sacrificing her only child and home for another man . . . The least she could have done was leave a note, or send some word over the years. "I don't ever want to hear her name again. She never loved me or wanted me."

Calinda sat down on the edge of the bed. "You can't possibly think such a terrible thing, Lynx. How could a mother not love her child? You're letting grief and resentment destroy you. She didn't betray you or desert you by dying," she tried to console him.

Lynx captured Calinda's hand and held it between two strong ones. "I know the truth, Callie, because she told me so, many times over the years. Laura Cardone was devious, cruel, and selfish. She proved she didn't love me or father. Her only desires were . . . money and power." Just in time, he caught himself before saying passion and Brax. "It's over, Callie; let it alone."

Calinda stared at him, reading the honesty in his anguish-lined face. "I'm so sorry, Lynx. I didn't know." A tear eased down her cheek, feeling she understood Lynx's rebellion and cynicism, feeling she now grasped Rankin's reluctance to discuss his wife and the past.

Lynx pulled her face down to his chest, stroking her hair. He tenderly whispered, "Don't worry about me, Callie; I'll survive."

Calinda lifted her head and gazed into his eyes. "But you deserve more than surviving, Lynx, especially how you're doing it."

"Do I deserve an angel like you, Callie?" he asked, kissing her, needing her warmth and touch to repel the agony she had revived.

When the kiss ended, Calinda smiled and said, "Yes."

"Because you feel sorry for me, pity me?" he asked.

"No," she murmured honestly. "I feel sorry for the suffering you've endured, Lynx, but I don't pity you. You're a very strong and brave man. Why is it so difficult for you to accept your feelings and deal with them? You have defeated everything but your worst enemy, yourself. Come home, Lynx; Rankin needs you, and you need him."

"What about you, Callie? Do you want and need me here?"

His mouth closed over hers. Calinda didn't resist his silent plea for her response. He pulled her over his body and down beside him. Eventually he was lying half on her eager body. Her arms went around his neck and she held him tightly to her. Their mouths meshed in unison; their bodies touched and pleaded. Their desires couldn't be ignored.

This time, Calinda was not dazed by drugs or sleep, but by forceful passion. This time, Calinda was aware of each caress and kiss, but mindless with smoldering desire. This time, Calinda wanted to learn why Lynx filled so much of her mind and heart. She needed to comprehend this fierce urgency, this bittersweet torment.

Lynx's hand drifted down to unlace Calinda's gown and expose her creamy flesh to his lips and quivering hands. She hadn't realized Lynx was nude beneath the sheet. She didn't resist when he eased her gown off and their fiery bodies made staggering contact. She only knew she wanted Lynx to halt this raging fire and end this tormentingly sweet agony. She surrendered to his blissful touch and possession.

Lynx had just enough presence of mind not to hurriedly make passionate and savage love to her. He had dreamed of her for weeks. His daring caresses tempted her until she was aquiver with urgent need. She moaned softly and writhed as his tongue lavished moisture on her firm breasts and his hands stimulated her womanhood. He murmured into her ear, "Do you want me, Callie?"

"Yes, Lynx, yes," she feverishly responded.

He entered her and rode wildly and freely until she stiffened briefly and then clung desperately to him. As if starving for him, she greedily encouraged him to feed her fiercely and quickly. When both were rapturously sated, Lynx was drenched in perspiration. He rolled to his side, mentally willing his drumming heart and swift respiration to slow to normal. Never had he felt as whole as he did at this moment.

Callie didn't mind the moisture on his chest as her fingers drifted over it and she laid her face against his damp shoulder. They lay quietly for a time, then Lynx propped on his elbow to study her. "Are you all right, Callie?" he asked, as if this was her first time to make love.

She smiled serenely and nodded. "You have a way of hypnotizing a woman, Lynx Cardone. Perhaps I should watch you closely and be on guard every minute."

Lynx tenderly caressed her cheek and smiled. "I hope that won't be necessary or desirable, Callie. You're the most intoxicating woman I've known.

Promise you won't leave here while I'm gone. I'll get back as soon as possible, then we can work out something about us."

"Must you leave?" she entreated, missing him already.

"Yes. I promised a man I'd do some work for him, but I can't tell who or where." His thumb moved back and forth over her lips.

"Is it dangerous?" she worried aloud.

"Living is dangerous, Callie," he side-stepped her question.

"You will be careful?" she insisted, knowing he wouldn't tell her more than he had stated.

"I promise. Give me your word you'll be here next time."

"I promise. I'd better go," she said reluctantly.

"Don't," he urged, hugging her tightly.

"Your father would be most upset and disappointed with me if he discovered the truth about us." She suddenly laughed.

"What's so amusing?" he inquired, eyeing her curiously.

"I don't believe this. I'm lying in bed with a near stranger, calmly chatting after making love. You are a wicked and potent temptation. You should be ashamed of yourself for demoralizing me. This is the most illogical and incredible thing I've ever done."

He chuckled. "Count me in. I'm just as astonished and confused. I'm glad I met you first. You'd best be on your guard, woman; I'll probably shoot the first cowpoke who looks at you sideways."

"How could I possibly notice him when my eyes are for you alone?" she quipped, caressing his smooth jawline.

147

"Just make sure you remember that while I'm gone. I wouldn't want to challenge some new sweetheart the moment I returned."

"Aren't you mighty possessive for a man who has no claim on me?" she teased, snuggling up to him, savoring his words and new mood.

Lynx shifted to remove a cross of pounded Spanish silver from his neck. He slipped it over her head and vowed, "That says you're mine." Lynx tried to ignore a stunning reality: he hadn't felt this happy, carefree, or excited in years. His only regrets were bad timing, mandatory silence, and a defensive reluctance to trust this woman so quickly and completely or his own unpredictable feelings. Until he was certain of what he wanted and needed, he must bind her to him without making rash promises or perilous confessions. A man would be a fool to douse such flames without a good reason . . .

"How shall I mark my claim?" she hinted playfully.

As he chuckled, she bit his shoulder gently. "There, that's my brand. However you read it, it says Calinda Braxton. Perhaps I could alter the bottom of the C/R branding iron and make one to use on you," she gleefully ventured.

"You wouldn't want to inflict such searing pain on me."

"Rankin told me it only smarted for a minute."

"On a horse or cow, but I'm a man," he amusingly wailed.

"That you are, Mister Cardone," she agreed dreamily.

Lynx's gaze fused with hers, then his mouth came down to begin a leisurely session of lovemaking . . .

Lynx's tongue drew moist circles around her breasts as she watched with smoldering eyes. Oddly, she felt no shame at this intimate and erotic behavior. The look in his gaze told her everything she needed to know at this special moment; this was love, their first love, love wild and free. Her heart surged with joy at that realization.

A radiant smile flickered over her face. Her fingers drifted through his curling mane, the ecstasy of their contact flooding her heart and soul. For a time, he seemed content to engulf her beauty and to lovingly stroke her satiny flesh. This moment had been long in arriving and demanded to be savored to the fullest.

When their play grew serious and hungers mounted, he entered her and held her possessively. Each blissful stroke urged another, then another. Soon they were caught up in the swirling vortex of fierce passion. As if submerged in water, he seemed to surround her completely. She wondered why she had ever resisted him. His love offered all she wanted or needed. Regardless of the past or future, Lynx Cardone was a vital part of her existence now. She loved him.

With skill and persistence, he timed their release perfectly. They clung together as rapture enslaved and rewarded them. Afterwards, he held her with such gentleness she wanted to cry with joy. She nestled into his arms, knowing she never wanted to leave them.

"You're mine, Callie," he whispered against her forehead.

"Yes Lynx," she instantly agreed, hugging him tightly.

Wrapped in each other's arms, they slept until passions demanded another feeding . . .

Chapter Six

When Calinda yawned and stretched contentedly the next morning, she discovered herself in her own bed! As her mind cleared of dreamy cobwebs, she recalled Lynx gathering her drowsy body in his arms and returning her to her room. She smiled as lovely memories of last night returned. It was definite; she was in love with Lynx Cardone. After his actions last night, surely he felt the same. She hopped out of bed and dressed, eager to see him. She prayed he hadn't left for the range yet, but he had promised to take her riding with him.

When she went downstairs, the house seemed empty. Finally she located Rankin in his office, poring over the ranch books. He glanced up and smiled fondly at her, quickly closing the books. She returned his smile, then asked if she was disturbing him.

"Not at all, Cal, come in. You look mighty chipper this morning." He opened a drawer and slipped the two books inside, then closed and locked it.

"I suppose I was out of sorts yesterday," she excused her mood. "I didn't see Salina or Lynx around," she remarked to withdraw information. She was trembling with excitement at seeing her love.

"Salina's gone into town with one of the men for supplies. I'm sorry to say, that son of mine took off for parts unknown at daybreak."

Calinda's smile faded. "He's gone?" she asked without caution.

"Is something wrong, Cal? You look pale," he said.

"He said he was taking me riding this morning. I guess he forgot he was leaving." Calinda didn't conceal her disappointment.

"He was in a strange mood last night," Rankin said. "How did you two get along?" he probed.

"Fine," she murmured, not really paying attention.

"He left me a note. Want to hear it?" he asked.

"No thanks," she almost whispered, her eyes sad.

"He mentioned you," Rankin tempted.

Her face brightened. "He did?"

"Told me to take real good care of you. I think you made quite an impression on my son. I was hoping you might encourage him to stay home. Seems he still has wander-dust in his boots."

Calinda blushed. "You two are lucky to have each other. Did he say when he'd be home again?" she asked, trying to sound casual.

"Afraid not. Maybe knowing you're here, he'll hurry back."

That news put a curious sparkle in her eyes and smile. Rankin suppressed his grin and pleasure. Clearly these two had something going. But why had Lynx taken off like that? Had Rankin's hints at marriage panicked Lynx into defensive distance? If Calinda changed her mind and asked to see the note, he would have to find some excuse to deny her. After all, Lynx hadn't really mentioned her in terms she should read. Was the fearless Lynx running scared of Brax's daughter? Or was Lynx avoiding his father's gentle co-ercion?

For the next few days, Calinda was depressed. She couldn't believe Lynx would make such passionate love to her, then leave without a word. He had shown trust in her by exposing such bitter and private feelings. Had he felt threatened by the revelation of his emotions? Had her sympathy and fiery responses merely been soothing for him?

As promised, Rankin found Calinda a chore to eat up time and energy. She was responsible for feeding and watering the new colts and their mothers. Later, she asked to help with the extra saddles to keep them in condition. Wherever possible, she took on little chores and performed them skillfully and eagerly. She cleaned and blued Rankin's guns, and she rode fence with him while he taught her more each day. As with Rankin, she came to love the openness and beauty of the landscape. But she missed Lynx terribly. After learning about the other event which occurred the day of her father's disappearance, she comprehended the two men's reluctance to discuss that agonizing time. How could she probe her father's actions without re-freshing the haunting memory of Laura? She let the matter slide for now.

When Salina became busy with canning fruits and vegetables for winter, Calinda found household tasks to drive her body to fatigue and her mind to distrac-tion. She helped one of the men in the floral gardens; she assisted with cleaning the balconies and outside furniture; she scrubbed the stone floors on the porches; and she made herself useful in many other ways. Still Lynx haunted her day and night.

Carly Jones, a dependable and amiable ranch-hand, worked with Calinda many times. He taught her to handle a lasso and small calves. Some days they practiced roping and shooting. Other days, she accompanied him on his fence rounds. It was imperative to locate any holes cut in the fences and to repair them quickly to prevent expensive cattle from being stolen or wandering off. Calinda came to realize that rustling and fence-cutting were common occurrences. After she learned to manage a wagon and team of horses, she frequently delivered barbed wire and supplies to the cowboys on the range.

Some days, when Salina wasn't present to prevent it or to harass her, she would prepare special treats or cool drinks and take them to the men who worked within riding distance of the house. The men became fond of her and her company.

During the first week of June, Calinda sought out Rankin to beg a favor. She handed him a letter and asked him to mail it for her the next time he went into town. "I wrote to the Simpsons," she told him. "I asked them to let me know if they heard from my father. I doubt it will do any good, but I felt it was the only action I could take."

Rankin smiled indulgently. "Why don't you go into Waco with Steve tomorrow? You can mail the letter and shop. You've worked hard these last weeks, Cal. Steve will look after you. You deserve a rest and diversion." Rankin wasn't worried about the Simpsons. He knew he would intercept any response.

Two days later, Calinda was in Waco, "Six-shooter

153

Junction." This large town was bustling with activity, prosperity, and people. Though Waco was quite modern, it wasn't uncommon to have a gunfight on the main street every day. A center for education and culture, Waco was often labeled the "Athens of Texas." It boasted of churches, opera houses, and flourishing businesses. There were many schools, including Baylor University. She was surprised by the immense size and architecture of the buildings, many flaunting lofty spires or turrets. There were stockyards on one end of town, for cattle being sent by train to the market. There were a variety of stores, and Calinda had a fat purse which Rankin had given to her.

Steve Garrison, a trusted ranch-hand and close friend to Lynx, took Calinda to see the sights after their arrival. Steve related tales of early longhorn cattle drives through this area before the railroads came. He told her how fencing and windmills had altered Waco's landscape and way of life. Besides cattle, this was a heavy agricultural region, with vegetables and cotton the main products. Calinda was surprised to discover a large Texas Ranger post at Fort Fisher. Perhaps they could offer help with her dilemma.

Steve hired a buggy and showed her the cotton mills, expounding on the days when "Cotton was King." He gave her a brief history lesson on Waco during the Civil War, adding that Confederate uniforms were made from local cotton and on machinery smuggled through the enemy blockade. He drove her to see the suspension toll bridge over the Brazos River which had been completed in 1870. Steve pointed out how many buildings and homes were constructed of Waco-made pink brick. She saw the McLennan County Court House, the Cotton Belt Depot, and the famous

Waco Square. Then, having business to handle, Steve left her to herself later that afternoon.

As Calinda was leaving a dress shop to return to the hotel, a pair of startled golden eyes trailed her movements. When she was safely inside, Lynx headed for his meeting. He kept wondering what Calinda was doing alone in a wild town like Waco. Surely she hadn't left the ranch? Later, he would check out this mystery.

Lynx pulled up a chair and sat down across from Major Jones. "Things going smoothly up Dallas way?" he queried absently.

"Peak is dogging the Bass gang. I'm going to need your help, Lynx. Murphy is ready to turn traitor to Sam. He'll need a contact."

"Where do I find him?" Lynx asked, propping elbows on the table.

"Sam's planning another big robbery. Murphy's going to inform me as soon as it's set. I'll need you to stick close until word comes in."

"You sure it isn't the James gang?" Lynx inquired.

"Yes. The Jameses are working out of Arkansas and Kansas right now. But we do have two other problems: Rube Burrow and Cole Stevens. Burrow has been hitting the Southern Express heavily. He's got Pinkerton detectives roaming the woods after him." Jones shoved some papers into his saddle-bag and focused his piercing eyes on Lynx.

"Burrow's description wasn't in the crime book."

"He's a mean one, Lynx; don't take any chances if you happen on him. Blue eyes as cold as winter; nerves like iron. He's tall and gangly, but strong as an ox. He thinks nothing of using his 44's on anyone. He also likes to use disguises, so he's hard to trace."

"What about Stevens?" Lynx questioned, leaning

back in his chair, his hands dropping across his lap.

"He's a sly one, Lynx. He hits banks, trains, and stages at their peaks. I don't see how it's possible, but it appears he knows when and where to strike. Mighty strange . . ." Jones murmured.

"Who's riding with him?" Lynx asked, coming to full alert.

"Six men and a skinny lad."

They talked on for a time, then Lynx left by the side door. He headed for the hotel. It was nearly nine o'clock by then. Lynx encountered Steve coming out of a saloon. He questioned his friend about Callie's presence, relieved to learn why she was in Waco.

Lynx decided it would be best not to see Callie and went to his own room in the same hotel. The longer he lay there thinking about her so close, the tenser he became. Why was he afraid to love her and trust her? Finally, he got up, dressed, and headed to her room.

Concluding it might attract the attention of others, Lynx didn't knock. He used his acquired skills to unlock her door and sneak inside. He walked to her bed and stared down at the lovely sleeping face. Could she betray him too? Could he handle her and the resulting situation if he allowed her to get too serious and too close? He clenched his teeth and turned to leave, as soundlessly as he had entered.

"Lynx?" Calinda spoke softly. "Is that you?" she asked, fearing she was asleep, dreading she wasn't.

He faced the shadowy bed, hands on gun-butts, boots planted apart. "It's me, Callie. I didn't want to disturb you. I saw you in town earlier, but I've been in a meeting. I talked with Steve; he explained what you're doing here. Must say, I was surprised to see you."

Fully awake by now, she recalled their last parting. "Why bother to say hello? You were too busy last time to say goodbye. You do have a cunning way of sneaking in and out when it suits your purposes. Just leave; I don't want to see you again. Ever," she added tersely.

"I didn't sneak out; I left you a note," he argued, expecting her anger, but not her coldness and rejection.

"You left your father a note; that isn't me," she told him. She removed the silver cross and threw it at him. "Take your little ruse and try it on someone else. I don't have time for users and liars."

"User and liar? What's gotten into you, woman? I told you in the note I'd be home within two months." Lynx was vexed at being insulted, challenged, and forced to explain anything. Just as he had feared, she was becoming possessive and demanding with closeness!

"The note you forgot to write?" she sneered.

"I left it on your pillow when I put you to bed, Callie," he snarled. "If you're playing games with me, I don't like it, woman."

She sat up. "There wasn't any note on my pillow."

Lynx's hungry gaze roamed over her partially concealed features. His tone softened. "Then look under the bed; it must have fallen off."

"I've cleaned that room many times; there wasn't any note."

Lynx came over to sit down beside her. "Is that why you're so angry with me? I swear, Callie; I left a note on your pillow."

"I never found one," she disputed his claim. "You could have said something before taking off. I didn't even know where you'd gone or for how long. You're

157

greedy, Lynx Cardone; you think only of yourself. I was a fool to trust you or let you come near me again."

"Didn't Salina tell you a man came for me early that morning?"

"No," she snapped at him like a testy diamondback rattler. "Don't go creating phony notes and messengers to pacify me."

The truth settled in. "That little *serpiente!* Just wait until I get home. Don't you see, Callie? She must have taken the note while you were still asleep. She wanted it to look like I took off without a word. Probably hopes it will send you running. Damn her!"

"Are you saying Salina took your note?" she asked skeptically.

"She must have. When Tom came by, I had to pull out in a hurry. It was dawn, too early to disturb you without exposing us. I didn't have time to hang around until you were up. Besides, I didn't want any trouble. I was afraid you would cry and beg me not to leave. Salina must have seen me write the note and put it in your room," he sullenly defended himself.

"You are wrong, Mister Cardone. I would never cry like a baby or beg for affection or attention from anyone. If I'm such a dark secret, then I'm not worth your time and energy. Afraid I might impair that carefree, cold-hearted image of yours? Are you ashamed to be seen with me, for anyone to learn we care about each other? I don't understand you at all, Lynx. I'm fine to sleep with, but nothing else?"

"That isn't true, Cal," he argued, witnessing her rising fury.

"Then what is the truth, Lynx?" she demanded.

"I'm enchanted by you, Cal. But right now, I just don't have time to deal with you," he murmured tenderly, but sternly.

"You certainly find time to sleep with me," she sneered.

"Damn it, Cal. I didn't force you into my arms. Both times, you were in *my* room and in *my* bed," he informed her, stressing his claims. "You're being unreasonable. You wanted me as much as I wanted you. I haven't misled you. What do you expect from me?"

"You think I'm chasing after you?" she asked incredulously.

"Are you?" he unwisely teased.

"You conceited ass, no. To think I actually felt sorry for you that night and wanted to comfort you. Was it only an act to disarm me?"

Calinda's forceful words struck Lynx the wrong way. In the heat of her anger, she hadn't meant them as they sounded to him. "You slept with me out of pity? What are you trying to do to me, Cal? At least my feelings were open and honest. I don't need your pity or self-sacrifice." He glared at her before standing up to leave. "I was a fool to get tangled up with another Braxton. If that's the way you want it, Cal, I'll leave you alone. Just remember, it was your decision."

As he stalked toward the door, Calinda shrieked in panic, "Lynx, don't go. I'm sorry; I didn't mean it like that. You're so darn sensitive! Oh, forget it! I'm tired of battling a situation and a person I don't understand."

Lynx came back to the bed and seized her by the shoulders. "Then what did you mean?" he insisted, staring down at her.

"I don't know. But I didn't yield out of pity. How could you even think such an awful thing about me? It's just that one time you behave like I'm special to you; then the next, you act as if you don't give a fig. I don't know where I stand with you," she vowed, frustrated.

The implications of her words stunned him. "What do you mean by, where you stand with me?" he anxiously inquired, stalling for time to think out the consequences of his explanation either way.

"You heard me," she murmured, compelled to press the issue now that she had foolishly opened it with this jittery creature.

"Are you falling in love with me, Cal?" he blurted out, then scolded himself for his bluntness.

"Does it matter to you?" she asked another explosive question, rather than dousing the fuse to the one already lit.

He sat down on the edge of the bed, his back to her as he pensively stroked his taut jawline. "Do you think we've known each other long enough to have such serious talks and feelings?" he asked, trying to handle the volatile subject without it blowing up in his face.

They had known each other long enough to spend two nights in bed together. Was intimacy easier to accept than deep emotions? Was he resisting a commitment to her? Did he feel a vow of love would entrap him, would entice her to expect marriage? He was being awfully hesitant and evasive. How should she interpret his moods and actions?

Calinda recalled how Lynx had looked and sounded when he had spoken of his mother. Had Laura Cardone actually denied this troubled man love? Had she scarred him so deeply that he resented loving a woman, resisted sharing himself? What had Laura done to Lynx to make him so cynical and defensive? How could she repair the damage?

Calinda had never confronted anything like this. Perhaps Lynx was just as emotionally assailed, confused, and panicked. If such was true, she shouldn't pressure or corner him. It was possible that Brax's desertion and selfishness inspired mistrust toward her.

"Lynx, I think it's best if we drop this subject permanently. I've been under a great deal of stress these last few months, and I suppose I'm still not thinking clearly. The situation between us happened too quickly and unexpectedly. You needn't worry about my pursuing you, because I won't. The smartest thing for me to do is find a way to search for my father. Under the circumstances, I don't think it's wise for me to live in your home. I'll speak with Rankin when I return and see what can be worked out about my leaving the ranch. I wouldn't want you to be reluctant to come home because I'm there."

Lynx turned to observe her for a lengthy time. She was serious. "Afraid I won't come home, Cal? Or afraid I will?" he speculated.

"Either way, the situation isn't right, Lynx. It's time I stopped being a coward and started making my own decisions. Rankin has been very kind and generous to me, and I'm grateful to him. Perhaps he'll loan me the money to make a new start on my own somewhere. Goodbye, Lynx; I should be gone before you come home again."

"You can't mean it, Cal. This isn't England. Haven't you seen and learned enough to know you can't up and leave the ranch? If we couldn't find Brax with a hot trail, how do you expect to locate him on one that's been cold for years?" he anxiously tried to reason with her.

"I don't know. But I plan to try. I'll start tomorrow

161

at the Ranger post. Perhaps they can tell me how and where to begin." Cal tried to master the telltale quivering in her voice and body.

"You'll be wasting your time, Cal. Rankin hired the best detectives around to look for Brax and . . . If they couldn't find him, you surely can't. You'll only hurt yourself and endanger your life." Lynx berated himself for pushing her into such a precarious action.

"Since you love to roam around, why don't you help me search for him? Why were you and Rankin so anxious to find my father?" she asked, abruptly aware of the determination revealed in his voice. They had paid detectives to search for a deserter of friendship?

"We wanted to solve the problem which made him leave. I'm not heading out on another futile chase, so drop this crazy idea."

"Is there something you and Rankin aren't telling me? I get the feeling there's more to Brax's departure than either of you have said. I sense bitterness and resentment when you two talk about him and the past. Why, Lynx? What really happened?" she implored.

"I've told you all I can. He's gone, and he'll never set foot on the Cardone Ranch again. If he dared to show his traitorous . . . Just drop it, Cal. You can have a good life on the ranch, if you'll just let the past stay buried. Please," he urgently coaxed.

Calinda shifted to sit beside him. "You hate my father, don't you? Why, Lynx? What did he do before he ran off? Please tell me the truth; I must hear it. Why did you say 'traitorous'?"

"Leave it be," he stated firmly, regretting his careless slips. "I don't want to hurt you, Callie," he added mysteriously. What was wrong with him? Where were his wits and self-control?

"If you don't tell me, I'll ask Rankin," she rashly threatened.

Pinning her face between his hands, he warned through clenched teeth, "Do so, and you'll answer to me, Cal. Rankin has suffered enough. He took you in and cared for you. You want to repay him by tormenting him? If you can't accept us and trust us, get off the Cardone Ranch. If you stay, forget about Elliott Braxton."

"But he's my father, Lynx," she reminded him.

"Was he ever a real father to you, Cal? If so, he would have contacted you and you wouldn't be wondering where he is now. He hurt and disappointed us, just like he did you." He forced devastating facts into her bruised heart, with a coldness and insensitivity which he hadn't intended.

Her chin and lips quivered as tears ran down her cheeks. "You despise me as much as him, don't you? Is that it, Lynx? Revenge? You can't get to Brax, so you're punishing me in his place? Befriend and charm, then reject, like Brax did to you? That's cruel, Lynx."

Her assumptions shocked him. The anguish and accusations in her eyes plagued him. He had said too much. Now, he must say more to correct matters. "You're wrong, Cal. It isn't like that. I'm not going into the whole story, but I will tell you certain facts. First, I want your promise you won't mention this or the past to Rankin again."

"What are you talking about, Lynx?" she asked, puzzled.

"Give me your word, Cal, or I won't tell you anything."

"You have it," she complied, her heart beating

wildly.

"Brax doesn't deserve your loyalty and love, Cal; he never deserved ours. He did some terrible things years ago. That fall before your father vanished, Brax and my father completed a very lucrative cattle drive, 1500 cattle at $30 a head. That next afternoon, Brax stole the $45,000.00 and our ranch deed from Rankin's desk. My father caught him packing to leave hurriedly, and they fought. Brax cheated him, beat him, and disappeared without a trace. Afterwards Rankin became cynical and remote. If a man couldn't trust his best friend, who could he trust? If a man who was like his brother could rob him and beat him, anybody could. Brax turned love and faith into cruel jokes. Those things are hard for a man to accept, Cal; they color his whole outlook on life and people. Brax escaped that same day, and he hasn't been seen since. After my mother . . . I searched for Brax. I never found him." Lynx had spoken the truth, but only selected parts of it. He had to persuade her to forget her search.

"Were you going to kill him?" she asked reluctantly.

"I don't know what would have happened if I had located him. I was angry and bitter. I loved your father almost as much as my own; I even spent more time with him than with Rankin. I had trusted him and respected him. I'd followed him around like an innocent, blind pup. He made fools of us. Men have been hung for a lesser offense. Rankin went through hell; first Brax, then mother. We thought it was over, until your arrival. We felt guilty every time you begged for answers, but we didn't want to tell you such terrible things about your father. Leave it be, Callie. We've all suffered too much."

"You're certain Rankin's hired men never located him and . . ."

She didn't finish, but her insinuation was clear. "No, Cal, he didn't have your father killed. When you first arrived, we both suspected Brax might have sent you to nose around. We wondered if he'd run through all that money and was scheming for more. Since you don't favor Brax, father wasn't convinced you were Calinda Braxton."

"If he didn't believe me and resented I might be a Braxton, why did he invite me to the ranch? Why does he want me to stay on there?"

"At first, to be honest, he wanted to watch you; I agreed. If Brax was up to something, you could clue us in or lead us to him."

"Why would he come back? If he wanted to reach me, he would have contacted me in England, long ago. Do you still want revenge after all these years? Is the stolen money that important?"

"I was like you are now; I was confused and I needed to know the whole truth from Brax. Betrayal is hard to swallow, Cal. After it happened, I went searching for him. I couldn't believe Brax would do such things without some reason. When I realized I'd never find him, I couldn't make myself go home that soon. There were too many painful memories at the ranch. In a way, I had chosen Brax over my father for years; I couldn't face Rankin with all that guilt inside. As time passed, I liked going from place to place and doing exciting things. It made me too tired and busy to be tormented. But every time I went home, I was reminded of mother and Brax. I needed to make a man of myself, Cal. I had to test myself, learn who and what I was. I needed to conquer my inner demons. I also needed to prove myself for Rankin. Like you said, Cal, grief and hate are vicious diseases."

"But what about me, Lynx? Where do I fit in at the ranch?"

He chuckled, slowly relaxing. "You're one bewitching and stubborn bundle. It didn't take long for us to realize you're nothing like Brax. You brought a change of pace, new life and sunshine to the ranch. It appears Rankin observed you too closely. He became fond of you, Cal. Course you're mighty hard to resist. When he decided he could trust you, he felt you should stay at the ranch. I think he's being selfish; he likes you and likes having you around. Besides, you can't be punished for being Brax's daughter."

"What about you, Lynx? Do you honestly want me to stay?"

"Frankly, I was furious and shocked when I came home to find Brax's child living in my home. I was fully prepared to hate you and determined to kick you out that same day. Trouble was, I didn't expect Calinda Braxton to be Callie. Luckily we had met, and most provocatively I might add. I found myself in a most uncomfortable position. There you were again, and I didn't know what to do about you."

"Do you think my father might return one day?" she asked, switching to a safer topic.

"I don't know, Cal. He nearly killed Rankin in that fight."

"Why would my father steal the ranch deed?"

"We suspected he might try to take the ranch by altering it. He loved the ranch and did a lot of work on her. Or he could use it to make a false sale to some rich fool. If the records office ever burned, we'd have a hard time proving Cardone ownership without it. It's impossible to say where it is or what he'll do with it. It's clear he didn't mail it to you for safe-keeping."

"Lynx, does it bother you that Brax is my father?"

He looked away. "Sometimes," he admitted. "I guess we don't want to see you in that light, but you seem determined to keep reminding us."

"You're still observing me and testing me, aren't you?"

He looked her straight in the eye and nodded. "Can you blame us? You invaded our lives and turned them upside down. You're forcing us to face emotions and decisions we're not ready to deal with, Cal. As for me, I care about you and want you; beyond that, I'm just not sure yet. It takes courage and daring for a man to accept a connection to an enemy." He was finally saying "I," instead of "we."

"I don't see you as man short on courage or daring. I seem to recall a very bold man in the Red Satin Saloon and the water shed."

"That wasn't daring, Cal. You just drove me past the point of control or wisdom. Both times you cunningly set up irresistible traps for me, and I rashly got caught," he jested.

"You poor thing, you must be exhausted from your struggles for escape," she taunted him playfully, forcing his confessions from her mind until later when she could absorb them.

He fell back to the bed and sighed heavily. "You're right." It was easier to corral and tame a wild mustang than Callie Braxton.

"Up and out, Mister Cardone, it's late," she hinted softly, knowing where things might lead if she didn't stop them. Lynx must learn that he couldn't stroll in

167

and out of her life at will. If he wanted her and she was important to him, then he needed to make it clear to both of them. If he was allowed all privileges without a commitment, he would stall making one. She would not force him into making a hasty decision, but she would avoid giving him reasons to evade one.

He turned his head to gaze at her, his expression revealing his imminent plans. "It's been weeks, Callie; I want you. I need you."

"Not tonight, Lynx. Too much has been said. I need time alone. Will you be around tomorrow before I leave?" she asked.

"No. If I go now, we won't see each other for a long time. Do you want me, Callie?" he asked huskily, waiting tensely for a reply.

"That has nothing to do with it. You've given me a lot to consider. We'll talk when you come home again, whenever that is."

Lynx felt she would relent if he ardently tempted her, but that wasn't fair. "Don't forget your promise, not one word to Rankin."

"I'll remember everything you told me. You have my word. Lynx, what about your mother? When did she . . ." she cautiously probed, knowing that harmful malady couldn't heal until excised.

"If you don't mind, Callie, I don't want to discuss Laura Cardone, now or ever. Let the past die, all of it," he said inflexibly.

Calinda read the anguish in Lynx's tawny eyes. She knew he had been describing his emotions and reactions as much as Rankin's. The two people Rankin and Lynx had loved most had hurt them deeply. Since she was Brax's child, she felt responsible for gleaning the truth or an explanation to ease their torment. Brax owed each of them that much. She knew she could not discuss this painful subject with Rankin, and she realized she could never borrow money from the Cardones to seek the man who had done such evil in their lives and home.

Lynx couldn't beg for her touch, so he left. Afterwards, Callie allowed his words to flood her mind, as tears flooded her eyes. It was hard to accept the truth and she resisted it. If what Lynx said was the truth, how could he and his father stand to look at her? There must be more to it. Brax's crimes might explain his lack of contact with her; perhaps he thought that if he wrote to her, they could trace him through his letters. But why had they pursued her father, unless to punish him? Why had they taken her into their home? Why would they think Brax might return to the scene of his crime? Curious inflections, questions, and looks from the two men returned to make an impression in her mind. Somewhere there were other pieces to this unfinished puzzle . . .

But there were realities Calinda couldn't ignore. Her father had abandoned her and ceased to support her, as if she meant nothing to him, with not one letter of apology or explanation. He had taken a path of crime, at the expense of good friends and his family. How could he do such wicked things? Surely there had to be more to the man her mother had loved and married, more to the man the Cardones had trusted and loved? What had changed her father? He had sacrificed everything and everyone; why? It was senseless.

The next day, Calinda went to the Ranger post. She asked to speak with the man in charge. Without giving facts she had promised Lynx to keep concealed, she explained her dilemma to Major Jones. He was kind, attentive, and patient. But he told her there was nothing the Rangers could do to help. He suggested she locate a picture of her father, then hire a detective to hunt for him. Lastly, he told her there was little, if any, hope of locating a man who had vanished long ago, adding that Rangers couldn't be involved in personal matters.

Calinda thanked him and returned to the hotel. She didn't have either a picture of Brax or any money to hire a detective. She was still trapped at the Cardone Ranch and dependent on them. Knowing this, she felt uneasy about returning there. To discover how tight her web was, she spent all morning seeking a job. By the time Steve was ready to leave Waco, Calinda knew she had no choice but to return with him.

Calinda didn't know that Lynx was having her watched, for her safety. When the man reported to Lynx after her departure, he was baffled and annoyed by her visit to Major Jones and her attempts to find work in Waco. Evidently she hadn't fully accepted his words and was still determined to locate her father. Too, she seemed resolved to leave the Cardone Ranch. Was it to elude him, or was she suspicious of them now? What if she sought work in Fort Worth, Dallas, or Wichita Falls? What if she pressed Rankin for more clues? Where was that critical ranch deed? What was Brax planning to do with it?

Lynx couldn't help but wonder if his mother was still alive somewhere. Had she ever regretted her traitorous actions? Had she ever been tempted to return home? After what his own mother had done to him, could he blindly trust another woman, rashly offer his heart and soul? Even to his beautiful and gentle Callie? Why was he reluctant to reach out and take something he wanted so desperately? Because he feared his dream would dissipate as wind-assailed smoke.

Lynx couldn't allow his love to desert the ranch or place herself in danger. But if she pressed his father for answers, Rankin would make her leave rather than tell her the whole truth. He headed to see Major Jones about a two-day leave, needing to settle this matter with Calinda before it was too late for all concerned. He cursed his careless revelations to her; he berated this weakness, this overwhelming and aching desire for her. How could he stop her departure and also distract her from the past? The problem was, he was on a tough assignment; it could be weeks before Jones gave him permission to go home. Time might be a new enemy . . .

Chapter Seven

Calinda had been home for less than two days when a harrowing episode began on Thursday morning. She had kept her word to Lynx; she had not mentioned their unexpected meeting in Waco and she hadn't asked Rankin any questions or dropped any clues. Calinda had returned late Tuesday evening; Rankin had departed early the next morning for Graham to meet with the Southwestern Cattle Raisers Association. He would be gone for over a week. Calinda was relieved by his absence — she needed time to adjust to the stunning information Lynx had supplied. Caught up in the excitement of her return and preparations for his departure yesterday, Rankin hadn't noticed a change in Calinda. But she was more observant and subdued, with a slight gleam of remorse and sadness in her eyes.

Shortly after Rankin left, Calinda had confronted Salina with her daring theft of Lynx's note. Naturally Salina denied the charge, a charge which told Salina the infuriating Calinda had been with Lynx in Waco.

The jealous Salina threatened to reveal their "wanton affair" to Rankin, shrieking that Rankin would never allow such goings on in his home with his son. Their volatile quarrel had nearly erupted into a fight, but Calinda had wisely prevented it by suggesting they halt their private war before Lynx and Rankin got involved and were forced to choose between them.

Salina had smiled deceptively. If her revenge was to succeed, she couldn't openly expose herself as a bitter enemy of Calinda's. Once Calinda was removed from their home, she must look innocent. Something strange had taken place between Calinda and Lynx in Waco, for the hated girl alluded to being afraid of the Cardones' rejecting her.

Calinda unknowingly stepped into Salina's long-planned scheme to be rid of her when she had stated unflinchingly, "I'm not leaving, Salina. I like living here on the ranch with Lynx and Rankin. Besides, I don't have a home or family anywhere. So you're stuck with me."

"What about your papa? You do not care if you find him or not. It was a trick to steal into this home," she hotly accused.

"That isn't true! While I was in Waco, I went to see Major Jones of the Rangers to gain their help and advice," Calinda shouted back at her, continuing angrily with the whole meeting. "And I'm not accepting charity from the Cardones! I've been working hard for my keep. I checked around in Waco; there weren't any decent jobs. I have no choice but to stay here, so stop trying to run me away."

"If you say so," Salina skeptically responded, her mind racing wildly with excitement. This was the event and time she had anticipated. She finally had an opportunity to send Calinda a misleading note about her father, a note to lure her into danger and to inspire trouble between her and the Cardones. It was perfect.

That next morning, Salina supposedly left early to go into town for supplies. After Calinda straightened her room, she went to the water-shed to do her laundry. When it was hanging on the line, she went to the kitchen to prepare a lunch of scrambled eggs and coffee, as she had skipped breakfast. Afterwards, she went to her room to rest.

There was an unpost-marked letter on her pillow. Calinda glanced around; her room was empty. Who had placed the envelope there? She hadn't seen anyone come near the house all morning. She lifted it and read it.

Miss Calinda Braxton,
    You must forgive this manner of delivery, but there are reasons which I will explain when we meet. I have uncovered distressing news of your father. You must come to the Keystone Hotel in Lampasas with all speed. The Butterfield Stage-line runs between Fort Worth and here. The trip will take two days. You must tell no one of this letter or your plans, even the Cardones. I cannot sign this note, but you asked my help and should know who has written it. Come quickly, before it's too late.

Calinda's mind was in a flurry of thoughts. Major Jones? Was her father in danger or trouble, or both? Why didn't the Ranger want the Cardones to know about his help? Of course, they would follow her and arrest her father. Did she dare go and meet him? If so,

174

would she finally uncover the missing link in this chain of events? But how could she disappear for days, five at least? She couldn't claim to be visiting friends or shopping for that length of time. She had enough money to carry out this journey, thanks to Rankin. But how would he and Lynx react to her seemingly traitorous actions? There was no simple answer to this crisis. Yet, this might be her last and only opportunity to confront her father and hear his side.

Calinda paced her room, trapped by indecision and worry. Suddenly she raced out and searched the house and surrounding yards, finding no one. She hurried to the stables to speak with the two men working there; they hadn't seen or heard anyone come or go. When they questioned her behavior, she smiled and told them she thought she had heard someone arrive while she was bathing, but found no one when she was dressed. They grinned when she cunningly hinted she thought Lynx might have come home. They shook their heads and said no. Calinda went to the house, halting by Salina's door to knock. There was no answer. Clearly Salina hadn't returned from town . . .

Calinda went back to her room to give this grave matter more thought. Two hours later, Salina slipped out of her room and stole into the supply shed. She carried several bags to the kitchen, loudly slamming the door on her last trip. Calinda went downstairs to find Salina putting away supplies. She asked the sullen girl if she had seen anyone around the ranch or on the road earlier this morning.

Salina turned to glance to her. "Were you expecting company? Lynx does not return home so quickly after leaving," she sneered, making it sound as if Calinda was hoping he had changed his ways now that she was here. "It would be fun with old papa away so long."

"I wasn't thinking about Lynx, Salina. Several times I thought someone was in the house, but I couldn't find anyone when I searched. Do you ever have bandits come around?" she tried to prevent any suspicion in the Mexican girl who was watching her strangely.

"We have rustlers on the range, but no *bandido* has dared to enter this *casa* to rob a Cardone. It must have been your imagination, or perhaps wishful dreaming," she hinted playfully.

"Perhaps," Calinda flippantly agreed to end the matter. She must make a decision this afternoon. If she could come up with an acceptable excuse, she could make the two-day trip to Lampasas, speak with Jones or her father, then make the two-day trip home. A five-day journey could be carried off before Rankin's return in six or seven days. If she could sneak off, the men wouldn't think anything about her absence on the range since Rankin wasn't home to escort her. The problem was Salina. That malicious witch would enlighten Rankin the moment he returned. Since Calinda couldn't lie to Rankin, it might spoil everything. What to do?

Calinda remembered her laundry and went to fetch it. When she returned to her room, Salina was standing near her bed with the letter clutched tightly in her hand, cunningly plotting how to help Calinda solve the problem of Salina.

Calinda entered the room and halted instantly. She raced forward, throwing her clothes on the bed and snatching the letter from Salina. "How dare you read my mail!" she shrieked at Salina. "What are you doing in my room? I told you never to set foot in here again."

"I came to make a truce. You are right about our

battles causing trouble. I sat down to wait for you to come back. I saw the letter on the bed. I could not help but see what it said. What does it mean?" she asked, pointing to the letter.

"Since you so boldly read it, you know as much as I do," Calinda snapped in irritation, viewing the girl as a kink in her plans.

"Are you going to meet him?" Salina inquired, eyes wide.

"How can I? Rankin and Lynx would be furious with me. I don't even know who sent it or how it got in my room."

"Who do you think sent it?" Salina questioned innocently.

"I suppose that Major Jones, the Ranger from Waco."

"Why does he want you to come in secret like a thief? Why would your papa not come here to see you?" Salina pressed.

"I don't know, unless my father is in some danger or trouble."

"But you said the Cardones would be angry with you; why?"

Calinda wondered how much, if anything, Salina knew about the past. "How long have you lived here?" she asked. "Did you work for Laura Cardone?"

"No. My sister worked here until she married. I took her place. You did not say, why will they be mad if you seek your papa? If you came to look for him, why do you not rush to answer this message?"

Calinda chose her words carefully as she said, "My father used to work here. He was Rankin's best friend. For some strange reason, he vanished five or six years ago. Rankin and Lynx were upset because he left suddenly without a word to any of us. He treated us badly, so they would be angry with me if I rushed to him now that's he's decided to come forward after all this time." Calinda observed Salina closely. If Salina had learned anything since coming here or her sister had revealed any facts to her, it didn't show on her face or in her voice.

"Men are silly creatures, so proud. How can you refuse over a quarrel so long ago? If your papa is in trouble, why would a Ranger send for you? He would arrest him. Perhaps your papa is a secret agent. That could explain why he moved so quickly, why he could not get in touch with you, and why they are helping both of you. *Si?*"

"Your sister never mentioned Elliott Braxton? He was called Brax. I would think sisters shared all secrets and gossip."

"She was my step-sister. We never liked each other. She always thought she was better than me. She hated her mother for marrying my father. She left home as soon as possible. She did not even tell me about the Cardone job; my father did."

"Do you think she would tell you anything she remembered if you wrote to her? I would like to know what happened to him."

"Then why do you not go to see him? Perhaps he will only confide in you. If he leaves on a mission again, you might never see him."

"My father couldn't be an agent, Salina. He was a rancher. Something happened to either drive him away or to scare him off."

"Then why do you not find the reasons which keep him from you?"

"I told you why," Calinda panted in exasperation.

"Which is more important, *senorita?* Your own papa or the Cardones and your life here on the ranch?" Salina artfully challenged.

"I see what you're trying to do. You want me to leave. You hope they'll be furious and will refuse to let me come back."

"I care nothing for your truth or papa. *Si*, I wish you to leave and never return. If you find your papa, perhaps it will be so. My tongue does not run wild. If there is a slim chance your papa will take you away from here, I will keep silent for you to chase it. Even if I told them about your trip, they would probably forgive you and I would look bad in their eyes. They take your side against me. There is time for you to seek your answers before *Senor* Rankin comes home. If you are here to stay, I also wish to know."

"Why would you cover for me? You despise me."

"I told you. If you cannot find your papa, you will remain. If that is to be, I wish to know now. Then I must decide if I am to go or stay. If your trip and success can bring home answers for both of us, then I beg you to go. If you resist because you do not want the Cardones to know of your search, then I will keep silent. But I swear to you, Calinda, I will deny I knew of your departure and its reasons. You must promise to never tell anyone I knew of your plans. If they discover your actions and question me, I will tell them it was none of my business. They said you were free to come and go. Who am I to stop you?" Salina shrugged her shoulders and sighed.

"What if I don't find him and return? You would seek trouble and spite by telling them or by threatening to tell them. I don't trust you." Calinda and Salina stared at each other. Calinda was so confused and intrigued that she couldn't observe this situation wisely. She was so desperate to hear the truth and to see her father just once that she unconsciously allowed herself to be charmed and convinced.

"If you return, then I must leave or we must make peace. If there is trouble, they will send me away before casting you out. You can clean the house and cook, and they like you more. You are the one not to be trusted, Calinda. You have come here and tried to take my place and my family," Salina accused grimly.

"That isn't true, Salina. The only reason they've been upset with you is because of the mean way you've treated me. I don't want to take your place. There's no reason we can't be friends. Why must you hate me so much?"

"Friends? You do not wish me to leave so you can take over the house? You do not wish to turn them against me?"

"Of course not. I've never seen a more qualified housekeeper and cook. I could never handle everything with the skills you do. You've been here a long time, Salina; they're very fond of you. They know how special you are and how hard you work. They also know you love them and love working here. If you're angry about Lynx, I'm sorry. Lynx has had a difficult time growing up. I've been trying to convince him to come home, that Rankin needs him on the ranch. But he wouldn't listen. If you think I'm chasing him, you're wrong." If Lynx was the major problem between them, Calinda wanted to clear the air today.

"You are very beautiful. I saw how he watched you. It was as I feared; he desires you. You are a lady, and *hombres* hunger for them. He will not come to me with you here," she voiced her jealousy.

"Desiring and loving are two separate things, Salina. Lynx doesn't love me. I'm not sure he's capable of loving any woman, at least not yet. I think his mother hurt him deeply; now, he doesn't trust any woman. He's afraid to feel anything or share himself. Even when he's ready, I doubt he would select me."

"But you also desire him, do you not?" Salina asked with a deceptively calm and sad voice. "If you wish, you could win him easily."

"I like him very much, Salina. But Lynx is a mistrustful man. We're very different. He is charming and handsome, but that doesn't justify love. I only want him to be happy."

"What if he chooses me? Would you stay here if he did?"

Calinda's face betrayed her answer, but she didn't voice one. "I don't think we should discuss him like this, Salina. But I will promise you one thing; I won't ever chase after him."

Salina had her answers. She sighed dramatically and nodded. "You are right, Calinda. A woman cannot force a man to desire or love her. But I will promise you something; I will go after him until the day he marries another woman. Until then, he is free to be taken."

Calinda couldn't suppress a smile. "You and Lynx are much alike, Salina. You're both proud and strong. You both know what you want and you go after it with all your might. I envy such daring." Calinda had caught herself before including mercurial and stubborn on her list of similar traits. Could she trust Salina? The girl's arguments were logical, even selfish; and Salina freely admitted to her feelings. Right now, they were both trapped in the middle. Calinda's quest

181

could solve many of their problems.

"Are you going to Lampasas?" Salina queried.

"I'm afraid to go, and I'm afraid not to go," she replied honestly. "I don't even know where it is or how to get there. It could be dangerous. If you recall, the first stage I rode here was robbed."

"You said you envied my daring and courage. If you challenge nothing, you win nothing. Find the truth, Calinda. Then we can settle this confusion between us. I swear to hold my tongue silent."

"But what if someone sees me or tells them? What if Rankin comes home early?" Calinda fretted aloud.

"I can not tell you what to do, Calinda. But I will help you. In doing so, I help myself. I can not risk earning their wrath, so I must deny everything if you get caught," Salina reminded her.

"If I don't get caught, you promise to say nothing? Even if I come back to the ranch?" Calinda pressed anxiously.

Salina withdrew a silver cross from beneath her blouse and held it tightly between her fingers as she said, "Upon this cross, I swear never to tell anyone where you went or why. If anyone should come home early, I will swear I know nothing of your departure. I swear only you will explain when you return, if you do."

Calinda sighed with relief and gratitude. Salina demanded, "Now, you hold the cross and swear you will say nothing of my knowing such things."

Calinda held the silver cross between her fingers and murmured softly, "I swear to tell no one of your knowledge or help." She released the cross and sat down on the bed. "Now, all I have to do is figure out how to get to this Lampasas."

"Manana, I must go to town to get more supplies. You can ride with me to the stage office. It will take you to Lampasas. But you must stay there or return in five days. I do not wish to lie to *Senor* Rankin unless it cannot be helped. Agreed?"

"Agreed. Thank you, Salina. I promise things will be better when I come home," Calinda naively and wistfully implied.

Home, Salina mentally sneered. *You will never return. Lampasas has many outlaws and dangers. One will surely claim you. He will see to it for me. Even if you escape this trap, you will return too late to keep their love and trust . . .*

"You must pack tonight. We will leave as soon as the hands have left for the day. It is best no one sees you leave with me." Salina eagerly planned the one-sided conspiracy.

"Will you have dinner with me tonight?" Calinda offered.

"That is not permitted, but *muchas gracias.* I have promised to see an *amigo.* If Lynx finds another woman, then I must be prepared with another man. I will soon be past my age of beauty when husbands are harder to find and trap," she teased happily, knowing her revenge and dreams would soon be met, denying Calinda's offer of friendship.

Calinda smiled and remarked, "You're very smart, Salina."

Salina left thinking, *more than you know, senorita. . .*

In Waco, Lynx was trying to reason with Major Jones, and having no success. For the past three days since Calinda's departure, he had been working feverishly to complete this present mission. Finally today, he had gained the information and names which Jones needed. He had asked for a short leave on Monday, but had been refused. Now, he was asking again Thursday, but was receiving new orders instead.

"I'm sorry, Lynx, but you just had a leave home. I can't spare you or another Ranger to take your place right now. I've got explosive problems all over the state threatening to go off at any time. I need you in Kimble County within the next few days. You're the only Ranger those men won't recognize. As soon as that fire's put out in Junction, you must come back here. From Murphy's reports, Bass is heading this way for the biggest job he's ever pulled. If we don't nail him this time, it could be ages before we sniff the right trail again."

"What's so vital in Kimble?" Lynx asked, annoyed but resigned. He had never been one to shirk his duty or to put personal feelings above them. Calinda would just have to wait another few weeks.

"You see all these letters?" he asked, directing Lynx's attention to the sliding stack on his desk. When Lynx nodded, Jones continued. "They're from terrified citizens, nervous local officials, and eagle-eyed Rangers. There's been a heavy rain of fear and crimes in that county. You name it, and Kimble has it: rustling, robbery, murder and beatings. There're so many outlaws operating in that area that the two Rangers I have assigned there can't handle all of them. It's like a viper's nest; little snakes crawling all over and hiding everywhere. You've got desperados working alone and in gangs. The citizens are banding together and carrying weapons. Could be another vigilante or regulator group forming. You know what that means: violence and lynchings. Innocent people get caught in the middle, Lynx. Those people are so touchy, a sudden thunderstorm could set them off. What few lawbreakers the sheriff captures are stolen from jail and hung. Some of those men could be innocent. Things are getting out of hand, Lynx. I need you to scout around and report to Ranger Clark with any news. No one else, Lynx, just Clark," he stressed.

"Yes sir. I'll pack and leave at dawn," he accepted his duty.

"Lynx, if it becomes necessary, use your badge. I don't want you killed down there. But I hope to keep you a secret a while longer."

"I understand, sir," he said, then left.

That night, all Lynx could think about was Calinda. He tossed and turned until he was tense and exhausted. He worried over his distraction, as survival demanded a clear head. He wasn't much good to anyone in this state, especially himself. Calinda was proud and stubborn. He recalled a gleam in her eyes which troubled him. If he pulled out at dawn and rode hard, he could swing by the ranch before heading to Kimble. If he could just see her and talk with her a few minutes, he could settle her fears and his nerves. If things were that bad down Kimble way, he might not come out of this one alive or soon. He must see her again before riding into the face of death. He had to make certain she would wait at the ranch for him. If need be, he would give her a good reason to hang around, a promise of marriage. If he really pushed himself, his arrival in Kimble would be delayed only a few days. What could possibly happen in three days to change things?

After all he'd done for the Rangers, they owed him this one lapse. He loved Texas, the Rangers, and the law. But he also loved something else now. He chuckled to himself at that realization and admission; he actually loved Calinda Braxton. He had wasted a lot of years and emotions, but not any more. He would complete these last three assignments, then go home for good. Rankin was a sly devil; this time he was right. Calinda was the perfect woman for him.

It was like a heavy weight had been lifted from his chest. He felt deliriously happy and excited. He would hurry home and confess his love for her, then secure her promise to wait for him. Rankin should be delighted with his decisions to marry and come home soon. In fact, it was time to confide in his father about everything . . .

Nearing town that next morning, Salina reined in the team of horses and told Calinda to get out. "If Rankin questions anyone, I do not want us seen together. Just get home by Tuesday."

"Thanks, Salina. If things do work out with my father, I'll send word to you. I'll sign the letter Maria. If they don't, I'll be at the stage office Tuesday afternoon. I'll hire someone to bring me out to the ranch. If Rankin's home, I'll handle everything."

"Do not forget your promise," she cunningly reminded Calinda.

"I won't. Thanks again. Goodbye."

"*Adios,* Calinda," the girl stated, thrilled by that word.

As Calinda made her way to the Butterfield Stageline, Salina headed for the telegraph office. Simultaneously, her deadly telegram was flying across the wires faster than the stage was carrying Calinda to her fate. By Saturday, Calinda would be at the Keystone Hotel and battling the dangerous surprise Salina had in store for her . . .

It was late Friday night when Lynx tied Star's reins to the hitching post before his home. He quietly entered the house, trying not to alert Rankin until he had spoken with Calinda. He found her room empty and her bed rumple-free. It was late. Where was she? His heart began to drum madly. Surely she hadn't . . .

He walked to Rankin's room, whose bed and room were also empty. Could they be at a neighbor's this late? Rankin's mutual absence calmed his tension. He would wait for them. He poured himself a drink and stretched out in a chair. But his peaceful mood was transient; he fumed as he imagined Calinda with another man. She was beautiful and available, perhaps hurt by him or desperate to flee this ranch. Jealousy chewed at him. The hour passed to midnight without their arrival. Could they be on a trip somewhere? That was unlikely.

Lynx hated to disturb Salina this late, but he needed some answers. His time was limited and precious. Was there a problem? Since Rankin was also missing from home, it would cover his questions at this hour. Besides, it didn't matter what Salina thought.

Salina opened her door without even asking who was there. She rubbed her sleepy eyes and stared at Lynx. "Lynx!" she squealed happily. "*Entrar.* When did you get home?" With Rankin and Cal gone, his timing was perfect. What a night they could share . . .

"Where is Rankin? I've been waiting to see him. I have to leave at first light."

"He went to Graham Wednesday for the cattlemen's meeting. He said to expect him home late next Wednesday or early Thursday. Shall I give him a message?" she offered.

"Did he take Calinda with him?" he tried to ask casually, his gut turning in dread. But he was too upset to care, even too distracted to notice the nearly naked Salina who was posing seductively before him.

"No. Are you sure you can not stay this time?" she coaxed. "You look tired, *amante,*" she noted, stepping closer to him.

"Then where is she?" he demanded, ignoring her sultry appeal.

"You have checked her room," she concluded petulantly.

"I did. Where is she?" he demanded again, wondering if she had left the ranch or was out with another man. Both thoughts rankled.

Salina rested her back against the jamb, causing her ample bosom to flaunt itself as she revealed Cal's departure. "*Senorita Braxton irse hoy.* She did not tell you?" she asked, feigning innocence.

"Where?" he shouted in disbelief.

"*Que se yo,* and I did not ask. I was ordered to leave her alone. You said she could come and go as she pleased. It pleased her to pack and leave today. Why are you screaming at me? I did not run her off. *Ciertamente,*" she stated defensively.

"She didn't tell anyone where she was going or why?"

"I can not speak for *Senor* Rankin. Why would she tell me; we despised each other. *Me allegre tanto,*" she expressed her pleasure.

"How? When?" he probed, his fury and panic rising by the minute.

"She was packing when I went to town for supplies. I came home, she was gone. *Es lastima,*" she murmured sarcastically.

"Damn right, it's a pity," he mocked to irk her. "Come on, Salina, surely she said something to you?"

"*Nada.* When I saw her last, she was holding a letter in her hand. She told me she was leaving. It was not my place to pry or stop her. Maybe the letter was from *Senor* Rankin asking her to join him."

"She would have told you. She didn't say anything about someone coming for her?" he speculated. Was Salina devious or only delighted?

"No. But she must return. I was curious, so I checked her room. She did not take all of her clothes," she hinted as if annoyed and disappointed. "*Que te pasa?*" she questioned his anxiety and interest.

"Who brought the letter?" he asked, recalling that curious fact.

She shrugged. "In case you forget, I have chores to occupy my time and attention. Maybe it was an old letter."

That couldn't be true, for he had thoroughly searched her room the last time he was home. Rankin was to check her mail, but he was gone. Where? Why leave secretly? "Tell me the truth, Salina," he demanded fiercely, grabbing her shoulders and squeezing tightly, suspecting she knew something she wasn't sharing.

"You hurt me, *diablo*. I know not where she is or why she left. I asked Charlie who took her away; he saw nothing. When I told him she had left, he asked

189

the other men. None of the hands took her away or saw her leave. At least they said they did not."

"Did Charlie say if there was a horse or carriage missing?"

"He checked; no. Someone must have come for her."

"Que mas? She didn't leave a note?" he suggested an overlooked clue as Salina shook her head.

"I saw *nada* when I cleaned. There is nothing more to say."

"You didn't by some chance get rid of it like you did mine?" he asked, his teeth clenched tightly as his rage increased. He captured her wrist and put pressure on it until she cried out in discomfort.

"No!" she panted. "I swear she left no note. If you do not believe me, look for yourself. Or ask her when she comes back."

"If she doesn't return, that would suit you just fine, wouldn't it?"

"Si! She causes trouble. I hope she never shows her face again. Why are you so eager to see her tonight? If you made her mad the last time you were home, she took her time leaving. She knows *Senor* Rankin will be home next week. Maybe she just took a little trip while he was gone. Maybe she has another *amante* somewhere."

Lynx threw her backwards against the door before he could stop himself. "Don't you dare talk about Cal that way! She'll be back."

Salina's eyes widened in astonishment. "You love her!" she shouted in spiteful jealousy. "You came home to see her, not Rankin." Salina burst into chilling laughter. "So, the wary Lynx has gotten himself trapped by a sneaky *zorra. Digame,* Lynx, what will you do if she has run off with another *hombre* and made a fool of you?"

"Calinda isn't like you, Salina," he stated insultingly.

"How do you know what she does when you are not home? She did sneak off. I wonder how she will explain it when she returns, if she does. *Que le vaya bien, bestia,*" she mockingly wished him good luck.

"If I discover you had anything to do with this, you'll be sorry," he warned, then stalked off.

He went to the bunk-house and aroused Charlie. He fumed when he got the same answers from Charlie as he had gotten from Salina. But Charlie added another alarming clue; Calinda's odd actions the day before leaving. Had she been expecting someone? Had she merely checked to see if the hands had noticed anything suspicious? He told Charlie to search for Calinda and bring her home if he found her, by force if necessary. Charlie was confused by those orders, but promised to carry them out, scratching his head as Lynx swaggered to the house.

Lynx couldn't sleep, so he mounted up and rode off. If Calinda had packed clothes, she wouldn't be returning tonight or tomorrow. The letter Salina had mentioned worried him. Could it be from Brax? Or the Simpsons? Did Calinda know where to locate her father? Had she gone to meet him? Rankin wouldn't send for her in secret or without an escort. Why would she rush off without leaving word? Maybe she just used Rankin's absence to flee the ranch. Maybe they had quarreled. No, Calinda would keep her vow of silence; she would wait for Lynx to return before leaving the ranch. Something was going on, but what? It was doubtful she would take off alone.

There was only one rational explanation: Brax. After what Calinda had gone through, she wouldn't hurry into danger without good reason. If Brax had returned and told her the truth, it would ruin everything. He wanted to search for her, but he didn't have the time. Without clues, it could take days or weeks to track her down. There was nothing he could do but wait and pray, pray she loved him and trusted him enough to return to the ranch. At least she should grant him the chance to explain and to prove his love. Since she had left things behind, it must mean she planned to return. There was another possibility; she might be looking for a job to halt her dependence on them. If so, she would send word or come back. All he could do was head for Kimble and Junction, then telegraph Charlie for news. He wished he hadn't come home; he was more distracted now than before!

Chapter Eight

The stage halted in front of the Keystone Hotel in Lampasas. Ensnared by conflicting emotions, Calinda had hardly noticed the changing scenery along her journey or the passage of time. Fortunately she had been the only passenger since the last stop along the Butterfield route. Yet, she hadn't given any study as to her planned response to her father. As if numb with shock, she had stared out the window for hours at land which was becoming harsher and drier by the mile.

She accepted her bag from the driver and glanced around. This instantly depressing town was small and crowded. She noticed the common western structures: the hardware store, the gunsmith shop, the smithy and stables, a bank, an adobe sheriff's office and jail, a saddle-shop, stage depot, barber shop and a bath house, two saloons and one cantina, a combination church and schoolhouse, and other mercantile and specialty shops, all of which were ramshackle or soon would be. Decrepit houses could be seen on either end of the dusty and pitiful town. The vegetation present was sparse and thirsty.

The hard-packed street was noisy with rickety buckboards, wagons, and mangy horses. Decaying hitching posts and murky water troughs were conveniently placed before each building. Calinda was distressed and alarmed by what her wide gaze discovered. What an awful place; why would anyone wish to live under such conditions? She had to admit the Keystone Hotel looked the cleanest, most durable structure in Lampasas.

What concerned and panicked her most was the abundance of squalid men. She saw men dressed in grimy and wrinkled clothes, men unshaven and unkempt in all manner, men loud and crude, men armed with one or two guns and sometimes knives and rifles. If there were any decent women around, she didn't see them. Several saloon girls were basking in the sun on porches overlooking the main street, resting or enticing passing males. Calinda couldn't believe their vulgar chatter or their indecent clothing. Three men halted to speak to her, eyeing her up and down and grinning lecherously. Others gaped at a distance or called their friends' attention to her. She promptly concluded she didn't like this place or feel safe here.

She ignored the offensive cowboys and walked inside the hotel to register. She questioned the bug-eyed, scrawny clerk about Major Jones. When he found his tongue and used it, he told her he didn't have any Jones staying there. She hastily inquired about Elliott Braxton and received the same reply. After telling the clerk she was expecting either or both men, she registered. She would freshen up and then find the sheriff of this disgusting and intimidating town. Evidently Jones had been delayed. Perhaps the sheriff had news for her. She didn't like the appearance or the mood of this town and its inhabitants; she would make her powerful contacts known quickly.

Calinda selected her most modest gown when she bathed and changed. She donned a bonnet to conceal as much of her face and hair as possible. She didn't want to draw any more attention than necessary to herself. She asked the clerk for directions to the sheriff's office, even though she knew where it was located. She was hoping he would suggest he escort her along that crowded street. He didn't.

Summoning her courage, Calinda left the hotel and walked down the wooden-planked walkway. Since there were saloons on both sides, she had no choice but to pass one or the other. Rowdy men were standing in the batwing doorways or perched on hitching posts, as if they had nothing better to occupy their time and energies in the middle of a workday. She recalled her mother saying that idle hands and bored minds were the devil's playland. Squaring her shoulders, she lifted her chin proudly to reveal false courage, then steadily continued her walk. Cowboys on horses slowed to observe her progress and beauty. The men she passed halted their talks to stare openly at her, some turning to watch the gentle swaying of her skirt as she moved away.

She received admiring glances and brazen greetings, all of which she haughtily ignored. As she approached the dreaded saloon, her heart began to run ahead of her. She increased her pace to get by it quickly.

"Howdy, Ma'am," one cowpoke said, flashing a broad grin.

Calinda didn't slow or speak. "Yer new 'round these parts, ain't you?" his friend attempted to catch her attention.

"What's yer big hurry? How's 'bout sharin' yer name and a little talk?" the first man tried again, reaching for her arm.

Calinda jerked it away and glared at him. "You will kindly keep your hands and words to yourself, sir," she admonished him.

"I'll swan', Pete, uh fancy lady," he remarked, not the least discouraged. "She don't cotton to us'ens. Uh plumb shame."

"Yeh, pretty 'un too," his shabby friend agreed.

"Caint blame 'er. Yer smells wors'n kee-arn," he joked merrily.

"You boys ain't pestering this lady, are you?" a steely voice spoke from behind her. "You need some help and protection, Ma'am?"

Calinda kept moving. The tall gunslinger moved forward to block her path, nearly causing her to tumble against him. "How dare you accost me, sir! Move out of my way this instant," she demanded.

A lop-sided grin captured and twisted his lips; his blue eyes sparkled with amusement and pleasure. His playful expression revealed two things: mischief and determination. "It's a hot and dusty day, Ma'am. Why don't we go to the cantina to wet our throats? Looks like you need a strong hand and fast gun to defend you against all these hungry wolves. Why I'd be obliged to take care of you."

"I don't need or want your assistance, sir. I'm on my way to the sheriff's office, and I can find it alone," Calinda informed him, fighting to control her tone of voice and trembling.

"You got a long wait, Ma'am; he's out at the Hardy Ranch. You'd best come along with me till he returns. This here ain't no safe town for a lady." His gaze leisurely scrutinized her.

Calinda watched the devilish lights play in his blue eyes. He wasn't dissuaded. "Then I shall return to the hotel and wait for him."

She turned to leave, but Clint Deavers wouldn't allow it. "Unhand me this instant or I'll scream," she warned.

Clint laughed. "Ain't no need to do that, Ma'am. Wouldn't matter anyway. See these guns? No man here would challenge them, including that lily-livered sheriff. Now you don't want to go making Clint angry. Let's have us a nice drink and get acquainted."

"I don't care to drink or converse with you. Release me!" she shouted at him, trying to pull free.

Clint patiently waited for her to realize she couldn't get away and no one would come to her aid. She looked around. No one had moved. Anyone watching them seemed afraid of going against those guns Clint had boasted of earlier. It was apparent she was defenseless. She wished she had the gun Rankin had purchased for her. If so, this ruffian wouldn't be treating her in this vile manner.

"If the sheriff is out, then perhaps my uncle has arrived. I can assure you he will not be bullied as these other so-called men. Do you know if Major Jones of the Texas Rangers has arrived to meet me?" She desperately attempted to trick this persistent man.

"Your uncle's a Ranger? He's coming here?" he asked, trying to conceal the panic which glimmered in his eyes before he could hide it.

So, she hastily decided, it was true; all men feared

the Rangers, even a solitary one. Her lagging courage returned. "Yes. Why else would I come to a horrible town like this! If you do not show me the respect due to a lady, my uncle will deal severely with you."

"He ain't here now, and he might not come," Clint called her bluff, grinning as if undaunted by her claims or the Rangers' power.

"When he does arrive, he will be furious at your treatment. Have you ever known a Ranger to be denied the man he seeks? And I can assure you, he won't rest until he finds you and punishes you."

"I think Major Jones will be happy I took such good care of you."

"I doubt Major Jones will view your conduct in that same light," she sarcastically sneered, sensing this man wasn't going to back down.

"Well, I tell you what, Miss Jones; when your uncle arrives, I'll be the first to see if he minds you having a drink with Clint Deavers."

"You'll be wasting your time, Mister Deavers. My uncle doesn't permit me to associate with gunslingers or strangers, nor to partake of strong spirits." With that refusal, she pulled her arm free and headed for the hotel, forcing her steps to be light and confident.

Once inside her room, she cried softly to release her tension and terror. She decided she would leave this horrible place tomorrow if Jones or her father failed to appear today. Why had Jones asked her to come to such a dangerous place and then be late? She was distressed by the terrifying confrontation with Clint Deavers. He appeared a man who didn't take no for an answer, one who would rebel against deceit and resistance. If he suspected her trickery and vulnerability, he might press her again. It was petrifyingly clear that the daring gunslinger feared only the Rangers, and there were none around.

When Cal finished her evening meal and stood to leave, she froze in trepidation as she sighted Clint Deavers leaning negligently against the doorpost, watching her every move. He tipped his felt hat and smiled seductively at her. He pushed himself away from the doorframe, winked and smugly swaggered outside.

Calinda wished she had known of his intense observation. If so, she could have prevented the telltale alarm from crossing her pale face. Her unmasked panic would inspire more aggressiveness in him. She wanted to know the truth, but not this badly. It was crazy to stay here. She shouldn't have come. She would leave in the morning.

Calinda sounded the bell on the desk many times before the clerk came to answer her summons. "Has there been any word from Major Jones or Elliott Braxton?" she inquired first.

"Nope," he said, vexed at being disturbed.

"I see," she murmured thoughtfully. "I don't wish to wait any longer in this awful place. I'll leave a message for them, if that's all right with you, sir. What time does the stage leave for Fort Worth?"

"Ten o'clock . . . next Saturday," he sluggishly replied.

"Next Saturday!" she exclaimed incredulously.

"Yep. She runs once a week, to and from Fort Worth, each Saturday," he said, unconcerned by her dismay.

"But surely there's another stage sooner?" she helplessly debated.

"Nope. Didn't you check the schedule back there?"

"I just assumed it ran every day or at least every other day. I was planning to buy my return ticket here, after I saw my uncle. He must have been delayed. Please don't take offense, sir, but I dislike your town. You have so many ruffians. It is not the place for a lady."

"Yep," he readily agreed. "This here area has the reputation as an outlaws' stronghold. I kin see why your uncle would come here, being a Ranger. But I don't gain a reason for him 'viting you to meet him." The weaselly fellow was looking at her oddly, doubtfully.

"I'm certain he felt I would be perfectly safe under his protection, even under his name alone. I'll send a telegram to Waco tomorrow and check on his delay," she announced shakily.

"Can't. Telegraph office ain't open on Sunday."

"Can I pay you to deliver a message to the sheriff? I don't care to walk those streets again with so many rude cowboys lining them."

"Can't tonight, but I'll take your money come sunup. Sheriff's out to the Hardy Ranch collecting a horse thief afore those Hardys stretch his neck. Anything else tonight?" he asked impatiently.

"Nothing, thank you. I'll speak with you in the morning."

Calinda went to her room and locked the door. Just to be on the safe side, she propped a chair beneath the knob and checked her window. Her room was on the second floor and had no porch, so she felt safe leaving the window open for fresh air. She fumed over the clerk's behavior; he almost appeared delighted over her troubles. She scolded herself for her carelessness. She hadn't even considered the stage schedule. What if neither man arrived? She was trapped here for another week! She was afraid to leave this hotel. But she needed to send a telegram and see the sheriff. With luck and a little money, she might get the sheriff to come here. If fate was agreeable, things might work out.

As the hour grew later and darkness engulfed the town, Calinda dared not undress for bed. She reclined on the lumpy mattress, but didn't close her eyes. Her heart refused to keep a normal pace, and she couldn't halt her tremors. How she wished she were sleeping peacefully in her room at the ranch, instead of lying awake here in this perilous town and quaking in terror.

As the clamor from the street below increased in volume, Calinda wondered what was taking place. Surely such rowdiness didn't occur every night? She rolled off the bed and went to the window. The wooden sidewalks and dusty street were filled with boisterous men. As her curious gaze travelled down the way, she noticed a group of about fifteen men who were the center of attention and the cause of the commotion. Her green eyes widened as she watched them.

The band of men was heavily armed, their heads and identities concealed by dark hoods. It didn't require a keen mind to realize something criminal and dangerous was taking place near the jail. Many of the men were carrying fiery torches. A gunshot rang out over the din of ominous noise. Then a man's screams and pleas could be faintly heard. Calinda didn't want to see what was going on, but she couldn't pull herself away from the open window.

From her lofty position, she saw a struggling man dragged from the jail into the street, then thrown into the dust. Masked men crowded around him, kicking

201

and cursing at him. She could make out only a few words: "Horse-thief . . . Get yore due . . . Example . . . Skittish sheriff . . . Law of the West . . ."

As if hypnotized by violence, she helplessly waited and watched. A rope was tossed over the beam which held the sign reading, "Sheriff's Office." A noose was skillfully made, then placed around the man's neck. He was squirming and shouting his innocence. Chilling laughter and shouts of "caught in the act" and "guilty as sin" rang out in answer. The lanky man began to cry in fear and plead for mercy. He was ignored and shoved to a waiting barrel. He was placed on the deadly perch, and the rope around his neck was tightened. The leader of the crazed mob shouted, "Die like a man, you filthy rustler! The sheriff ain't gonna stop us; he's anxious to live a day longer!"

The leader kicked the barrel from beneath the man's feet. The beam groaned in protest of the weight placed on it with this wicked deed. The alleged rustler's body jerked spasmodically and gagging sounds left his lips, then he was still silent. The group quieted down as they watched the limp body sway to and fro. Shortly, they dispersed, slowly parting as if leaving a friendly barbecue. The crowd which had witnessed and encouraged this foul action gradually scattered. Soon, only a few men were left on the darkened street along with the body which continued to swing aimlessly in the still night.

Calinda's attention was drawn to a sudden flash of light directly across the street from her window. She went rigid as the dancing flame of a match revealed the man's face as he lit a cigar. His face was held upward and his hat was pushed back from his forehead. He seemed to purposely hold the lighted match close to his face so she could identify him. He stepped into the street, his taunting gaze never leaving her window. He swept off his hat and grinned. "Goodnight, Miss. I'll see you tomorrow," he smugly vowed, then headed for the Mexican cantina, patting the late telegram in his pocket.

Calinda couldn't move or scream. As Clint Deavers passed the suspended body, he laughed coldly and started the dead man to swinging again. The rope and beam sent forth their combined sounds of eerie warning. She inhaled raggedly, knowing that repulsive rogue would definitely be around tomorrow. Before she left the window, a man approached the body and cut it down. He carried it inside the jail, then appeared once more to return the barrel to its proper place under the water spout on the corner of the jail. Tears began to ease down her flushed cheeks as she fearfully watched the pale moonlight glittering on the silver star which announced him as the town sheriff. *My God,* she sobbed silently. *If a man of the law can't halt a lynching, how can he possibly help or protect me?*

That night was the longest one Calinda had ever known. When she dozed, she was plagued by nightmares. Once, she slipped into restless slumber for half an hour, to awaken in a drenching sweat, sobbing and thrashing on the bed. She splashed her face with tepid water, then sipped some to moisten her aching throat and dry mouth. She could almost hear Lynx's past warnings echoing across her weary mind. Why hadn't she listened? Why was she so obstinate and impulsive. When she got back to the ranch, she would never leave it again! She began to cry once more. What if they wouldn't let her stay this time? If she couldn't get out of Lampasas until next week, she'd never be able to keep this futile quest a secret.

Finally about four in the morning, Calinda fell asleep from sheer exhaustion. The rapid sound of gunfire around ten o'clock jerked her to full awareness. She jumped up and ran to the window. She instantly berated herself for looking. In the street below, Clint Deavers was lazily replacing his pistols in their holsters. Down the street, two men lay dead or wounded, while Deavers hadn't received even a minor scratch. "Take 'em away, my good man; they won't be troubling me again," he told the black-garbed undertaker.

The door to the jail opened and the sheriff came forward. "Dang you, Clint Deavers! I done told you to do your shooting out of town," he declared, as if mildly correcting a mischievous child.

"Now, Sheriff, I didn't start anything," Deavers innocently remarked, a tone of indulgence and a total lack of respect lacing his strong voice. "What was I supposed to do? Let them two gun me down? It was a fair fight, two against one. Ask anybody; they drew first. I was only defending myself."

"Yeh, like you claim every time you hand over a dead body. I'm trying to gain some peace and order in this town, Clint. I can't have you battling on the street all the time. What am I gonna do with you?" The sheriff could have been talking to himself.

"Ain't nothing you can do. I drew last. I can't help it if I'm faster and better. If I wasn't, ole Greeley there would be stuffing me into a pine box instead of those two." Clint discussed the two killings as if they were a joke.

"One day, it is gonna be you if you don't stop challenging any man who looks at you sideways. You're itching to get killed, Deavers, and some man's gonna oblige you," the sheriff warned.

"There ain't a man alive who can beat my guns from their holsters. You gonna arrest me?" he teased lightly.

"For what?" the sheriff scoffed, then ambled away muttering.

When Clint focused his attention on Calinda's window, she quickly ducked behind the curtains. Clint laughed merrily as he watched their enlightening movement. "Sorry about the noise, Miss Braxton. I hope I didn't disturb your sleep. Care to join me for supper?"

Before thinking, Calinda slammed the window shut. She could hear the satanic laughter from Clint Deavers at her foolish action. "Is that fearless uncle of yours here yet?" he shouted at her.

Calinda shuddered. He was making fun of her, trying to frighten her. He knew her name—evidently he had questioned the clerk. What had that stupid man told him? Even if Deavers knew her name, he couldn't be sure Major Jones wasn't her uncle as alleged. There was no way for him to know the truth . . .

She was hungry and she needed to send a message to the sheriff, even if it was ridiculous. That old man would never antagonize a ruthless gunslinger. Cal was afraid to leave her room, but she couldn't remain locked in here for a week. It would be wiser to show a brave front and try to continue her bluff.

Calinda went to see the obnoxious clerk to hire his service. She was disconcerted when the stolid man informed her he was too busy to run an errand for her, even with pay. She argued and reasoned with him, but she couldn't change his mind. When she turned to enter the area where food was served, Clint Deavers was poised in the open doorway. He strolled forward and smiled confidently.

In a lazy drawl, Deavers asked, "Having problems, Miss Braxton? Looks as if that uncle of yours has forgotten all about you. Now he shouldn't go letting a pretty thing like you go roaming around in such a dangerous area. Ready to settle for my help and company?" he murmured suggestively, tugging on one of her shiny chestnut curls.

Calinda slapped his hand away and commanded, "Stay away from me, Mister Deavers, or you'll regret it. My uncle was probably delayed on Ranger business, but he'll arrive very soon. You might use your guns and colorful reputation to frighten the local people, but I'm not afraid of you. And I don't like you. So keep your hands off me, or you'll discover what an excellent shot I am."

Deavers captured her hand, finding it cold and shaky. He was a man who depended on his keen observations and instincts to stay alive. He could read Calinda's panic at twenty paces. He noted the enlarged pupils of her deep green eyes. He watched her moisten her dry lips several times. He caught the rapid rise and fall of her chest. He could see the throbbing of the pulse in her neck. Too, the letter which the clerk had refused on his orders was quivering in her tight grasp.

Calinda yanked on her imprisoned hand, but Clint didn't release it. He chuckled, then said, "That's the first time I've ever been challenged by a woman, a beautiful one at that. Where you want this showdown to take place, Miss Braxton, in the street or in your room?"

"You vile creature," she gasped. "Leave me alone."

"I can't rightly do that, Calinda. You have me all heated up over you. You don't mind if I call you

Calinda, do you?"

Calinda stared at him. He was playing with her, mocking her. "Yes, I do mind. You appear a proud man, Mister Deavers; won't it damage your ego and reputation to harass a lady because she rebuffs you and your rude manner?" she icily struck at his immense pride.

"Just think how it will improve my 'reputation' and 'manner' when I win you over. Haven't been turned down by a female yet."

"There's always a first time, Mister Deavers, and this is it. I'm sure you try to terrify any woman who catches your gaze. But I gravely doubt any one of them would . . ."

When she flushed and stammered, he laughed. "Well, Calinda, people usually do try to keep on my good side."

"You don't possess one," she scoffed, her disdain visible.

As it was noon by then, several men entered the hotel to eat, including the incompetent sheriff. He walked like a rolling wave, his slumped shoulders reminding her of the curl on its crest. She called him over to them. "Sheriff, would you please tell Mister Deavers I do not wish his company or conversation, today or any other day. He seems intent on forcing both on me."

The sheriff's eyes rolled backwards in irritation. "Come on, Clint, ain't you had enough fun and excitement for one day? Move along," he ordered, his voice lacking any serious conviction or force.

"I was only offering my protection and assistance to Calinda," Clint insouciantly replied, retaining his grip on her hand.

207

Calinda knew it was time to press her advantage and get away from this man. "Release my hand! Sheriff, my uncle, Major Jones of the Rangers, will hold you responsible for this mistreatment."

"Your uncle's a Texas Ranger?" the sheriff asked nervously.

"That's correct, sir. I came here to meet him, but he's obviously been detained. Mister Deavers has been harassing me since yesterday. I would appreciate it if you would handle this matter promptly," Calinda demanded boldly.

"Head on out, Clint. We don't want no trouble bringing Rangers to Lampasas. You can see the lady ain't interested in you," the older man cautioned, sounding serious this time.

Clint shrugged as if the sheriff's words had been convincing. "I guess you're right. I hear you're gonna be mighty busy between now and Saturday. Guess you won't be in town too often this week," he spoke casually, but Calinda seized his implication and paled.

"That's right. I got to head into the brush and see if I can flush out those other rustlers. But I don't want no trouble from you while I'm gone. I'm leaving Deputy Barnes in town," the sheriff told him, unaware of the part he was playing in Clint's impending scheme.

"Old Barnes?" Clint jovially hinted, then chuckled wickedly. "Why old Barnes is fifty if he's a day."

"What's wrong with that? So am I," the sheriff muttered.

"Why, I think he's the best man you could leave behind. I'll be seeing you later, Sheriff. Calinda," he added, then nodded. A guileful leer spread over his face after revealing how helpless she was.

"You want to sup with me, Miss Jones?" the sheriff offered.

"Yes, thank you. I was planning to see you today and discuss my problem. I headed for your office yesterday, but you were out. That's when I ran into Mister Deavers; he's been pestering me since. Your townspeople aren't very friendly or helpful," she stated grimly.

After they were seated and served, Calinda told him her carefully constructed story. The sheriff sympathized with her, but said there was nothing he could do to solve her troubles. She concluded this man was a discredit to his badge and to law and order. She felt no respect or confidence in him; he was useless to this town and to her. She knew her only safety lay in sticking to her false claims. She dared not trust this man with the truth. It was also futile to plead for his protection, so she didn't. She was tempted to flaunt Lynx's name for added protection, but changed her mind. An egotistical man like Deavers might try to use her peril as a challenge to Lynx.

As they finished their meal in stony silence, the sheriff stood up to leave. He lingered to offer, "If you'll write out a telegram to your uncle, I'll send it out for you." He smiled affably.

Calinda was pleased and relieved. Since she had been told the telegraph office was closed today, she assumed her message would go out in the morning. The sheriff sat down again for another cup of black coffee while she borrowed pen and paper from the sulky clerk to write out her message. Cornered, she fretted over how to word the message to indicate her dangerous position without making Jones think she was touched in the head and without giving away her deceitful claims.

Finally it was ready. Cal handed it to the sheriff and withdrew the money to pay for it. He accepted it, bid her farewell, then left, promising to bring any response which came in later. She quickly made her way upstairs before Deavers could return to torment her. As before, she propped the chair under the doorknob.

Deavers watched the sheriff head for the telegraph office and enter. He decided to check out this action before seeing the beautiful redhead again. He waited until the sheriff had left and disappeared into his office. He ambled over to the telegraph office.

"What's doing, Slim?" Clint asked the chubby man behind the desk.

Slim glanced up and tensed. He didn't like this man who wore his guns low on his hips and tied securely to his muscled thighs. Slim pulled his beady eyes from the roguishly handsome face and chilly blue eyes. "Nothing, Clint. Kind of quiet today."

"I saw the sheriff leaving a while back. Did he hand you a telegram to send out?" he asked, his expression relentless.

"Yes," Slim hesitantly replied. "It wasn't about you," he quickly added.

"The sheriff made a mistake, Slim; he doesn't want that telegram to go out after all. Just hand it to me and I'll take it over to him." Clint didn't even try to make his lie sound plausible.

"You know I can't do that, Clint; it ain't legal," Slim weakly argued. "Anyway, it's too late; I just tapped it out."

Clint's eyes narrowed and frosted. His rigid stance exposed his anger. "What did it say? Where did it go?" he demanded coldly.

"Clint, please. You know that ain't allowed. I could get in big trouble. Telegrams are the same as U.S. Mail; they're protected by law. It was personal business for some lady stranded here."

"Smart people say the law is made by the strongest man and fastest gun," Clint hinted lucidly, pulling out one of his weapons and lazily fondling it as he spoke. "I got my eye on that little gal, Slim. If she's planning to leave town, I need to know. Who's to know if I take a look-see at her telegram?" His voice was smooth and firm.

Slim knew from observation that Clint always spoke and acted in this deceptively calm and sportive manner when he was seething with lethal fury. What did it matter? "Just don't you tell anyone," he acquiesced, fetching the handwriting sheet.

Slim could tell that Clint didn't like what he was reading by the way he moved his jaw from side to side and frowned. Slim shook his head, delighted he wasn't in Miss Calinda Braxton's shoes.

Clint's sharp mind took in the facts on the page:

Major J.B. Jones, Fort Fisher Ranger Post, Waco,
Came to Lampasas as your letter requested. No Elliott Braxton. No Major Jones. Why? Town unsafe. Stranded. No help in sight. Please explain delay. Must return home. No stage for six days. Send message promptly. Hurry.
Calinda Braxton, Keystone Hotel, Lampasas.

Clint's gaze lifted to pierce the distance between him and the stocky man who was trembling in dread. "You're positive this has already gone out to Jones in

211

Waco?"

"I'm sorry, Clint, but the sheriff said it was important."

So, Clint reasoned, that old buzzard wasn't as dumb as he seemed. He was trying to help Calinda, even if that meant bringing a Ranger here. Clint glanced over the missive again, then chuckled. He had the girl worried and frightened. It would take days for anyone to arrive, if Jones didn't think her crazy. Still, the weird telegram might stir Jones's curiosity. If his time was limited now, he should halt this silly game with that ravishing flower. Clint glared at the station agent. "When the answer comes in, Slim, you best bring it to me first. Understand?"

"You'll give it to her after you read it, won't you? If they find out she didn't get it, them Rangers could get nosy and nasty."

"I'll see she gets the message, loud and clear, Slim." Clint's chest rumbling with laughter, he strolled out into the afternoon sun. This was turning out to be a most rewarding favor . . .

Dusk began to lightly drop into dark shadows. Calinda had been sealed in her room since mid-day. If a response didn't come tomorrow, she would be on slippery ground. Perhaps Jones had run into trouble; perhaps he wasn't coming; perhaps he wasn't in Waco to receive her urgent plea for help. If he was absent, would anyone read his messages, or hold them until his return?

Calinda had spent the last two hours huddled by the window, remaining out of sight, watching for any sign of Clint Deavers. What kind of town and people were these? A lynching on Saturday night and a gunfight on the main street on Sunday morning . . . A town where a villain held more respect and authority than the law . . . A town where a decent lady wasn't safe . . . This peril and fear reminded her of her danger and situation in Fort Worth. Since coming west, she had found no safety or serenity except at the ranch. When a knock sounded on her door, she jumped and nearly screamed.

When she didn't answer it, the sheriff called out, "You in there, Miss Braxton?"

Calinda rushed to open it, sighing in relief. She never thought she'd be delighted to see this particular man. It was strange how a person could get extremely hungry when sitting around with nothing to occupy her mind or hands, and her stomach was growling softly.

"I wanted to drop by to say there's been no word yet. I been busy, so I came over to eat before heading home."

Calinda quickly asked, "May I join you? I haven't eaten yet."

"Surely, Miss Braxton," he replied, suspecting why she hadn't left her room. He had heard the scraping of the chair on the floor when she had removed it. Poor child . . . But he was retiring next month, and he was finishing his duty without endangering himself. A man would be a dead fool to challenge Clint Deavers, and he didn't want to be one. More accurately, he didn't want to be another notch on a gun. He had done all he could for her; he had sent her telegram.

They talked little as the meal was consumed. While they were having coffee and pie, Calinda asked about the violence she had witnessed last night. Recalling the fragility of men's egos from the stage incident, she didn't ask why he had done nothing to stop it. She listened as he talked of rustlers and armed citizens resisting the outlaws. He even excused his cowardice last night by saying they would have killed him if he had interfered; one man was no match for a riled mob with loaded guns and functioning on hatred.

"If you think this town is wild and lawless, Miss Braxton, you should visit Junction in Kimble County. It's south of here, two day's ride. This town is peaceful compared to Junction. I'm too old for this job. I'm retiring next month when the election is held. Gonna do myself some fishing and hunting. Gonna read some books and rest plenty. This job needs a man with iron in his back and courage in his blood. I used to have plenty of both." He sighed heavily. It was difficult for a man to accept growing old and useless.

Calinda watched his sad expression. Her heart went out to him. She couldn't blame him for her crisis or for wanting to survive. She smiled warmly and thanked him for his help. As he was leaving, he whispered, "I wouldn't worry about Deavers tonight. He's over to the cantina. Once into a card game, he usually stays the night."

She smiled gratefully and thanked him again. Before going up to bed, she approached the clerk about some water for her room. She wanted to freshen up before turning in. The clerk groaned as if in pain. She was shocked when he told her there were buckets by the door and guests were responsible for fetching their own water.

"Surely the hotel charge covers such services?" she argued.

"Just the first day, Miss. We ain't got time to do more 'an cook meals and clean rooms after that," he lied.

214

"You can't be that busy; you have only three guests. Shall I pay extra?" Cal sarcastically asked, feeling he was cheating her.

"Don't have time, Miss. I was turning in. The well's by the door and there's a light. See you tomorrow."

Calinda gaped at him as he hurried to his room. What a rude and selfish man! Surely he could take a moment to fetch water for her, at least go along with her. She hesitated to go for the water. But it was humid and hot today, and she knew she would rest better if she washed off before bed. The sheriff had said Clint was busy for the night. And no one else had bothered her since Clint had made it clear he was pursuing her.

Calinda went to the door and unbolted it. She picked up a bucket and walked outside, finding the well nearby as informed. She lowered the pail, allowed it to fill, then drew it up again. She dumped the water into her own bucket. Before she could lift it, she noticed a man's legs behind her as she leaned over for it.

Cal shrieked in alarm, straightened, and whirled around. "How dare you sneak up on me!" she declared in a strained voice.

A sinister chuckle escaped his mouth before he teased, "I do believe your temper is as fiery as your hair, Missy."

Calinda was filled with panic. She deserted the water bucket in a vain attempt to hurry inside and bolt the door. Just as she reached it, it was slammed and locked from the inside. Taken by surprise she crashed into it, wincing in pain as she forcefully struck the immovable object. She hammered the door with her balled fist. No one responded. Terror seized her wits and dazed them.

Cal realized a trap had been set for her, and she had

215

naively fallen into it. The clerk was definitely involved, but was the sheriff? She slowly turned to face her tormentor. She tried to imagine any way to battle him and escape, but her petrified mind refused any assistance.

Clint walked forward purposefully. He halted before her, placing an outstretched hand on either side of her shoulders, resting his palms against the sealed door, confining her between two well-muscled arms. His boots were planted apart, his body lax. Calinda's hands were clenched into fists, positioned near her chest for impending defense. Her respiration had increased, her efforts to conceal her panic futile.

Clint leaned forward as he spoke, his face ominously close to hers. She could feel his warm breath and smell the whiskey on it. "I thought it was time you and I had a private talk," he hinted. "You've been avoiding me, Calinda, and that don't sit well."

Calinda rammed her shoulder against one arm, trying to break his confinement. When that failed, she pounded his chest and shouted, "Leave me alone! Let go of me! My uncle will kill you for this outrage!"

Clint laughed wickedly. "Plenty of men have tried. I been real patient with you, Missy. Why don't we stop this horsing around? I bet your blood is just as fiery as that temper and hair."

"Not for you! Get out of my way!" Cal screamed at him, rashly grabbing for one of his pistols. When Clint imprisoned her wrists, she shrieked, "You're hurting me! When I get free, I'll kill you!"

"You're wasting your time and breath," Clint warned huskily.

"You'll be wasting more than that, Deavers, if you lay one finger on Cal," another voice spoke through the shadows.

Deavers spun around with lightning speed, his fingers touching his guns. Calinda bolted toward the stirring voice as she cried out, "Lynx! Where are you?" she asked, straining to find him.

"Here, Cal," Lynx verbally directed her toward him.

She ran into his arms and embraced him. "How did you find me?"

Lynx kept his arms hanging loose at his sides, his fingers limber and ready. "What's going on here, Cal?" he asked, alerting Clint to their acquaintance. "I've been tracking you for days, woman. Why the hell did you leave home? What are you doing outside this late? I should thrash you soundly for falling for such a dangerous trick."

Calinda assumed Lynx was referring to Clint's trap, but Lynx was setting one of his own to avoid a bloody conflict. He was fully aware of Deavers' short temper and lethal reputation. Lynx's mind was working fast as he tried to analyze this crazy situation.

"I'm sorry, Lynx," Calinda murmured apologetically, then briefly explained about Jones' letter and her perilous journey.

Clint remained stiff and alert, straining to catch their muffled words. There could be only one man with that unusual name. But what was his connection to this girl? Why hadn't he been warned about Lynx?

Calinda realized Lynx was up to something when he declared angrily, "I saw the letter on your dresser at home. You're a foolish woman, Cal. Don't you realize it was a trap to lure you here? I had a drink with Jones in Waco three days ago; he was heading for Dallas. If he wrote you, he would have said something when I talked about you. He didn't send that letter. Why didn't you wait and talk to me?"

Clint moved forward a few steps. Lynx slowly turned Calinda to face Clint, holding her left hand behind her. She felt him slip a ring on her finger as he asked Clint, "Are you in this kidnapping plot, Deavers? If so, you'll answer to me," he threatened coldly.

"What kidnapping? She came here on the stage to meet her uncle. We were making friends until you showed up. Get lost, Cardone."

"We were not!" Cal shrieked, blurting out how Clint had been terrorizing her since her arrival.

"I ain't never known you to fight over a woman, Cardone," Clint remarked.

"This one I will; she's my wife. Somebody lured her here with a phony letter, and I plan to discover who and why," Lynx alleged.

"She ain't your wife; she's Calinda Braxton. Who you trying to fool? If she was married to Lynx Cardone, she would 'a tried to use your name to scare me off," Clint debated smugly. Cardone had to be lying; nobody was fool enough to dupe Clint Deavers . . .

"I didn't owe you any facts about me!" Calinda stormed at him. "I thought I was here to meet my uncle. If I had mentioned who my husband was to a man like you, you would have caused more trouble just as a challenge to him. I'm surprised you didn't notice this while you were harassing me," she sneered, holding up her hand for the gold ring to twinkle in the moonlight.

Calinda had immediately comprehended Lynx's scheme to avoid violence. She recalled his past words about trying to settle disputes without bloodshed:

"I've never killed an innocent man. If I didn't keep a cool head, I wouldn't be able to hesitate until the last minute before firing."

To prevent distracting that cool and cunning head, Cal waited tensely to see if Clint would buy their story and relent. Calinda shivered in fear, recalling how Clint had easily gunned down two men at the same time. Clint was dangerously arrogant. Was Clint too vain or dull-witted to realize a peaceful compromise was not a defeat? Was Lynx faster? Could her love talk Clint out of a fatal confrontation? Lynx would never reveal cowardice, but why risk his life for her?

Chapter Nine

Time seemed irrelevant as the two men stood there deliberating their next moves, as if nonchalantly deciding if life or ego was more important. Calinda turned and eased her arms around Lynx's waist and snuggled her face against his brawny shoulder. Perhaps this show of affection would influence Clint's decision. "I'm sorry, Lynx. I promise I won't ever leave home again without your permission. But your business was taking so long, and the letter sounded urgent."

Lynx allowed her to speak freely, hoping her words and actions would entice Clint to walk away. Clint was vain and quick, but he wasn't stupid. To date, Clint had been sly enough to carry out his crimes without being apprehended. Lynx fretted, *if only my reputation wasn't greater than his* . . . That alone could encourage Clint to fight him. But Calinda was in danger; she could get in their crossfire. If anything happened to Lynx, she would be at Deavers' mercy. Lynx was self-assured and talented, but there was always that one chance that another man would be faster or craftier. If it became necessary, should Lynx use his badge to prevent deadly trouble? How would Lynx explain revealing himself over a woman and a gunfight? He prayed Calinda wouldn't be a witness to his lethal self-defense. As for himself, Lynx wasn't afraid or insecure. In fact, it required immense self-control to prevent him from beating Deavers to a pulp.

Clint had seen Lynx Cardone in two gunfights and was aware of his speed, accuracy, and fearless courage. As much as it rankled, he knew Lynx could probably beat him to the draw. Clearly Lynx knew and wanted this girl; Lynx wouldn't back down. It was a rule of survival: know your enemy and his skills. "Seems there's been a misunderstanding, Cardone; I didn't know she was married. I don't fight men over their wives, even one this beautiful and tempting. I ain't got no quarrel with you," Clint skeptically informed Lynx. But Clint wasn't convinced of Lynx's legal possession of this treasure. Someone owed him a satisfactory explanation for this deception . . .

Lynx knew better than to insult a man's pride and courage over a sensible move. But Lynx didn't trust Deavers or that gleam in his eyes, a curious glimmer which implied Clint had a wicked secret. "Know anything about that phony letter?" Lynx asked.

"Don't know anything about a letter or kidnapping. Nobody's made a move against her. You got me to thank for keeping her out of danger. If I was you, I'd give her a good spanking and scolding. Could be your little woman was just running off," Clint gibed boldly.

"That's a lie!" Calinda shouted at the gunslinger.

"He's only teasing, Cal; settle down," Lynx advised

221

astutely, the situation still tense. "Let's go inside and figure out this puzzle," he suggested, affectionately cuffing her chin. "You've got plenty of explaining to do, woman. See you around, Deavers. If you hear anything about this mix-up, I'll pay well for the information."

Deavers turned and stalked off without replying. "You all right, Cal?" Lynx suddenly asked, noticing how pale and shaky she was. She nodded faintly. "Let's get inside before Deavers changes his mind."

As Lynx reached the door, Cal said, "It's locked. Someone slammed it and bolted it after I came out for water."

Lynx's hand was already on the knob, which opened easily. He half-turned to gaze at her. "Maybe it was stuck," he hinted oddly.

"It was bolted! Slammed in my face and locked!" she shrieked in confusion, stressing her points angrily. "That mean clerk wouldn't fetch any water for me, and the sheriff told me at dinner that Clint was busy for the night. It was a trick to get me alone!"

"Could be," Lynx too calmly agreed. "Deavers could have threatened them into helping him. I'll check into it tomorrow. Naturally they'll deny it, but I can tell if they're lying. Even so, Cal, what do you want me to do about it? Shoot all of them as punishment?" He had spoken lightly, but his expression was grave.

"You mean you can't do anything? But I could have been hurt or killed. Or worse! I know that sneaky clerk was in on this plot," Cal heatedly accused, then told Lynx of his previous mischief.

"Sounds logical, but we couldn't prove his guilt. How do we ride out of town after making such charges against so many men? I know you're angry and upset, Cal, but sometimes justice isn't worth the cost. I'm here now, and you're fine. If you want me to press it, I will. I just want you to understand the consequences. I have a tall reputation, Cal, and men fear it. They might tell me what they think I want to know. In that case, some innocent person could be accused and injured. It's over; do you need to press it?"

"You don't understand, Lynx. He was going to attack me. I don't understand your code of justice. Why are men like that allowed to go around terrorizing people, forcing them to do evil things, then get away with it? If they aren't arrested and punished, they'll keep on doing as they please. What about another unsuspecting woman who comes here? She might not be as lucky as I was."

"I keep trying to tell you things are different out here. If you're going to stay in Texas, you'd best learn that quickly to avoid danger and trouble. Next time, help might not arrive in time. Let's get inside and you can fill me in," Lynx said firmly, taking her arm.

When they were safely in her room, he demanded, "Let me see that letter; maybe the handwriting will give us a clue."

"I don't have it; I burned it," Cal told him anxiously.

"Cielos, Cal! How can I solve this mystery without a clue?"

"I was afraid someone would find it," she excused her action.

Lynx angrily snarled, "You mean Father or me! Why the hell would you take off like that alone? Tell me what it said, word-for-word."

Calinda slowly complied, watching the anger increase in his tawny eyes. "Who delivered the letter?"

Lynx inquired.

"I don't know." Cal told him how she'd found the letter, then related her search of the house and grounds, then her questioning of the men. "Why would Major Jones do this to me?"

"I can promise you it wasn't from Jones. He would never send you to a dangerous place like this. If he discovered any news of Brax, he would have contacted the Cardones, not you. Aren't you forgetting Brax is on the run from the law? He stole a great deal of money and assaulted my father," he reminded her icily.

"Then who sent it?" Cal fumed in exasperation.

"Whose help did you ask for besides Jones?" Lynx pressed her.

She reflected for a time, then responded, "Only the sheriff in Forth Worth. I've been at the ranch since then. But it's no secret who I am and why I came here. Are you positive Brax couldn't have sent it?"

"If he's here, he would have shown himself by now."

"What if he was waiting to see if I was followed or if I told someone? It said to come in secret," Cal reminded the furious man.

"No way, Cal. Seeing the danger you were in with that Deavers, Brax would have come to your aid," he stated, oddly defending her father. "Why in blazes did you pack up and leave?" the query stormed out of his taut lips.

To lessen his fury and irritation, Cal explained her motives. When Lynx debated them, she added, "Don't you see, Lynx? I haven't seen Brax since I was four. You've told me the horrible things he did, but they're only words. I didn't witness those events; they don't seem real to me. I must learn what changed him. A man doesn't suddenly rob and beat his best friend without some desperate reason. Something panicked him and drove him away. You knew him for years; could you have been so wrong about him? Don't you care about the truth? I owed him this one chance to explain. He's my father! I also wanted to uncover the past for you and Rankin. It can't end until it's resolved. If I had waited around for your return, he might have panicked again and left. If I had brought you with me, he might not have revealed himself. I know it was impulsive, but there wasn't time to think clearly or to lollygag. Surely he knows you hate him and would kill him on sight." she finished breathlessly.

Lynx didn't deny her last statement, hurting her. "You've got to give it up, Cal; it's too dangerous. Someone is after you. It's lucky I stopped here tonight; I almost by-passed Lampasas."

"What are you doing here?" Cal promptly asked, intrigued.

"I was heading for Junction to see a man. I should have been there by now. I would have if I hadn't swung by the ranch to check on you," he sullenly declared.

"Why did you go to the ranch?" she inquired curiously.

"I was worried about you. I wanted to make sure you were all right. I was stunned when Salina told me you'd packed up and left without telling her anything. I suspected she was lying. I forced the truth out of her. I had to make sure you hadn't left me or Father a note. She told me about a letter which enticed you away," Lynx told her.

Calinda stiffened. "What did she say? How did she know?" she gingerly pressed to see how much Salina

225

had revealed.

Lynx repeated their conversation. Calinda decided Salina had kept most of her promise, but why had she mentioned the letter? Surely she wasn't afraid of Lynx. But if he had been furious, it might have slipped out in panic. It really didn't matter; at least he knew there was a letter. For a time, he hadn't looked convinced.

"Did you leave a message for either of us?" he questioned.

"No. I thought I could get here and back before either of you realized I had left," she admitted contritely. "There's been so much conflict between Salina and me that I doubted she would say anything about my short absence. How was she to know Rankin hadn't given his permission? Besides, it would make it appear she was only trying to cause more trouble. It really doesn't matter now, you know everything."

"Are you certain Salina didn't leave that note on your bed?" Lynx questioned suspiciously, a revealing scowl on his face.

Calinda wondered if Lynx was intentionally casting doubts on Salina. Was there a reason he didn't want them to become friends? "She couldn't have. She left early that morning for supplies. Salina didn't get back home for several hours. While I was washing clothes, it appeared as if by magic. I searched the house and grounds, but couldn't find anyone. I even questioned your men, nothing."

"I know; I questioned them too," he calmly disclosed. "You can be very sly and impulsive, Cal. I underestimated your cunning and daring."

Calinda feared he was about to question her as to how she slipped off the ranch, and she couldn't improvise a believable tale under this pressure. To distract him, she asked, "If the letter is gone and Jones didn't send it, how can we learn who did?"

"We can't. From now on, don't you ever set foot off that ranch without telling me or Father. You might have an enemy trying to get rid of you," Lynx stated to frighten her into compliance and caution. This situation was perplexing. He sensed she was withholding other facts, but didn't press her. It struck him she was trying to explain without lying, and he didn't want to compel her to begin. Later he could pull more information from her. As he did frequently, she was attempting to tell only the facts she wanted him to know and in such a manner as to inspire the desirable conclusions. Still, Brax could be behind this weird incident . . .

"What if Rankin doesn't want me to stay there when he learns what I've done?" Cal speculated worriedly. "I can't get back before he returns, and I can't deceive him. He'll be hurt and angry. I didn't know the stage wouldn't run again until Saturday. I'm stranded here. When must you leave for Junction?" Fear brought moisture to her eyes.

"If you think I'll leave you here with Deavers or some other enemy around, you're loco. Damnation, woman! You've ruined my tight schedule. First that rash trip home, now this new delay. There's no choice; I'll have to take you back to the ranch tomorrow. I'll send a telegram to Junction explaining things. Some excuse, a mule-headed female!" Lynx growled in consternation.

"Why did you stop in Lampasas?" Cal probed again, thinking this stroke of good fortune very strange. Who had lured her here? How had Lynx timed his arrival and rescue so perfectly?

227

"I told you. I've been riding for two days and a night trying to make up the time I lost worrying over you. I was so exhausted, I had to stop here. Lampasas is on the trail to Junction. When I hitched up out front, I heard the commotion out back. Needless to say, Cal, I recognized that voice of yours. I didn't have the vaguest idea what was going on or why you were here." His gaze was penetrating.

"Then why did you rescue me?" she asked foolishly.

"*Que demonios!* I might not know you well, Cal, but I do know enough to realize you wouldn't be tangled up with Deavers," he said, shaking his tawny head in exasperation.

"Why did you slip this ring on my finger?" she pressed to see if her conclusions had been accurate, gazing at the golden circle.

"That's the only reason he relented. I've had it a long time; a man who owed me money used it as payment for a job. It's been like a good-luck charm. I knew Clint would think twice before fighting over another man's wife, especially mine. You see, Cal, sometimes a colorful image is valuable," he teased light-heartedly.

"What if he finds out you tricked him?" Cal fretted aloud.

"I don't want to alarm you, Callie, but this didn't end it with Deavers. He'll seek another time and place to get to me, and you. A man like Deavers doesn't give up something he wants that easily, and he wants you and my notch on his reputation. As soon as I send that telegram in the morning, we'll head for home," he announced.

"Will we get there before Rankin?" she ventured quizzically.

"I doubt it. He'll probably think you took off to look for a job."

"That isn't true; I couldn't lie to him," she protested.

"Don't worry about it tonight, Cal; I'll take care of everything. If he isn't home, I'll leave him a message. I've got to get to Junction before I lose this job and my boss's respect. Let's turn in; I'm exhausted." Lynx walked to the chair and began to undress.

Cal gaped at him. "You can't sleep in here. What will people say?" she argued his bold intentions, suspense washing over her body.

"Are you forgetting about Deavers? Wouldn't it look suspicious if a husband didn't sleep with his wife? I'd like to get out of Lampasas without more trouble. Nobody knows the truth about us."

"What about when they discover we aren't married?"

"Doesn't matter what they think or say," he stated casually.

"It does to me!" Cal snapped. Having a secret affair was one thing, but flaunting it was another. "Are you sure you didn't lure me here so you could play around again?" she hinted saucily to ease her tension.

"Sounds like a crafty idea, but I'll have to disappoint you. I never expected to find you in my path. You had me worried, Cal. If I'd had the time, I would have hunted you down and strangled you."

"It does seem odd that we keep running in to each other."

"You're right about that. You sure you aren't pursuing me? Was there a letter, Cal? How do you keep track of me and set up these meetings?"

She laughed, relaxing as time passed and his nearness assailed her senses. She played along with his

229

joke. "It isn't easy, but I'm doing fairly well so far. But this time I outsmarted myself; I didn't plan on exposing us to Rankin. If he beats me home, the game is up."

"I hope not. I'm enjoying the chase," Lynx replied, pulling her into his arms. She laid her face against his thudding heart. "Ready to turn in?" he murmured, his lips against her hair.

Her gaze turned serious. The moment she had dreaded, yet fiercely craved, had arrived. She yearned to taste and share his beguiling tenderness and torrid passion; yet, she feared another flight of mindless ecstasy. When he caressed her body and stole her breath and reason with intoxicating kisses, she was as eager and pliant as clay in a gentle sculptor's hands. He controlled and designed her responses as deftly as a treasured piece of earthenware in a master potter's grasp.

When Calinda didn't verbally respond, Lynx gazed down at her, reading the unspoken submission in her eyes. His tawny gaze studied her indecision. His hands slipped into sunny red hair on either side of her head and tilted her face upwards. Her lips were parted as if to speak, but no words came forth. She didn't want to say no, but neither could she boldly say yes. Her dreamy green eyes locked with his, as two emeralds sinking leisurely into a tranquil pool of amber liquid. Mentally poised on the edge of a shadowy region, she feared to wave aside the obscuring veil to seek what her body and heart desired.

Mesmerized by his powerful gaze, Cal did not move or resist when Lynx undressed her, nor when his admiring gaze wandered over the creamy flesh before it. His hands went to her shoulders, then lazily slipped down her arms and over to her waist. He leaned forward to tantalize her warring senses with moist kisses on her breasts. She stiffened and inhaled as the blissful sensation attacked her spinning mind. His lips came up to fasten hungrily to hers.

Like an artist's tools, his lips and hands moved lightly over her body, preparing and honing and creating a prize worth possessing. When he leaned backward to look into her passion-gazed face, Calinda's arms around his waist shifted to withdraw his shirt from his pants. Longing to make contact with his virile frame, she shamelessly unbuttoned it with quivering fingers, then eased it over his broad shoulders and allowed it to float to the wooden floor. Her palms flattened against his coppery flesh and drifted from his throat down a hard chest covered with curling hair down to a flat stomach, only to begin her stirring journey upward again, this time to ease over darkly tanned arms with their smooth and powerful muscles.

Lynx shuddered as he tightly controlled his rising passion which strained at the crotch of his pants. He caught her hands and brought them to his lips, placing kisses on each finger tip and in each palm. "I want you, Cal," he murmured in a tight voice, recalling her last rejection, dreading another one.

"I want you, too," she promptly concurred, quivering.

Lynx swept her into his arms and deposited her on the bed. He hastily removed the rest of his clothes and his boots, then reclined beside her. His mouth seared over hers, branding it his. Her head dug into the pillow as his lips continued down her neck to place his mark of ownership on every inch they encountered. Ever so lightly his fingers moved over one breast point as his lips drew magical nectar from the other one, to

231

later shift from one to the other driving her wild with pleasure. Even if this was wrong, Calinda didn't care.

Soft moans of urgency escaped her lips as his exploratory mouth sensuously travelled down her chest to tease at her navel as his seeking hands mapped out the silky territory along her thighs and most private region. As his hands climbed a small peak located there to travel back and forth with stimulating resolve, she sighed in tormenting ecstasy and clung to him, pleading for this hunger to be sated. When Lynx had her straining against him with a fiery intensity which matched his own, he dared to enter her.

Each time Lynx partially withdrew and briefly hesitated to cool his rampant flesh, Cal groaned as if fearing the feverish object would never again plunge into her receptive and entreating body. Her body was a savage blending of ecstasy and torment. As she fervidly matched her pace to his, he huskily cautioned her to master her ardor.

His warnings were futile. Cal writhed beneath him, tightening her grip around his body, twisting her mouth into his. "Don't, love," he pleaded hoarsely. "I'm barely restraining myself. You're driving me wild, Callie. I can't hold out much longer. Be still a minute."

"It doesn't matter, my love. Take me now. Now, Lynx," she sobbed passionately into his mouth.

As love's music played over their minds and bodies, its tempo increased in pace and volume. Blood pounded in their ears as urgency consumed them. Faster and louder the strains filled the room, until a powerful crescendo thundered in her ears. Their fused bodies worked in perfect unison as love's strings yielded the sweet chords of a pleasure beyond words. Never had love's tender passion sent forth such romantic and stirring notes, such a harmonious blending of spirits.

Contented and sated, they nestled together in spite of the heat and their damp bodies. The mood demanded a silent touching and sharing. Safe and happy, they gradually surrendered to slumber's arms.

After dressing and eating the next morning, Lynx began preparations to leave. "You stay here with the door locked until I return," he ordered softly. "Don't open it to anyone but me. I'll be ready to pull out after I get you a horse and send that telegram. Keep this in case you need it," he commanded, giving her one of his pistols.

Lynx headed for the stable to make a deal. Once the purchase of a sleek sorrel was completed, he told the man to have both horses ready to leave in fifteen minutes. He handed him the saddle purchased on the way to the stable, then left.

At the telegraph office, Lynx wrote out his message to Major Jones in Dallas and told the agent to send it out while he waited. Knowing the code, he always made certain his messages went out exactly as worded. He listened to the clicking noises of the metal key as the words formed in his mind:

Advise Clark of three-day delay. Trouble in Lampasas. Calinda lured by foe. In danger. Rescued. Returning her to ranch. Will head out from there. Hold her message for me. Excuse delay. Will explain later. L.X.

"Miss Braxton didn't receive any answer to her telegram to Jones?" Lynx questioned, furtively watching the apprehensive agent.

233

"No sir. I guess he didn't get it yet. I was supposed to give it to the sheriff and he was to take it to her." The man fidgeted.

"What did Clint Deavers say about her telegram when he read it?" Lynx queried astutely, reading the man's alarm.

The pudgy man went pale and quivered. "I can't allow anybody to read other people's telegrams. It ain't legal."

"I'm in a big hurry, so I'll only ask this once more," Lynx sought to intimidate the man into a confession. It was doubtful Clint hadn't either demanded the telegram or its contents, not after the way he had been chasing and frightening her. "Did he stop you from sending it? Or just read it later?" Lynx had pulled out his Bowie knife and was carefully passing his finger over the sharp blade.

"Her telegram went out; I swear it, Mister . . ."

"Lynx Cardone," he nonchalantly ended the man's ignorance, but birthed his mounting panic.

The man sank into his chair, growing paler if possible. He stammered, "I . . . sent it . . . out while the sher . . . sheriff was still here. You can . . . ask him."

"But Deavers did force you to let him read it? I know he's a dangerous man; I don't blame you for giving in to his demands," Lynx cunningly reasoned with the terrified agent. "I can assure you, I'm more dangerous than he is if I'm crossed. This baby can peel a man's hide as skillfully as an Apache. Calinda's my wife, and I want to know if Deavers saw her message."

"He'll kill me," the man blurted out in unleashed fear.

"I won't tell him you confessed. I'll be leaving town as soon as you speak. I like to know when to guard my

234

backside. You know this Deavers has been after her. I want to get her out of town before he presses me. I'll deal with him the next time we meet, when my wife's safely at home. Speak up, my good man."

The agent jerked open a drawer and pulled out the copy of her telegram. "Here, this is what he read. He threatened to kill me if I didn't give him the response when it came in. But it hasn't; I swear it."

"I'm sure of that; Jones is in Dallas, not Waco." Lynx skimmed the contents of her urgent message. Evidently she had told the truth, most of it. He tossed it back to the agent. It fluttered before Slim could seize it, then it noisily crackled in his sweaty grip.

Lynx took a pen and paper from the counter, then scribbled another message on it. He held it out for the agent and ordered, "Burn the first one. If Deavers comes in to check on mine, give him this one."

"Burn it?" the man echoed. "But that's against the rules."

"Burn it right now," Lynx demanded, then watched the man hastily comply. "Do as you're told, and Deavers won't suspect a thing. If he's planning on calling my hand after we ride out, that should send him in the wrong direction. He'll figure I tricked him, not you."

The nervous agent read the message:

Found Calinda. Lured to Lampasas. Both safe. Returning her to ranch. Swinging by Waco. Seeking Jones' help. Will discuss trouble. Must solve plot. Arrive ranch four days. Lynx.

The phony telegram was addressed to Rankin Cardone near Fort Worth. The man glanced up at the towering and cunning Lynx. He grinned and nodded. "I'll handle it, Mister Cardone." Slim wondered if he should tell Cardone about another telegram, but quickly decided he didn't want to get involved in a conflict between two famed gunslingers.

"I'm sure you will. I'd hate to swing by here again soon." His implication was clear. Lynx smiled to calm the man, turned and left.

Before returning to Calinda's room, Lynx made a call on the sheriff and the hotel clerk. He let them know how furious he was with their actions. He informed both men the Rangers would receive a full report on the happenings here in Lampasas and their parts in them.

Clint Deavers watched Calinda and Lynx ride out of town on the trail heading toward Waco. As Lynx suspected, Clint went to the telegraph office and demanded to see his message. The clerk handed the phony words to Clint, who read them and grinned wickedly.

Clint headed for his rented room behind the Mexican cantina. He packed a saddle bag and headed out of town to skirt the Waco trail and find a perfect spot to ambush them. Clint rode swiftly and purposefully, allowing Lynx time to feel confident in their escape and to lower his guard. What man, even a husband, could retain a clear head with a beauty like that beside him? Clint knew Cal and Lynx had spent an envious night together in the same room. If he could lay a trap for Lynx and get the drop on him, he just might allow Lynx to witness his lusty pleasure before killing him. That should punish the smug gunslinger for thwarting his plans and for forcing him to settle their dispute with words only. Too, with Lynx's life in danger, that fiery redhead should be willing to do anything to save her lover's hide.

Five miles out of Lampasas, Lynx motioned for Cal to follow him as he left the deserted road to head off across rugged country, a loamy terrain which discouraged all life. He quickened his pace, compelling her to pursue his galloping steed, denying any chance for conversation. Her bag, tied securely to his saddle, bounced precariously as he nudged Star into a steady run. Her sorrel needed little encouragement to tag along. Her tender buttocks were bruised as the saddle pounded against them along the rough and hasty route. Her dress kept pulling free of its confines under her thighs to flutter wantonly in the breeze which their rush created.

The pace continued for thirty minutes until he spotted a cluster of trees with their branches which hung like an umbrella. Lynx headed that way, halting and dismounting beneath their concealing shade. When Calinda reined in, she was breathing hard; perspiration was trickling down her face and neck and was gluing wet curls to her face.

Lynx helped her dismount, grinning as she mopped the moisture from her upper lip and forehead, then inhaled and exhaled slowly to steady her respiration. Her cheeks were flushed and her clothes were damp. He pulled the canteen off his saddle-horn and offered her water. Calinda accepted it and drank greedily.

As Lynx took his turn at the canteen, she asked, "Why the rush? And why did we leave the road? This route is awful."

Lynx sat down and motioned for her to do the same. He told her about the incident at the telegraph office and his precautions. She stared at him, then asked, "Do you think he's trailing us?"

"Nope. If I know Deavers, he'll get ahead of us and set a trap along the Waco road. By the time he figures out I've tricked him, we'll be long gone. Plus, I have to get you home as fast as I can. I'm late for a meeting in Junction. You sure are a lot of trouble, Cal."

"You're the smartest and bravest man I've ever known, Lynx. I appreciate your help. I'm just sorry I'm detaining you. Are you still angry with me for coming here?" she coyly wheedled.

"Damn right, I am! Do it again, woman, and I won't be so lenient or understanding," he thundered at her.

"You don't have to get upset again. I explained and apologized." Cal realized she was twisting the ring round and round. She pulled it off and held it out to Lynx. "Thanks for loaning me your magic charm."

"Keep it; with that impulsive and defiant streak, you might need it another time." His voice became mellow and mocking as he ventured, "Tell me, love, what can I say or do to make certain you don't pack up and run off again? Even if another letter arrives and claims to be from Brax?"

"I've learned my lesson, you mean brute. If Rankin doesn't toss me out, I'll stay put this time." She turned her back to him.

"I need to make sure I can trust you," he murmured thoughtfully. "How can I hold you there without locking you in your room?"

Cal whirled and watched him in astonishment. Lynx sounded serious. "I know," he finally spoke again. "You need a home and a family. Why don't we change your name to Calinda Cardone?"

"You want me to become your sister?" she cried.

"Cal, Father's been on my back for two years about settling down. He says it's past time for me to find a wife and have my own son. Why not? That would settle both our problems," he reasoned flippantly. "When we get to the ranch, I'll marry you before I head out again. It's perfect," he smugly congratulated himself.

"Marry you?" she echoed in disbelief.

Observing her reaction, Lynx playfully chided, "You don't have to make my proposal sound like an insult, Cal."

"Then don't issue it like one!" she panted in distress, anticipating a spiteful game. "You make marriage sound like a joke or a business deal: my safety and life on the ranch in exchange for appeasing your father and producing a Cardone heir. Marriage is very serious, Lynx."

Lynx threw back his golden head and laughed heartily. "I suppose I did word it a bit strangely. I conceitedly assumed you were in love with me. Aren't you?" he challenged, grinning devilishly.

"Are you in love with me?" Cal parried his question.

"Why would I ask you to marry me?" he avoided responding. "Have you got something against marrying me and staying at the ranch?"

"Of course not. I just didn't expect a proposal from you," she anxiously confessed.

"Neither did I. That little trick gave me the idea. Sounds like a perfect solution for both of us. Well?" he pressed for her answer.

"I thought you recently said we didn't know each other well enough to have such serious feelings and conversations. I thought we agreed to drop this subject. We hardly know each other, Lynx."

239

"I didn't agree to any such thing, Cal. Besides, once we're married, we'll have plenty of time to get acquainted." His tawny eyes gleamed with passion and suspense. "Father won't make you leave the ranch if you marry me. He'll think you ran off to seek a job; I pursued you and convinced you to marry me so I could hold you captive. He'll be thrilled by the idea. As soon as I finish these two . . . jobs I agreed to do, I'll be coming home for good. It'll be easier for us to live in the same house if we're married," he hinted suggestively.

"If you get killed, what then?" she speculated in dread.

"You win either way. Father would never cast out my loving widow," he replied, then chuckled at her look of astonishment.

"It's crazy, Lynx," she muttered anxiously. He hadn't declared any love for her, but maybe after they were married . . .

"I know, but it sure sounds enticing. I love challenges, Callie, and you're one stimulating vixen to tame. Does it take that long to give a simple yes?" he teased roguishly when she eased into silence.

"It isn't a simple question," Cal blurted out.

"How about we analyze this matter carefully? One question at a time. Do you want to stay at the ranch?" Lynx began. Cal nodded. "Do you . . . Shall we say, find me desirable?" She flushed and nodded. "Are you at least deeply fond of me?" Her flush deepened in color, but she nodded. "Then why not marry me?"

She hesitated, then murmured hoarsely, "All right."

"You sound like a person heading for the hangman's noose. Is it so difficult to say, I want to marry you, Lynx," he teased.

FIRST LOVE, WILD LOVE

"I want to marry you, Lynx," she complied, then grinned. "I also have a penchant for challenges, but I doubt anyone could tame you."

"Then it's settled. We'll tie the knot as soon as we make home."

"Are you positive you want to do this, Lynx?" she asked quietly.

"Yep," he stated laughingly. "That should keep you bound to me and the ranch. Let's get moving. I don't want Deavers to catch up and alter our plans. My time's fleeing fast. If we don't hurry, I'll lose any time with my bride." A lazy grin crossed his features.

"You're a rake, Lynx Cardone," she chided him, warming to his insinuation. She watched the beguiling grin deepen on his bronzed face, then settle in his smoldering eyes.

"I know, but you love me anyway," he remarked blithely.

"You're right," she concurred saucily, sticking out her tongue.

Lynx gazed at her, then pulled her into his arms. "I wonder what our first child will look like when your red hair mixes with my blond," he speculated happily.

His gaze was tender and seductive. He kissed the tip of her nose. "If he looks anything like you, he'll be irresistible," she said.

"And if she favors her mother, she'll be utterly enchanting."

His mouth closed over hers, sealing their bargain most provocatively. When senses began to enflame to a danger point, he pulled away and huskily warned, "If we don't get moving, Deavers could find us in a most perilous position. You're clouding my senses."

"Are sure you'll have to leave the ranch so quickly?"

241

she asked, recalling last night in vivid and stirring detail.

He chuckled, restraining his passion by sheer force. "I promise to get home without delay, Cal. Just trust me and wait for me."

There was an odd inflection to his voice, but she dismissed it. "Be careful, Lynx. I would die if anything happened to you," she raggedly confessed, caressing his cheek.

"As long as I know you're waiting for me in safety, then I can keep a clear head. I'll be all right. I have lots of sons to make."

Their gazes fused and locked. They laughed and embraced. "Since we can't start them here, we'd better ride," she boldly hinted, confidence born from his proposal and disarming mood.

With merry laughter ringing, they mounted up and headed off again. With luck, they could make the ranch by tomorrow evening. He would stop by the next town and send Rankin a telegram. This news should entice his father home by Tuesday night. He wanted Rankin there for the hasty wedding, and he needed to explain a few things . . .

Chapter Ten

Lynx and Calinda rode hard all day with few stops. When they did halt, it was mostly for the horses to rest or drink. Nearing six o'clock, they entered the town of Comanche, shortly before the telegraph office was to close. Lynx tied their reins to the hitching post, then guided Calinda inside the small building. She collapsed wearily into a chair while Lynx wrote two telegrams, one to Rankin in Graham and one to Ranger Clark. He waited patiently as the agent sent the messages over the wire. He paid the man, thanked him, and turned to collect his woman.

Calinda's head was resting against the wall, her eyes closed. Her respiration was so steady that he thought she had fallen asleep. He nudged her and called her name, "Cal?"

She stirred, her eyes fluttering open. "Yes?"

"Let's get some hot food before we head out again," he suggested, helping her to rise.

"Head out?" she wailed. "Aren't we going to spend

the night here?" When he reluctantly shook his head, she grimaced. "But we've been riding hard all day; I'm exhausted. I need a bath and some sleep."

"Sorry, *pelirrojo,* but we're overdue now," he reasoned, smiling.

"Can't your schedule be changed?" she pleaded.

"You've already delayed it by six days. We'll eat and rest, then move on. You'll have plenty of time to laze around when we get home. You want to wait in the hotel restaurant or go with me to see about our horses?" he asked, leading her outside to talk privately.

"I'm sticking with you, Cardone," she quickly stated. "But I don't see why we can't get a bath and sleep for at least a few hours," she added peevishly, frowning at him. "You didn't allow much rest last night," she pointedly refreshed his obviously lagging memory.

"You know why, Cal; you're not thinking clearly," he chided.

"I'm too tired and dirty to think at all," she came back at him.

"I promised to be in Junction last Friday night. Here it is Monday, and I'm on my way to the ranch with you. By the time we get home, marry, and I head out, it will be Wednesday. If I break my neck, I'll be lucky to reach Junction by this coming Friday."

"What difference does it make, Lynx?" she questioned irritably.

"I promised to do a job there, four days ago," he replied.

"You have the ranch; why do you need to work for other people?"

"That isn't the point. I gave my word to help

244

a friend."

"A man doesn't marry every day. Under the circumstances, can't you break it or change it?" she wheedled.

He sighed heavily, then stated unrelentingly, "No, Cal; I can't. A man's word is his bond and respect; without them, he's worthless. I'm doing all I can to solve two problems at the same time. Don't be selfish and stubborn; please," he added to soften his demands.

"You're not being fair," she gently scolded, inhaling wearily.

"You're the one who isn't being fair, Cal. First you pack up and run off into danger; then, you treat me like this after I toss everything aside to rescue you, escort you home, and marry you. I made promises before all your problems cropped up to delay them. I'm doing my damndest to help and protect you first."

"We've been through this before. I promise to be a good girl from now on. Will a few hour's rest be that terrible?"

"Then be good and stop pressuring me," he coaxed fretfully.

"All right. Even if you drive us into the ground, I won't say another word," she declared sassily. "Let's eat; I'm starved. You did say we have time to fill our tummies?" she sarcastically stated.

He groaned in exasperation. "Fine," he agreed crisply.

Lynx walked away from her, seizing the horses' reins to lead them to the stable for rest and care. He began strolling down the street, the horses following him. Cal watched him, then rushed forward.

"You beast! You're mean and cruel, Lynx," she

accused.

He glanced over at her and grinned roguishly. "Then perhaps you should give my proposal further consideration. If you prefer, stay here and rest, then take the stage home. I could head for Junction tonight, then you can give me your answer when I make it home."

Cal halted in her tracks, but he kept walking. Leave her alone in this strange town? Risk Deavers catching up with her? Delay their marriage? Perhaps change his mind altogether? Was he that annoyed with her or merely that rushed? Falling for his crafty ploy to put some energy into her fatigued body, she ran to catch up to him. She grabbed his arm and forced him to stop. "Are you serious?" she demanded, eyes glittering in doubt. "Your proposal was a trick all along!"

"If you want to marry me any time soon, Cal, it has to be Wednesday. No matter how I feel about you, I'm keeping my word. If you can't accept that, you don't know me or love me at all. You'll be safe here until the stage arrives. If we can't make the ranch late tomorrow and marry Wednesday, then I'm wasting my time by going home. I'm putting you first as long as I can. Well, which do you want: me or sleep?" he challenged.

"I don't know why, but you," she confessed, frowning.

"Good," he responded, smiling at her and tenderly caressing her cheek. "Come along, woman. One day we'll look back on today and laugh. You're a demanding vixen, *pelirrojo*."

"What does *pelirrojo* mean?" she bravely inquired.

He chuckled. "Redhead. In case you ever need to use it, *'yo te quiero'* means 'I love you,' " he slyly added, winking at her.

They left the animals to be fed, watered, and

rubbed down. They headed for the hotel to eat a hot meal. Lynx didn't permit her to linger over it, even though she tried to stall. As they remounted, Cal groaned. "My fanny and back are killing me. It's obvious you're used to driving mindless cattle, not people."

"I'll rub 'em good when we get home. You can stretch out on my bed and relax while I ease those pains and aches. Or I could give you a rub-down in the tub," he hinted seductively.

"With a promise like that to urge me on, let's get going." She knew she couldn't change his mind, so she wisely relented.

They laughed and rode out of Comanche. They moved steadily through the night, then halted at dawn to catch a short nap. Lynx knew he couldn't push her any harder or faster. But an hour later, he had her up and going again, amidst grumbles and pleas.

When Calinda realized they were heading straight to the ranch, she argued his plans once more. She wanted to stop at the hotel in Fort Worth, to bathe and change clothes. Cal told him she couldn't arrive at the ranch filthy and exhausted. When Lynx adamantly refused, she scolded him and pleaded for some consideration. When he wouldn't budge, she sank into peevish silence for the rest of the journey.

It was nine o'clock when they reached the Cardone house. A flurry of talk and actions commenced instantly. Charlie hurried over to take care of their horses and to greet them on their safe return. Rankin came outside, staring at them with a mixture of confusion and pleasure, his probing gaze going from one to the other.

Salina was about to rush out to greet Lynx, but faltered when she saw Calinda at his side. Her eyes widened in disbelief. How had Lynx found her? How had she gotten away from Clint? Rage filled Salina at the sight of her thwarted plans. She whirled and returned to the kitchen to complete her chores before they entered the house. She would flee to her room and stroke her fury into cautious calm while she made new plans for this vexing girl.

Numerous questions rolled past Rankin's lips before Lynx could answer the first one. When Rankin halted breathlessly, Lynx said, "Calinda's exhausted, Father. I've been pushing her hard. We'll let her bathe and turn in. I'll explain everything."

"You all right, Cal?" Rankin asked worriedly.

"I'm fine, sir, just numb and sleepy. I'm sorry for the trouble," she apologized, smiling faintly.

"What trouble?" Rankin asked, intrigued.

"I'll explain later. You want me to get you some food, Cal?"

"Just some sherry after I bathe. I'm too tired to eat."

"You go to the water-shed; I'll fetch you some night clothes," Lynx offered unthinkingly.

She blushed. "We aren't married yet, Lynx. I'll fetch them."

"You two are getting married? No joking?" Rankin pressed, hoping his surprise plans hadn't been made unwisely.

"Si. Mañana." Lynx and Rankin exchanged a curious look which Calinda noticed but didn't analyze.

Cal went to get a clean gown and wrapper. She left for the water-shed as the two men entered the house to talk. She didn't linger in the water, but bathed quickly. After dressing, she sneaked into the house and up the stairs. She was asleep the moment her drowsy head and sore body touched the comfortable bed.

When Lynx tapped lightly on her door, she didn't answer it or call out. He peeked inside. He smiled to himself, then downed her sherry in one swallow. He joined his father, a serious talk long overdue.

Rankin opened the conversation. "I must admit I'm delighted with your plans, son. But I'm a little confused and surprised. Why the rush? Where did you and Cal go?" Since the telegram had stated Lynx would explain everything, Rankin hadn't questioned him since his unexpected return at mid-day.

Lynx stroked the two days of stubble on his face, then ran his fingers through his mussed hair of ripened wheat. "Fix us a brandy while I get comfortable," he entreated. He removed his spurs, hat, and guns, hanging them on the hooks by the door. He dropped into a chair and accepted the glass from his father.

Rankin sat down near him and waited impatiently for the news. "I don't quite know where to begin, Father; there's so much to tell," Lynx stated mysteriously. As he stalled to choose his words, Rankin suggested he begin with their sudden marriage plans.

"Calinda . . . Now there's a fetching and exasperating problem. You've been trying to get something going between us ever since her curious arrival. You've been after me for years to marry, settle down here, and give you a grandson for the Cardone line. As you hinted the last time I was home, Calinda Braxton is the perfect choice, for many reasons," Lynx told his father.

Their gazes touched and spoke mutely, knowing Lynx's meaning and agreeing with it. "Is that why you're marrying her?" Rankin asked.

"Hell, I don't know myself. I hadn't imagined Lynx

Cardone settling down with a wife anytime soon. But she's here now, and a marriage can solve many problems for all of us." Lynx drew in a long breath, then released it, aware of the weighty burden on his shoulders.

Rankin observed his son; for a man known for his self-assurance and control, Lynx looked edgy and indecisive. "Are you doing this for us, or do you love her?" Rankin boldly inquired.

Lynx stiffened noticeably. Just in case he was misjudging Calinda and her motives, he couldn't confess such powerful emotions this early. He had been wrong about Brax and hurt his father deeply. Now, he was accepting Brax's child into his life. "She's a beautiful and spunky lady. I find her desirable and intriguing. She's bright and charming, easy and fun to be around. She's proven she has the mettle and stamina for living out here. From what I've witnessed, she'll make a good mother and a pleasing wife. She has a lot to offer. It seems logical. As for loving her, I'm not sure I would recognize that emotion in me."

"Does she love you?" Rankin dauntlessly continued.

"I think so," his son muttered in response, sounding wishful.

"Why else would Cal go off with you?" Rankin reasoned. "Cal's a lady, and ladies don't usually act so boldly or impulsively."

"She didn't," Lynx informed him. "She packed and left; I tracked her down." Lynx carefully allowed the incident to unfold for his startled father, explaining how he had convinced her to marry him and to stay put on the ranch. He even told him the phony story he and Calina had created for Rankin, then swore his father to secrecy. "With a home and family here, she won't take off again. With us, the house, and children to occupy her time and hands, she'll forget about Brax and the past. Besides, I honestly don't want her hurt anymore."

"Then you're sure she's genuine?" Rankin said happily.

"Unless she's the best actress around, I think she is. But I sure would like to know who sent that letter and why," he said, a look of puzzlement filling his eyes.

"You're positive there was a letter? And that she burned it?"

"Yes," Lynx readily answered. He explained about her telegram to Jones, then added he would investigate it further.

"If Brax has wheedled Jones' help and friendship, he won't tell you anything, son. Running off like that is mighty queer."

"If there's a man alive I can trust, it's Major Jones." Lynx stared his father in the eye as he finally disclosed his secret identity as a Texas Ranger. While Rankin was speechless, Lynx continued with tales of his past, present, and imminent assignments. He let his father know he had two remaining missions to carry out before he would be coming home to settle down permanently.

"Why didn't you tell me? Does Cal know?" Rankin asked, stunned and thrilled. His son, the famous Ranger who used the coded star? Pride and respect flooded Rankin's heart.

"Cal doesn't know anything about me. She thinks I'm a famous gunslinger and carefree rogue. She won't learn anything until my work is over, if then. It might be best to keep my identity a secret, in case the Rangers need me again in the future. You can't tell anyone, Father, not even hint at it. I'm sorry I couldn't tell you sooner, but my role was safer and stronger with my father treating me as the rebellious son. If you'd gone around with that proud smile, it could have been dangerous for me and my missions."

"Why are you telling me now?" Rankin probed.

"These next two missions are tricky and deadly. If I don't . . . get home again, I wanted you to know the truth about your son. Few Rangers know my cover, and no one else. I report to Major Jones; that's how I know I can trust him. If anything had happened to me, he would have contacted you with the truth." Lynx continued with his present orders. "Now you see how late I am? I'll have to pull out as soon as the wedding's over. I know it's moving too fast, but I've got to keep her on the ranch. I want both her and the ranch, Father," he stated simply.

"If you're not in love with her, son, you're wavering on the edge of it," Rankin said. "I'm proud of you, Lynx."

"Maybe I'm just too wary to trust anyone, especially a mysterious female, and certainly a Braxton. I can't risk feeling too much for her until I'm positive it's worth it," Lynx candidly admitted.

"I know what you mean," Rankin concurred. "She does have a way of stealing your affection. I pray she deserves it."

"The only step she might take now would be a letter to or from the Simpsons. Make sure you intercept all mail except from me," Lynx cautioned once more. "I'll try to keep you informed as to my location. If she says or does anything unusual, send word to me. I'll sign myself as Wade. Now, all I have to do is round up the preacher for the wedding."

"That won't be necessary, son. He's coming here for the wedding at two o'clock. I also invited a few of our closest neighbors. Can't have a Cardone married without a little show." Rankin smiled.

"But I've got to pull out right after the wedding," Lynx argued.

"To marry in secret could inspire gossip. If anyone tries to hang around past four, I'll send them on their way. It'd look strange if you ride off in front of them. Anyway, son, you need some rest. Why not leave early Thursday?" Rankin suggested.

"Valgame Dios! She surely has complicated my life."

"If you leave after the wedding, that means no time alone with your new bride. I doubt Calinda will accept such treatment. Besides, it might be wise to work on a son before heading into danger," Rankin hinted slyly.

Lynx caught himself before confessing to past work on a son. He suddenly realized this hasty marriage was best for another reason: what if Calinda was already pregnant? He was shocked at having overlooked that possibility. He recalled his fears in the Red Satin Saloon about a shotgun wedding, then chuckled at the private joke.

"What's so funny, son?" Rankin asked.

"Who would have ever thought Lynx Cardone would marry Elliott Braxton's daughter?" he parried the loaded question.

"It's one of the smartest moves you've made, son. Looks as if we'll finally out-smart Brax, ironic justice. You do realize the legal implications in marrying Cal? A wife can't harm her husband?" When Lynx ruefully nodded, Rankin added, "We'll make a nice family."

They exchanged smiles, then shared hearty laughter.

"Well, this future groom is bone-weary. We'll talk in the morning. Goodnight, Father. Pretty soon, you'll be sick of having me around daily. You and I do have a way of challenging each other. Maybe we're too much alike," Lynx devilishly speculated.

Like Calinda, Lynx scrubbed quickly and went to bed. Shortly, the entire house was asleep.

Rankin and Lynx were up and drinking coffee when Salina entered the kitchen. She glanced at both men, pondering their smug grins and cheerful moods. If Rankin was furious with Calinda, he didn't show it. Salina puzzled over what had taken place in Lampasas and after their return last night. She dreaded what Calinda may have said to the men. Yet, if they were annoyed with her, they didn't offer any clues.

"Ready for breakfast?" she asked.

They both nodded. "Is the *senorita* up yet?" she inquired, trying to sound casual, turning her back to conceal her expression.

"Not yet. We're letting her sleep a while longer. She's got a busy day ahead," Rankin hinted, laughing merrily.

"Busy day ahead?" Salina echoed suggestively.

"Cal and Lynx are getting married at two," he stated.

"*Ca . . . casada?*" she stammered the devastating word, whirling around to gape at the insouciant Lynx.

Rankin declared, "That's the size of it, Salina. I want you and Charlie to help get the house and food ready. We'll be having neighbors over for the wedding. See if you can round up some flowers to brighten things up a bit. It isn't everyday a Cardone gets lassoed."

"Hoy? Por que? How can we prepare for a *boda* on such short notice? When did this happen?" Salina questioned, stunned and distressed. *Se quieren mucho?* No, they could not be in love!

"We'll have to make do; Lynx is leaving in the morning," Rankin nonchalantly stated, grinning mischievously at his son.

"Que te pasa?" she queried, fearing Calinda was pregnant, or claiming to be to force a marriage with Lynx.

"Nada. Why wait? I asked and she accepted. I'll be coming home to stay within the next two months. A wedding ring will hold her put till then," Lynx humorously alluded.

Although Lynx was laughing roguishly, Salina knew something was going on between them. She pressed boldly, doubting him, *"Que se ha hecho de el astuto solo lobo?* You asked her?"

"Si," he replied, furtively watching her for revealing clues.

"No importa. I did not realize you and Calinda were *enamorado, tomar casamiento en consideracion,"* Salina deviously explained her surprise at their wedding plans, having failed to score with her mocking taunt about the careless snaring of the Lone Wolf.

"Surprised me, too," Lynx declared playfully. "Calinda didn't feel right staying on here. When she packed up and left to find a job, I went after her and forced her to come home. A wedding ring's the only way to keep her where she belongs. I was getting used to that vixen."

Salina realized Lynx hadn't mentioned love. He made it sound as if he was going to any measure to just to keep her on the ranch. Why? Did it have something to do with this Brax and the past? Did he want to prevent her from locating her father? It was awfully suspicious . . .

Feeling she must respond, Salina murmured, *"Que le vaya bien."* He would need good luck, but she would never congratulate him.

"Gracias, Salina, I'll probably need it to tame that wild filly."

Salina set to cooking their breakfast, her mind working steadily and maliciously. There was nothing she could do or say to halt this event. Evidently Calinda had lied about her reason for going to Lampasas. That flame-haired witch had somehow compelled Lynx to marry her. Even if Lynx was bewitched by Calinda, he wouldn't rush into a confining marriage, unless there was a vital reason. If Salina confessed her lies to Lynx about the letter and trip, Lynx would think she was trying to cause trouble. She dared not do anything which might entice them to fire her. She must stay here to sever this marriage!

Salina decided on her future path. She would disarm Calinda with feigned resignation to this marriage and gradual friendship. She would keep her eyes and ears open to solve this riddle, then use the information gleaned to destroy Calinda and win Lynx. Time, cunning, and patience were all she needed. No, she hastily concluded; she didn't have time. A *bebe* could complicate matters further! How dare that haughty bitch enjoy what Lynx had denied her for years! *Jamas!*

While the men were discussing ranch matters after breakfast, Salina eased upstairs to awaken Calinda. She needed to learn what Calinda had said to Lynx. She aroused the sleeping girl, putting on a controlled expression. "You must get up, Calinda; they have planned the wedding for two," Salina revealed to the sluggish girl. "The neighbors have been invited, and there will be a *fiesta*."

"What?" Calinda shrieked, coming to full awareness. They had altered the plans without even consulting her? "But I thought Lynx and I were riding into town to see the preacher there. A wedding here? Guests? But I don't have an appropriate dress," she fretted nervously.

"Use one of Laura's," Salina suggested, wanting to slap her foe. "I must start the cleaning and cooking. First, I wanted to know about your talk with Lynx. What did you say about me?"

Calinda explained the terrifying incident to Salina, omitting personal parts. Salina in turn related Lynx's arrival and fury. "I mentioned the letter before thinking. I have never seen him *hecho una furia*. I told him it might be an old one. He was *cierto* it was not. Could he figure out who sent it?"

Calinda asked for a translation, then told her no and why. She apologized for getting Salina involved. "Well, it did prove valuable; Lynx proposed," Salina remarked.

"I suppose so, but he was furious with me. I can't blame him. It was a stupid idea. Thanks for the help, Salina," Cal said, throwing the covers aside and getting out of bed. She would need to hurry.

"Why do you marry Lynx, Calinda?" the girl inquired gravely.

Calinda blushed, then replied, "I'm sorry if you're upset with me, Salina. I didn't mean for this to happen. But Lynx is so . . . irresistible and forceful. I do love him. I know this is awfully sudden, but I don't have any choice. If I stall him or refuse, he might never ask me again. He's so proud and obstinate. I just wish there was more time and he was staying home."

Salina didn't press her luck by asking if Calinda was pregnant. She shrugged and sighed. "I should not be shocked. I saw the way you two stared at each other. Knowing Lynx always gets what he desires, I should have realized he wouldn't release you; he wants you badly."

Becoming uneasy with this intimate conversation, Calinda smiled and said, "I'd better get busy. Thanks again, Salina."

Salina glared at her back as Calinda stood before the closet trying to select a dress for her wedding. *You might marry him today, my cunning foe, but you will not keep him long,* Salina mentally plotted.

When Calinda went downstairs, Lynx and Rankin were out riding. She ate breakfast, sensing she would be too nervous and busy to eat before the wedding. She washed her hair and bathed, then sat on the balcony in the sun to dry the vibrant curls. She had selected a teal blue gown in satin, one of Laura's prettiest. She spent most of the morning in her room preparing for this major change in her life.

Lynx didn't come to Calinda's room, but that didn't surprise her. After most of the guests had arrived, Rankin came to fetch her. He stood back and admired her beauty and softness. The rich blue gown complimented her creamy coloring, golden-red hair, and dark emerald eyes. The billowy skirt swayed gently when she moved, sending forth a muted rustle. Her slender waist looked as if he could reach around it with two hands. He complimented her on her choice, knowing whose gown Calinda was wearing, bitterly recalling the last time he had seen it.

"I hope it's all right, Rankin. It was the only one which seemed appropriate. You don't think Lynx will mind, do you?" she fretted.

"Certainly not. Why would you worry?" Rankin inquired, pondering if Calinda knew something she shouldn't.

Calinda lowered her lashes as she told him how displeased and upset Lynx had been the last time she had worn one of Laura's gowns. She modestly didn't tell what kind of gown. "I don't favor her, do I?" she asked, that horror suddenly entering her anxious mind.

"Not at all, my dear. Lynx favors his mother a great deal: the same eyes and hair, the same expressions. Sometimes when he smiles or laughs, it's like a small echo or mirror of Laura's. Maybe that was why he and I had such conflicts after she . . . was gone. Maybe I saw too much of Laura in our son," he murmured remorsefully.

Calinda was warmed by the confession. There was such anguish in his eyes and voice, emotions Rankin rarely exposed. It gave her another insight into the troubled past, especially into the relationship between these two men. Had Lynx mistaken his father's unconscious resentment as a lack of love and need? Had Rankin unknowingly punished his son for Lynx's love for Brax? Perhaps Lynx had also blamed Rankin for driving Brax away, perhaps suspecting jealousy as the motive. Had Lynx somehow blamed his father for Laura's early death? Surely it was tormenting to gaze into a matching face of a lost loved one. How sad they had taken their grief and bitterness out on each other. How tragic to waste so many years and so many emotions. Perhaps she could draw them closer. Evidently time had eased some of those pains and differences, for they appeared to get along fine now. If only Lynx would halt his roaming and come home. If only Rankin would gentle his grip to prevent Lynx from needing solitude and excitement elsewhere. If only they would talk to each other and work out their differences, or wisely accept their similarities.

Cal grasped his arm and smiled into his face. "But things are better now, Rankin. I've seen the love and rapport between you two. Lynx has changed since those wild days; he's a very special and strong man. When he comes back to stay, I know everything will be wonderful."

"You love him very much, don't you?" Rankin asked.

Cal flushed, but felt she should admit such an emotion. After all, it was their wedding day. She wondered how Lynx had responded to this same question, for surely his father had broached it. "I've never met any man like your son, Rankin. He's handsome, charming, smart, and brave. He swept me off my feet. I hope our sudden plans didn't upset you," she hinted.

"Not in the least. Surprised me, yes; but I'm delighted, Cal. Lynx and I had a long talk last night and this morning. Before we know it, he'll be home to stay. Until then, you and I can have fun running this ranch. He did tell you he must leave first thing tomorrow?"

"Yes," she replied sadly. "I tried to change his mind, but he wouldn't listen. Seems your son is a proud and stubborn man."

"If there's one thing I know about my son, he's a man of his word. Lynx has always been reliable and relentless. If he gives his promise to do something, he'll fight the demons of hell to keep it. That speaks highly of a man out here, Cal. Lynx made some promises before you came along, now he must keep them. If he didn't, he wouldn't be the man you love. Be patient and understanding while he's gone. He'll come home as soon as he can; he'll have a pretty wife to lure him back quickly. You ready to come downstairs?"

"I'll be there in a moment. Is everything ready?"

"I think you'll be amazed and pleased," he said, sparking her curiosity.

After Rankin left her alone, Calinda sat down on the edge of the bed. What was going on between them? Why was Rankin expounding on Lynx's good traits and defending his departure? Rankin's sudden change of heart about his son's behavior inspired speculations. Getting married wasn't the answer, for Lynx was taking off almost immediately. If they didn't have guests, he probably would. In Rankin's eyes and mind, how had Lynx gone from carefree rebel to "reliable" and unquestionably honest and honorable? Until now, Rankin had been arguing and threatening Lynx to come home; now, he was coaxing her to be "patient and understanding." Evidently Rankin knew where Lynx was heading and why, and he clearly agreed with Lynx's motives. If Lynx could confide in his father, why not in his wife? She was miffed and disappointed. It was almost as if they were conspiring to keep secrets from her, conspiring to hold her on the ranch. That was ridiculous, she hastily decided. Maybe her jittery nerves were playing tricks on her mind. She must join them before they wondered what was keeping her. As Cal removed the silver cross Lynx had given her, she abruptly realized it matched the one which Salina wore. She stiffened. Instantly, she scolded her jealousy and suspicions, dismissing them.

When Calinda gracefully walked down the steps, she was amazed and pleased, as Rankin had stated. The house was filled with beautiful and colorful wildflowers. Delicious odors from the kitchen assailed her nose. She could hear laughter and muted conversation coming from outside and the next room. She summoned her courage and entered the room. It was crowded with people. Had they invited everyone nearby?

Lynx glanced up and grinned. He came forward with agile steps. He caught her cold hands and smiled into her tense face. He leaned over to kiss her cheek, whispering, "Relax, *querida;* they aren't here to devour you. Let's give 'em a good show of love and happiness."

Cal met his gaze and smiled faintly, his last words echoing across her mind. "I'm scared stiff," she murmured to hide her doubts.

"Me, too. But we've gone too far to back down now," he teased.

Several neighbors came over to congratulate them. Calinda smiled and spoke genially, her anxiety seeming natural for a bride. Soon, Rankin announced it was time for the ceremony. The crowd gathered on the veranda as Calinda and Lynx were directed to stand before the preacher. Within a blurred twenty minutes, Lynx was slipping the gold band on her finger again, this time for good.

As she stared at it, he lifted her chin and kissed her soundly. Cheers went up as they parted. A bright flush greeted Lynx, who chuckled in 'amusement. "Well, Mrs. Cardone, how about a toast?"

The party began. There were platters of barbecued

beef and pork, fried chicken and baked ham, bowls of fresh beans and peas, stacks of "rowsinears" as they called corn-on-the-cob, fragrant bread, and mounds of creamed potatoes. Besides steaming coffee and tea, stronger spirits were offered in abundance. Afterwards, there were many tempting desserts to choose from, or a slice of wedding cake. Calinda stared at the lovely cake which was Salina's prized creation.

The new bride nibbled on the food Lynx placed in her hands or lap. She chatted with neighbors, accepting their compliments or teasing jokes. She carefully sipped very little wine, knowing how long this day might be. With the assistance of her new husband, she looked every inch a happy bride very much in love.

But Rankin's plans for a short celebration were thwarted by merry neighbors. Several men had brought along musical instruments. They joined together to encourage dancing. Without rudely ordering everyone to leave, Cal and Lynx had no choice but to go along with their friends' good intentions.

As the bride was enticed to dance with many friends, the hour grew late. She had danced several times with Lynx, but it was always a lively tune. With all the excitement, they were granted little time alone. As Calinda was dancing with Rankin, she longingly gazed at Lynx who was genially chatting with friends.

Rankin whispered in her ear, "I'm sorry, Cal. I know this is stealing most of your time with Lynx. But our friends don't know he's leaving at dawn. They should start heading home soon."

Cal looked up at him and smiled. He, too, had good intentions, but costly ones today. "Everyone loves a party, especially a wedding. They'll hang around as long as possible. Don't worry about it."

Rankin caught his son's eye and sent him a message to join his wife. When Lynx claimed her hand for a dance, Rankin asked the musicians for a slow tune. A devilish grin flashed over Lynx's handsome face as he gathered her tightly against him.

Cal mildly protested, but he didn't loosen his embrace. She sighed and accepted what she felt was an immodest closeness even for newlyweds. As they seemingly floated around the grassy area, Lynx boldly kissed her forehead, then nuzzled her ear.

"Lynx, stop that," she softly warned. "We're in public."

"Maybe they'll take a hint and leave," he said.

"It wouldn't matter, if you stay home another day."

He looked down at her and taunted mischievously, "Missing me already? Afraid you won't have enough of me tonight?"

Calinda stared at him. "What's gotten into you?" she asked. "Have you been drinking too much?"

"I'm trying my damndest to stay loose, but thoughts of getting you alone are tying my nerves into knots. You look beautiful today, Cal. I could almost make love to you right here," he informed her.

"Behave yourself; you're embarrassing me," she scolded, but a telltale tremor passed over her.

"I could behave, if I didn't recall our last night together. You realize tonight will have to last us for weeks?" he hinted wryly.

Calinda was about to make a naughty comment, but realized they were the only ones dancing. As she gazed around, Lynx did the same. He threw back his head and chuckled, then hugged her tightly. Before she realized what he was doing, he boldly swept her into his strong arms and announced to the laughing crowd, "If you folks don't mind, my bride and I will take our leave. Please continue." With that, he carried her into the house and up the steps to his room.

Shocked by his conduct, she didn't speak until he dropped her on his bed. "How dare you do something like that to me," she ranted.

"If I hadn't, they would stay around half the night. Damnit, Cal, you're driving me wild. If you think that embarassed you, this would have more," he declared, pointing to the bulge against his tight britches. "See what you were doing to me out there? When the music ended, we were in trouble. Don't worry; they'll find it amusing."

Calinda's face was as fiery as a sunset. Lynx murmured, "You're the first woman who's ever stolen my self-control. I started thinking about tonight, and nature took over. What are you doing to me, woman? I must not have the same effect on you, but I'm as heated up as a piece of dry wood in a roaring fire."

Calinda's anger was replaced with passion. She grinned and replied, "You don't affect me like that because we don't have the same parts, my darling husband, in case you haven't noticed."

"I have noticed. That's why my pants got so tight and uncomfortable. Let's just see if I can inspire a similar effect."

Lynx pulled her to her feet, turned her around, then started unbuttoning her dress. "What are you doing?" she asked in alarm.

"Getting us ready for bed," he cheerfully replied, continuing his task at hand.

"Bed," she shrieked. "But we have guests outside. Surely you don't plan to stay in here while they're still out there?"

"Why not?" Lynx fenced, spreading kisses over her neck.

"They'll know what we're doing," Cal wailed anxiously.

"Maybe it'll heat the men up so they'll race home to do the same thing," he mirthfully teased her.

"You're awful, Lynx Cardone," she declared.

"But you're ravishing, Mrs. Cardone," he retorted.

"This is embarrassing, Lynx. What will they think about us?"

"We're married, Cal. This is a natural act to follow a wedding."

"But during our own party?" she debated, turning to face him.

"In less than six hours I'll have to ride out for weeks. Do you want to spend most of it entertaining guests who should have enough intelligence and consideration to go home?" Lynx reasoned.

"But they don't know my beloved husband is deserting me right after our wedding," she countered angrily.

"Let's don't quarrel tonight, Cal; time is short," he coaxed, easing her dress and chemise down to torment her senses.

He gently kissed each soft tip, then travelled up to eagerly devour her parted lips. The palm of his hand moved over her breasts, enticing them to crave their lingering pleasure. When his lips roamed to her ear and asked, "Do we stay here or return to our party?", she was lost.

"You win, Mister Cardone, but most unfairly," she helplessly relented. She freed herself to finish undressing, then returned to his waiting bed. He was quickly out of his clothes and lying beside her.

"I'm going to miss you terribly," she murmured

against his shoulder. "When people find out you left so quickly, they'll think something's wrong between us. It isn't natural for a bridegroom to leave home the day after his wedding, a hasty one at that. They'll probably think I'm pregnant," she apprehensively speculated.

"You could be, Cal," he said softly, lifting his head to gaze down at her. At her shocked expression, he teased, "That does happen when two people make love, and this isn't our first time."

"But . . ." She actually paled and shuddered. "Is that why you married me before heading off again?" she fearfully questioned.

"No, love. I didn't even consider it until last night. But it isn't impossible. Would that upset you, Cal?" he asked seriously.

"No, I just haven't thought about a baby."

"Our baby," he corrected her, then smiled warmly. "Promise me you won't go running off again, not even to chase after me."

"I promise. But do you have to leave?" she entreated a last time.

"We'll talk about it later. Right now. . ." he hinted, then seared her quivering flesh with fiery kisses and burning caresses.

He shifted to lie half atop her. His mouth came down on hers, exploring and tasting the sweet desire within her. He embraced her so tightly and fiercely that she feared she couldn't breathe, but didn't care at that moment. Eagerly seeking her unbridled response, Lynx hungrily took her mouth with skill and resolve.

Cal's arms had encircled his waist and her hands slipped up his back. How intoxicating he was, as some potent drug which dazed her. Surely there wasn't a spot on her body that he hadn't set to tingling with his tantalizing actions. She was alive with molten flames, as was he. Lynx seemed to control and stimulate the very essence of her being. His warm breath caused her to tremble as he murmured words of passion into her ears. His insistent hands roved her sensitive body, as if stirring each inch to life and awareness.

As his hands became bolder, they soared over her slender and shapely figure. Soon her entire body urged him to conquer and claim her willing territory, to invade it, to explore it, to map it, and to declare it his sole possession. Wild and wonderful sensations attacked her senses, enslaving her. Cal wanted to savor this special union, but her need was too great to linger.

Her hand went into his hair and drew his mouth closer to hers. As his hand provocatively slipped down her flat stomach to seek out the secret place that summoned his skills and heightened his desires, Cal moaned and writhed in unleashed passion. Her fingers roamed down his sleek sides to brazenly claim a prize she had not dared to touch before tonight, a prize which possessed the power and talent to drive her mindless with pleasure and blissful torment. She stroked it gently, relishing its warmth and smoothness. His body shuddered as a groan came from deep within his muscled chest.

Moments later, Lynx shifted between her parted thighs. His body so taut and enflamed, he swiftly and urgently entered her. The contact was staggering to his senses. He moved leisurely and deliberately, fearing his self-control would vanish too soon.

Her hands wandered up and down his strong back, feeling the muscles rippling at his movements. As Lynx probed her body again and again, she arched to meet each entry, moaning at each exit. Her responses told Lynx when she was ready to conquer her rapturous challenge. He increased his pace and invaded her with a savage gentleness.

A muffled cry of victory was torn from Cal's lips as the powerful release claimed her. As if a signal to charge his own defenses, he quickly and eagerly pursued her successful journey. His body shook with the force of an equally potent release. His mouth engulfed hers, blending them as one until every spasm had ceased and his body was as sated as hers.

They snuggled together in his bed, caressing and kissing until their passions were reborn. They made love once more, slowly and relentlessly. Lynx murmured instructions into her ear, which she quickly and readily followed, increasing their pleasures. When they lay exhausted and moistened in each other's arms, he whispered fiercely, "You're mine, love; I'll never let you leave me. If you did, I would hunt you down and . . ." When he realized what he was saying, he made a light joke of it. "I'll hunt you down and punish you by tormenting your body and senses. I'll make you beg with hunger, then refuse to feed you. I'll make you burn with desire, then let the flames go undoused."

Cal twisted her head to gaze over at his roguish expression. "That kind of torment runs in two directions, my love. Whyever would I leave you; you're mine now. But if you don't come home soon, I'll punish you in said manner when you do show that handsome face and virile body," she laughingly threatened.

"I promise you, when I come home, we'll be too busy for games." He kissed her lightly, then they fell asleep without moving.

It was mid-morning when Calinda stirred, smiling contentedly. As dreamy memories flooded her mind, her body responded with rising passion. Her lips hungered for his; her body flamed to join with his. As Cal turned over, her hand reached out to touch her love. She sat up, the covers falling to her lap, exposing flesh which quivered with desire. She looked around, but Lynx wasn't in the room. She snuggled into the softness of his bed, waiting to see if he would return soon. She held out her arm to gaze at the gold band which thrilled her soul.

When time passed, Cal decided she must dress and look for him. Lynx was more than likely eating breakfast or talking with his father or making preparations to leave. That last thought spurred her into hasty action. It never crossed her mind her husband would ride off for such a lengthy separation without awakening her to say goodbye in a proper manner for deliriously happy newlyweds. Cal hummed merrily as she pulled on a paisley dress. She hurriedly brushed her hair, then rushed downstairs, to discover Lynx had ridden off before dawn.

Chapter Eleven

To make matters worse for Calinda, it was Salina who informed her of Lynx's departure. Salina gave the facts in succinct words, her tone crisp and mocking. The Mexican girl offered Calinda nothing more. Calinda would not dismiss her pride to press the girl, who was inexplicably hostile again.

As she was about to prepare her own breakfast, Calinda did ask where Rankin was this morning. If there was more to learn about her husband, she would do so from her new father-in-law.

Salina told her that Rankin had gone into town on business. Calinda was forced to ask when he would return. Salina stated indifferently, "*Buenas tardas,* late afternoon," she clarified.

When Calinda reached for an iron skillet, Salina asked frostily, "What are you doing?" When Calinda said she was going to cook her breakfast, Salina snapped, "Not in *my* kitchen. No one works in here but me. What would you like this morning, Mrs. Car-

271

done?"

At Salina's caustic tone and bold order, Calinda looked at her. "What's wrong with you, Salina? I always do this. If you think you'll have to wait on me now, that isn't true."

"I do not plan to wait on you, Mrs. Cardone. But I allow no one to take over my kitchen or prove I'm not needed anymore."

"This isn't your private domain, Salina. Lynx and I are married now. I can enter and work here anytime I choose," she stated defiantly.

"*Senor* Rankin and Lynx do not agree. Before Lynx left, they talked of me. They said I was needed and wanted. They said, just because you live here now, it changed nothing, *nada,*" Salina joyfully emphasized her allegation. "That means, you are still a guest and I am in control of this *casa.* If you do not believe me, ask *Senor* Rankin. In fact, I dare you to ask him. Your husband is gone, poor thing."

Calinda's mouth fell open at her hostility and daring. "I thought you and I had a truce, Salina. Why are you being so hateful?"

"A truce and peace are *mucho diferente,*" Salina replied.

"So, it's back to the secret war again?" Calinda surmised angrily. "I doubt Rankin and Lynx will accept your demands and spite."

"They know me longer than you. If you tattle or treat me badly, they will think you try to run me off. I will see they do not believe you. This was my *casa* and family *primero.* You are foolish, blind."

"How dare you! Lynx and I are married now," Cal shrieked.

"I know not how you forced him into marriage, but

272

it was not love. If Lynx married you, he had *bueno* reasons. Did you claim to be *encinta,* with child?" she coldly challenged, glaring at Calinda.

"No! But even if it were true, it's none of your business! Lynx proposed on the way home from Lampasas, and I accepted."

"Pero por que, that is what I wish to know," she sneered.

"When Rankin comes home, we'll have a long talk about this," Calinda warned the surly girl, mutely praying she wouldn't get pregnant too soon and give Salina cause to gloat.

"Do so, *senora;* I care not. I will tell you what else *Senor* Rankin said this morning. He said be nice to you; he does not want you to run off again. He does not want you to know Lynx told him all about your *poco aventura,* little adventure, in Lampasas. *Senor* Rankin thinks you will be upset and *nervioso* around him," she murmured balefully, placing her hands on her rounded hips.

"I don't know what you're trying to prove or pull, Salina, but I won't allow it. Lynx is my husband, and you'll have to accept it. I won't allow you to be rude or cause trouble."

"Your *esposo?*" Salina scoffed. "Tell me, *Senora* Cardone, do you have any idea where he is right this minute, or when he will be home, or what he is doing? No. I wonder how much a husband loves his wife when he keeps his life a secret from her. Must be nice to have a hot-blooded wife at home, then be able to roam around the state doing anything you please, with anyone you please," she hinted audaciously and crudely. "I wonder who he is with today . . ."

Fury and resentment surged through Calinda. She

nearly slapped the girl, but realized she couldn't dispute the statements. "When Lynx comes home, we'll settle this matter once and for all, Salina. I'm going to confess everything."

A cynical smile claimed the girl's lips. "He already knows everything, Cal. Did you really think I would lie to my love? Tell him the truth. He knows you deceived him before. To confess now will only inspire suspicions for your change of heart. He will think you are the one trying to pull a trick. You will look the trouble-maker."

"You have the arrogance and gall to threaten me! To blackmail me! You're a fool, Salina. Lynx would never take a servant's word over his wife's." Calinda and Salina glared challengingly at each other.

"I proved I can be trusted, but you have not. I do not plan to blackmail you, *Senora* Cardone. I just want you to stay out of my path until Lynx grows weary of you and tosses you out. Lynx is used to freedom, privacy, and lots of women. Once he comes home to stay, you will strangle him with your constant presence and demands. I doubt you are woman enough to hold his interest very long. I will do my work and bide my time until that day comes, which it will."

"You're wrong, Salina; I'm here to stay. I love him," she boldly confessed to vex Salina. "He married me, didn't he?"

"We will see, will we not, Cal? I bet you will be gone before the fall round-up. Lynx will never change. Even if he permits you to hang around for a respectable image, you will tire of his ways."

"I don't want him to change; I want him just as he is. I'll never tire of him, and I'll make sure he doesn't get bored with me."

"Would you care to know where your loving *esposo* has gone?"

"I know," Calinda declared smugly. "To Junction."

Mirthful laughter filled the quiet kitchen. "The business in Junction was lost because of you. He goes to Waco to meet with Major Jones, something to do with your telegram to him. You see, *Senora* Cardone, your trusting *esposo* is checking out your wild story."

"No, Salina, he's trying to discover who sent the phony letter."

"No, Cal, he does not believe you," Salina refuted.

"Lynx knows there was a letter which lured me there!"

"He knows there was a letter, but he is not convinced it was a trap as you pretended. Two reasons: he knew it was not an old letter because he searched your room on his first trip home; and you suspiciously burned the letter to prevent him from seeing the message and the handwriting. He is what I call a devoted *esposo*," she scoffed.

"I don't believe you! I'll ask Lynx when he comes home."

Salina laughed maliciously. "I would not corner a fierce wolf. Lynx is sly, ruthless, and deadly. Do you honestly think he will confess such things to you? You play the fool! He will lie to you or attack. Will you risk either reaction?"

"If such things are true, how did you learn them?" Calinda questioned, her sarcastic tone voicing her doubts of Salina's honesty.

"I saw Lynx searching your room, and I heard him tell his father many things. That is how I know you will not last long. If I am right, Lynx married you to

275

trap you here while he investigates you. It is strange they do not want you seeking your own father . . . I wonder what they hide from you . . ." she mumbled thoughtfully.

"At least you're being open with your resentment and hatred. If I ever catch you spying on any of us, I'll force a choice between us. No matter who wins or loses," she told Salina, then went to Lynx's room to do some heavy thinking.

Calinda paced the floor as distressing questions stormed her mind. Lynx hadn't left a note this morning. Did he feel he owned her now, that it wasn't necessary? Perhaps he had given Rankin a message to pass along to her. But why had he confessed the truth to Rankin, then sworn him to secrecy? If such was true, it was painful.

Why was she allowing that vicious girl's statements to haunt her, to inspire mistrust? Why had the men drawn Salina into their schemes and confidence? If Salina had repeated Rankin's words accurately, they didn't want or plan for Calinda to take over anything. But she was Lynx's wife, the new mistress of this house! How could they allow a mere servant to have more authority and power?

Had Salina lied to her? Had Salina deviously misled the two men? Had that tempestuous Mexican girl told Lynx everything? If so, no wonder Lynx didn't trust his wife. Cal didn't like him searching her room, but she couldn't blame him for his mistrust back then. But now? Investigate his own wife? Was there a vital reason for marrying her quickly and holding her here on the ranch? Yet, she begrudgingly agreed with Salina; they were withholding facts.

Calinda knew she had trusted that sly vixen too easily. Perhaps Salina knew more than she was telling; she was behaving awfully smugly and brazenly. If there was future trouble between them, Salina would try her best to make certain Calinda was blamed for it. Calinda scolded herself for being so trusting, naive, and gullible. She should have known that little witch wouldn't take their marriage calmly. As surely as the sun was up, Salina was plotting and practicing more mischief. It would be wise to keep a close eye on that devilish girl.

Calinda was distressed and alarmed by their deceptions and her husband's sneaky departure. So much for his statement of discussing it this morning. He had avoided a scene by slipping out early. She vowed to clear the air with everyone the moment Lynx came home.

Rankin returned shortly after five. He was in a cheerful mood, smiling and chatting with the subdued Calinda. He grinned and teased her about missing Lynx already. He told her he had gone into town to send telegrams to their distant friends, to reveal Lynx's marriage. He didn't tell Calinda he had sent the announcement to newspapers over the state, nor that he had done so to take a last stab at luring Brax out of hiding. If anything would draw Brax out of concealment, his daughter's marital entanglement with a Cardone should do it . . .

Calinda asked Rankin where Lynx had gone and when he was expected to be home again. Rankin sighed and told her, "He was heading back to Junction, if it isn't too late to carry out his . . . business there. What do you say to some cards and sherry?" he tried to distract her, but they both caught his slip.

Calinda pretended not to notice it. She smiled and

277

nodded. As they played cards and sipped sherry, she asked Rankin what kind of work Lynx did. Her head was lowered to prevent Rankin from noticing her close observation. "He used to take odd jobs for excitement and a good reason for staying away from home. Now, he's trying to locate two bulls for breeding. In cattle country, it's important to keep good blood in the breeding line. He'll be traveling around to several ranches to check out their stock. Plus, he's setting up the plans for the next cattle drive to market."

"How long will he be away?" she continued, knowing Rankin was deceiving her.

"I would venture a guess at three or four weeks. Are you mad at him, Cal?" Rankin asked anxiously.

"I'm just disappointed that breeding bulls are more important than a new bride," she said, letting him know she was indeed rankled. Evidently her new father-in-law had forgotten that both men had vowed the honorable and reliable Lynx was heading south to keep a promise which his pride demanded he fulfill. Now, Ranking was telling her Lynx was merely checking out bulls and round-ups! Didn't he realize such lies didn't excuse Lynx's hasty flight and absence at this special time?

"Is something bothering you, Cal?" he asked in panic.

She glanced up, her expression innocent. "No, I was just studying my hand. Someday I'll have this cunning game under control. I'm never sure when to bluff or fold. It's difficult to tell which hand is better." Rankin didn't realize that Calinda wasn't referring to their card game, but he did note the odd inflection in her voice.

"Maybe your concentration is bad tonight," he

teased.

"I think you're right. Yesterday was a busy day and late night. I think I'll turn in, Rankin. See you tomorrow." As she stood up, she halted to ask, "What about my new duties around the house?"

"New duties?" he queried confusedly.

She laughed brightly. "I am Lynx's wife now, the new mistress of the Cardone Ranch. Surely I will assume part of running the house?"

"That isn't necessary, Cal; Salina can handle everything. You don't need to slave here when we have an excellent housekeeper and cook. Why don't you spend your time re-doing the bedrooms? You could also use some new clothes. It's the custom to visit the neighbors and get better acquainted, to invite them over occasionally for dinner."

"You make it sound as if I'm to be a hostess and decoration around here," she jested cunningly. "I should learn how to run the house, Rankin. What if Salina got sick or left? I would be lost; I hardly know where to find anything," she reasoned logically for his reaction. She waited for Rankin to think up a good excuse.

"We could make do for a few days if she took ill. But why would Salina leave? She loves it here."

"She's a young and pretty woman, Rankin. She might find someone to marry. If so, she would want her own home and family."

"Salina marry?" he mocked playfully. "That girl's too wild; she likes too many men to settle for one. She doesn't strike me as the wifey, motherly type. Is there some problem between you two? Do you want her to leave?" A look of concern washed over his face.

"That isn't what I meant, Rankin. I don't want to take her place; I doubt I could run this house alone. I haven't had any experience. I just wanted to help out and learn everything. That is the custom for a wife, isn't it?" She laughed softly to disarm him.

"Only if she isn't lucky and wealthy enough to have a servant. Salina's a feisty girl, Cal. She doesn't like anyone in her way. Could you wait a while before making your new role known to her? Let her get used to having you here. If she starts to feel unwanted or in your way, she might take offense and leave. As you said, you can't run this big house alone. Just give it some time," he coaxed.

"But she won't even let me help with little things, Rankin," she softly argued, her fears and doubts concealed from him. Besides Salina had been given plenty of time to get adjusted to her presence.

"She's just insecure right now, Cal. Your arrival and marriage have been shocks for her, big changes. She'll settle down. Just relax and be patient. Besides, you'll need your energy and rest if a baby comes along," he hinted, grinning wistfully.

A baby, Calinda mentally sneered. *How can I get with child when my husband isn't around enough to make love to me!* "If it will cause dissension, I'll do as you say. But I'll need something to occupy my time and hands."

"There'll be plenty of work when Lynx comes home."

Calinda want to scoff, but what about until then? She didn't. "I suppose so. Goodnight, Rankin," she said in a muffled voice.

Leaning against the wall outside the open double-doors, Salina smiled to herself. She stealthily made her way to her room, concluding Rankin had played right into her devious scheme and put Calinda in a wary and uncomfortable position. That should teach Cal a thing or two!

When Calinda got to her room, she sat in the middle of her bed, ensnared by depression and worry. Evidently Salina had spoken accurately; that deduction infuriated and troubled her. Something was terribly wrong in this house and with the two men. Perhaps she shouldn't have married Lynx so hurriedly, so impulsively. It almost appeared they had more confidence in Salina, more affection for her, more fear of offending her than Calinda. She needed to unravel this mystery confronting her, but first she needed more evidence or clues. She fretted over this new situation. Just as she was solving one puzzle, a new one appeared; or was it merely unexpected pieces to the old one? It saddened and alarmed her to suspect she couldn't trust her new family.

To prove her new position, Calinda dressed for bed and went into Lynx's room. She would show that little witch! Let her do all the plotting and grinning she wished, but it wouldn't change things. After all, it was a natural arrangement, one which might irritate Salina. Hopefully that vixen would squirm in her bed downstairs, knowing Calinda was occupying Lynx's room and bed right above her. That should teach her a much needed lesson! Calinda wasn't normally a spiteful person; but something was troubling her deeply, something which she didn't quite recognize or comprehend.

Calinda spent a restless night in her love's room. His manly odor still lingered on the wrinkled sheets. The masculine decor loudly announced its intoxicating owner. She was haunted by his past presence and his tormenting absence. She fretted over the facts which she had discovered today. Her body hungered for his touch; her heart cried at his actions; her mind spun with the plaguing riddle.

Cal awoke early, the bed rumpled from her tossings Having slept little, she was jittery and fatigued. After pulling on her clothes and brushing her hair, she closed the door and reluctantly went downstairs for coffee, relieved Salina wasn't around. When she returned to Lynx's room with the cup in hand, the door was standing open. She went inside to find the room empty. She stared at the sheets which showed the signs of their heated night of lovemaking and the vivid evidence of her restive night alone. Besieged with anger, she yanked off the sheets to change them.

"What are you doing now?" Salina shrieked at her from the doorway, startling Calinda. "Get out of here; I have work to do."

"If you aren't blind or simple-minded, Salina, it's obvious I'm changing the sheets," she quipped bitterly.

"That is my job. This is Lynx's room; I am responsible for cleaning it. Go back to your room where you belong," Salina commanded.

"This is my room, too! I'll take care of it from now on. As Lynx's wife, here is where I belong and plan to stay. Don't set foot in here again without my permission!" she shouted at the venomous girl.

"Did Lynx say you could move in here?" Salina brazenly pressed.

"He didn't have to! I'm his wife!" she stressed to vex Salina.

"He will be angry. He loves privacy."

"If he didn't want me around, he wouldn't have married me, idiot! I'm moving my things in here today," she sassily informed Salina, outraged and angered by the girl's audacious behavior.

"I wouldn't until he agrees," Salina told her.

"You don't honestly think we'll have separate rooms or that he'll kick me of *our* bedroom?" Calinda sneered smugly.

"Do not forget I warned you. Even so, I am the housekeeper. You do not fool me, *puta*. If you are trying to hide the truth, you are *tarde*. Either you did not sleep with him, or it was not the first time. There is no virgin's blood staining them," she vulgarly announced.

Calinda was shocked by Salina's unforgivable language and actions. "How dare you, you bitch!" Calinda screamed at her.

Suddenly Rankin was standing in the doorway. "What's going on in here? Cal, I could hear you screaming all the way downstairs."

"Tell him," Salina wickedly suggested. "About the sheets," she maliciously added, her insinuation clear to Calinda.

Calinda mastered her poise and temper, knowing she had rashly stepped into Salina's trap. "I'm sorry for my outburst, Rankin. I'm just tired and edgy this morning; I didn't sleep well last night. Something I ate didn't sit well in my stomach. I suppose I'm still adjusting to Salina's spicy cooking. I was trying to *explain* to Salina that I prefer to take care of mine and Lynx's room, that I would like some privacy in here. I was annoyed when she barged in without knocking, then *ordered* me to leave and let her do my chores. I'm not accustomed to being waited on like a baby or invalid; I will perform my own personal chores. Salina feels I'm usurping her authority and position by changing the sheets on my own bed. I hardly feel it's important to quarrel over such a small task. When Salina disagreed, I asked her to stay out of my room, to never enter again without knocking or asking permission."

"Then why the shouting and screaming at her?" he asked, sure Cal wasn't telling him everything.

"She informed me it was Lynx's room and I would need his permission to move in here. Is that true, Rankin?" she challenged, her gaze piercing and frosty. Salina had forced this confrontation, so she could face the consequences. If they preferred to side with Salina, it was best to know immediately. Calinda's nerves were frayed and sensitive. At that moment, she didn't care what truth spilled forth; she didn't care what Salina exposed or alleged. Salina was trying to intimidate and torment her, and Calinda was pressed against the wall.

"I don't know what's gotten into you two women, but this argument is silly. Settle down, Cal. It was a simple mistake. Salina is used to coming and going at will; she probably forgot you would be in here. It sounds awfully unfriendly to order her to never enter this room. You're just tired. Why don't you let Salina clean up in here while you rest? If you demand your privacy, she won't come in here again. Salina knows Lynx's quirks; she assumed he would like to be asked about the move before it takes place," he stated diplomatically.

Calinda's gaze slipped over Rankin's shoulder to witness the taunting sneer on Salina's smug face. "I will take care of this room myself; I prefer total privacy in here. Surely with the entire house under her control, she has more than enough to keep her busy?" she stated distinctly, stressing most of her words, refusing to back down or soften her chosen stance. She would discover just how much power that little witch possessed!

Rankin sensed a deeper problem here than either of them revealed. He wondered how he should handle it. Was it simple female rivalry? "Of course you can have full control of your own room, Cal, if that's what you demand," he stated finally, using words which nettled Calinda. "But I do wish you would try harder to get along with Salina. She did a marvelous job with the wedding party and decorations yesterday. And she does work hard for us."

"I offered Salina a truce, Rankin; she doesn't want one. She seems intent on making me feel a stranger here, an undesirable one at that. She takes offense at everything I say or do; she constantly corrects or scolds me like a bratty child. I don't plan to spend my days walking on eggshells around her. If she dislikes me and my presence so much, perhaps she would be happier working elsewhere."

"*Senora* Cardone, surely you do not ask him to fire me?" Salina carefuly wailed, phony tears coming to her cold eyes. "I was only trying to help you. Why do you despise me? The Cardones are like my family, the ranch like my home. Where would I go?"

"I have never despised you, Salina, but I do resent your hateful attitude and surly manner when no one else is around. I also dislike your phony politeness and friendliness when they're present. Your two faces are wearing thin. Either accept me here and be friends, or one of us should leave. If we can't be friends, at least stop being my enemy. I'm not taking any more of your insults and threats. If Rankin and Lynx hold more affection and respect for you than me, then perhaps you

were right moments ago when you said I didn't belong
here." Calinda glowered at Salina; *let her get out of
those charges,* she decided.

Salina realized she had pushed too hard this soon;
she slyly relented. "*Perdon* if I treated you badly. Perhaps I am overly tired and tensed from the extra work
from the wedding. It will not happen again. I am a
bossy and out-spoken person by nature; I did not
mean to anger you. I will try not to be so sensitive to
your help. Would you like for me to wash those sheets
for you?" she sweetly inquired.

Calinda saw through her ploy to make her the vil-
lainess. She smiled and nodded. "If you mean it, Salina, that's fine with me. I'm even willing to meet you
more than half way. I have tried to convince you I have
no intentions of taking your place or encouraging you
to leave. When Lynx comes home and we start a family, we'll all need your loyalty and help. Then, after the
baby comes, I'll need to spend most of my time with
our son, or daughter."

"*Bueno,* that's a start," Rankin complimented both
women, sighing in relief, ignoring the seriousness of
their conflict. "I'll see you two later; I have some work
to finish."

After he left, Calinda reached over and gathered the
sheets. Tossing them to Salina, she smiled confidently
and stated, "Thanks for the help, Salina. Where are
the clean lines kept?"

"I will bring them," the girl replied, observing the
dauntless Calinda with new vision. It was clear this
cerdo would get in the mud to battle if pressed. Salina
knew she had underestimated Calinda's determination. She must be more careful in the future . . .

Calinda spent the afternoon moving into Lynx's

room. She took possession of drawers unused or nearly empty. She placed Lynx's clothes in the drawers down the left side of his dresser, then placed hers in the drawers down the right side. Since there was little space available in his closet, she left most of her dresses and gowns in the other room. She hung her daily garments of shirts, vests, riding skirts, and pants in his room. If Salina dared to inspect the two rooms, she would find Calinda settled in with Lynx.

Cal was pleased with her accomplishments. But one small drawer near the top of the dresser kept attracting her attention. Since it was locked and she hadn't found a key, she assumed he kept private possessions inside. Her curiosity chewed on her all afternoon. What did it contain? Why was it locked? Secrets about Lynx? She couldn't break it open, so its secrets remained hidden.

For the next few days, Calinda and Salina were on their best behavior. They were polite around Rankin, but avoided each other when he wasn't present. Calinda found things outside to occupy herself, trying to keep out of the path of Salina and her baleful tongue. Rankin foolishly believed things were going fine between them.

But Calinda was determined to reveal poise and confidence. If Salina got to her, she didn't let it show. The same was true with Salina. If Calinda wanted to perform some household chore, she would cunningly wheedle in front of Rankin, compelling Salina to comply. Too, Calinda furtively observed everything, learning more and more about the house, watching Rankin and Salina.

Calinda would take advantage of Salina's occasional absences. She would practice her cooking skills, but wisely give the food or treats to the working hands. Sometimes she would entertain the men with tales of England or the East, or read stories to them, or play games with them. The men came to appreciate and accept her company. She quickly realized she was winning them over with her kindness and charms. As she worked around the ranch, the hands noticed how her skills increased. She was always willing to take on or share in any chore, no matter how difficult or dirty, gaining her their respect and friendship.

A week had passed without even a note or telegram from Lynx. Calinda pretended not to notice, but it pained her deeply to be ignored or taken for granted this quickly. She had gradually learned to sleep peacefully alone in the new room.

When Lynx was mentioned, Calinda exposed her loneliness and disappointment to Rankin, but concealed her vexation. She didn't challenge Rankin's explanations or excuses, but Lynx wouldn't have the same leniency when he came home! As the days passed, she came to realize that Rankin was caught in the middle of her dispute with Salina and her baffling husband. She couldn't hold him responsible for either, so she gradually relented and pressed for a closer relationship. He had suffered greatly in the past and she didn't want to cause him more pain.

Rankin instantly warmed to her overtures of friendship. As their bond tightened, Salina became more secretive with her hatred and picking at Calinda. The early days of July were dry and hot. Many times an afternoon swim became part of Calinda and Rankin's schedule. When weather-confined to the house, they played billiards, talked, read, and played cards.

As Rankin relaxed and opened up his emotions to

Calinda, a mellowing took place. As Calinda spent more time with him and observed him, she was disarmed by his warmth and admiration. She chided herself for past suspicions, not allowing any new ones to take hold in her mind. She was content, except for her husband's absence. Clearly his father felt a loyalty to Lynx which he couldn't break or betray. She finally accepted that facet of Rankin. It was apparent Rankin was extremely fond of her and enjoyed her companionship.

But each time Calinda dusted her room, the locked drawer fascinated her. To date, Lynx had been gone for nine days, nine days without contacting her, nine days of Salina pointing out that fact. Did the drawer contain some secret to Lynx's work or character? He would be furious if she opened it. And she knew how.

During a stifling night when a violent thunderstorm prevented sleep, Calinda's curiosity was overwhelming. She took a curved knitting needle and jimmied the lock. She slowly opened the drawer and peeked inside. She was surprised to find it contained boyhood treasures: a watch, a rabbit's foot, two sets of snake rattles, a raccoon tail, the ear of a mountain lion, an Apache necklace, a rusty knife, a child's toy, and other such objects. Why would he keep a drawer with such innocent souvenirs locked? Her gaze touched on two objects of interest, the watch and two jealousy-inspiring lacy handkerchiefs.

Cal lifted the gold watch and studied it. It was rather large for a boy and clearly expensive. She pressed the button to flip open the cover. Her gaze widened as she read the incredible inscription:

"To Lynx, a son I never had. Brax. 8/17/72"

Her hand trembled as she stared at the portentous

289

wording and the date. It didn't make sense. If her father had loved Lynx that much, how could he leave soon after that date? When and how had such affection turned to bitterness and hate? Why did Lynx despise and resent Brax so much, when Brax had clearly adored him? An irrepressible and unbidden pang of envy assailed her. A parting memento?

Cal returned the tormenting watch to the drawer, then reached for the lacy kerchiefs, monogrammed with lovely "LC." As she lifted them in her quavering grip, another object caught her eye. "No, it can't be," she murmured. She threw the kerchiefs aside to pick up the mesmerizing item. She examined it closely, then opened it. Tears slipped down her cheeks; her heart drummed wildly. How could this be possible? Why would he keep it from her? How had he gotten it?

Her mind was spinning with confusion and anguish. Cal stared at the tiny golden circle: her precious locket, the one stolen during the stage hold-up, the one which had cost the guard his life . . .

Chapter Twelve

Calinda mindlessly walked to the bed and sat down, her brain too stunned to think about anything or anyone, too dazed to ponder this monumental discovery and its meaning. She didn't want to think about this devastating mystery; it was too painful.

She blankly stared at the locket for a lengthy span. Her finger traced the delicate artwork; her misty eyes roamed the smiling couple — her parents — who stared unseeingly back at her. When she could no longer shut out her accusatory questions, she asked herself why Lynx would do this cruel thing to her. She had told him about the stolen locket; she had related its precious meaning, her anguish at its theft. Even if he had come upon it accidentally, he must have known it was hers; he must have recognized her father's picture inside. Why had he hidden it from her? Why hadn't he returned it?

Why? Why? Why? the words echoed across her warring mind, as loudly and ominously as the rolling thunder outside. How could he possibly explain this foul deed? Did she mean so little to him? Why had he married her, if he was going to treat her so vilely? Where was he? What was he doing? With whom? The mystery surrounding Lynx grew larger and darker. Calinda realized how very little she knew about her husband. Who and what was the man who held her soul in his grasp? His secrecy and reputation stormed her tortured mind. Surely he was not an outlaw?

Cal wept until exhaustion claimed her, to free her from her agony and doubts. By the time the sun rose, Calinda was plagued by relentless suspicions. Lynx had been gone two weeks. This demanding enigma was rapidly becoming a cruel maze. Each time she pursued a liberating path, she found herself facing an obscuring hedge, more lost and confused than before. When would she escape and what solution would greet her senses?

Calinda felt she must get away from the ranch for a while, away from Rankin and away from Salina and away from her torment. She dressed in a tawny pants-skirt, a dark blue shirt with colorful designs in sunny yellow, and western boots. She snatched her felt hat off the rack and headed downstairs. Salina had better watch her step and tongue today; Calinda was ready to explode from tension and fatigue.

Fortunately, Salina was busy in the water-shed with the laundry. Calinda walked to Rankin's office and knocked. Rankin opened the door and smiled. Calinda only faintly returned it, her thoughts vividly somewhere else. She told Rankin she was riding into town to shop for the day. She requested that Charlie go along as her driver and escort. Naturally Rankin agreed.

Calinda left immediately, without breakfast or coffee. She would eat in town while she settled her nerves. Charlie hitched up the carriage and helped her up into it. They headed off toward town. An unseen rider quickly mounted up and rode off swiftly behind them.

Charlie tried to make conversation with Calinda, but she was quiet and distracted. As they rounded a bend in the road, Charlie hastily reined in the horse. He grumbled at the fallen tree which was blocking the road. It would be impossible to go around it. He told Calinda he would move it aside, then jumped down to do so.

From the nearby rocks and trees, masked riders surged forth and surrounded them, their guns pointing at Charlie and Calinda. Charlie wisely didn't go for his weapon, seeing they were out-numbered. "Take our money and ride off," he suggested to the outlaws. "If Mrs. Cardone is injured, you'll be chased to hell and back," he warned.

"We know who she is," one desperado announced. "Take her," he gave the order to a mounted outlaw near her side of the carriage. "The Cardones will pay plenty to get her back safely."

A kidnapping? Her, for ransom? Leave with these vicious men? As the man reached for Calinda, she carelessly pulled her gun from its holster to defend herself. Taken off-guard, the outlaw responded with a blow from his pistol to her forehead. She screamed and lost consciousness, falling sideways on the padded seat.

Charlie moved to aid her, but the leader warned, "Move one muscle and you'll die. Take Cardone a message. Tell him I want $50,000 for her return. I'll give him three days to come up with the money. Monday,

I'll send him a message where to deliver the money. If he comes after us, we'll put a neat little bullet hole through her head."

"But Lynx isn't home. We don't expect him back for another few weeks," Charlie fearfully told him.

"Then old man Cardone can handle it for him," the leader snarled.

"But that's a lot of money to gather in three days," Charlie argued, dreading the coldness in these men.

"Then I suggest he get his ass to town before the bank closes today," the leader responded casually. "Take her," he shouted again.

Charlie watched the gang ride off with Calinda. He jumped into the carriage and raced wildly for the ranch to inform Rankin. He jumped off the carriage and ran into the house, yelling for his boss.

Rankin hurried out of his office to see what the commotion was. Charlie babbled almost incoherently. Rankin hushed him, then told him to slow down and speak clearly. His eyes widened and his face paled as the daring tale came forth. "Get the sheriff! They won't get away with this outrage! The posse will hunt them down and shoot 'em!"

"That won't do no good, boss. They could be anywhere by now. You'd best try to get the money before they contact you. They mean business, boss. They'll kill her for sure," Charlie wailed anxiously.

Before Salina could come inside and learn the truth, Charlie and Rankin were heading for town at breakneck speed. Rankin went to the bank first, to arrange for the money. He told the banker he would return shortly, after he sent Lynx a telegram in care of Jones.

Three hours later, Rankin was sitting in his office, worrying and praying. He had the money, and the telegram was on its way to Lynx, if Jones could locate him. All he could no now was wait and hope.

Calinda gradually struggled to seek freedom from the tormenting black void which had imprisoned her for an hour as the outlaws galloped toward their hideout. Nearing it, on rugged terrain, the men had slowed their pace to a leisurely ride. Her head was throbbing, her body was being shaken to pieces. She had just enough wit about her to remain still and silent until she could clear her dazed head. She comprehended her dangerous situation and uncomfortable position: she was lying on her stomach across a man's thighs, the man who had kidnapped her. The rocking motion came from the steady walking of his horse. Her injured head and bruised ribs aggravated this humiliating and painful position. She dared not attempt any struggle until she could think of a promising escape plan. Cal was not amused by the thought which flashed across her mind; during the last robbery and knock on the head, the bandits had stolen her possessions, not her. She endured this agony and listened as they talked freely, assuming her still out to the world and their words.

"You know Cardone's gonna come after us. Taking his woman and demanding $50,000 won't sit well. You think it was smart to strike on him? He ain't one to tangle with," one man remarked.

"Don't matter. He'll never find us in here. Farley's been covering our trail. After we get the money, we'll lay low for a while," the leader replied. "After we split the money equally, we'll have ten thousand dollars apiece," he added, telling Calinda there were five of them to defeat. Impossible.

"What about that payroll stage to Abilene? We still gonna take it Friday? Oggie said it leaves Fort Worth about ten."

"Yep. We'll strike right after she slows to cross Big Sandy Creek. That ought to give us plenty of money for a long rest."

"Sandy Creek?" the man shrieked. "Ain't that too close to Rangers? They'll be madder'n a dogie caught in a barbed fence!"

"That's why it'll work; who would suspect a robbery in that area?" the leader boasted, chuckling with pride in himself.

"Did Little Red scout it out good?" a third man asked.

"Yep. Won't be no problem," he smugly stated.

"Little Red know about that bundle in your lap?" he teased.

Cole Stevens glanced down at Calinda, eyes slipping over her shapely figure and striking hair. "Little Red suggested it. But Red didn't want her harmed, unless we can't avoid it." He winked at his men.

"Harmed, or touched?" the second outlaw teased, then burst into lecherous laughter, the others quickly joining in with amusement.

"Neither," Cole sneered, as if Little Red had anything to say about his gang or plans. But Little Red did offer certain advantages.

"The way Little Red handles that six-shooter and fiery temper, I wouldn't challenge either. I wonder if all redheads are hot-blooded."

Little Red's britches are getting a mite too big. It's time for the boss to cut 'em down to size, he mused to himself, growing weary of Red's bossy air and his men's tauntings. Red could never be a leader!

Calinda almost sighed in relief. Whoever this Little Red was, she prayed he held the power to control these crude men. For certain, it wouldn't do for her to antagonize them, especially Little Red.

As the outlaws began joking about their daring attack and the hopeful results of the kidnapping, the whole story unfolded for Calinda. Could Rankin get his hands on that much money? Would they truly release her afterwards? Where was her husband? If he had been home, this danger wouldn't have befallen her!

Calinda couldn't ride in this position any longer. She felt it best to alert them to her arousal. She began to moan softly and move gingerly. The leader halted his animal to lift her into a sitting position before him. Her hand went to her temple and she winced with pain. She opened her eyes and looked around. "Where am I? What happened?"

Cal pretended to be too weak and fuzzy headed to struggle for escape. She glanced around, observing four men with masks. "Who are you? Why did you kidnap me? And hurt me?" she asked sluggishly.

Cole Stevens related the facts she needed to know, prompting her to act stunned and alarmed. She gave the same arguments Charlie had given to them; Cole laughingly debated each one. "Just be a good girl, and you won't get hurt. Before you know it, you'll be at home."

"Surely you wouldn't kill an innocent woman for money?"

"Nope. But we will if we don't get it," Cole said to frighten her.

They rode on for another thirty minutes, weaving

around tall boulders and scattered trees until a wooden shack came into view. Cole reined in and dismounted, then lifted her down. To carry off her part, Calinda swayed precariously and grabbed his right arm to steady herself.

To her amazement, the leader said, "Sorry about that, you shouldn't have gone for a gun. You've got a nasty cut and bruise."

"What did you expect me to do when you attacked us? How was I to know you didn't plan to rob and murder us? My head aches. May I have some water?" she asked politely, drawing on her manners to disarm him and force him to realize she was a lady. He was a confusing, complex man. He was cruel and cold; yet, his eyes and voice could wax warm and gentle at times. Could this man murder her? Was he second in command to this absent Little Red?

"Let's get you inside. I'll see if I can round up a bandage. I'll warn you now, Calinda Cardone; don't try anything foolish. If you do — " He halted dramatically to imply a deadly warning, then left the ominous threat hanging in mid-air.

Calinda was taken inside, through a large room, and into a smaller one. After she was given water, she thanked the carefree leader. He smeared something on her wound, saying it was an Indian remedy, then bound her head with a bandanna. He tied her wrists securely, then told her to lie down and rest.

When she asked his name, he laughed merrily and stated, "You don't want to know that, little lady. If you learn who we are, then we can't free you later. Don't get up or leave this room. Savvy?"

Cal nodded and thanked him for his assistance, inwardly wanting to spew forth threats and curses on his sable head. She knew it was best to play the delicate and gentle-minded beauty to inspire any hope of escape. She couldn't say how Rankin would respond to this danger. Had he contacted Lynx? Even so, Lynx could never find her. She could only pray for the Cardones' cooperation, or a daring escape.

The door was pulled to an angle which allowed the men to remove their masks without Calinda seeing their faces. She dared not risk learning their identities, just in case the leader kept his word.

Later, she was given food and water by the masked leader. After she ate, she was bound again. Her headache was lessening by the hour. She closed her eyes and fell asleep.

When Cole came to check on her, her steady respiration told him she was resting peacefully. He stood beside the bunk for a time, staring down at her. She was very beautiful. Her skin was fair and unblemished. Her hair sparkled like a roaring blaze. Her eyes were as green as spring grass. Her lips were the kind which drew a man's eyes to them. The tip of her dainty nose turned up slightly. Her voice reminded him of sweet music. How had Cardone captured this fragile creature? Why had this lady married a man like Lynx Cardone? Maybe Little Red was right: no family, no money, no home. But Little Red was a thorn in the side to be removed very soon.

Cole dashed aside tuggings of fierce desire for her. For some crazy reason, he liked her. She was spunky and bright. But if he laid one hand or lip on her, Little Red would punish her for tempting him. The minute his back was turned, Little Red would be maliciously handing her over to his men for their pleasure.

Cole wondered if it was time to send Little Red

down another path, a separate one from him and his men. Little Red had proved valuable to his gang, but was getting cocky and demanding. Cole didn't like anybody infringing on his leadership and manhood. If Little Red could be dumped before this job was over, perhaps . . .

He shrugged his shoulders and left the room, closing the door. He and his men played poker and drank until late, then turned in.

In Dallas Saturday morning, Major Jones sent one of his Rangers to fetch Lynx at the hotel. He was pacing the floor when Lynx arrived, an uncommon action for the steely-nerved and calculating man. Lynx noted this curious behavior, then asked, "Trouble, sir? I was packing to leave for Waco. I shouldn't be far beind Bass and his men."

Jones halted his wanderings to meet Lynx's steady and probing gaze. "You recall that suspicious incident with your wife recently?"

"You mean that phony letter and Lampasas?" Lynx asked. Why was Jones bringing up that matter again? They hadn't been able to come up with any logical explanation or additional clues. Since Lynx had left home, he hadn't even been allowed to write or telegram Cal, to avoid giving away his location. Jones had hinted she couldn't come chasing after him if she didn't know where to look.

"Evidently someone did lure her there, but not to find Braxton."

"You know something I don't," Lynx hinted warily.

"A telegram came for me last night, but wasn't delivered until this morning. Your father wanted me to locate you and send you home. Does that mean he knows all about you?" Jones questioned calmly.

Lynx sighed heavily and nodded, giving his reasons for confiding in Rankin. "Is it that important, sir? He'll keep it to himself."

"I'm not worried about Rankin, Lynx. It's your wife."

"My wife? What has she got to do with this? Father wouldn't tell Cal anything about me and my work," he said confidently.

"Calinda's been abducted by outlaws. They want $50,000 by Monday. Do we let your father handle the ransom? Or do we send you home?" Jones waited patiently for that fact to settle in.

That news was like a perfectly landed blow to a tender gut. Fear, alarm, and fury attacked Lynx. "Was she injured? Do they know who's involved?" he inquired tensely.

"No. You think you should take care of it?" Jones asked.

Lynx almost shouted, Are you loco! Nothing could stop him! "Even if Father pays the ransom, they might not release her. I've got to head home, sir. Maybe I can ferret out the snakes. If she's harmed, I'll track them down and kill 'em," he vowed coldly. "I'll head for Waco the moment she's home safe."

By noon, Lynx was riding hard for the ranch, fear his companion. He halted only once: to eat, flex his muscles, and rest Star. He fretted over who had taken Calinda and worried if she was all right. No doubt she was as furious with him right now as she was terrified. As he drank from his canteen, his keen senses heard a branch snap behind him. In one flash of action, the canteen was tossed aside, he had whirled around, and his gun was in his hand. A challenging bullet whizzed past his shoulder; his gun quickly answered.

The man howled and struck the ground, then writhed in pain. Lynx waited but a moment before going over to the fallen back-shooter. When Lynx shot or killed a man, he wanted to know who and why. He searched the man's pockets, finding a handwritten note. He read it, then stuffed it into his pocket. He would deal with the contents of the note later; right now, time was short and imperative.

Blood was flowing from a chest wound on the cutthroat. The man was groaning in pain, pleading for help from the very man he had tried to murder. "You'll get help after you tell me who you are and why you tried to kill me," Lynx snarled. "If not, I'll stand here and watch you bleed to death."

Lynx's nerves were taut as he heard the man relate his tale. At one point, the man decided to keep silent. Lynx booted him in the ribs, demanding his answers. The man grimaced in agony, but stubbornly refused, appearing afraid to reply. Lynx pulled his large knife and declared he was going to give the man a few more wounds to increase his bleeding and suffering.

The man related the facts, sensing Lynx meant what he said. By then, the man had lost a great deal of blood and was very weak. Lynx was all too aware of his fleeting time. Should he leave this filth here to die, or should he carry him back to Fort Worth to the doctor? If he patched him up and left him, the man might miraculously survive. If he took the time to find the doctor or sheriff, it could be too late for Calinda. The man probably wouldn't survive the ride.

Lynx withdrew his father's urgent message and read it again. This was late Saturday; Calinda had been taken yesterday morning. The ransom was due Monday—that gave him one day to ease his father's worries, to get the whole story from him, and to save Cal. Lynx wasn't usually a man without mercy or sympathy, but too much was at stake. This man had tried to kill him, just to rob him. His decision was unavoidable. He gritted his teeth and mounted up, leaving the outlaw to die there.

As he rapidly covered the dusty trail, he kept thinking about the first time he had met Calinda Braxton Cardone. Clad in a red gown, she had appeared part woman and part child. Even when he sought every chance to steal even a blissful moment with her, his duty was always coming between them, tearing them apart without even an acceptable excuse. From that first meeting, he had instinctively known he must change drastically to win her. A gunslinger and a lady, the words flashed across his mind. He grimaced in wry humor; it was as if he were being compelled to surrender his silver spurs to gain a lady who had innocently worn red satin on a fateful night. Was the trade-off worth it? Yes . . .

As Lynx raced to rescue his love, he was consumed by worry, fear, and anger. He kept thinking, *what will I do if anything happens to her?* His tormented mind refused to even guess.

Chapter Thirteen

Calinda was slipping in and out of light slumber when she sensed someone near her. She forced her mind to clear and her eyes to open. The bandit leader was propped lazily against the wall near the bunk, one ankle crossed over the other, his arms folded over his chest, his mask securely in place over the bridge of his nose. His sparkling sapphire eyes told her he was grinning beneath that red bandanna.

Cole shoved himself up and walked toward her. Calinda shrank away from his approach. He saw her fearful response and halted. "No need to be afraid, Calinda," he coaxed playfully.

"You kidnap me, terrify me, threaten to kill me — then say I shouldn't be afraid?" Cal disputed skeptically, her gaze detecting a lean and hard physique beneath those dusty and snug garments.

"I didn't know if I should let you sleep or wake you up for breakfast. Hungry?" he asked, hunkering down beside the bunk.

Calinda's eyes flew to the window. The sun was shining brightly. It was morning! "What time is it?" she asked, sitting up.

"About ten, Why, are you going some place?" Cole teased.

"That's very amusing," she scoffed angrily, glaring at him.

He chuckled. "Don't worry. You'll be leaving me soon."

Calinda wondered if that was disappointment in his voice. "Have the Cardones agreed to pay the ransom?" she asked, sounding doubtful.

"I gave them until Monday noon to get the money together."

"If they refuse?" Cal speculated, eyes misty.

"Why would they refuse?" Cole reasoned confidently.

"They might. That's a great deal of money, and they haven't known me very long," she answered.

"From where I stand, you're worth it," he said too warmly.

"Maybe not to them," Cal disagreed. "If they refuse, will you really kill me?" she questioned seriously.

Cole's eyes narrowed in deep thought. "I suspect you married Cardone for protection and security. But why did he marry you?" he boldly questioned, watching her startled reaction which implied, how did you know that? Cole was intrigued when she actually blushed.

"I married him because he asked me. Why else?" she sneered.

"But why did he ask you?" Cole pressed the proud beauty.

"You abducted me for money, not my life story," Cal parried his too nosy question. "When will you know if they accept your terms?"

"One of my men will bring their answer tomorrow night. If all's set, they'll be told where to leave it Monday. I've got two . . . men watching the trail and town to prevent a double-cross," Cole responded. "You're afraid they won't pay, aren't you?" he challenged.

Her flush deepened. "If they can get the money, they will," Cal stated, but her tone and look belied her words and confidence.

"Where's Lynx? When's he expected home?" Cole demanded, his tone insinuating close knowledge of her mysterious husband.

Calinda looked out the window. "I don't know. His father said he was away on business. Could you open the window? It's stuffy."

"What kind of business?" Cole continued, pushing up the sash.

"Something about buying new bulls," she answered. "Do you know Lynx?" she abruptly inquired.

"How long has he been away?" Cole asked another question, to her dismay and rising tension. "When is he returning?"

"He left the day after we . . ." She caught her foolish slip and changed it, "after he settled some business at the ranch."

"You mean, the day after you married him, don't you?" he astutely challenged, his curiosity piqued. "Some marriage," he sneered.

Calinda wanted to hide when her face went crimson. "I need to be excused. May I go to the little house?" she asked.

Cole gazed at her turned head. Why would a man

leave his bride of one day, if he loved her? Could Lynx Cardone love any woman? It wasn't a secret he normally avoided them. Maybe his father had selected this girl for a respectable wife. Maybe old man Cardone had used some hold over Lynx to force their marriage. If so, Cardone might pay for her return, but Lynx might not . . . Perhaps it was best Lynx wasn't home. Just maybe those two had trapped this girl. That could explain her fear of them not paying. If Lynx refused to meet his terms . . . No, Lynx wouldn't let anyone take his property, whether he valued it or not. This sweet little game would serve two purposes: victory over Lynx and plenty of money. He smiled . . .

Cole went to the door and told his men to cover their faces. He came back and untied Calinda. She swung her legs off the bunk and rubbed her chafed wrists, remarking on the rope's excessive tightness. Cal followed him to the wooden out-house. After warning her against recklessness, Cole stopped a short distance away. As she relieved herself, Calinda peeked out cracks in all directions to assess her surroundings. Her predicament didn't look good.

She returned to Cole's side, wincing as she tested the injury on her forehead. "Still hurt?" he inquired as if honestly concerned.

"It throbs when I move. Why am I so dizzy and weak?" Cal asked, setting her plans into motion. If they felt she was disabled, they wouldn't expect her imminent actions.

"He cracked you pretty hard. Let me look at it," he said, removing the bandage. Cole studied the swollen area which presented a small cut, reddish blue coloring, and dried blood. As his gaze lowered to hers, his hands propped on his hips. "Should heal nicely."

Her right hand lifted slightly, then went back to lock with the other one. "Why didn't you jerk off my mask, Calinda?"

She blushed and lowered her head. Cole grasped her chin and lifted her head, drilling his blue eyes into her green ones. "Well?"

"I remembered what you said about surviving if I couldn't identify you and your men. I was just wondering how an outlaw looks." To disarm him and win his sympathy, she related the stage hold-up incident.

"And you believed me?" Cole queried strangely, eyes alert.

"I don't have any choice. I pray you'll keep your word."

"I will, Calinda, unless you force my hand."

"What if . . ." Again she halted. "I'm hungry. Do prisoners get to eat around here?"

Cole guided her back to her confining room, then brought the food prepared by one of his men. Cole didn't like the way she was getting to him, so he left the room. As Calinda ate her meal, she pondered this perplexing and dangerous episode. She had better keep quiet and remote from now on; that bandit leader was getting too friendly. He was mistaking her desperate attempts to save her life as flirtation. She had unwisely thought a man would have more trouble slaying a friend or someone he had gotten to know. But her scheme might go awry. He was developing a gleam in his eyes which troubled and frightened her. He wasn't feeling sorry for her; he was feeling desire for her. When would this Little Red arrive and prevent problems?

Supper came and went, with dusk on its tail. As the

hours slowly crawled by, Calinda became panicky. Her fate would be settled in less than two days. She had already decided she wouldn't plead for her life, nor offer this outlaw any bribe to spare it. If he attempted anything before killing her, she would fight him to the death.

What troubled Cal most were the two men in the next room. They were becoming restless and rowdy. They had been playing cards and drinking for most of the afternoon. Several times their leader had entered her prison to chat with her, annoyed when she rebuffed his company and conversation. The last time, two hours ago, he had snarled, "Don't talk, little lady, some things don't require it," then stalked out and slammed the door.

Suddenly the door opened slightly and the bandit returned. Alarm filled Calinda when he strolled over to the bed and sat down. He stared down at her, the expression in his eyes concealed by the darkness in the room. Her face was illuminated by the light from the other room, her fear plain to Cole. "What happened to all that trust, Calinda?" he asked, his voice blurred by whiskey. "Why this sudden freeze?"

Tears glimmered on her lashes. "Please go away," she whispered.

"What if I say no?" Cole fenced, watching her terror mount. He shifted to light the lantern on the table by the bed.

"You promised . . . to return me safely," Cal reminded him.

"Did I say that, Callie?" he taunted mischievously, trailing the back of his rough hand over her smooth cheek.

"Yes, you did," she replied, her voice strengthening.

309

As he casually let his finger drift over her quivering lips, Cole murmured, "Well, I tell you what, Calinda Cardone; if I get that money, I'll set you free just the way I found you. If not . . ."

Cole placed his finger against the throbbing pulse on her neck. When Cal tried to move away from his touch, he chuckled, placing his hands on the bed on either side of her, causing him to bend forward. "You know, you're a very beautiful woman, the best I've seen. If I don't get paid with money, I might think of some other way for you to buy your freedom. We've still got another whole day to become good friends." His meaning needed no further clarification.

"Don't waste your time or energy," she vowed softly, her voice quavering, her respiration erratic. "I'm not a saloon harlot."

"Your life's worth lots of Cardone money, but nothing else? I'm sure my men will demand some kind of reward if the Cardones refuse payment. Course, my men don't bother good friends of mine. Think we can become good friends, Callie?" he asked, stressing "good".

"I'll let you know at noon Monday," she bluffed him to stall for time, to keep him away from her as long as possible. She recalled the two missing men, knowing she would have five to deal with on Monday.

He chuckled smugly. "Then we'll talk at noon, Callie," he surprisingly agreed. He stood up, stretched, and headed for the door. At it, he hesitated to say, "I'll leave this open, just in case you get a wild notion to test my patience and temper. But I hope you won't."

Cal snuggled her face into the pillow, tears rolling down her cheeks to be absorbed there. She would never come out of this alive. Lynx probably thought she had been raped and abused by now. He wouldn't want a ravished wife back in his arms. Even if they did pay for her release, it would never be the same between them. They had begun their relationship with a stormy breach between them, one which had widened with time.

Calinda kept remembering that odd letter; it couldn't have been from this gang, for she hadn't been a Cardone then. She reflected bitterly on the locket and Lynx's mysterious life. How could they ever find love, happiness, and trust when he kept so much of his existence and self from her? Maybe she was just a pleasing convenience.

Her gaze aimlessly shifted to the window, then froze abruptly, her lips parting as she inhaled in astonishment. Lynx! He lifted a finger to his lips and shook his tawny head to signal her to silence. Was she dreaming? Hallucinating? How had he found her in this den of outlaws? What if they caught him? Her warring emotions ceased to battle within her; her painful relections halted their keen study. Resentment and anger fled as she stared at the man so near to her.

Cal lifted her head to glance at the door into the other room. It was standing ajar, but she couldn't see into the next room. Her gaze went back to Lynx outside the window. His features were taut with determination and fury. He smiled encouragingly, white teeth gleaming at her. He examined the window, deciding it would be noisy to open. His gaze went to the lantern and analyzed its revealing danger. Calinda watched him closely, comprehending his two obstacles. Lynx suddenly moved aside, removing himself from her view. Why did he go away, she fearfully wondered.

Cal had her answer when the leader strolled into the

room. "Want any coffee?" Cole asked moodily.

"No, thank you," Cal responded faintly. "I'm tired, and my head is pounding again. Could you lift the window for some fresh air; it's smothering in here."

"And let you get hurt sneaking out during the night?" he teased.

"If you tie my hands to the bedpost, I couldn't possibly escape," she suggested sassily. "Besides, I'm not stupid. You would kill me."

Cole came over and tore a long strip from the dirty sheet. He took her hands and secured them to the post. "That should hold you."

Cole lifted the window sash and propped it open. When he leaned forward and gazed outside, she nearly fainted. He inhaled the muggy air, then came back to her side. "Anything else, Callie?"

"Will you put out the lantern? I want to go to sleep."

"You're just full of demands tonight," he murmured. "One good deed without a nice reward is enough. Now, if I was to get a little kiss, I'd be glad to help you."

Calinda tensed in dread. If she didn't kiss him, he wouldn't douse the lantern to safeguard Lynx's rescue attempt. If she did, he might get aroused and demand more than a mere kiss. How could he be so nice, then turn so mean? One minute he was gentle, the next savage. What to do? If he tried to attack her, surely Lynx would try to stop him. If Lynx tried to stop him, there were other armed men to confront. They could both be killed. She hesitated in doubt.

"What's wrong, Callie? Don't trust me to have self-control?"

"You'll give me your word of honor, just one kiss?"

"My word of honor, just one kiss, until Monday," he added.

"But if you remove your mask to kiss me, I'll see your face."

"Not with the lantern out. Well?" he eagerly pressed.

"All right," she reluctantly acquiesced, wondering how Lynx felt about this necessary action.

Cole doused the light, then lifted his mask when he was near her lips. His mouth seared over hers in a demanding and greedy kiss, to which she didn't resist or respond. Cole forced her lips apart, fusing his mouth to hers as if to devour her. He made the kiss last as long as possible. When his mouth left hers, he taunted, "That wasn't a fair deal; a kiss can't be one-sided."

She replied angrily, "You gave your word. You didn't say I had to respond."

"I said, if I was to get a little kiss, not take one," he argued.

"That wasn't a little kiss," she snapped, feeling duped. "You're trying to trick me; I shouldn't have trusted you."

"Maybe you're right. But Monday at noon, make sure you understand my meaning," Cole warned. If he wanted her to be willing, he couldn't press her tonight. Anyway, he had all day Sunday to work on her resistance and hopes. He walked out, whistling.

Calinda's gaze went from the nearly closed door to the darkened lantern, to the open window. She had done all she could; the rest was up to Lynx. Her heart was racing happily; he had tracked them down and was going to rescue her, just as in Lampasas. Funny, every time she was in trouble or danger, Lynx inexplicably showed up to help. She waited; he didn't appear at the window. Had they seen him and captured him? She trembled with growing suspense. She fretted over the perilous full moon which might expose his presence.

A towering shadow moved before the window. She held her breath as Lynx stealthily crawled through it. He stood up and paused, cocking his head to listen for a minute. Her eyes grew large with astonishment; he wasn't wearing his guns or boots. If that outlaw entered the room again, Lynx would be helpless! Was he so self-assured that he felt he could lick three men with his bare hands?

Lynx gingerly moved forward, careful of creaking boards. He bent over her, placing his lips to her left ear. He whispered, "Don't talk or move, Callie. I'm getting you out of here."

Lynx withdrew a large blade from his waist, then severed the roped binding her wrists. Cal wanted to throw herself in his strong arms, but didn't dare move as ordered. He leaned over again, saying, "Be still while I take off your boots."

Lynx removed one, then the other, bobbling the second one before he had control of it. She tensed in alarm, then relaxed. The intoxicating rogue grinned playfully, as if this was a game. He scooped her up in his arms and set her down near the window. Her clever love reached for some blankets and fashioned them into a body-like roll on the bed. He placed her boots in a position which indicated she was lying on her side. He covered the handmade dummy with the dirty sheet, except for the boots which were peeking out near the foot. He took her hat and placed it where her head should be. He stepped back to eye his creation. In the darkness, it should pass for Calinda's frame.

Lynx grinned in satisfaction. That should give them time to escape, if Cole Stevens didn't try to enchant her again tonight! Naturally Lynx had recognized the man's voice. When Calinda was out of danger, he would take care of Stevens and his reckless gang.

Lynx warned her again in silence, then slid her out the window. Cal waited anxiously as he agilely eased over the sill and joined her. He caught her head between his hands and pulled it forward. She was piqued when he didn't kiss her, but only whispered, "See those rocks over there?" He pointed to them and waited for her to nod. "Get behind them pronto, but don't make any noise. I'll stand guard. If I don't come right behind you, get the hell out of here fast."

Calinda flung her arms around his waist, briefly craving his comforting contact. Lynx hastily seized her arms and loosened her grip. He warned, "We don't have time for that, Cal. Get going."

After what she'd been through, Cal yearned for a moment of solace. It had been weeks since she had seen him and touched him. Cal was too distraught to consider their danger. At that time, all she could think about was the safety of his arms.

At her hesitation, her murmured into her ear, "If you don't get moving, we'll be caught and shot. I didn't risk my life for nothing."

Calinda jerked her hands from his brawny chest, then glared at him. She whirled and headed for the assigned hiding place, gritting her teeth as the sharp rock snipped at her socked feet. Lynx stepped behind the corner of the shack and waited there until she vanished from his sight. He stepped back to the window, then fished a small object from his pocket. He placed the tiny silver star he had removed from a broken pair of spurs on the windowsill where Cole would be sure to notice it. He reached behind a bush and lifted Farley's gunbelt, digging an impression of a small star into the scuffed leather, symbol of justice and the unknown Ranger. He hung it over the sill, then snatched up his own gunbelt and boots.

As quietly as possible, Lynx hurried to join the waiting Calinda. Once concealed by the large boulder, he dropped his boots to fasten on his gunbelt, tying a holster down to each muscled thigh. He pulled on his boots. He glanced at her and smiled broadly. "So far, so good, Callie. Let's move out before Cole realizes that isn't you in that bed."

"Cole? How could you know him with a mask?" She despised the suspicions which chewed viciously at her, inspiring rash anger.

"I recognized his voice when he was trying to seduce my wife. Don't worry; I'll repay him after you're home safe," he vowed coldly. "How's the head? Did they . . . hurt you, Cal?"

"Some scrapes and bruises, nothing serious," she replied. When his hand reached out to move aside her hair to check the injury, she twisted away from his touch and panted, "We don't have time for that! It's fine; just a little crack on the head. How did you find me?" she demanded, her voice exposing a strange note of accusation. "I'm surprised you took the time from your busy schedule. But I suppose a man like Lynx Cardone prefers to pay such debts with vengeful pride rather than money. No promising bulls for sale?" She had remembered all at once how he had deceived her. Was he an outlaw? What if he were killed or captured? How could she live without him? Fears and doubts clouded her reason and compelled her to strike out in fury and spite.

"What are you babbling about, woman? I think that

lick on the skull is playing havoc with your senses. I've finished my work in Junction; we trapped some fence cutters and rustlers. I was heading home when a man tried to back-shoot me, one of Cole Stevens' men. That's how I learned about the kidnapping and your location."

"I see," she murmured skeptically. "What happened to that code of honor amongst thieves, to die in brave silence?"

"I told him I'd kill him if he didn't speak up and fast," he casually informed her, wondering at her frigid manner.

"How did you know he had anything to tell you?" she pressed.

"I'll explain everything later. We can't stand here jawing. Follow me," he commanded, then headed off into the scattered rocks.

Calinda decided his story sounded a little too incredible and convenient. Why had Stevens called her Callie? As in Lampasas, Lynx had appeared just in the nick of time to rescue her from peril. By generous fate or Lynx's unknown purpose? It was past time for some truthful answers. When they reached home, she would demand them. Her stockinged feet began to gingerly pick a path between sharp rocks and cacti in pursuit of her exasperating husband, dressed in satanic black as usual.

When Lynx turned to realize how far behind she was and why, he hurried back to her. He scooped her up in his arms and walked off with her, despite her muted protests. "There isn't time to argue, Cal. Just shut that lovely mouth and follow my instructions."

She fell into stony silence. When he set her down, she murmured sarcastically, "You don't seem very glad

317

to see me safe and sound, dear husband." She knew she was being asinine, but couldn't halt it.

"In this predicament, I'm not," he growled. "You're one bag of trouble, Calinda Braxton."

"It's Calinda Cardone, in case you've conveniently forgotten."

"I haven't forgotten. If I had, I wouldn't be here tonight. I've been waiting around for hours until dark. It's been driving me wild."

"How did you locate me so quickly?" she inquired.

"I'll tell you later. For someone just rescued from killers, you sure have a funny way of showing your appreciation," he scolded. "What's gotten into you, Cal? You sound like I'm responsible for this dangerous situation." His gaze searched her expression, trying to unravel this curious puzzle.

"You are. If you'd been home where you belong, instead of gallivanting all over the countryside in search of adventure, they wouldn't have dared kidnap me. Obviously this golden band isn't a magical charm. I believe you said for me to stay home where I'd be safe and happy. Well, dear husband, I haven't been either. I hate Texas. It's a land of violence, deceit, and peril. I shouldn't have agreed to marry you or remain on the ranch," she bluntly informed the startled man. She kept herself from adding, *if you can't be honest with me.* She was tired of secrecy and separation which she didn't understand. *If he loved her . . .*

"You did, so you'll have to make the best of both. Come on; I'm sure Father's half out of his mind by now." He mounted up. He held out his hand and told her to mount before him.

Calinda didn't want to be in his line of vision or within his stimulating embrace. She much preferred his less demanding broad back. "I'll be more comfortable riding behind you."

"You'll also be in the line of fire if they discover you're missing and come after us. Stop behaving like a spoiled child, woman. We've wasted precious escape time as it is."

The tension too much to contain, she angrily vented some of it, "How do you expect me to act after what I've endured? I could have been ravished or murdered, for all you care."

"If I didn't care, my rebellious wife, I wouldn't be here." His amber eyes narrowed. How could she blame him for this crime? Why was she so cold, sarcastic, and ungrateful? For the first time in his life, he had experienced real fear and a lack of confidence in his own abilities. He was trying to save both their lives, but she was determined to pick a silly fight! Maybe it was a reaction to her shocking ordeal. But they had to get out of here; if they were caught, that star left behind would expose his identity.

"If you're shot in the back, I don't want to be left alive to face those crude men. Let me sit behind you — they might be reluctant to shoot a woman. They think I'm a valuable prize," she reasoned fearfully.

"You're worth far more than fifty thousand dollars. But they'd kill both of us before allowing us to escape. I'm larger and stronger. I could survive a bullet in the back easier than you could. Now, hush and get up here," he ordered firmly, his gaze daring her to refuse.

"All right," she agreed, placing her hand in his.

Lynx gave Star his lead. The animal sensed danger from previous training and experience, and walked for a lengthy distance from the hideout before picking up his pace. At a steady gallop, they made the ranch in less than three hours, time for her silly anger to vanish.

The moment they arrived, Calinda and Lynx were surrounded by gleefully shouting people. In a flurry of excitement and greetings, the daring tale of their escape spilled forth.

"I shore am glad to see you, Mrs. Cardone," Charlie stated.

"Not as happy as I am to see your face again," she replied.

"How did you find her son?" Rankin shrieked. "I had the money all ready to go at their signal. I guess you got my telegram?"

Calinda glanced at Lynx. Rankin had sent for him? He had known Lynx's location? Lynx smiled at his father, then nodded. Calinda's anger and hurt returned two-fold at that news. Lynx related the incident on the trail with Farley, whose pocket contained the instructions for the delivery of the money, the message to be delivered to the Cardone Ranch Monday at noon. "I'm sorry I couldn't stop by and tell you my plan to rescue her; there wasn't time. When I discovered it was Cole Stevens behind it, I headed for his hide-out. I doubt Cal would have been safe for another day and a half."

Calinda captured the dual meaning to his statement. How did Lynx know Cole Stevens so well? Why not, both were noted gunslingers! Had uncanny luck aided Lynx's rescue, or was there more to it? Perhaps her roguish love had connections to many outlaws. After all, there was the stolen locket in his possession. She wanted to challenge him about it, but was afraid to let him know she'd searched his room.

"You're a courageous and cunning man, son,"

Rankin affectionately complimented Lynx. "You're a lucky girl, Cal."

Dazed by their deception, she murmured, "I want to thank you for offering to pay them so much money, Rankin. I'm just relieved you didn't lose it. I promise to be more careful in the future. Right now, if you'll excuse me, I want to get out of these filthy clothes and take a soothing bath. This has been quite a harrowing experience, and I'm exhausted." Suddenly, she felt utterly drained.

"I'm sorry we didn't protect you better, Cal," Rankin apologized.

"It wasn't your fault. Lynx, I did hear something you should pass on to the sheriff, if this Cole doesn't change his plans now," she began, then related the overheard details for the robbery Friday.

"I doubt Cole and his gang will be smart enough to alter those plans. The sheriff or Rangers can set up a trap and take 'em Friday. Wouldn't do any good to return to their hideout; they've cleared out of there by now." He looked at his father and said, "You'd best post guards around the ranch, just in case Cole doesn't give up easily. Cal, make sure you stay within sight of the house until Cole's gang is captured."

"You needn't worry; I will. Goodnight." She entered the house, passing Salina without a word or nod. Gathering her needed items, she went to bathe. Afterwards, she would sleep in her old room. The strain of her many ordeals demanded solitude. She feared the reasons for Lynx's dishonesty and the effect it was having on their relationship.

Both Lynx and Rankin noticed Calinda failed to hug or kiss her heroic husband. They went into the study and closed the door. "Is something bothering

321

Cal? She was acting strangely."

"Then it wasn't just my imagination. I don't have the vaguest idea, father, unless the tension of this ordeal. Maybe she'll settle down after a bath and a sherry. She's been a little peeved since the moment she saw me. I don't know what's going on, but I'm glad she's safe. She had me scared out of my wits."

"Tell me everything," his father coaxed, wanting to hear of his son's intelligence and daring.

Lynx went through the whole episode in minute detail.

"You left one of your marks behind? What happens when they learn Lynx Cardone snatched his wife from their evil clutches? They'll know you're the unknown Ranger. That wasn't smart, son," Rankin scolded him.

"I was too furious at the time to think clearly. Anyway, by Friday, Cole and his men will be under the Rangers' control. I'll head out at first light for the Rangers; we'll be ready and waiting for them to strike. I have a personal score to settle with Stevens."

"Tonight, you have something else to settle, with your wife."

"You haven't given Cal any hints about me or the ranch? I'm worried about the way she's acting and looking at me."

Rankin filled in Lynx on the happenings since he left weeks ago. Lynx was troubled by the conflicts between his wife and Salina. "I don't think Salina should be allowed to treat my wife like that, father. I know Salina's a valuable servant, but not irreplaceable. I don't like her harassing Cal. You think Cal's merely upset by Salina's attitude? Cal might be disturbed by what she views as ill treatment from us if we allow Salina to pester her. Cal's a proud, stubborn woman. It's only natural for her to want to run her own home, at least be in control of it. It's unfair to allow Salina to have more authority. I think we'd better settle this tomorrow before I pull out."

"I guess you're right, son," Rankin concurred.

Salina had just made her way near the open doors, to boldly eavesdrop on the men's conversation. She tensed and fumed at their last words. If she didn't soften her covert attack, that little bitch would force a showdown! Too bad Lynx had bravely rescued her!

"You don't think there's any way she's learned anything, do you?" Lynx worried aloud. "Salina doesn't know anything to maliciously pass along, does she? For certain, something has my wife inflamed."

"You're forgetting, Marie was away for several days during the trouble with Brax. She couldn't reveal anything to Salina."

As the two discussed what had taken place years ago, the staggering truth was devoured by the greedy Salina. When Lynx said he was going to talk with Calinda, Salina waited until he left the room before slipping away from her hiding place. She danced around her room, hugging herself, congratulating herself for her good fortune. So, that explained why Lynx and Rankin were so desperate to keep Calinda here, to hold her captive with a wedding band, to prevent a search for Brax? If something happened to Calinda . . . Surely their shows of affection were phony, just devices to ensnare her, to disarm her? Surely they hated the daughter of the man who had done such evil to them? No doubt they were waiting for the proper time to get rid of her . . .

Lynx went to his room; Calinda wasn't there. He went to the next room, both the hall and balcony doors were bolted. He tapped lightly and called out, "Cal, are you all right? I want to talk to you."

Why had she returned to her old room? he fretted anxiously. When she didn't respond, he warned, "If you don't open the door, I'll do it myself. You've got some explaining to do, wife."

Calinda walked to the balcony door and unbolted it. "I'm tired, Lynx. What can't wait until morning? Or will you even be around then?"

"I'd like to know why you're being as chilly and aggressive as a blue norther?" he stated, moving her aside to enter the room.

The weary girl turned and gazed at him. Dare she demand the truth? She closed the door and came forward to stand before him. "You're most selfish and inconsiderate, Lynx. You know what I've been through since this terrifying incident began. Why do you insist on talking tonight? I just want to relax and unwind." Her cloudy gaze prevented his piercing eyes from ascertaining her crazy mood.

"We're both drained. I've been crazy with worry, Cal. I've had little sleep or rest in days. If I was unresponsive back there, I'm sorry. I just wanted to get you away safely. I've missed you, woman."

"You had enough time to give me plenty of insults, terse orders, and scoldings. That wasn't what I needed or wanted. But I am grateful for your second timely assistance. It appears you know a great deal about outlaws, Mister Cardone."

"What's that supposed to mean?" he demanded, piqued by her tone and manner. "I told you how I found you."

"Ah, yes, the miraculous clue to my misfortune and location," she murmured skeptically. "You do have an uncanny way of showing up in the nick of time, don't you? First the saloon, then Lampasas, and incredibly at the scene of my captivity. You must possess immense insight, luck, and intelligence. I'm learning quite a number of lessons, my talented husband," Please remove my doubts, she prayed.

"I don't like the insinuations in your frosty tone, Cal."

"And I don't like being kept in the dark about my own husband," she instantly retorted. "Mainly, I don't like being deceived."

"What are you talking about, Cal?" he asked seriously. His baffled gaze eased over her tumbling chestnut hair, her stormy green eyes, and her silky skin. Her complexion looked as if she hadn't been out of the house since her arrival in sultry Texas.

"The next time you leave home, which is probably at dawn, you should get your excuses to match your father's. Even Salina knows more about you and your movements than I do. I suppose you've never heard of letters or telegrams home?" Cal hinted in rising vexation.

"You knew I was heading for Junction to do a job delayed by a willful and crafty young lady. I don't know what my father said, but he was probably trying to ease your concern and loneliness. But you're right about my leaving at dawn; I'm going to set a trap for Stevens. Besides what he did to you, he's wanted for numerous crimes. I'm heading over to the Ranger camp to see that he's put out of action for good. I know I should have contacted you sooner, but I kept thinking I would be finished and heading home any day. It won't happen again, Cal; I promise. Now, what's this about Salina?" he asked, returning to a clue which had caused her eyes to glimmer with fury.

.Wanting to clear the air and make her position a known fact to all of them, Calinda revealed what Salina had said to her. Lynx tensed, realizing Salina must have discovered information to use to her advantage. He must caution his father to avoid any future conversation which might be enlightening and hazardous. He would deal with Salina's brazen conduct!

"Listen to me carefully, Cal, I swear to you I went to Junction to help a friend. Afterwards, I rode to Dallas to meet another friend, to complete one last promise so I could come home. As soon as I warn the Rangers about Stevens, I'll head for Waco and be done with this separation. I know you said you would handle matters with Salina, but clearly you haven't. If you let that tempestuous girl order you around or insult you again, I'll turn you over my knees and spank you. If she's going to treat my wife like that, then she'd best get the hell out of my home. The first time she ordered you out of your own kitchen, you should have flung a skillet at her, preferably a hot one. And don't ask her which chores you can have; do whatever you please. Rankin's just become dependent on her, but I don't think he realizes how bad it is between you two. I'm deadly serious, woman. You'd best recall, you're the wife and she's the servant. As for moving into my room, you didn't need to ask. In fact, I'd have been awfully hurt and curious if you hadn't. Trust me a while longer, Cal. I just need a few more weeks, then I'll be home for good."

"You have so many secrets, Lynx; you're like a total stranger to me. How can I trust you when you don't trust me?" she asked sadly.

"I'll explain everything when the time is right, Cal.

I'll be frank with you; there are certain things I can't tell you at present, some things I don't want to tell you, and some things I'll never tell you. But I will say enough to explain matters, to justify what I'm doing right now. I just need a little time and privacy for a while longer."

"You've been shutting me out of your life ever since we met. You expect blind faith and unquestionable loyalty. Don't you understand how difficult and demanding that is over such a long period of time and distance? I'm weary of all the excuses, deceits, and mistrust. I'm so confused and exhausted, I don't even know if it's worth it anymore." She sighed heavily in frustration.

"There's more to it, Cal," he speculated astutely, reaching to pull her into his yearning embrace.

She moved aside, denying him his quest. "Don't, Lynx. I'm not in the mood to be touched. Tonight, I need some time and privacy," she informed softly. She turned away from him, locking her arms over her abdomen, closing her eyes, and inhaling raggedly.

His hands gently grasped her shoulders. "I'll be leaving soon, Cal. We've been through hell. I need you," he stated huskily. Even if she didn't want to make love tonight, he wanted to hold her tightly and kiss her time after time. He wanted to vanquish her coldness and painful rejection. He wanted her to feel the love within him.

"What about my needs?" she challenged in a hoarse voice.

"If I've hurt you and disappointed you, Cal, I'm truly sorry. If you don't feel like making love, at least come to bed with me. I need you near me tonight. Do you realize how close I came to losing you?" he asked, his voice and gaze tender and compelling.

"Would it really matter if you did?" she asked shockingly, alarming him with the gravity of her dejected tone.

"How can you even ask such a question?"

"If you care so much, why have I seen my husband for less than a day since our blissful marriage? If you care so much, why haven't I received even the tiniest note? If you care so much, why do you keep your life a secret from me? If you care so much, why are you leaving within hours after I escape from the jaws of death?"

"If I don't head for the Rangers tomorrow, this might be our last chance to snag Cole Stevens and his gang. Don't you see, Cal, the timing is perfect to capture him? Do you want me to allow him to go on killing, robbing, and terrorizing the countryside? Perhaps kidnap another woman?" he questioned in exasperation.

"Do your duty, Lynx; I won't try to stop you. I won't cry or plead or scream. Just don't expect me to calmly accept your running in and out of my life whenever it suits your fancy. I hate this place; I wish I had never come here," she falsely vowed.

"You don't mean that, Cal. You're just upset and tired."

"Yes, I do mean it. It's been awful since the first day of my arrival. How do you think I should feel about Texas? I was robbed before I even got to the ranch," she placed the bait on her hook.

"I know you're angry about the hold-up. I wish I could find your possessions. I can't. The sheriff never caught who was responsible."

"I don't care about the money or clothes or other

things, just my locket. I told the sheriff he could keep everything as a reward if he could only locate and return my locket. It means so much to me," she said, dangling the baited hook before him.

"I'm sorry about the locket, Cal."

"No, you aren't. And stop saying you're sorry. If you were, you would help me find it," she continued to fish for the response she wanted so desperately.

"How am I supposed to do that?" he asked strangely.

"You're very successful at solving mysteries about me. You seem to be acquainted with plenty of outlaws and gunslingers. Find out who has my locket and get it back for me. Maybe my locket will turn up in as timely and unexpected a manner as you do," she tried another area.

"I wish I could hand you the locket right now, Cal."

Calinda turned and faced him. Her heart began to thud heavily, "Why can't you, Lynx?"

"Because I don't . . ." He halted and stared at her. He had a gut feeling she was trying to imply something. But what?

"Perhaps I should teach you how to complete sentences, my devoted and heroic husband. Shall I assist you? Because I don't have it?"

Lynx's heart skipped a beat. He stiffened slightly. He grabbed her chin and forced their gazes to fuse. "You know, don't you?" he asked simply, fearing the worst.

"Yes, my loving husband, I know you have it," she replied, her gaze never leaving his as it narrowed and hardened. "But what I would like to hear is why you kept it from me, knowing how I felt?"

"Why did you open that locked drawer, Cal? Why?"

he demanded.

"I wanted to know who and what my husband was, since he refuses to tell me."

"I don't believe what I'm hearing," he stated softly.

Calinda observed the unexpected reaction on his bronzed face; he actually looked betrayed and disillusioned. She had thought he would be furious, but he was hurt. "I wanted and needed to understand you. Why do you keep me at arm's length? Why do you and Rankin feed me false tales and words which even a starving fool would choke on? I'm not stupid. Is it me, Lynx; is there something terrible about me?" she inquired in a near whisper.

"All right, Cal, I'll tell you about your locket. I took it off a man I fought in Dallas. He was a member of Sam Bass' gang, the ones who held up the stage. When I went to see the Rangers to give them the information, Major Jones asked me not to give away their identity yet; they're tracking him down to capture him. That's how I knew Jones didn't have anything to do with that letter. I had the locket with me when I found you in Lampasas risking your lovely neck to find Brax. I didn't give it to you for several reasons. First, I didn't want you to have a picture of Brax; I was afraid you would use it to hire a detective to search for him. A search would cost you lots of money, futile time, and more anguish. I wanted you cut off from the past so you would stay here with us. Second, I didn't want you wearing it here. I saw Brax's picture inside. I didn't want my father and me having that constant reminder flaunted in our faces. Last, I didn't want to explain how I came to be in possession of it. Your image of me was already dark; I didn't want anything to make it worse. Believe it or not, I was planning to return it some day. I knew how much its loss pained you; I couldn't throw it away."

Oddly, Calinda felt he was telling the truth. "What about the watch? I'm so confused about the past, Lynx."

"Some day, I promise to tell you everything I know, Cal. Please, not tonight. We've been through hell for three days. If it bothers you that much, I'll give you the locket right now. Just don't wear it for a while longer," he urged.

"Keep it for me. As long as I know it's here, that's all that matters. You're a very complex and puzzling man, Lynx Cardone."

"I suppose you're right, Cal. I've never had to answer to anyone before now. Maybe I am too damn proud and stubborn. Sharing and loving come hard for me, I've had no experience," he teased.

"I think certain kinds come too easily, Lynx. You share yourself and your skills with your friends. And you positively know a great deal about loving," she murmured, her implication clear.

"If I promise to try harder at everything, am I forgiven?" he coaxed, trailing his fingers over her silky cheek. "You're a challenge to me, Cal; and I'm having a devil of a time accepting it. Taking you into my life and heart requires heavy changes; it's difficult, love."

"You drive a hard bargain, Lynx. Stop grinning at me like that, or I might forget my anger. You're a heartless devil and you know it. When it comes to you, I must be a naive and gullible fool. You're dangerously irresistible." She returned his smile, mellowing as time passed. She should have waited for his explanations before jumping the gun. He had a beguiling way of justifying anything. When he was near and enticing, all other thoughts fled her mind.

She yawned and stretched, her lids droopy and her body going lax. "Let's go to bed, husband; I can hardly hold my eyes open."

"No wonder, it's nearly morning," he said, tugging on a stray curl, leading her into his room. "To bed with you, wife."

She looked up into his arresting face. "But you'll be leaving soon."

He chuckled. "Not before you wake up, love; I promise."

She smiled as he pulled the covers over her, then kissed her lightly on her injured forehead. He undressed and joined her, pulling her into his possessive embrace. He kissed her tenderly, then murmured, "Go to sleep, *Llama de mi corazon;* you're safe now."

"I love you, Lynx," she murmured drowsily at his endearment, leisurely sailing off on a peaceful journey to dreamland.

"*Yo te quiero,* Callie, *mi vida, mi aliento, mi corazon,*" he responded, but she didn't hear him. He was relieved she had accepted his truthful explanation about the locket. With loving determination, he was gradually constructing a bridge across the river of mistrust and bitterness which kept them apart. In the near future, he would complete his compelling task when he removed the final obstacles between them. But he must be very careful to allow nothing to destroy his steady progress; for she was indeed his love, his life, his breath, and his heart. Soon, Lynx was fast asleep.

Chapter Fourteen

It was approaching noon when Calinda awoke. Subdued rays of sunlight gently pierced the translucent curtains on the balcony doors. She sat up, staring down at the empty place where Lynx had slept. Had he broken his promise and left without telling her? Had the abduction and rescue been stygian dreams? No. Cal flung the covers aside and jumped up to search for an inexcusable note.

The door opened quietly as Lynx tried to steal inside without disturbing Cal. When he saw her standing by the dresser, he smiled and closed the door. *"Buenos dias,"* Mrs. Cardone," he said warmly.

A bright smile flickered over her face. "I was looking for a note, Mister Cardone; I feared you had left already," she confessed.

"I promised I wouldn't leave before you could give me a good scolding for my terrible behavior lately," he teased, strolling toward her. "But I was beginning to think you were going to sleep away all our time together. I was trying to be patient," Lynx ventured merrily.

"It must be awfully late. Why didn't you awaken me?"

"You needed your sleep, *mi amor.* I gave my word to remain. You've got to learn to trust me, Cal," he advised, stopping within inches of her, assailing her senses with his arresting aura.

"I know," Cal contritely replied. "I suppose all newlyweds go through this demanding period of adjustment and confusion."

"Hungry?" Lynx hinted, his amber eyes sparkling as sunbeams dancing upon a glass of golden sherry.

Hungry? Cal mentally challenged. *Certainly not for food!* How could she think of anything when he was standing before her wearing nothing but a wrapper around his hips! It was obvious that he often went shirtless, as his appealing body was darkly tanned from the waist up. His taut flesh was as smooth and firm as hardened taffy. His muscles were flexible and strong. Not an ounce of excess fat marred a frame Apollo would envy. Despite having been in so many fights, his splendid body was scarless.

Lynx reminded her of a magnificent male animal, lithe and sleek. He was as quick and nimble as a prized stallion. His arms and legs rippled with each movement. His shoulders were broad, his chest covered with a dark gold mat of curly hair. His stomach was flat and taut, his waist narrow. Cal smiled as a crazy thought touched her mind; he even had pretty feet.

As her brazen study travelled up from the floor, it hesitated briefly on the noticable bulge beneath the wrapper which covered him. Her respiration quickened; she warmed and tingled. When her gaze reached his handsome face, his parted lips exposed even ivory teeth that added charming allure to his sensual smile. His tawny eyes smoldered like a pool of amber liquid. As if his gaze was magnetized, it drew and held her tightly.

His hands cupped her face, a thumb moving over her lips in a provocative manner. "You're beautiful, Callie. Do you have any idea how you affect me?" he asked huskily, his voice thick with passion.

Her hands came up to rest on his chest. She murmured, "I hope the same way you affect me, Lynx."

His hands wandered up into her fiery hair, relishing its satiny feel. He pushed aside the curls falling over her temples, his gaze locking on the contusion and angry red line. His eyes chilled and squinted. "I should kill him for hurting you," he stated glacially, a deadly gleam telling of his inner rage.

Cal snuggled her face against his furry chest, her arms slipping around his taut body. Lynx was so tall compared to her medium frame that he could lay his face on the top of her head, which he did after kissing it. "Don't think about it now, Lynx. Our time is so short." She lifted her head to look up into his features. "Can't you wait until the holiday is over? Thursday is July fourth. There's going to be a celebration in town; Rankin's taking me. Couldn't you join us, at least a few hours? Surely everyone wonders why a new bride is always alone."

Lynx sighed heavily. "If I stay, Cal, there's no way I can get to the Rangers to trap Stevens. If he steals that money, he'll lay low for a long time. Don't you see I have to do this, for all of his victims?"

As much as Cal wanted to debate his logic, she couldn't. She knew from experience how dangerous

JANELLE TAYLOR

that outlaw was. "I'm sorry, Lynx. I won't ask again. Of course you're right. But I don't have to like it," she added laughingly, punching him in the back very softly.

"How do you like this, Mrs. Cardone?" he asked playfully, nibbling at her ear. "Or this?" he added, searing his burning lips over hers. His deft fingers removed her gown, then pulled her naked body to his bare chest. He groaned at the staggering contact of her warm flesh against his cool body. As he shifted from side to side to tease her sensitive breasts with his hairy torso, he hinted knowingly, "Or this?"

"I can think of something better," Cal hinted bravely. "If you have time to return to bed," she speculated seductively.

He leaned backwards to study her inviting expression. "Then show me what you have in mind," Lynx coaxed eagerly.

Cal took his hand and led him to the rumpled bed. She released it to straighten the covers. She glanced at him and smiled, "Would you care to lie down first?"

"At your pleasure, *Llama de mi corazon, mi cuerpo*," he retorted, stretching out on the inviting bed.

"What does that mean?" she probed in undisguised curiosity.

"Flame of my heart, my body," he sensuously responded.

Calinda sat down beside him, grinning mischievously. Salina's words about his growing bored with his wife kept racing through her mind. If he ever did, it positively wouldn't be today. She would show her adventure seeking husband what excitement and fulfillment he was missing at home! If she dared to use the

336

stimulating actions which she had overheard at school and from careless English servants . . .

"Then relax, my love, and let me discover what pleasures you," she hinted suggestively, emerald eyes dancing with intrigue.

Lynx stared at her suspiciously. "If I didn't know any better, I'd think you were up to something, Mrs. Cardone."

Calinda felt very confident and daring today. Her senses were alive with suspense and desire. Her hand casually roamed over the hard mound which was concealed from view as she innocently replied, "It appears, my love, that you are the one . . . up to something. I wonder what it could be," she murmured, coyly pursing her lips.

When Lynx reached over to draw her down to him, she pushed his entreating arms aside, saying, "Relax, love. I'm in full command."

His eyes glittered with amusement and interest. His arms fell back against his pillow on either side of his head. "If you're brave enough to become the leader, I'll gladly surrender that rank."

Calinda lay half over his body, her breasts threatening to burn holes in his chest. She dropped feathery kisses over his nose and eyes. She confined his head between her hands, seeming to attack his mouth with feverish intensity. As she drifted from his lips to one ear, then back to his mouth to eagerly trace each inch in the other direction, he moaned in rising need of her. As his arms instinctively reached for her, she chided, "No, my tempting mate. I must teach you how to relax, how to enjoy new experiences."

"Relax?" Lynx taunted skeptically. "How can I possibly relax when you're heating me up to a boiling point?"

"Then you'll just have to control yourself and simmer a while longer, Lynx. This is fun." She covered her giggling mouth.

"You're a sadist, love; you're just trying to torture me," he playfully accused, chuckling in pleasure.

"Torture you?" she murmured. "You call this punishment?"

"Nope. I call it sheer heaven," he admitted raggedly.

"Then you best savor your brief visit; perhaps this will entice you to return sooner," Cal easily scored a point in her favor.

Her lips created tremors as they worked their way down his neck, nibbling at the hollows there, then at his shoulders. He stiffened briefly as her tongue drew moist circles around his breasts, discovering the unknown fact that his could be as susceptible and sensitive as hers. She took his left hand and kissed each finger, then his palm. Each spot she touched and teased tingled and flamed. For a man who was well versed in sex, Lynx was learning something new and exciting.

When one of Calinda's hands trailed lightly over his taut stomach and released the wrapper to encircle his manhood, he shuddered and groaned with tormenting bliss. His hips squirmed as her light journey tickled over his groin area and upper thighs. Ever so gently she caressed the two round objects beneath his vividly aroused manhood. As her hand slipped up and down the pulsing shaft, he wanted to grab her and make savagely sweet love to her. Thrilling to this unexpected facet of his modest wife, he dared not halt her dauntless adventure.

Lynx's blood surged with fiery life when she moved

to drop brazen kisses on the throbbing, rearing stallion. He was quivering all over, his body a sheet of tingling sensations and roaring flames. "Blazes alive, Callie, you're driving me wild," he stated breathlessly.

After a few more stirring kisses and caresses, she moved up to his face. "Then douse our flames, my love," she wantonly entreated.

He rolled her to her back, assailing her breasts with intoxicating skill. He wanted to see her passion glazed eyes and flushed cheeks as he gave her mutual satisfaction. He lifted her legs and shifted to his knees near her buttocks, sinking his aching shaft into her receptive sheath, burying it to the hilt within her quivering body.

As Lynx tantalizingly invaded her body over and over, he inspired fiercer yearnings within them. His control was sorely strained from her daring trek. Cal moaned in urgency, her head rolling from side to side as he masterfully explored that molten region. As a sleek and powerful mustang, he rode up and down her dark canyon which presented no obstacle against his wildly rapturous invasion.

Back and forth he galloped the distance of her womanhood, mutely enticing her to follow his lead. He hungrily claimed and branded his private territory which willingly yielded to his control and ownership. He charged forward with daring and skill, then retreated slightly for another successful assault.

Calinda was fascinated and bewitched by the erotic sight of their bodies blending to seek fulfillment, fusing as if they would never part. Mesmerized, she watched the wickedly wonderful motions. Her darkened gaze went up to his, their eyes joining to speak silently of shared needs and emotions, of seemingly predestined love.

When their passions reached the point of no retreat or denial, he urged his tightly reined manhood to race for the summit of victory which loomed before them. With confidence and talent, he galloped toward it, setting his pace to allow her to arrive at their destination only seconds before him.

A muffled cry of triumph left her throat as she topped ecstasy's peak, quivering and savoring her victory before sliding down the other side into the peaceful valley which compelled her forward. He freed her legs to lower himself on her damp body, his mouth taking hers as he thundered after her approaching contentment. He extracted the sweet nectar of love from her lips until his body was sated.

At last, he lifted his head and met her glowing eyes. His expression became serious and thoughtful. "What is it about you, Calinda Cardone, that makes you so unique and enchanting? You can't imagine how many nights I've lain awake thinking about you and a moment like this. Sometimes your face appears before my eyes even during the day. Sometimes I want you so badly it scares me. Other times I wonder what I would do if I lost you. You're like a part of me; I feel denied when I'm away from you. Pretty soon, you'll get sick of me and my constant demands on you. Because when I come home, I won't let you out of my sight for more than an hour."

"I can hardly wait," Cal happily announced. "As to getting sick of you, that day will never dawn. As implausible as it sounds, I love you and want you with all my heart and soul." The confession had accidentally slipped out, but she didn't correct or withdraw it.

"I'm probably the luckiest man alive to have you.

340

Have I ever told you how glad I am you came? You're the most important thing that's ever happened to me, Cal. I never knew such feelings existed in me. No woman had even lingered in my mind, but you. Do you comprehend what a terrible distraction you are?" he teased.

"I would prefer to be a wonderful attraction," she quipped.

"I'm gonna have to keep a sharp eye on you, woman. If I don't, you'll be leading me around like a horny bull in mating season."

"Then we should both be overjoyed that you possess such stamina and talents, my love." Her verdant eyes twinkled. "Now, all we need is time to take advantage of them. Just remember I'm waiting at home."

"That's one of my problems, I can't seem to forget it when I'm away. You take up so much of my time and attention, I work slowly and carelessly. You're a dangerous obsession, Callie."

Her features softened with a contented smile. "Good."

"Now that one appetite has been fed, how about some breakfast?"

"Only if I can prepare it," she hinted. "But first, I need to visit the water-shed. I might find it difficult to concentrate on cooking with your manly fragrance clinging to me."

Lynx chuckled. "You're a wanton hussy, my fetching wife. What's happened to you? You were never this carefree before."

"You happened to me, Lynx Cardone. Besides, we're married now. Am I behaving improperly for a wife? God, how I've missed you," she wailed, throwing her arms around his neck, drawing his mouth down to join with hers. "I can't bear the fact you're leaving."

"We're matched perfectly. We'll have a wonderful life together. Your appetite is as insatiable and ravenous as mine."

"It's your fault; you created it. If you're sorry, you've only yourself to blame. Since you're home so rarely and briefly, there isn't time for modesty or manners. I'd best stuff myself before my tasty food leaves again. Alas, how shall I face another period of starvation?"

Lynx threw back his head and chortled. "What's so amusing?" she asked, staring at him as the peals of joyful laughter subsided.

"I never knew a woman could be so much fun, especially not a wife. A man's supposed to feel trapped and bored, but you don't permit it. You never cease to amaze me, Callie," Lynx avowed.

"I hope I never do, my love."

As his mouth leisurely feasted at her breasts, she teased in rapidly rising passion, "I thought you were hungry."

"Starving, but not for breakfast just yet."

Her fingers tousled his dark gold hair. A tranquil sigh slipped out of her chest. He set a deliberately titillating pace to arouse her to another quest for rapture. Locked in each other's arms, they invaded the heady realm of passion's ecstasy and easily conquered it.

Her boldness most rewarding, Cal didn't protest when Lynx joined her in the overly large bathtub. They splashed and played as two children, laughing and teasing, soaping and rinsing each other. When Lynx's laughter would increase in volume, she would giggle and caution him to lower his voice. He would wink at her and declare he didn't care who heard him, after all they were married.

Lynx sat on the submerged wooden seat and pulled her down across his lap, her spread legs dangling over his thighs. Cal hugged him tightly as he trailed his lips over her shoulders and neck. When he fastened his mouth to a taut breast, she glanced down at his face. His eyes were closed dreamily as his lips and tongue played on the tiny summit. How was it possible to want him again so soon? How did his mere touch tempt her beyond reason? As if they hadn't made love for weeks or months, her body fiercely craved his.

When a hand sneaked below to investigate a small peak there, she lay her cheek on the top of his head and snuggled against him. Even if the water had been ice cold, it couldn't have cooled her body and passions. "Lynx, I want you so much. Why are you tormenting me here?"

"What's wrong with here, Callie?" he inquired thickly.

"We can't make love in a bathtub," she replied sultrily.

"Why not?" he debated, looking up into her glazed eyes.

A look of astonishment claimed her features. "You can?" she asked seriously, naively.

Lynx chuckled softly as he shifted his body and entered her, seizing her hips and gently forcing them tightly against his groin. Her eyes widened, then she burst into muffled laughter. "If you were home for longer periods, my love, you could teach me such lessons."

"You'd be shocked by how much I can teach you,

343

Callie."

"I doubt it. But I'm a bright and willing student," she whispered, causing him to shudder with anticipation as her tongue traced the contours of his ear before working on his sensitive earlobe.

Lynx artfully stirred her passions for a time, then withdrew. "Why did you stop?" she asked in lucid disappointment.

He stepped out of the tub and placed a padding of thick linens on the platform. He reached for her, lifting her out of the tub and placing her on her back on the make-shift bed. He entered her again as his mouth took possession of hers. Soon, they were riding the stormy waves of passion which eventually crested and ebbed into a serene pool.

Afterwards, he returned her to the tub and washed her from head to foot. After completing his own bath, he dried her off with a provocative slowness which threatened to re-whet her greedy appetite. "Now, Mrs. Cardone, does that earn me a sturdy farewell meal?"

"That, my love, earns you anything you desire from me."

"I think I've tied myself to a lecherous and demanding vixen. Are you trying to kill me, woman?" Lynx gleefully accused.

"I don't want a single hair on that devilish head harmed. I was just trying to give you a sample of Calinda Cardone, so you'll hurry home again. At least, maybe you'll be as lonely and miserable as I will."

"I knew it," he declared. "You're trying to disease me and drive me wild with discomfort. You know my only cure and appeasement is you. You're a sly vixen, Callie. Whatever shall I do with you?"

"Love me and keep me forever," she responded instantly.

"If I ever wanted to do anything more in my life, I can't imagine what," he informed her, grinning.

They returned to Lynx's room to dress, then Calinda cooked Lynx a big breakfast. As they were eating and chatting in the kitchen, the back door opened and Salina strolled in, her hips swaying and her lips sending out sultry messages to Lynx. She came to the table and spoke to Lynx, totally ignoring Calinda.

"I am late returning, Lynx. I see your *esposa* is feeding you properly. Will you be here for dinner?"

Lynx's left hand captured Calinda's right one beneath the table and squeezed it. "If you don't mind, Salina, Cal and I would like to be alone while we eat. We have some talking to catch up on before I leave soon." His smoldering gaze engulfed his wife's joyful expression.

"I have supplies to put away, Lynx. Surely I will not be in your way?" Salina reasoned petulantly, trying to spoil their contentment.

"I'm afraid you will, Salina. Run along until we're finished."

At his playful dismissal, Salina actually blushed for the first time in her life, a scarlet covering of mingled anger and embarrassment. She glanced at the serene Calinda who was forcing her loving gaze to remain locked on her love's face. "If that is what you want," she hinted.

Calinda was determined not to look at Salina and gloat smugly. Her heart was singing with happiness. Lynx placed their interlocked hands on the corner of the table, causing Salina's eyes to widen.

"That is what I want, Salina. Your chores can wait for me to say goodbye to my wife. Run along, and

345

close the door behind you."

Salina unknowingly gritted her teeth. "Would you like anything before I am tossed out? Coffee? More food?" she asked sassily.

Lynx glared at Salina. "You're getting a wee bit large for your fancy britches, Salina. I think you're forgetting who lives here and who just works here. One of those positions can change quickly," he warned subtly. "I was asking nicely. But now I'm telling you; get out of here before I lose my temper. If I need or want anything else, I have a most capable wife sitting beside me. I think it's past time you realize Calinda Cardone is the mistress of this house and ranch; don't force me to remind you again. I'm fully aware of your *hinchado*."

"But," Salina opened her mouth to dispute his statements.

"No buts!" he snarled. "You think I don't know how you've been treating her. I'm surprised she hasn't fired you or punished you."

Salina bit her tongue to keep from blurting out, she wouldn't dare! "What has she been telling you?" Salina asked, emphasizing the "she". "I do not understand why you act and talk this *salvaje* way."

"I spoke with Rankin about the conflict between you two. Callie didn't want to cause trouble, so she's kept silent. From now on, I'm demanding she tell me everything. She's been taking your crap for months to avoid problems. No longer, Salina. If you work for the Cardones, that includes my wife. If you can't endure her, then I suggest you start looking elsewhere for another job," he stated coldly.

Salina paled. "Where would I go? I have lived and worked here for five years! Where? How?"

"Things have changed, Salina, but you're refusing to accept those changes. It's time you decide if you want to remain with us."

"Lynx, let me give you my side," Salina entreated fearfully.

"Alto! Ya se acabo! That's what I'm talking about!" he thundered, switching to English for his wife's benefit. Exasperated, his fist struck the table, sloshing coffee from their cups, causing both women to jump in surprise. "There are no sides to be taken! I've never met anyone easier to get along with than Cal. If you give it some help, you two could get along fine. Is that clear?" When Salina nodded, he said, "Good, now leave us alone."

Salina left quickly. Lynx looked over at his wife, frowning. "Think I was too harsh?" he speculated.

"I should say yes, but I can't. I don't know if that scolding will help or hurt. But I promise to do my best with her, Lynx. She just resents me so much. Thanks," she murmured sweetly.

"It will help if you constantly remember you're a Cardone."

She lifted her left hand and gazed at her ring. "I will."

Calinda stood in the yard watching Lynx ride away from home, failing to move until even his dust vanished. She sighed, this time happily rather than angrily. For the first time, she was convinced they had a bright future together. She resolved that nothing and no one would dampen her gaiety or destroy her trust and happiness.

Today was Monday, July 1, 1878. With good luck and smiling fate, Lynx should be home before the end of this month . . .

Chapter Fifteen

As the days passed, Rankin noticed a pleasing change in Calinda. There was a serene glow to her cheeks and a happy sparkle in her eyes; she hummed merrily as if the entire world was in love and at peace. She didn't appear the least worried about her close call with peril. It was obvious; Calinda was deeply in love with Lynx.

As they talked, dined, and played cards, her laughter was bubbly and frequent. When Lynx was mentioned, a twinkle filled her eyes and spread warmth over her face. They didn't discuss his location or purpose. They merely enjoyed each other's company and wit.

To Salina's surprise, Calinda didn't become bossy and smug. It was as if Calinda was content to let Salina continue with her chores in her own way. When Calinda wanted to perform a particular task or help with one, she didn't ask; she simply did it. Salina couldn't believe the lack of gloating in the victorious Calinda. The new Mrs. Cardone seemed too preoccupied to notice what went on around her or be troubled by any menial problems.

Salina wisely accepted this curious behavior, observing it closely with intrigue. Until things settled down, she would make herself as unnoticeable as possible. She would be as quiet as a field mouse and as sweet as wild honey! Her time would come . . .

When Thursday arrived, Calinda told Rankin she didn't want to go to the July fourth celebration in town. She explained her motives for wanting to stay home, which included her absent husband. She told Rankin she didn't want to risk running into any of Stevens' men or Stevens himself, just in case they had hung around this area. When Rankin debated her points, Cal reminded him she couldn't identify any of the bandits. That notorious outlaw could stroll right up to her face, and she wouldn't know when to scream or run.

"They lost $50,000 on me, Rankin, surely more than any stage carries. They might try to snatch me again. I'd feel safer and happier here. I would be asked buckets of questions about Lynx's constant absences; I hate making phony excuses. I'm not a good liar or actress. I don't want people playing guessing games or starting rumors. Besides, it's hot and noisy in town. I heard you assign half the hands as guards this morning and half of them for this afternoon. I'll be perfectly safe."

"I suppose you're right, Cal. But I'll miss you with me today. It'll be hard to explain your absence since we don't want to let anyone know about the kidnapping. I warned Salina and my men not to say anything to anyone." But Calinda didn't know the real motive behind keeping it quiet, to protect Lynx's identity. Still, he didn't want any gossip about his family. From what Lynx had said, he had rescued Calinda just in the nick of time to spare her any degradation.

So, the holiday passed with Calinda under heavy

guard, reading a book while Rankin had a merry time in town.

Under Ranger McNelly's leadership on Friday, Lynx and Tom Peters set a trap for Cole Stevens and his gang. Five miles before reaching Big Sandy Creek, they halted the stage. The three passengers were taken aside to be picked up after the foiled robbery; they were to wait in the wagon until the lawmen returned with their prisoners. The three Rangers hid themselves inside the coach and headed to defeat the outlaws. McNelly told them to wait until the stage was stopped and the bandits were nearby, to shoot anyone who tried to escape.

All went as planned. As the driver slowed to ford the wide creek, the stage was approached by four heavily armed outlaws. As instructed, the driver and guard didn't make any precarious moves.

"Throw down that strong-box, and we'll be on our way without any shooting," Cole ordered the driver, lazily propping his crossed wrists on his saddle horn, his gun pointing negligently into the air.

The guard struggled to lift the heavy metal box and tossed it to the ground. Instantly he and the driver sank into the protective area in the shotgun box at their feet. The coach door sprang open, McNelly bravely exposing himself as Tom and Lynx simultaneously appeared in the windows. The three Rangers sent forth warning shots.

McNelly shouted, "Rangers! Throw down your guns or be killed!"

Two of the outlaws quickly obeyed, tossing away their guns and lifting their hands. Oggie and Will didn't want to challenge such deadly odds. As if prearranged, Little Red and Cole Stevens fled in opposite directions. The three Rangers bounded from the stage. Tom trained his two pistols on Oggie and Will. Glancing in both directions, McNelly shouted to Lynx. "You take Stevens! That way."

McNelly knew how much Lynx wanted to defeat his foe, so he fired at the fleeing carrot-haired Little Red, winging him with skill.

Lynx fumed at Cole's flight. Lynx wanted to yank Cole off his saddle and beat him senseless. Without Star to pursue him, Lynx had no choice but to shoot or let Cole make his escape. He aimed his Colt and squeezed the trigger twice, striking Cole in the left thigh and right arm, the one gripping his reins. The bandit wavered and fell off his horse, the frightened animal continuing his terrified pace.

Lynx rushed to where Cole had fallen. Cole was holding his wounded arm across his stomach and gripping the profusely bleeding wound on his leg with his left hand. When Lynx swaggered to where Cole sat in agonizing pain, Lynx towered over him, grinning in pleasure.

Cole stared at him. "What the hell are you doing here?"

"Helping the Rangers clear this land of rattlesnakes," Lynx sneered, kicking his injured leg, recalling Cole's treatment of Calinda.

Cole grimaced in anguish. Lynx snarled at him, "You'd best be glad you didn't hurt my wife any worse than you did, Cole, or you'd be choking on your own blood right this moment. The Rangers will put you away a long time, if they don't hang you, you bloody bastard!"

Cole scoffed, "You're just riled that Unknown Ranger saved her instead of you. Did the little wife fall for that courageous man?"

"How could she? She's in love with me," Lynx stated smugly.

"Didn't look that way to me. She was even willing to do anything I said to earn her freedom. She's a damn good kisser with fiery blood."

"Forget it, Cole. The Ranger was outside the window when you forced her to kiss you to gain some fresh air. It might interest you to know that's why she asked for the window up and the light out. If her hands hadn't been tied, she would have scratched out your eyeballs. She said she nearly puked when she followed the Ranger's orders."

Cole stiffened in fury. "That good for nothing bitch! If I ever get my hands on her again, I'll . . ."

Lynx grabbed Cole by the front of his shirt and yanked him to his feet. He delivered several blows into Cole's face and gut with lightning speed and forceful strength. "I'll kill you if you even think about her in passing," Lynx warned ominously at Cole's threat.

Cole doubled over with pain. Blood seeped from cuts at the corner of his mouth and left eye. A shirt sleeve and pants leg were saturated with crimson liquid. "If I ever get loose, Cardone, I'll kill you for this," he mumbled, spitting blood on the dry ground.

Torn between a desire for revenge and a duty to justice, Lynx scathingly declared, "If those Rangers weren't standing over there, Cole, you'd be a dead man. I'm a fool all right; I should have come alone and dealt with you. I'll see that you either hang or rot in prison. Mark my words," he vowed confidently.

When Lynx dragged Cole over to the waiting stage, Cole began protesting his beating, claiming a man wasn't guilty until tried.

McNelly glanced at the bloody Cole and stated calmly, "I didn't see Cardone lift a finger against you, other than to prevent you from escaping after an attempted hold-up which I personally witnessed and will testify to in court. Seems I was busy with your surprise."

Lynx gaped at the belligerent and lovely female with fiery red curls. Little Red was a woman! He promptly realized how the successful scouting was carried out. Who would suspect an attractive woman of spying! His astonishment mounted when he learned her name, Callie O'Hara. "So you're Darlin' Nelle's cousin," he murmured reflectively, absorbing the image of past misconceptions. Two fiery-headed Callies.

"So you're Calinda Braxton's husband," she sneered hatefully. "Too bad Cole didn't let his men work her over good. I doubt a Cardone would have taken back used goods."

McNelly glanced at Lynx, but Lynx merely smiled satanically at Cole and Callie. Lynx hoped McNelly didn't suspect the truth. With each mission, more Rangers were discovering his identity and more people were suspecting it. He wished he could confide in McNelly, but he needed to keep silent a while longer. The more who knew, the less effect he had. Since Tom was Lynx's contact with Jones, Tom was one of the few who knew who left that warning mark behind. How he wished he could tell Cal.

McNelly promised to take care of Cole and his men before Lynx headed out for Waco to catch up on the news of the Bass gang. From Murphy's traitorous reports, the gang was heading south from Dallas, their target either Waco or Round Rock. Murphy was to let Jones know something definite this week. Lynx had been ordered to remain at Waco until word arrived. Before leaving the Rangers, Lynx sent a telegram home, telling Rankin and Calinda about the defeat of the Stevens gang. He said he would send word again when possible.

Lynx paced his room in Waco for three days before word came from Murphy, saying the target was the bank at Round Rock on Friday, either July 12 or 19, according to how things looked in town when they arrived. Most of the time Lynx could cover his involvement with his gunslinger reputation as a paid assistant or as a favor to a Ranger friend. But this mission would unavoidably reveal his identity to several noted lawmen. On July 8, Lynx rode out of Waco, heading for Round Rock to meet with Major Jones and other famed Rangers.

It was Lynx's assignment to mingle in the saloons, watching for any sign of Bass or his men. When Friday the twelfth came and went, it was concluded Bass would strike the next Friday. An urgent message came from Murphy: Round Rock Bank on the nineteenth.

Lynx had a week to while away in that rowdy cowtown. He missed Calinda and wanted to get home. None of the Rangers were allowed to send telegrams or letters out of Round Rock—it was vital that they maintain a low profile. The days were arid and boring; the nights, long and stuffy. For the first time in his Ranger career, Lynx became edgy and restless. It had been over two weeks since he'd been with Calinda, with over another week to go before he could even think of heading toward her arms.

At the ranch, things were going much the same for Calinda and Rankin. With the capture of the Cole Stevens gang, Rankin didn't lower his guard. He was concerned over another outlaw trying where Cole had failed. Calinda often went riding with Rankin or helped with the stable chores. When the day was too hot or was rainy, she found tasks inside to occupy her mind.

Lynx had sent a telegram on the sixth, but nothing since then. She fretted over his safety and the lack of word from him. Neighbors came to call several times, giving Calinda a chance to get better acquainted and to entertain. Twice she and Rankin went to visit friends of his, staying for dinner both times.

It had been seventeen days since Lynx cheerfully rode away from the ranch. As if in a lull before a powerful storm, Calinda and Salina had practiced good conduct. They had been careful to avoid arguing or fencing; even their thinly veiled insults had ceased. They were civil to each other even when Rankin wasn't around. It seemed as if each was finally resigned to the other's role in the Cardone house.

As the days slowly drifted by, Calinda experienced mild discontent and loneliness; she was too inactive. She missed Lynx terribly, but she also missed female companionship and the engrossing facets of society and civilization. She longed for exciting evenings at amusing plays, elaborate dinners, and gay parties. She missed the enthralling shops which larger towns offered. She loved Rankin and the ranch, but there was little to do but dreary chores or the same masculine games each day. Cal was educated and vivacious; she missed fascinating people and enlivening events. She liked the hired hands, but there was little in common with them. Amusement here might include a swim in the pond or a raucous game of horseshoes. If she were really lucky, there might be a taxing dinner or barbecue where the conversations centered on cattle, horses, the weather, or violence. The people here were kind and nice, but their sole interest appeared to be daily existence. Surely she would get accustomed to the monotonous routine and lack of diversions. If only she had at least one female friend, but the women here were too busy for such relationships.

Calinda wondered if the hardships, sacrifices, boredom, and loneliness were the factors behind Laura's misery and malicious behavior. Had Laura taken her unhappiness out on her husband and son? Calinda recalled Lynx's allusions to Laura's love of money and power; out here, those were critical defenses, means for survival. She couldn't be right, for Laura had been blessed with her husband's and son's presence.

When word failed to arrive from Lynx, Salina's old suspicions surfaced and blossomed. She told herself that nasty scene in the kitchen had been for Calinda's benefit, to further disarm and enchant her. Evidently Calinda didn't feel secure in her role, or she would be taking over by now. Was Calinda afraid to test her importance? Perhaps Lynx had given her a scolding in private, warned her to behave or be sent on her way. Still, Calinda was settling in too firmly. Something had to done to shake her confidence and trust. Salina's resentments had festered with time and suppression; they were ready to burst open and spew forth their viciousness. Salina couldn't forget that revealing conversation between Rankin and Lynx, those dark secrets in her favor . . .

It had been pouring rain for two days, and Calinda was confined to the house. Lightning slashed across the dark sky. Violent claps of thunder rattled the windows; twice, windy gusts blew them open, allowing rain to soak the floor. The house was immaculate; laundry had to be postponed. There was little to do; Rankin was in Fort Worth on business.

Calinda had read constantly for the past two days. She was bored and tense. An idea came to her restive mind; she could clean the attic. Attics were always fun. Hidden treasures were discovered; adventures could be imagined. Perhaps there was something of value stored there, perhaps old furniture which could be re-finished and used. Perhaps it contained boyhood prizes of her husband, items to warm her heart and lighten her mood on a dreary day. She almost invited Salina to go along, for she had been pleasant lately. Since they were the only two women around, it was foolish to be enemies. Calinda decided against it, dreading her invitation would send Salina off on one of her unpredictable tirades. At least, they were speaking and not quarreling. Perhaps in time . . .

Calinda took a lantern and mounted the steps. Once inside, she glanced around. She grinned in pleasure. The attic was filled with boxes and trunks, old furniture, and such. She inched her way around, peeking here and there. She abruptly laughed. Never had she thought the day would come when a musty, cluttered attic was the highlight of her existence! But it would be different when Lynx came home.

To her disappointment, most of the trunks were empty. She realized those were the ones which had contained Laura's clothes. Two other trunks were sealed by rusty locks. There was an interesting crate of old books which she could check later. She found a beautifully carved wash-stand which would be lovely if refinished. She found boy's clothing, snuggling them to her heart. She wondered what it would be like to have her own child, Lynx's baby. There were two crates of old toys, some in excellent or fair condition and others irreparable. She trailed her fingers over a cradle, trying to envision her love tiny and crying inside of it. There were odds and ends which should be discarded.

On the far wall was a painting covered with a moldy sheet. Cal removed the filthy covering, sneezing as dust scattered around her. She stared at the exquisite woman in the portrait. The woman was small, but very shapely. Her skin looked as if the radiant sun itself had kissed it gently with a golden tan. Her silvery gold hair hung to her waist, curling ever so slightly. Her eyes appeared as tawny as precious topaz. There was no doubt; the woman was Lynx's mother.

Calinda moved closer, holding the lantern up for more light. If the oils didn't lie or exaggerate, there was a vivid sparkle of life in Laura's exquisite face, especially her compelling eyes. Her features were delicate, she had a face which could stun a man speechless. Lynx definitely favored his breathtaking mother. Cal understood what Rankin had meant by seeing Laura in Lynx's smile and twinkling eyes.

As Calinda turned her head to one side, she observed a curious aspect which she hadn't noticed at first glance. On closer study, there seemed to be a softly provocative countenance about Laura Cardone. Perhaps it was the artist's interpretation or a trick of the lighting. But Laura's expression and pose created an impression of untameable wildness, a radiant and carefree spirit, a playful seductiveness. It was as if Laura knew she was a beautiful creature who could take or give if it suited her purpose, a woman accustomed to having her way. How Calinda wished she had known this unique woman.

Standing there, Calinda couldn't imagine this ravishing beauty as a deprived pioneer in a raw and dangerous land, or screaming in pain in a lonely mountain shack while giving birth to Lynx, or tranquilly enduring the kind of existence which Calinda was living now. Laura Cardone was a woman who seemed to belong in expensive gowns and jewels, in a large town where civilization was at its peak, or on an English estate with countless servants and a husband with the king's ear. Laura Cardone definitely didn't appear the cowgirl type.

Laura must have loved Rankin deeply to share his earlier days in this rugged territory. Rankin must have loved her, for he still carried scars from her death. And Lynx, how could this vital creature deny all love for her only son? Could it be she hadn't wanted children? Could it have been the harsh circumstances around his birth which caused her to resent him, to avoid having other children? Surely some tragic misunderstanding was at the bottom of their problem? Oddly, Laura's image didn't imply arrogance, but immense pride and self-assurance. Calinda couldn't find any traces of coldness and cruelty. Obviously, Laura had changed drastically after the flattering portrait.

The painting was splendid, but the heat and moisture were taking their toll. Had they placed it here to keep from facing it each day, a painful reminder of her loss? Would seeing it again re-open those unhealed wounds? It was too costly and beautiful to be ruined in the attic. If they didn't want it hung downstairs, she should at least clean it and store it properly. One day, the anguish would be gone; one day her children would like to view their grandmother.

Calinda carried the painting downstairs to the kitchen. She carefully placed it on the table to scrub gently. She would return it to the attic and cover it tightly to prevent damage. As she worked, Calinda wondered about this ravishing creature.

Also bored, Salina was straightening the pantry. She heard Calinda come into the kitchen. Strange noises reached her ears, enticing her to investigate. When Salina moved to glance into the kitchen, she couldn't believe the sight before her wide eyes. Surely Calinda wasn't planning what she thought! Rankin and Lynx would be furious when they came home, to find that treacherous harlot's picture hanging again! Salina smiled maliciously. *Let Cal do as she pleased* . . .

Another thought flashed through Salina's wicked mind. They would simply claim grief and take it down. They would never tell Calinda the truth. Somehow she needed to inspire mistrust in Calinda. This was the perfect moment to expose one damaging secret . . .

Salina sauntered into the kitchen, sighing wearily. "If you will not tattle, I will sneak a brandy," she murmured. "What are you . . ." She dramatically halted and gaped at the object of Calinda's attention. "Where . . . did you get that?" she stammered as if shocked.

Calinda glanced over at Salina, puzzled by her behavior. "What's wrong? I'm not harming it. It shouldn't have been hung in the attic; it's nearly ruined. Perhaps a good cleaning will have it lovely again."

"You cannot hang that down here," Salina fearfully mumbled, staring at the painting as if mesmerized by a horrifying demon.

"You look as if you're seeing a ghost, Salina. It's only an old painting of Laura Cardone, a very good one. It would be terrible to allow it to deteriorate," she explained.

"What are you planning to do with it?" Salina continued her game to spark Calinda's intrigue. Matters had gone so well between them recently that Calinda shouldn't suspect a thing. Salina was aware of Calinda's friendly overtures and genial manner lately. Salina had been pretending to gradually mellow toward Calinda. For the past two days alone, she had compelled herself to converse politely with Calinda.

"I don't know. Why?" Calinda asked in rising intrigue. Salina was behaving so strangely—she looked panicky; why?

"If I were you, I would put it back this *momento,*" Salina advised, her voice strained and her gaze wary.

Calinda halted her work to look at Salina. "Why?" she asked.

"*No importe,*" Salina stated, her gaze staying locked on Laura.

There was a knock on the front door. Calinda said she would see who was there. It was one of the hands checking on them for Rankin. Salina peeked around the corner, watching Calinda speak with Charlie, then close the door and head her way. She hurried over to the painting and stared down at it, muttering, "If she knew the truth about you and her papa, you traitorous *puta,* she would burn it."

Salina turned to fetch her brandy from the front room. She jumped as if startled by Calinda's presence and a quizzical stare. "Who was it?" she asked, trying to sway Cal. "Want a brandy?" she offered.

"What truth, Salina?" she demanded tacitly.

"Truth?" she repeated, her black eyes darting around as if trying to think of a hasty explanation.

"I heard you. What about my father and Laura?"

"I do not know what you are talking about," Salina declared, exhibiting phony panic and noticeable dishonesty.

Calinda walked over to the table and gazed down at the image. "Why did you call her a traitorous *puta?* What is a *puta?* Why did you say I would burn it if I knew the truth?" Calinda pressed stubbornly.

"You must have misunderstood me. I was just . . . just

muttering about a saloon girl in town who is making eyes at my *hombre*," the Mexican girl alleged saucily.

"You're lying," Calinda charged.

Salina forced herself to look even more edgy and secretive. "Do not be silly. Do you want a brandy?" she asked again, acting as if she were trying to pacify Calinda.

When she tried to leave the kitchen, Calinda seized her arm and prevented her flight. "I heard you plainly, Salina. Now tell me what you were talking about," Calinda persisted. "What do you know about my father? Don't lie to me," she commanded sternly.

"I never met your papa; he was gone before I came to work here. My chores are finished. I will rest for a while. Do you want me to cook your dinner tonight?" the malicious girl offered sweetly.

"What I want is an explanation, now," Calinda demanded.

"About what?" Salina stalled intentionally.

"Damnit, Salina! If you don't speak up, I'll question Rankin."

Salina inhaled sharply and rapidly shook her head. "No, you cannot!" The words seemed to burst forth uncontrollably. "I am in *mucho* trouble here because of you. Have you not noticed how good I have been lately? You will spill your guts the minute *Senor* Rankin or Lynx returned, just like you did about Lampasas," she accused.

"I didn't tell Lynx anything except what we agreed on. You're the one who betrayed our bargain!" Calinda retorted angrily.

"No, I did not! I only said I did to aggravate you."

"But why?" Calinda inquired.

"I wanted to make you miserable, to leave. I never expected them to ask you to live here. I was shocked when Lynx married you. I love him for years; then you stroll in and take him without even lifting a finger to snare him. Things were fine until you came. I was happy; they were like my family. But you have changed everything; all they care about is you and keeping you happy. I know part of the trouble was mine. I wanted to prove you did not belong here with us. Maybe I am wrong, but I do not trust you."

"If I've made you unhappy, Salina, I'm sorry. It wasn't intentional. You've known Lynx for a long time. Can you blame me for falling in love with him? But I don't want to push you out. Why can't we make a fresh start and become friends? We're the only women for miles. It would be fun to work together and talk. Is that impossible?"

"It is too late, *senora*. We have been too mean to each other. We could never trust each other," Salina cunningly hedged.

Challenged, Calinda argued, "That isn't true, Salina."

"You would suspect everything I say or do. If I confided in you, you would run to the Cardones, and they would get rid of me. I feel I live on borrowed time here. I have tried to be nice to you since Lynx left, *si?* But I do not see how we can become *amigas.*"

"I've proven I can be trusted, Salina. Haven't I tried to ease your concerns and stay out of your way? I can see how these changes have been difficult for you, but you must accept them. Please."

As Salina pensively mused on Calinda's words, Calinda asked, "What are you trying to conceal from me about my father?"

Salina shifted nervously. "If I dared open my mouth, you would tell them. You could not help it. You would insist on more facts or try to solve the problem. You cannot. What is done is done, *senora*. Forget about your papa and the past. It is trouble for all of us."

"If you weren't here, how could you know anything vital? Do you spy on the Cardones?" Cal asked, trying to trick Salina into a defensive disclosure.

"No!" Salina shrieked. "But I could not help but learn certain things over the years. Sometimes they forget I am around and talk too freely. But I do not listen at door cracks, so do not accuse me of such."

"What did you overhear, Salina?" she insisted firmly.

"I cannot repeat it," Salina defied her demand.

"I'll ask Rankin to explain your statements, if you don't."

"If you speak to him about this, you will be *mucho* sorry, *senora*. If he does not lie to you, you will regret forcing the truth from him. Do not remind *Senor* Rankin or Lynx you are a Braxton. Hide the picture and forget Laura Cardone and your papa."

Something about the provocative inflection on those two names linked together inspired suspicion in Calinda. Both left the same day. Lynx had called her father traitorous; Salina had called Laura traitorous. Everyone refused to discuss either. "I might be sorry later, Salina, but I'm going to unmask the truth."

"You do not hear me, *senora;* everyone will suffer. They will demand to know how you discovered such clues. I will be fired, perhaps beaten!" she blurted out anxiously.

"I swear to you I'll keep silent," Calinda vowed desperately.

"Not after you learn why he ran!" Salina shouted at her.

"I promise you, I'll never mention either of them or

the past if you'll tell me what you know," Calinda tried once more to convince her.

"*Demonio!* I am trapped between devils and demons!" Salina ranted. "If I keep silent, you will talk with *Senor* Rankin. If I speak, you still might. Either way, I am doomed. Why did you have to come here causing trouble and digging up the past? Why would you even take my word? You will think I lie just to hurt you! There is no guessing what they will do to me. You are too damn tender-hearted! You will try to ease their pains; I know you will," she panted, as if that trait were an insult. Both girls jumped as thunder crashed nearby.

"If you lie to me out of malice, Salina, I'll make you sorry."

"That is the problem! You will think so," she charged heatedly.

"This has gone far enough. If you don't explain yourself, I'll speak to Rankin the minute he returns. If you tell me, I give you my word I won't repeat it to them, no matter what it is."

Salina guilefully paced the floor, fretting and thinking. "All right, *senora,* but I warned you. *Primero,* I need a brandy." She fled into the other room and quickly downed two glasses, pouring another to sip. She handed Calinda a sherry. "You might need that, and you must sit down," she advised gravely.

Salina roamed the spacious area for a time. Calinda said, "Stop stalling, Salina." Salina turned and met her probing gaze.

"I was trying to decide where to begin," she murmured.

"Why not at the beginning?" Calinda suggested, annoyed.

"I do not know the beginning, only the end. I know

why your papa vanished, and I know why the Cardones hate him."

Salina sank into a chair, acting as if this confession was weighty. "Your papa was *Senora* Cardone's lover. When *Senor* Rankin discovered their affair, he confronted them together *en cama,* in bed. There was a terrible fight, and *Senor* Rankin was injured. While he was unconscious, your papa stole money, *mucho* money, and escaped. Lynx was the one who found his bloody papa. Lynx loved your papa. You can imagine how the truth hurt him. Your papa betrayed them, used them, and destroyed their family. Can you see how *Senor* Rankin felt when he learned his wife was whoring with his *amigo? Peor,* in his *cama,* his *casa?* That is why Lynx hates women and does not trust them," she vowed.

Calinda was gaping at her in stunned disbelief. Salina went on, "How could they allow you to step foot in this *casa* after what your papa did to them. I suspected *venganza,* revenge; they could punish or trap your papa with you. As a *presa,* they could lure your father out of hiding. But when Lynx married you, I was confused. He would not go that far to punish *el enemigo.* He must love you to lose his freedom."

When Salina halted to catch a breath, Calinda still remained silent and stiff. "Do you see why they will not speak of the past and your papa? Do you see why you cannot hang that picture? I will never understand why they did not burn it and her things. Why would *Senor* Rankin give her clothes to you, to see such reminders of that *bruja?*"

"What is a *puta?* A *bruja?* What happened to Laura? Did Rankin kill her in a fit of rage? Did she take her own life? She was too young to die naturally. If my father loved her enough to do such things, why leave her behind?" Calinda questioned in a strained voice.

"If you repeat this, I will deny every word. That grave on the hillside is for protection, to save face. *Bruja* is witch; *puta* is whore. *Senora* Laura is not dead; she ran away with your papa. She sacrificed her *casa, esposo, nombre,* and *hijo* for your papa. She has sent no word to Lynx since she left. That is why he went to roaming the countryside, searching for them. *Acaso* he still looks for his *madre.* When *Senor* Rankin healed, he told everyone your papa had run off to new pastures; he said *Senora* Laura died of a sudden illness. Very few people know the truth. See why I feared to speak such words?"

"How could they do such a cruel thing? If they loved each other, why didn't Laura divorce Rankin and marry my father? How could she desert her own child? Never see him again? Never communicate with him?" Cal reasoned in anguish.

"Your papa did the same to you and your *madre, Senora* Cal," Salina added softly, to send her incisive point home.

"It can't be true, Salina," she argued against the searing truth.

"You must tell no one of our talk. *Tener cuidado,* be careful. Do not keep reminding them you are Braxton's *hija.* Your papa will never return here and risk his life. He dares not contact you and give away his location. Forget him; you have sided with the Cardones."

"I can't! I must learn why it happened," Calinda stated dejectedly.

"Why does anyone fall in love? Why is anyone selfish and cruel? There are no *bueno* answers to such questions. If you go seeking more answers or your *mal* papa, you will lose Lynx and *Senor* Rankin," she warned anxiously. "You are lucky to live here, more so to have

Lynx."

"How could they stand to even look at me?"

"You know the truth. Can you stand to look at them? Does it change your *amor* for Lynx?" she craftily pointed out such emotions to gain Calinda's trust and imperative silence. Let Cal be plagued with doubts and insecurities, but suffer in agonizing silence.

"Where could they be?" Calinda mused aloud.

"Anywhere, *Senora* Cal. They would be *loco* not to put a great distance between them and the Cardones."

"But what about that letter for me to come to Lampasas?"

"*Acaso* that is why Lynx was so alarmed. He knew it could not be from your papa. Do you think Cole Stevens sent it?"

"No. Maybe it wasn't from my father, but it might have been from a contact of his. If I was being lured into a trap by an unknown enemy, nobody showed up to seal it. Still, I'm glad Lynx came along," she murmured gratefully.

"That was lucky for you. It did teach you how danger-ous this area can be and how much you need the Car-dones. It also inspired Lynx to marry you. So, it was not all bad," Salina dropped little seeds to take root in Calin-da's mind and to grow entangling vines there.

"Are you positive that's what happened, Salina?"

"I can only repeat what I heard; I cannot swear it is true."

"You're right about one thing; I can't discuss this with them." Calinda missed Salina's satanic smile.

It was working beautifully. Salina asked, "Would you like me to put that picture where it belongs, in that dark attic? You did not say; do you want me to cook dinner before I leave?"

"Leave?" Calinda inquired.

"I go to town. A *buen mozo vaquero*," Salina lied skill-fully.

After Salina interpreted her words about meeting a very handsome cowboy, Calinda said, "You go along and dress. I can take care of dinner and the portrait. There's little else to do tonight."

Salina headed for the door. She stopped and glanced at Calinda, relieved Calinda was too distraught to remind her of the storm outside. Within the hour, Salina would be forcing Lynx from her mind in the arms of some man yet to be selected for that urgent purpose. Besides, her body was aching for a man's passionate touch. "You have no reason to trust me, *Senora* Cal, but I swear your papa and *Senora* Cardone ran away together. You will not tell?" she pressed, as if anxious.

"No. Thank you, Salina. Would you like to borrow a dress to wear tonight?" Calinda generously offered.

"I do not wish to wear anything of that *puta's*," she refused.

"Neither do I," Calinda concurred absently.

Salina tensed in panic. "If you stop wearing them and start acting strange, they will know something is wrong," she speculated.

"Not if I buy new clothes." Calinda solved that dilemma.

"It must be nice," Salina sighed dreamily, envious.

"I'll buy you a new dress, too," Calinda decided aloud.

"You must not; that will look just as odd," Salina remarked.

"Not if we keep it a secret," she refuted, smiling faintly.

"I do not think we wear the same kinds of clothes," Salina discouraged any show of kindness from her rival.

"Then I'll give you the money to select your own."

"*Por que,* why?" Salina asked seriously, amused.

"An offer of friendship," Calinda declared honestly.

"Perhaps I have been wrong about you," Salina hinted.

"Maybe we've both been in error," Calinda added, smiling.

"See you in the morning. Do not forget to lock up," Salina reminded her, sauntering out of the room. She wanted Calinda to be alone in the quiet house, to have privacy and time to think . . .

Calinda sat in the shadowy room for a long time, then went into the kitchen. She lifted the portrait and stared at it, trying to envision this woman in past reality. She mentally placed Laura beside her father, or how he had looked long ago. Truthfully, she might not even recognize him today if she passed within a foot of him! Surely he had changed with time and age.

Was selfish, wanton love the answer she had been seeking to his disappearance? Real love was precious and rare; could the desire for it entice such cruelty and betrayal? Had they been so desperate to be together? Or had they simply fled out of discovery and fear? Hadn't she and Lynx deserved just one letter from them? Were they still alive somewhere? Had they regretted their decision, if only once? Were they happy? How could they be happy when they had obtained it with the sufferings of others?

Calinda never doubted Salina's words; for that shocking revelation logically explained her father's actions and the Cardones' behavior and innuendoes. Although she felt Salina had told the truth, Cal helplessly suspected malicious motives. She returned the portrait to where she had found it, wishing she had never laid eyes on it or

Salina had tricked her into pressing for the truth. She wandered around the house, locking and checking doors and windows. She went to the room shared with her husband when he was home. She pried open the drawer and withdrew her locket. She opened it and studied the stranger.

"Why, Father? How could you do such evil things?" she asked.

She sat down on the edge of the bed, sobbing. How she wished Lynx were here to comfort her. Yet she couldn't even hint at this devastating discovery. How could she pretend she didn't know? How could she keep it from him? Still, she must.

Now that she knew the truth, their silence was understandable. A mingling of male pride and affection for her had imprisoned their tongues. In fact, they had never said Laura was dead. They always said "gone" or "left." It was painfully clear why they didn't want to talk about Laura or Brax or the past: they were all interconnected. Laura's betrayal had crushed Lynx; he had justifiable reasons for doubting her love. The truth explained so much about Lynx. He had cause to be bitter and cynical.

Calinda was glad they had met before he learned her identity. If they hadn't, Lynx would never have given them a chance. "Oh, Lynx, I'm so sorry for what Brax did to you. I wish I could erase the past and your pain, but I can't. Let the past die. Please don't punish us for our parents' deed. Please don't seek revenge against them."

Punish, the word rang across her mind. Her weeping abruptly subsided. "Stop it!" she ordered herself. "Don't even vaguely consider such vile thoughts." But the speculations grew larger and wilder in her warring mind as the storm outside increased its fury. Revenge . . .

Cal couldn't deny they had wanted to keep her at the ranch. She couldn't rationally explain her hasty marriage. She knew they had kept the truth from her, had tried to stop her search.

It couldn't be true! Lynx wouldn't marry her just to lure her father back. A more ominous thought forced itself into her dazed mind; would he entrap her with love and marriage, then seek revenge or appeasement by copying her treacherous father's actions? Could Lynx hate her father that deeply, that obsessively? Could Lynx seek to repay Brax by destroying his child? Were Lynx and Rankin in on some treacherous plot? But who was their intended victim, her or her father? Was she only a pawn in a vindictive game?

Calinda's mind raced backward to her arrival, then slowly walked forward to this moment. She didn't like what she was thinking. What had Lynx said that day when she ventured, "Love me and keep me forever"? He had replied, "If I ever wanted to do anything more in my life . . ." Wanted to do? Had he ever said, I love you? He usually said, "need" or "want." Was physical desire enough to compel marriage? No. She analyzed the damaging clues.

The locket . . . Had Lynx been one of the bandits that day? Had he known who she was that night in the saloon? Positively, he wasn't that roguish and lecherous leader. But were they friends? Was he a merry bandit, seeking daring challenges while keeping his identity a secret? Was that why he had kept the precious necklace from her, preventing discovery?

The letter . . . Had Lynx planted that mysterious letter to lure her into danger, danger from which he would rescue her, danger which would bring her under his control? A rescue to indebt and beguile her? Was Clint

Deavers another friend and assistant?

Waco . . . How had they accidentally run into each other? Had Rankin informed Lynx of her visit, to allow Lynx to work his charms on her? Had Lynx been watching her to see if her father would contact her? Lynx had discouraged her about seeking the Rangers' help. Why?

Cole Stevens . . . Had Lynx planned that terrifying scheme? What new lesson was it supposed to teach her? Cole had called her Callie. Had Stevens truly been captured? Perhaps Lynx had warned his outlaw friends!

Lynx had too many secrets, too many connections to dangerous men, too many timely rescues! The newspaper announcements . . . Were they crafty enticements for Brax?

"No!" she cried out in torment. Why was she doing this to herself? It was all a series of coincidences and strokes of good fortune!

Calinda remembered something Lynx had said about mistrusting her in the beginning. Surely they didn't think she and her father were plotting some mischief? For what? They knew Brax wouldn't return here; he had taken Laura with him. They couldn't possibly believe she would help Brax and Laura alter that missing deed to steal the ranch!

If Lynx didn't trust her, why would he marry her? If anything happened to him and Rankin, the ranch would be . . . hers. *My God,* she fretted, *surely they wouldn't set themselves up as targets for Brax and Laura?* If the Cardones were removed, those two could return home and take everything. That logic was insane! Or desperately evil and vengeful . . .

Calinda forced such terrible speculations from her mind. She knew and loved both Lynx and Rankin. They could never plan and carry out such evil. Her mind was playing tricks on her. It must be the gloomy solitude and the violent storm, one which was raging as wildly outside the house as the emotional one inside of her.

They might have mistrusted and disliked her in the beginning, but not now. It just wasn't possible. Surely they were only protecting her from anguish and themselves from shame. Missing puzzle pieces were causing her imagination to run crazy. She returned the locket and went to bed, ordering herself to forget this entire day.

Chapter Sixteen

By Friday, July 19, there were six Rangers hiding out in Round Rock: Major Jones, Dick Ware, Tom Peters, George Harrell, Chris Connor, and Lynx Cardone. In addition to the Ranger force, the sheriff and several deputies were available. It was decided that the Rangers would remain concealed, but the local lawmen would move around as normal to prevent suspicion. The waiting had begun when the bank opened; it was presently mid-afternoon.

Connor was visually scouting the street from the grimy windows, the other men relaxing after their turns. They had consumed cold ham and biscuits, washed down with strong coffee. As time continued to crawl by like a sluggish snail, someone said that Bass had probably changed his mind. Murphy had reported that Bass and his men were watching him like a hawk, so something must have gone awry.

The deputies were milling around aimlessly, or so it appeared to the innocent eye. The day was hot and clear.

Each man sensed this could be his last one and mentally prepared for a deadly confrontation.

"Anything, Chris?" Jones inquired from his chair.

"Three cowpokes just rode in. Stopping at the saloon. No sign of trouble or Murphy." Connor's eyes scanned the entire street.

"From the last message, there should be four of them. You all have Murphy's description; he'll be impossible to miss."

In the saloon, Sam Bass and two of his men swaggered over to the wooden bar and ordered whiskies. They headed for a table and sat down to relax. Trying to get a message to the Rangers about the change in plans, Murphy had claimed his horse had a sand crack in his front hoof, halting by the stable to get help. The nervous traitor stalled for a lengthy spell, just in case he was being watched. He had to locate a lawman and tell him the robbery would take place tomorrow; he wanted out of this perilous bargain as quickly as possible.

Two deputies walked over to the saloon to check out the three strangers, one waiting outside and one entering. The deputy nodded to the bartender and wandered about the nearly deserted saloon. When he came to the strangers, he remarked genially, "I see you cowpokes are still toting yer sidearms. Ain't allowed in town. Check 'em with the barkeeper or ride on through. Ain't seen you fel . . ."

The deputy didn't complete his sentence before one of the outlaws drew his gun and fatally shot him. The deputy waiting outside looked over the batwing doors. He, too, was killed instantly by the panicky gang, the frail wood splintering as two bullets blasted through it and into the unsuspecting lawman's body. His torso struck forcefully by the gunfire, the second deputy was hurled backward into the dusty street. The outlaws raced out the door and fled toward their horses.

Ware shouted, "Bet it's them!"

The Rangers surged out of the building, opening fire and shouting instructions to halt. Seaborn Barnes was struck by a lethal bullet before he could cross the dirt street. Bass took a direct hit and staggered. Frank Jackson reached the horses and mounted frantically. Seeing Bass was wounded, Jackson fetched both horses and helped the injured Bass to mount. Both men galloped out of town, bullets and dust flying all around them. Out of range, the shooting ceased.

When the dust and suspense settled, Murphy revealed himself, reminding Jones he was their helper and was supposed to go free. A small posse was formed under the leadership of the Rangers. They quickly pursued Sam and Frank. The lengthy chase was on . . .

The search continued far into the night, until it was too dark to see anything. The posse camped to rest and eat. At first light, the search was on again. Around noon, Tom sighted a fallen man beyond them. When they reached him, the man proudly informed them he was the notorious Samuel Bass.

When they reached town with the wounded outlaw, Sam was questioned about Jackson. A man of curious honor, Bass refused to betray one of his men. He endured his agony without complaints. By Sunday morning, the infamous Sam Bass was dead. As if fate had stepped in, Sam died on his twenty-seventh birthday on July 21, 1878.

When Sam was buried on Monday, the whole town turned out for the short ceremony, behaving as if it were a mournful occasion. His colorful and daring exploits were related time and again. Flowers were placed near his tombstone. Several witnesses were teary-eyed. Strangely, it seemed they were laying to rest a beloved legend.

Lynx noticed a photographer as he made picture after picture of the historical episode; as usual, he tried to conceal his presence. Normally he avoided exposure with ease and skill, but today he knew he had been captured on film several times. Only two Rangers present knew why Lynx was there, so he could slip away without joining the victory celebration. In Waco, he would send a telegram home as soon as the reports were signed and filed. First, he needed to locate that photographer and see if he could confiscate that perilous film — that would force him to hang around another day. This secrecy was a pain in the neck! At the earliest, he could make the ranch by Friday.

While Lynx was completing the business of Sam Bass in Round Rock, Calinda was experiencing her second and third shocks in less than a week. Since her stunning discovery about Brax and Laura, neither she nor Salina had mentioned it again. Salina had been calm and cheerful, pressing her advantage by revealing a genial acceptance of Calinda, delighting Rankin and fooling him completely. The guileful Salina had even begun to use her nickname to display fondness.

The day after that stunning incident, Calinda had been pensively reserved. Rankin concluded she was missing Lynx and working too hard. For Calinda did push herself for the next five days with chores, any task which would drive her body to exhaustion so her mind could rest at night. She adamantly refused to recall that devastating episode, blocking such thoughts from mind when they tried to assail her. She kept telling herself all would be fine when Lynx came home. She told herself there were logical explanations for each coincidence or deceit.

On Tuesday, she had labored hard polishing saddles in the barn. She had gone riding with her father-in-law later. When she entered the house to gather her things to bathe, Salina hastily approached her. The Mexican girl glanced behind her to make certain she was alone. "I did not think *Senor* Rankin should see this. The man delivered it while you were riding; it is a letter from England. You must see this, too, before *Senor* Rankin comes home," she added, handing Calinda the newspaper. "I feared he would hide it to avoid a problem."

Calinda's brow lifted inquisitively. "See what?" she asked, gripping the Simpsons' fat letter tightly in her shaky hand.

Salina pointed to the story about the slaying and burying of Sam Bass. Calinda met her curious gaze and said, "I don't want to read about violence and outlaws."

"Just look at the pictures," Salina encouraged slyly.

"No," Calinda refused, recalling her perilous episodes with Cole Stevens, the stage bandits, and Clint Deavers.

"Lynx is in several of them," Salina came to the point.

Calinda almost snatched the paper from her. There were three printed photographs and a lengthy account of the deadly drama. The first picture was taken immediately after the shooting. People were crowding around a dead man lying in the dusty street; in the background was Lynx Cardone. The next picture was taken when the wounded Sam Bass was brought into town after his capture; Lynx was standing beside Star in the left corner. The last picture was at Sam's burial; standing again in the background was her missing husband. She hurriedly scanned the story which told of a daring shoot-out with five Texas Rangers: Peters, Connor, J.B. Jones, Harrell, and Ware. Two bandits had been killed and one had escaped. Cal remembered Lynx telling her Sam Bass had robbed her stage and stolen her locket, now in Lynx's possession. Why was Lynx at the scene of another Bass crime? Attending the funeral of a friend? Had Lynx been involved in this foiled crime? She scanned the story once more; there were no mentions of Lynx.

"Why would Lynx be in Round Rock?" Calinda wondered aloud.

"He is always where there is danger or excitement. Too bad he did not help them and become famous. Sam Bass is a legend."

"He was an outlaw, Salina; he robbed and killed," Calinda softly chided her. "So much for all the enlarged tales about Rangers. I was led to believe it merely required one Ranger to handle such a tiny battle with only three men. How far is this Round Rock?"

"I think a little less than two hundred miles south of Fort Worth."

"But he was only sixty miles west when he sent that telegram! Why would he go that far away? It'll take him days to get home."

"Is he heading straight home from there?" Salina guilefully asked.

"How should I know? He doesn't tell me anything!" she panted, before thinking. "He just said he would be back in a few weeks," she tried to correct her rash outburst. "I guess I'm just tired and hot."

"It is all right, Cal. It must be irritating to learn your *esposo's* whereabouts from a *periodico*. It is time you learn, *hombres* can be thoughtless creatures at times, especially in those circumstances."

"I suppose you're right. I'll get my bath now."

"What about the letter?" Salina hinted curiously.

"I'll read it later. If I know the Simpsons, they probably want money or a favor. Frankly, I'm not in the mood for them."

Salina returned to the kitchen while Calinda went upstairs. She locked her door and sat on the bed. Cal tore open the envelope and withdrew a nearly illegible note and another unsealed letter, noting the vaguely familiar handwriting on the envelope which bore no return address. She expected the note to be from the Simpsons; it wasn't.

Missy Calinda,
   I promised ye any news of ye papa. I be leavin me work here and caint gits in no more trouble. I be cleanin the lady's room and found this here letter hiding there. They be wrong to keep it from ye. I prays it be good news. I won't be here to send no more letters to ye.
Martha

Wrong to keep it from me? she mentally questioned. Calinda wondered what the baffling message meant from Martha Drummond, a dear servant in the Simpson household who had befriended her for years. When she had left England, sweet Martha had promised to forward any news from or about her father. Perhaps she should at least send news about her marriage. She glanced at the enclosed letter. Who would write to her from America in 1872? America, 1872 . . .

Suddenly Calinda went pale; her hands began to tremble so violently that the paper rattled noisily. Could it be . . . She ripped open the envelope, flipping the page the check the signature. Her vision blurred with tears as her father reached across time to haunt her.

Her hands sank to her lap. She leaned her head backward and closed her eyes, inhaling and exhaling several times to slow her racing heart. They had dared to read her letter, then steal it! Why not burn it? They had lied about not receiving any word! But why hide it and keep it for years? Did they plan to return it some day? What didn't they want her to read? Yet, what news needed saving? Dare she read it after all these years? 1872, the year he had left her existence . . .

My dearest daughter Calinda,

I write you this letter with great sadness and guilt. I will be leaving the Cardone Ranch soon. How I wish you could see it, my child. My heart is heavy at such losses, too many sacrifices. I have worked hard to earn something special and beautiful; now I must walk away forever from a dream too costly to claim.

I know I have been remiss as your father. I beg your understanding. I know you will find this difficult to believe, but I love you with all my heart. Forgive the pain and loneliness which you have endured because of me, my selfishness, my cowardice. For they still rule my world, and I must say farewell for a long time. One day, I promise to locate you and explain my coming actions. At present, I can offer you nothing but my love and prayers as I go to seek a new life. Where, I do not know.

I beg you not to hate me or forget me. I also ask that you do not seek to find me, for it won't be possible. I have given the Simpsons ten thousand dollars to care for you until you wed. Find true love, my precious child, for it is the richest of all dreams.

When the time is right, I will contact you through the Simpsons. Only in a life/death crisis, contact Kyle Yancey, a lawyer in Austin (Texas). Remember my love.

Your devoted father

Calinda stared at the date: August, 1872. So, the Simpsons had lied to her; his letters had ceased, but money had been sent: ten thousand dollars less than six years ago! How guilty they had made her feel over every shilling spent on her education, entertainment, and clothing. How dare they steal from her! They were no better than these western bandits. Then, to send her away with less than fifty dollars was criminal. She would rather those bandits had taken it than her so-called family. Evidently, Thomas had wasted her money along with his. It would serve him right to become destitute. If he dared to beg one sixpence from her, she would sneer in his face. All those years of feeling abandoned by her father, when he had sent money and word . . .

From the date and wording of her father's letter, he must have been planning to leave the ranch before Rankin's discovery of his foul deception. The "sacrifices" he must "walk away" from must have been Laura and Lynx and his life here. But he dallied with Laura too long and got caught. He was right; he was selfish, a bloody coward. True love? she scoffed. He didn't know the meaning of real love. Real love wasn't selfish, or cruel, or destructive.

How dare Brax try to condone his actions. How dare he ask for her love, understanding, patience, and forgiveness; he didn't deserve any of them! "How cunning you are, Father. You never mentioned your wanton affair. Your blood money couldn't replace what you took from me! I hate you," she vowed sadly, weeping softly.

Distraught, Cal tore the letters to shreds. "That's what I think of you and your promises. I don't need you or your love."

As Salina had speculated, Rankin didn't show her the paper or even mention it. Cal toyed with her food at dinner, staring at her plate. Resentment flooded her. She didn't know who or what to believe anymore. She felt deceived and dejected. She no longer knew what was truth or reality. She was trapped in illusion, helplessly waiting for others to make their dreams or desires known.

"Cal, is something bothering you?" Rankin inquired in concern.

"When will Lynx be home, Rankin?" she asked a question instead of responding to his. "This waiting and silence are stifling."

"I would imagine very soon, probably the end of the week. You miss him, don't you?" he teased happily.

"If he doesn't return soon, I might forget him," Cal scoffed, dropping her fork to her plate and sighing heavily.

Taking her statement as a joke, Rankin chuckled. "It's just the heat and humidity. You aren't used to them yet."

"Does anyone ever get accustomed to such conditions?" she debated his words. "I'm so bored. I think I'll ride into town tomorrow and go shopping. I might stay a few days and have some new clothes made, if that's all right with you."

"But Lynx should be arriving in a couple of days," he remarked.

"So? I've waited around for him for weeks. The least he can do is wait a day or two for me. He shouldn't worry; at least he'll know where I am," she sneered irritably.

"Are you feeling all right, Cal?" he asked, watching her.

"Stop staring at me; I'm fine," she responded.

"Spite is a two-edged sword, Cal," he warned softly, worried about her state of mind.

"I wouldn't know; I've never drawn or used that weapon," she commented flippantly. "I'll go crazy if I don't get some relief."

"Is there trouble between you and Salina?" he ventured.

"No; we're getting along fine now."

"I know you, Calinda Cardone; something isn't right," he insisted.

"Do you, Rankin?" she asked strangely, gazing at him.

"I think I do," he said.

"Sometimes I don't think I even know myself." Why was she calmly accepting this offensive treatment? Why was she too fearful to challenge Rankin and Lynx for the truth? Why forget about Brax?

"What do you mean?" he inquired, leaning forward to listen intently. Was it merely the demands of Lynx's absence on a new marriage and bride? She looked so melancholy, so insecure.

"Nothing. I'm just moody tonight. I'm sorry."

Calinda didn't go into town that week. She worked in and around the house until Friday afternoon, then took off to go swimming in the pond over the hill. As she swam in the oblong body of water, she reflected on her letter to the Simpsons which she had given to Salina this morning to mail when she went into town for supplies. Thankfully Martha couldn't be punished for her aid. By now, Salina should be home and the strongly worded letter should be on its way to the Simpsons.

Cal tried to imagine their reactions to her demand for an accounting of the $10,000. She stated if she didn't receive an accounting and the balance due, she would turn the matter over to a lawyer. She told them her father was away on business; and by the way, she was married now to a wealthy and powerful man who would see that justice was done. She really didn't expect to hear from them, but maybe the threat would prevent future contact. Where had Brax gotten that money?

Calinda left the soothing water and stretched out on the grassy bank. She closed her eyes and gave herself over to dreamy relaxation. Her life was such a puzzle, with a mysterious golden stranger at the center of it. She loved him and wanted him, but could she trust him?

Cal's body felt light and drowsy. His lips were sweet and stirring as they softly captured hers. She sighed as her arms automatically encircled Lynx's body, greedily sealing her mouth to his and embracing him fiercely. As his lips drifted down her cheek to nibble playfully at her ear, she slowly aroused to learn she was not dreaming.

Her startled shriek of his name sent his ear ringing. Lynx raised his tawny head and shook it, grinning down at her. Her gaze slipped over his tousled hair which reminded her of wind tangled stalks of ripened wheat. His coppery features were lined with mischief and warmth.

"When did you get home?" Cal asked, without even a slight trace of a pleased smile. Her hands fell to the ground near her head, palms upward. Her expression was guarded and her eyes fathomless.

A pang of disappointment surged through Lynx as he witnessed her lack of a happy greeting. If he didn't know any better, he might be tempted to think Cal wasn't glad to see him. He flashed her a wide grin, deciding she was just peeved with his long absence. She shouldn't act so surprised; he had sent a telegram to expect him Friday. To make certain he reached home today, he had ridden as if the demons of hell were chasing him. Lynx was nettled by her chilly reception.

"Just in time to grab a fresh horse and ride over here," he informed her. "I tossed my things in our room, turned Star over to Homer, and high-tailed it to see my wife."

When he leaned forward to drop a kiss on the tip of her nose, he teased, "You shouldn't lie around like this, Cal; it's dangerous." He motioned to her dark blue shirt with missing sleeves and her cut-off jeans with their ragged bottoms which exposed most of her shapely calves. He chuckled when she looked annoyed.

"I'm fully clothed, Lynx, and perfectly safe," she told him, pointing to the gun lying in the grass near her.

Lynx refuted, "You were asleep, love; I did sneak up on you. But I was referring to the scorching sun and this cloud-white flesh."

Calinda placed her hand in the middle of his sturdy chest and pushed him aside to sit up. "Afraid I'll freckle instead of tan?" she said, her mind elsewhere.

He placed his elbows on the grassy earth to recline slightly with his torso propped up, one knee bent with a boot resting near his buttocks. "I've never seen a redhead with even a threat of golden skin."

"In your numerous travels, I'm certain you've met plenty of them. Have you seen your father?" she inquired casually.

"Nope. Don't tell him, but you're the one I wanted to see."

He sat up beside her as she challenged his husky claim, "If that were true, Cardone, you'd stay home more."

Lynx made the mistake of grinning ruefully and teas-

387

ing, "Been missing me and it's got your dander up? Well, I'm here now." He leaned forward to rub his lips over a bare shoulder.

Calinda jerked away and stood up to leave. "I need to bathe and dress. It's getting late."

He bounded to his feet and caught her wrist to stop her. "Let's stay here and talk, Cal; we can skip dinner," he coaxed, his voice thick with rising passion, his eyes dark with it.

"I skipped lunch, so I'm starving," Cal responded tersely.

"I'm starving too," the playful rogue replied, reaching for her.

Calinda stunned him when she shoved his arms away and glared at him. "Is that all you care about? Sometimes I think that's the only reason you come home for brief visits! You run in, stuff yourself, then ride off again until hunger pangs nibble at you. In case you don't know it, Mister Cardone, a marriage requires more than sex!"

"What's gotten into you, Cal? You feel the same way about me. We need each other. If you're riled because I've been away so long, I'm sorry. I got home as soon as possible."

"How do you expect me to welcome you, my devoted husband? We've been married forty-two days, of which I've spent one and a half with you. Since we met seventy-five days past, I've been generously given a total of six days in your company, mostly in your bed. Is that all I'm good for, Cardone? We don't have time to discover each other."

"All I've wanted for weeks was to be home with you, Cal. I made promises, and I have friends who needed me," he reasoned.

"You also made promises to me! I needed you! Obviously your stimulating life and friends are more important to you. So go hug and kiss your carefree life and snuggle up to your numerous escapades of daring and danger. Obviously they give you more satisfaction than I do. Why even bother to come home?" she shrieked at him. "I'm sure you were having more fun and excitement in Round Rock."

"Round Rock?" he echoed anxiously. Damn! That photographer must have printed his picture. How else would she know about Round Rock? How could he explain to her without lying? Lynx had managed to keep a low profile at countless Ranger victories, until Round Rock. He didn't know Jones was gaping at the papers this very moment, praying no one would start adding up such damaging and enlightening figures.

Lynx captured her chin and lifted her head, probing her gaze which was a baffling mixture of sparkling fury and misty anguish. "My God, Callie, have I hurt and disappointed you this much?" he asked.

"How could you? You aren't around long enough to do anything to me or for me. I didn't even know when you'd be home."

"What about my telegram?" he debated.

"That was weeks ago. Or does time pass too swiftly and happily to notice? I see you didn't receive any scars from your run-in with Cole."

"I'm talking about the telegram from Waco two days ago," he clarified, his own temper steaming.

"What telegram? If one arrived, your father hasn't mentioned it. He also didn't mention your visit to Round Rock. You take a very good picture, my love. Your handsome face was emblazoned all over the paper he thought I didn't see before he concealed it. Three of them, all in Round Rock where the action was. Is there some reason your whereabouts should be kept secret from your wife?"

He murmured thoughtfully, "What did the paper say?"

"I'm sure your father saved it for you. For some reason, he didn't feel I should see it or your telegram. I wonder why."

"There's an explanation, Cal," he stated softly.

"Isn't there always some tidy excuse to explain away your mysterious life? When you're ready to come home to me, really come home, Lynx, let me know. Until then, don't trouble yourself."

"What's been happening here, Callie?" he probed in dread.

"Such as?" she questioned innocently.

"You're angry with me about more than my absence. Would you please explain?" he asked quietly, a worried frown lining his forehead.

The weeks of suspicions, demands, boredom, and loneliness attacked her very soul. So much had been kept tightly constrained. Tears began to ease down her cheeks. "It isn't working, Lynx."

"What isn't working, Cal?" he asked, pulling her into his arms.

She rested her flushed face against his chest as she sobbed in anguish, her shoulders trembling. How could she get answers without questions, questions which she dared not ask? When she brought her tears under a small measure of control, she lifted her face and stated simply, "Us."

"What about us, Callie?" he sought to comprehend her meaning.

"Don't you understand, Lynx? There is no us, because you won't allow it. I don't know you at all, and you don't know me," she stated hoarsely. "How can we work on a real marriage like this?"

"I'll be home for a week this time, Callie. Then, I only have one last promise to fulfill before I'm here to stay. Bear with me a while longer. Please," he urged her.

"Why? Will it change anything?" she challenged dejectedly.

"I hope our love and desire don't change. I thought you felt the same way. Are you trying to say you don't love me? You want out of our marriage?" he asked fearfully, dreading her response.

"My feelings aren't in question; yours are," she told him.

"But you know how I feel about you," he argued, confused.

"No, Lynx, I don't," she replied honestly.

"Por Dias, woman! I love you. I need you. I want you. Whenever I'm away from you, I think I'll go mad before I can get home. I dream of holding you, kissing you, making love to you. What more do you want from me? You're the most important thing in my life."

"That isn't how it looks to me," she contested painfully.

"How can I prove it to you, Callie?" he asked seriously.

"Show me with actions, not words," she replied bluntly.

"But you just spurned my touch," he pressed in bewilderment.

"I know you find me desirable, Lynx. I wasn't referring to sex. You don't let me share your life. You tell me nothing. You stay gone for weeks. Did you hear what I said? Less than two days out of forty-two since our marriage. Just six out of seventy-five since we met. And you ask why I doubt your affections and loyalty?"

"I swear by all I hold dear and sacred, Callie, I love you with all my heart. I don't think I could survive if I ever lost you. I didn't even realize I was capable of feeling such powerful emotions, of knowing such fears, until I met you. You're the most wonderful and exciting thing to enter my life. If I've given you reasons to doubt me and my love, I'm sorry. I never intended to hurt you or shut you out. When this last job is over, I promise to tell you everything."

Calinda gazed into his entreating eyes, eyes which declared his honesty and love. What a fool she had been. How wildly and crazily her imagination had tormented her. There was no vengeful plot against her. Lynx was trying to change, with difficulty. He loved her . . .

Cal smiled at him, tears glistening on her lashed. "Do you know that's the first time you've ever said such things?"

Lynx chuckled. "I suppose I've always been a man of few words. I thought you knew how I felt about you. I guess a man should speak his mind once in a while, even if it's hard to learn how. Well, Calinda Cardone, I love you, pure and simple love you. It scares the hell out of me, even shocks me, but it's true," he declared roguishly.

"I know what you mean, my love." she concurred. "But it's more frightening when you feel it's one-sided."

"When we get to the house, we'll see why Rankin hid the telegram and paper. If I know my father, probably to surprise you. I believe you said you were starving, Mrs. Cardone. Let's go home."

"Would you believe my appetite has changed drastically?"

A beguiling grin flickered over his arresting features. "In what way, Mrs. Cardone?" he queried huskily.

Calinda unbuttoned his shirt to the waist, then snuggled against his firm chest. "I bet with a little cunning and investigating, you might gain a clue," she hinted seductively.

Lynx grasped her chin to lift her head, fusing their gazes. "Is sex all you think about, Mrs. Cardone?" he teased.

"Only for the next week," she saucily replied, her lips meeting his as his arms surrounded her.

They sank to the grassy earth, their love shared at last . . .

Chapter Seventeen

As Lynx spread enticing kisses over Calinda's face and mouth, her body was consumed by a great need for him. He was so absorbing, filling her mind with thoughts which prevented any distractions, consuming her body with urgent passion, blinding her warring heart to all emotions except her love and his nearness.

During their mild argument and blooming of desires, dusk gradually wrapped them in an ever-darkening blanket. Without taking his lips from hers, Lynx gathered her in his arms and carried her to a copse of small oaks and placed her there for privacy, his lithe body partially covering hers. It was possible someone might come riding by or might come to search for them when they failed to respond to the dinner bell; yet ravenous emotions demanded to be fed and sated.

Within a few minutes, Lynx had removed her scanty garments and his own clothing. Semi-surrounded by bushy trees and cloaked by shadows, Calinda felt no modesty or resistance. She had doubted his love and suspected his motives; she needed to destroy those feelings. She clung to his sinewy frame, thrilled by its wondrous contact with her tingling flesh. She yielded to his lips, intoxicated by their ability to stir her senses to a wild frenzy. She vanquished all worries and mistrust, allowing her love to lead her where he willed.

The sun could have blazed down upon them and revealed their feverish actions to the entire world, and she couldn't have prevented their imminent union. If anyone had confronted them, she would have been too engrossed with him to notice their arrival. Lynx filled her senses as no other force had ever done, not even air or life itself.

He was so strong, yet his touch was as gentle and light as rays of sunshine dancing over her quivering flesh, its heat warming her very soul. Her body seemed as helpless as a blade of grass being swayed to and fro by a powerful breeze. Her will was as pliable as dough in a baker's hands.

Like a daring and skillful explorer, he let his hands search her enticing regions. They travelled, mapped, invaded, trespassed, conquered, and claimed nearly every inch of her willing body, as his lips did simultaneously with hers. A welcomed interloper, his tongue forded her lips and tasted the eagerness of her mouth. Accepting him as a seasoned and talented guide, she followed his lead.

Yet, Lynx didn't enter her unguarded paradise too quickly. He tantalized and stimulated her appetite until she pleaded for his expedition into that conquerable territory. At last, he boldly eased inside the dark passage which was moist and trembling with anticipation. His manhood journeyed from end to end many times, often swiftly, then with tormentingly sweet leisure. He calculated how long he needed to bring her to the point of victory at his side, then lovingly labored at that pace.

Their bodies and spirits united to strive for that rewarding goal, they sought it with stirring suspense. Soon, the moment of ecstasy seized them and carried them away on waves of blissful rapture. They lay entwined until respirations returned to normal and a quiet contentment filled them.

A light breeze played over their nude bodies, cooling and refreshing them. "Thank God I don't have to leave soon because I couldn't," he murmured softly into her fragrant hair, nuzzling her ear.

"A week is very soon, my love," she debated tranquilly.

"In another month, we'll forget all these separations. We'll never be apart again, Callie. Wherever I go, you'll come with me. I'm eager to work on some little Cardones," he teased mirthfully.

"Ah, ha," she playfully mused, "so that's why you married me."

"Why not?" he genially accepted her jest. "I can't think of a better choice for the mother of my children."

The moment the word "mother" left his lips, she noticed a slight tensing in his body. Knowing the truth, her heart ached for the anguish he had endured because of Brax and Laura. Never would she treat her children in such an evil manner. "You'll make a wonderful father, Lynx. I can envision you now, trying to teach our son to ride and herd cattle. I only pray you don't share any of your wandering spirit with him; I'd like him to hang around longer than you. One expert gunslinger and carefree roamer is enough for me," she teased.

"He'll never have a reason to leave, Callie; I'll make certain."

Although Lynx didn't know she caught the dual meaning in his statement, she responded to it as she gazed into his impenetrable eyes, "So will I, my love; I swear it."

There was a haunting gleam in his eyes when he tenderly coaxed, "Please don't ever get weary of life on the ranch, Callie. I know trading silks and towns for jeans and dust is a big change for you. But don't lose faith in me, in us. If you're unhappy or angry, tell me quickly. Don't let bitterness fester until it sickens you and drives you from me. I don't know how I would survive if you ever walked away from me, if you stopped loving me. It's damn scary to love and need another person so much," he whispered in a deeply emotional tone.

Cal snuggled into his protective arms and hugged him tightly. "How can you even think of such an impossible thing?" she softly scolded him, but she knew why. "You would have to take a whip to me to drive me away from your side. I love the ranch and jeans. Who needs silks and civilization when I have you? I love you, Lynx, and nothing will ever come between us again."

Lynx's sharp mind picked up her last word and mentally questioned it. "You mean nothing I say or do will change things for us?" he tested for more information.

Cal twisted her head to meet his probing gaze. "What could you possibly do or say to shatter our love and promises?" she parried his oddly voiced question. "I'm holding you to your vows, Lynx. If you break them, I'll make you sorry," she warned merrily.

Her innocent threat brought a curious reaction to his face. "You trying to intimidate me, wife?" he asked, failing to mask an odd concern. "If I don't ride straight, what would you do to punish me?"

"I don't need to use energy planning for something

which will never take place. If you love me and want me, why would you try to damage our relationship? One day, I want to know anything and everything about you. All right?"

"Nosy little critter, aren't you?" he insouciantly claimed.

"Only because you make it necessary. One day I want to hear all of your secrets," she whispered conspiratorially, then laughed.

"I doubt it, Callie. If you knew them, I would lose you for certain. I'm really a devil in disguise, after your beautiful and trusting soul," he murmured huskily.

"Then your wicked task is over, Sir Demon; you own me body, heart, mind, and soul. What more can I offer to win you for eternity?"

"That's quite a valuable collection, woman. You sure you trust me to take care of them?" he ventured, chuckling with renewed life.

"If I can't trust you, Lynx, then I can trust no one," she stated gravely, her voice muffled and strained.

Lynx captured her quivering chin, alarmed by the moisture on her lashes and the panic in her voice. "Do you trust me implicitly, Cal?"

She glanced away as she light-heartedly declared, "Why shouldn't I? You're my husband, perhaps soon to be father of my children."

"Is there something I should know, woman? You've been acting awfully strange and tense," Lynx speculated an impending announcement.

"About what?" Cal asked, her fretful gaze and voice guarded.

"A baby?" he hinted cleverly. "Is that why you're so edgy?"

"Not that I know of, Lynx," she replied honestly, delighted his keen mind was running in that false direction. She cautioned herself to relax and to avoid bringing up any stressful points. She had been attacked by too many pains and problems lately. Soon, he would be home permanently; then, they could discover each other and share their lives. During this visit, she wanted to prevent quarrels.

Clever and perceptive, Lynx knew she was keeping something from him, something which was plaguing her deeply. Maybe they just needed time together to teach her to accept him and his words. He hadn't been much of a husband, lover, or friend since their marriage. Her hesitation and mistrust were natural. He would give her the time and love she needed to win her loyalty and contentment. He would grant her the time to come to him and talk openly about what was troubling her. His many secrets and separations couldn't help but distress her. In time, she would understand them. She had said to "prove" himself to her; he would make every effort to do so. Yet, her unhappiness and boredom tormented him, panicked him. He could never release her. He allowed the matter to pass for now.

"Let's freshen up in the pond, then get something to eat. I'm starved. If you want me to hang around home, you best take real good care of me, Mrs. Cardone," he teased her.

"Do you know how much I love you and need you?" she asked.

He cupped her face between his hands and studied her serious expression. "More than anyone else in my life, Callie," he answered.

For a brief moment, her eyes misted and her lips quivered. He thought she was about to cry, but she controlled that reaction. "Are you so miserable here at the ranch,

Callie? Is it me?"

"I just miss you so much, Lynx," she confessed raggedly.

"I'm sorry, love. It won't be much longer," he promised.

She flung herself into his arms and whispered fearfully, "I hope not. I'm so afraid something will happen to you."

His embrace tightened as he said, "Nothing will happen to me, love. Please don't upset yourself like this."

"Every time you leave, I fear it will be the last time you hold me, or kiss me, or I see you. Am I so terrible or life here so dreary that you can't stay home very long?" she challenged.

Her insecurities and loneliness flooded her words, startling him with their depth. "Look at me, Callie," he softly commanded.

When she did, he stated distinctly, "I love you, woman. If you don't believe anything else I say, at least know for certain that's the God's truth. I promise to take you with me if I ever leave again. If you'll recall, I do keep my word," he hinted slyly, grinning at her.

"I hope so, my darling. But if you start this secretive roaming again, Lynx, I might not hang around to be convinced of your love and needs. I can't live like this much longer, me always waiting alone and in fear while you gallivant around the countryside for reasons you can't even share with me. That isn't a good marriage or a real commitment; it's only a convenience for you. I'm going to trust you to keep your word, unless you prove otherwise. One final separation," she compromised softly.

The haunting words sounded as if they had been carved from her soul with an incisive honesty and sent forth with much agony. "I won't let you down, Callie. One last trip," he concurred joyfully.

"I pray you mean it, Lynx. If I ever discovered you didn't, I would leave that very day. I want so much to know you, to understand you, to share everything with you, to help you, to love you blindly."

"Is there any reason you can't?" he questioned.

"You," she stated simply. "You don't allow it to happen."

"Then prepare yourself to be stormed with answers and love," he playfully warned Cal. "Bargain?"

"I've been ready and eager since that night we met in the saloon. Did you honestly think I was Callie O'Hara?" she asked merrily.

"Yep, but that wasn't such a terrible mistake after all. It did get us acquainted before . . . Did you know Callie turned into an outlaw?" He hurriedly tried to cover a slip which she had caught. He went on to reveal the Irish lass' unmasking during the hold-up and her planning of Calinda's kidnapping. He was surprised when Calinda's intrigue was small. Watching her intense observation of him, he lazily rolled into the telling of the Round Rock incident, alleging himself as a witness and spectator without outright lying.

"That's what I meant earlier, Lynx; you're constantly in danger."

"I'm perfectly safe. Haven't you seen me with these Colts?"

"What's the saying about there's always someone else faster?" she craftily rebutted his confidence. "A reputation as large and colorful as yours is mighty tempting to a rising legend. Perhaps I should come along to guard your back."

"No way will I endanger your life again, woman. I'll

kill the first man who threatens you," he warned ominously.

"How soon do you propose to defend me at such a distance? As we both recall, you weren't around when Cole Stevens grabbed me," she reminded him, her fishing expedition in full swing. With the right bait, she might catch some enlightening answers or clarifying clues.

"I did rescue you, my ungrateful and demanding wife," he retorted, his intuition alive and working overtime.

"You do have that stimulating ability to sense when I'm in peril. We must have a mental link, or fate is guarding us. And I am most appreciative of all you do for me, Lynx. But alas, I admit to being demanding and selfish; I want more," she stated comically.

"Do you deserve more from me, you sly vixen?" he taunted.

"All you have to offer," she replied smugly.

"Demanding and selfish don't cover the half of it, woman."

"We'll see, won't we?" she cheerfully hinted.

"I think I'm in deep trouble," Lynx playfully sighed.

"You are, Lynx. You haven't seen anything yet. Let's get moving before we miss dinner," Cal reminded him.

They quickly bathed and dressed. She was mounted before he could assist her. "See you at home, love," she threw over her shoulder as she raced off across the meadow, heading for the rolling hill beyond.

Lynx jumped into his saddle and raced off in pursuit, easily catching up with her. She slowed her pace to ride beside him. "You're a damn good rider, Callie," he complimented her.

"Good shot, too," she informed him. "Maybe good

enough to challenge you," she laughingly added.

"I'd be a dead man; I'd never be able to draw a weapon on you."

"Any kind?" she speculated with a giggle.

"If I can help it, Callie, I'll never hurt you."

"Bribery and flattery are sly tricks to win my favor."

"I have it, don't I?" he smugly declared.

"Yes, my love, you do," she readily agreed.

When they arrived at the stable, Charlie took possession of their horses. They locked hands and strolled to the house. They were greeted by a grinning Rankin. "I see you found her, son. She's been fretting over your arrival for weeks. I saw you in the papers from Round Rock. I didn't dare show them to Cal; I didn't want her tearing off in search of her adventurous husband and getting into danger again. I even kept your telegram a secret; I wanted her to be surprised tonight," he cunningly enlightened Lynx.

"You underestimate my wife's intelligence, Father; she knew about both. She's been annoyed with us for keeping her in the dark. She's been raking me through the fires," Lynx replied in that same sly communicative way, failing to deceive an alert Calinda.

"I'm sorry, Cal," Rankin said. "Now I see why you've been so irritable and distant with me. We won't trick you again."

"Any food left from dinner?" she asked, dropping the nettling game. "We're both famished."

"In the oven. Salina's gone for the night."

Calinda stopped her pleased response from leaving her lips. "You relax, dear husband, while I get it ready. Talk with Rankin."

"We can talk later or tomorrow. I'm not letting you out of my sight in that crazy mood," Lynx informed her, a gleam of mischief in his tawny eyes. "I'd best learn my way around this house again."

Together, they set the table, retrieved the food, and sat down to eat. Hungry and weary, Lynx and Cal ate in relative silence. Afterwards, Lynx helped her with the dishes. "Watch it, Lynx, this could become a habit with me. I like having you around."

"Excellent. Would you like to take a walk?" he offered.

"Not tonight. That work and swim drained me. I think I'll turn in. You coming along, or staying to talk with your father?"

"I'll be along shortly, love. I think I should speak with my father for a little while tonight," he said, stroking her silky hair.

"I'll be waiting," she murmured, smiling seductively at him.

"I'm counting on it," he responded, his smile tugging at her.

Calinda went to their room and dressed for bed. While she waited for Lynx and Rankin to visit, she read and dozed. If only she'd known he was coming home today, she wouldn't have worked so hard. Now that she was bathed and fed, her fatigued and sated body was lax. After thirty minutes of straining to focus on the book, it fell into her lap and closed; Calinda was fast asleep.

Downstairs, Lynx and Rankin were sipping brandies and chatting about the ranch and impending round-up. They discussed his recent adventures and accomplishments. Lynx told his father that his last mission was to trace Rube Burrow and apprehend the vicious bandit. After which, his career as a secret Ranger would be complete. They spoke about children and Calinda. Time passed as the two mellowed men really talked for the first time in years, enjoying each other's company and intelligence.

Rankin leisurely filled in Lynx on the happenings at the ranch, each man delighting in the women's truce. But Lynx fretted over the moods of Calinda's which his father revealed. Evidently she wasn't as happy here as he assumed or hoped. But things would change soon . . .

When Lynx noticed the late hour of midnight, he hurriedly downed his brandy and bid his father good-night. He mounted the steps with eagerness, his loins throbbing at the thought of what awaited him. When he slipped into his room, he was dismayed slightly to find her sleeping peacefully. Her position and the book indicated she had tried to wait for his appearance. He could hardly blame her, for his father had enlightened him as to how hard she labored each day.

He eased out of his clothes and doused the lantern. He gingerly slid into bed and drew her into his arms. She sighed softly and murmured his name, her eyes never opening. As soon as Lynx forcefully cooled his smoldering passion, he joined her in slumberland.

An early riser, Lynx was up and eating with Rankin shortly after dawn vanquished the shadows of night. When Rankin suggested he ride to the north pastures with him, Lynx accepted, thinking Calinda would sleep late.

But, as if her body-clock was attuned to his presence, Calinda was awake and up by eight o'clock. She dressed and went down to join her husband. She was peeved to find he had left at seven-thirty. When he hadn't returned by lunch, she grew annoyed. So much for spending time with her while home! She fumed, *no doubt I'll only get him at night!*

Lynx and Rankin found traces of attempted fence-cuttings in three locations. It would be wise to plant guards at those areas tonight. Rankin told his son that he suspected at least one hundred steers had been rustled during the last three weeks. Whoever was behind it seemed to know their routine, their weaknesses, and strengths. Rankin asked his son to help solve this crisis while he was home, if he didn't mind.

When Lynx returned to the house near four in the afternoon, he discovered his wife had gone riding alone. Considering her past jeopardy and the allusion of rustlers nearby, he was furious with her. "What the hell could she be thinking to go out alone!" he snarled.

"Probably hoped to link up with her beloved," Salina hinted.

Lynx turned and scowled at the Mexican beauty. "I'll make sure she doesn't do it again," he stated confidently, his jaw set in angry lines.

"She does it all the time. She has not found trouble yet," Salina remarked, hoping to halt his future demand which could foil any distant plans to place Cal in danger. "She is a grown woman, Lynx; she carries a gun. She will resent your harsh orders, treating her like a *nena*. She gets bored around here with nothing to occupy her days and thoughts. Riding on the ranch is far better than going to town for a diversion."

"How do you know she's bored?" Lynx inquired sternly.

"Anyone who does ranch chores or cleans attics must be at their wit's end for amusement. Any other female would be sewing or such. Sometimes I think Cal wishes she were a man. If she were, she would roam around like you do," Salina stated with phony giggles.

"She cleaned the attic?" he queried tensely.

"*Si*. And she polishes saddles, drives the wagon, feeds animals, and you would not believe what else. Sometimes, she even helps in the house, when the wifey mood strikes her. She is actually a good cook; did you know that?" she hinted slyly, knowing he was distracted by her guileful hint. How she wished she dared tell Cal everything . . .

"No, I didn't," he replied absently, then excused himself.

As Salina assumed, he headed for the attic to check out a nagging dread. It was clear his wife had found his mother's portrait. He worried for a time, then dismissed his anxiety when he realized she couldn't know anything about Laura. It would appear natural for them to remove such a haunting picture. He stared at his ravishing mother for a long time, wondering if she had ever regretted her decision. He tormented himself with questions. Did she ever think about him? Did she ever want to contact him or come home again? Was she even alive and well? Why had she given up so much for Elliott Braxton? Had it been worth her present life? Would he ever learn her fate or see her again? God help him if Cal was anything like Laura.

Lynx threw the sheet over the painting and went to the study to toss down two brandies. He must not think about his mother; she wasn't worth the mental energy or his concern. Yet, new apprehension chewed at him. What if his lovely Cal became that restless and unhappy? What if life here was too demanding, empty, and despicable for his love? Would Cal run away from him and the ranch? No, Cal loved him.

"Lynx," Salina called out from the doorway.

He turned slowly and caustically responded, "Yes?"

"There is something you should know about Cal. After the past trouble between us, I was not sure if I should tell you. I was afraid you might not believe me or think I am only trying to start more trouble. I am not, honestly. She and I are becoming friends, but I worry about you. If you repeat what I say, she will never trust me again and we will return to battling every day. Maybe she has already told you about it," Salina slyly speculated as if nervous.

"Stop dodging cowflops, Salina; spit it out. What about my wife?" he demanded, stressing Calinda's position to him.

"Did she tell you she got a letter from England?" she opened the vindictive conversation. If she were going to halt this marriage farce, she needed to inspire conflicts on both sides, but cautiously.

"When?" he asked, his question admitting his ignorance.

"Tuesday, the same day the papers arrived with your pictures in them." Salina went on to repeat Calinda's words and actions that day, and Calinda's curious moods afterwards. "If you question her about the letter, she will think I spy on her for you. She will make certain I learn nothing more to tell you. Besides, she might be waiting for the right moment to tell you. Whatever it said, it surely had her upset. She sent the Simpsons a letter yesterday. She asked me to mail it. You might be furious with me, but I saved it for you."

"Where is it?" he growled coldly, piqued by their conspiracy.

"In my room. Did I do the right thing?" she fretted aloud.

"No, Salina, you didn't. If you ever tattle on her again

or betray her confidence like this, you're fired. Calinda is a Cardone now. Don't ever presume to spy on her or trick her," he stated icily, even though he was relieved to see at least one letter. He sat impatiently while she fetched it. He would search their room for the other one, but Cal had doubtlessly destroyed it. Why hadn't she mentioned it yesterday? No matter, he couldn't give Salina any weapons to use against his wife or any power to deceive her. If Cal needed watching, his father would handle that dreadful matter. Anyway, Cal would probably tell him the truth before the week was out.

Lynx snatched the letter from Salina's hand and glowered at her. "Don't you ever do anything like this again. Just to prevent any conflicts, we'll forget about today. Understand?" he warned.

As he left the room, Salina smiled maliciously. She knew he was going upstairs to tear open the letter and devour its contents. He didn't have her fooled one bit. He simply didn't want her to know how much he mistrusted his little wife. He wouldn't tell Cal anything; he would watch and wait for the instant to pounce on her. As she worked, she hummed, envisioning her seeds sprouting in his mind.

Lynx paled and shuddered when he read the sarcastic and intimidating message about her father's 1872 letter which had been kept secret from her for years. His eyes widened as he scanned the contents which included her vow to expose their deception to her father, her threat to make trouble for their theft of the $10,000 balance which her father had sent for her support, the announcement of her marriage to him, her allegation of their possible theft of other letters from her father, and a warning to never contact her again.

Lynx couldn't believe what he was reading. Surely

there was a logical explanation? Who had sent her a letter from Brax, even an old one? He was puzzled and worried. What had it said? Where was it?

He studied the letter and its implications. What had Brax revealed to Calinda? What had her so secretive? Why had she gone to the attic and examined his mother's portrait? *My God,* he worried, *did Brax tell her the truth?* He paced the room like a caged beast. Suddenly, he laughed at his foolishness. No, Brax hadn't confessed; her behavior proved she still loved and trusted her husband . . .

Between his secretive absences and the unexpected letter from the past, no wonder Cal was distracted and moody. She would tell him later, he concluded. Lynx went to the water-shed to bathe and dress for dinner. He waited for his wife's return.

Knowing she would bathe when she returned, Calinda had left her things on the shelf in the water-shed. When she came to the house afterwards, she was carrying her damp and dusty riding clothes. As she passed through the kitchen, she spoke to Salina, but didn't ask about her husband. She headed upstairs to hang the garments on the balcony railing to dry before placing them in the laundry.

"I see you made it home safely," a mellow voice teased from behind her as he propped negligently against the doorframe.

Cal halted and turned, her expression impassive. "Did you think I had run off?" she retorted, lacking any smile or merriment.

"It's dangerous to ride alone, Cal," he mildly scolded her.

"I've grown accustomed to being alone, my wayward husband. I'm surprised you had time to notice I wasn't around."

"I've been home for several hours. What took you so long?"

"Nosy critter, aren't we?" she copied his quip of yesterday.

"Just concerned, love," he replied, staring at her oddly. "Anything wrong, Cal?"

"What could possibly be wrong now that my husband is home and generously granting me his precious time and attention?"

"Can we take that stroll now and talk?" he suggested, needing to comprehend her new mood and to stroke her ruffled feathers.

"I should help Salina with dinner," she responded warily. Why was he looking at her in that curious manner? Why the interrogation?

"Salina's done it alone for years. Surely she can manage tonight. I'd like to spend time with you, Cal," he seemingly wheedled.

She appeared to ponder his invitation for a short time, then shrugged in resignation. "Why not? Let me hang these out to dry first. I'll be down shortly." She hurriedly vanished from his piercing gaze.

When Cal returned, Lynx hadn't moved from that spot. He waited for her to descend the steps, watching her with a smile. "You could let me explain my tardiness before getting so angry," he teased.

"You don't owe me any excuses, Lynx," she told him, then walked outside without waiting for him to tag along.

Cal sat down in the yard swing and gazed off across the hills, recalling the night she hadn't dared sit in this swing with him. He came to join her, frowning at her petulance. She didn't appear to be listening as he related

411

his reasons for being gone nearly all day. When he halted, she didn't debate or comment on them.

Calinda wasn't being attentive. She knew he was telling the truth, and she had no real cause to me mad or unreasonable. The letters were plaguing her. If she and Lynx were going to have a new beginning, it must be with honesty and openness. She couldn't fool him; he sensed something was troubling her. It would be a lie to say everything was fine; yet, she couldn't confide too much this soon.

"Cal?" he said for the second time before breaking her stiff concentration. "What's wrong, love?"

She inhaled deeply, then released it slowly. "Lynx . . ." She hesitated, then turned to meet his worried gaze. "Something happened while you were gone. I . . ." she faltered again, then related the letter episode in a quavering voice. "I was so confused and distressed I ripped it to shreds. I should have saved it for you to read; I'm sorry. I don't trust the Simpsons; I'm furious with them. I wrote and told them so. I couldn't tell them the truth, that I don't know where my own father is. Maybe if they think I have you and him they'll leave me alone. I know I'll never see that money, and I don't care about it. How could they be so cruel and evil? They made me feel like a lowly beggar all those years. At least I understand why they took the care to have me well-educated and clothed; they feared my father might turn up someday. How do I know that was the only letter from him? What if he wrote and told me the truth or where he is now? I hate them!" she shrieked in renewed anguish at their deceits.

"Don't worry, love. I'm glad their tricks sent you to me. Tell me what the two letters said," he coaxed gently, trying not to distress her further, needing to hear her repeat her letter accurately.

412

She regained control of her poise and speech, relating her letter nearly verbatim and then exposing the contents of her father's. For some reason, she didn't tell him about Kyle Yancey in Austin, although that was undoubtedly the reason the letter was kept. She told herself it was to prevent him from chasing that fleeting clue. She focused a tormented gaze on his unreadable one. "What could he have meant by guilt and sacrifices? He sounded as if he loved it here; why would he leave? What dream would be too costly to claim? He said he was a selfish coward, but I don't understand. Was he trying to buy my forgiveness and love, Lynx? Surely after so many years, he could have contacted me?" the questions tumbled out with hopes he would match her trust and confide in her. She had opened the door; would he walk inside and join her or would he close the door instead?

"You think he was referring to being guilty about stealing the money and sacrificing his life here? He had dreamed of a ranch in Texas; could that be what he meant by walking away from one?" When she didn't respond either way, he continued, "He proved he was selfish by his treatment of you, and he was a coward to leave after the theft. He made himself a criminal, Cal; to contact you might involve you in that life of running from the law. If he's still alive, love, he may never try to reach you. I know that's painful, Cal, but you must face it."

Calinda lowered her gaze, tears clouding her vision. Not at his gentle and torturous words as he assumed, but at his cunning way of deceiving her with questions which were intended to sound like speculative answers. When Lynx lifted her chin, she burst into tears and nestled her face against his chest. She sobbed quietly, praying he could one day confess his own anguish to her. If she could bare her inner soul to him, why couldn't he do the same? Perhaps it was more humiliating and painful to him, for he had lived it and not read it. Perhaps he feared it would alter her feelings for him.

Lynx embraced her tightly. "Don't cry, love. You have me now. I'll never desert you or hurt you, Callie," he promised tenderly.

She looked up at him, her face streaked with tears. "Will we ever know the truth, Lynx?" she asked sadly.

"I hope so, Callie; God, I hope so," he agreed honestly. "I wish I had been here when you needed me. I'm sorry you went through it alone."

"You're here now," she said, smiling up at him.

"Try to forget about it, Callie; it only brings pain and unhappiness. We have our life to think about," he reminded her.

"Yes, we do. I feel better now that you know. I was afraid to tell you; I know how the past disturbs you. I thought I could ignore it, but it kept haunting me, I felt I was being dishonest with you. There are too many secrets between us, Lynx. One day, I hope it won't be this way. I hope we can tell each other everything, anything."

He chuckled. "If that's a hint for my confession, it'll have to wait a while longer. Please, love," he entreated. "A few more weeks?"

To his relief and surprise, she smiled and nodded. "Do you think that $10,000 was part of the money stolen from your father? I would feel terrible if it was used on me." Surely the mention of the stolen money explained why the letter had not been given to her.

"I don't know, but it doesn't matter. What better investment than in my wife? Forget the money and the Simpsons."

"Will you promise me two things, Lynx?" she asked mysteriously.

Intrigued, he nodded. "Promise me the past is dead and you won't go looking for my father again. But if you do accidentally run into him, walk away without trouble. Please do this for me, for us. Don't allow him or the past to come between us."

"I will, if you'll promise the same things," he offered.

"I promise," she stated quickly.

"I promise," he vowed, smiling at her. He couldn't change the past. Nor could he kill Brax if he confronted him; to do so would place a wedge between him and his wife. Brax had taken something special from him; but in a way, Brax had replaced it with something more valuable. Besides, the letter revealed something Lynx hadn't considered before; Brax had intended to walk away alone. Something had changed Brax's mind: either Laura had done so, or Rankin had caught them saying farewell. Whatever the reasons, it was over now . . .

Chapter Eighteen

That night Calinda and Lynx had made passionate
love for hours, to awaken the next morning to another
fiery and leisurely bout of sensual pleasure. Calinda
felt it was best to accept her husband as he was until he
could effect drastic changes in his life and thoughts.
With her love and loyalty proven, that day couldn't be
far off.

When they came down for breakfast, they appeared
utterly happy and bewitched with each other. The am-
orous looks and cheerful banter between them vexed
Salina. Evidently the sly Calinda had confessed everything and disarmed Lynx. Did Calinda have a new and
powerful hold over him? She wondered why Lynx
kept Calinda around, now that he had everything he
wanted from her. Was there another vengeful challenge to be met? Salina was more determined than
ever to devastate their marriage, to make certain Cal
learned why this golden treasure had pursued and
married her . . .

Calinda and Lynx went riding after breakfast, to return later for a picnic lunch to carry to the pond. Calinda raced upstairs to retrieve her outfit for swimming; Lynx took care of another task. While they were gathering needed items for their outing, Salina set one of her plans into motion before packing the envious basket . . .

Lynx tied the basket and other bundle to his saddle and mounted. He grinned at Cal and challenged, "Beat me to the pond and you can share my lunch." With that playful statement, he clicked his tongue and raced off toward the end of the corral to wait at their starting point.

Calinda jumped into the saddle. Before she could knee her chestnut roan, he frantically pawed the ground and reared, flaying his hooves in the air and neighing in outrage. The saddle shifted to the right and Calinda was thrown to the hard ground. Manuel ran forward and grabbed the horse's reins before he could trample her legs. Before anyone could notice, he furtively removed the burr which he had planted beneath her saddle. He quickly removed the loosened saddle and tossed it aside, then guided the animal over to the fence and tied his reins.

Salina's first cousin went to Calinda to assist her. "Are you all right, *Senora* Cardone? Anything broken?"

Seeing the incident, Lynx came racing back to her, hopping off Star's back and rushing to his fallen wife. "What happened? Are you hurt, love?" he inquired apprehensively, kneeling beside her.

Calinda was still struggling to breathe, the wind knocked from her lungs by the heavy thud. Finally she nodded. Lynx helped her to stand. She rubbed her right hip and winced. "Just banged up a bit. The horse went crazy when I mounted, then the saddle slipped."

"Didn't you check it after our ride? You know it loosens after a swift run and good sweat," he chided her perilous oversight.

"I did check it after we returned. It was snug. Why would he act like that?" she inquired, nettled by his scolding, suspiciously eyeing the contented beast at the fence.

"I'll check him out," Lynx said, then went to see if there was a problem. He examined the saddle and found nothing. He studied the horse for any injury. Manuel had wiped the spot of blood from the sharp burr, leaving no evidence of its previous presence to alert Lynx.

"Everything looks fine," he told his sore wife.

"Except me," she retorted. "My fanny feels terrible."

"Think I should fetch the doctor to check you over?"

"Don't be silly. It wasn't my first fall, and won't be my last. What I need is a soothing swim. How about I ride with you?" she asked.

He grinned. "That's the craziest trick to finagle a ride, woman."

"Got to get your undivided attention some way," she teased, attempting to restrain her wild imagination. Who had intentionally loosened her girth?

He chuckled as he helped her mount behind him. "Slowly, love, no slapping this sore rear with a bouncing pace," she hinted merrily.

At the pond, Lynx eyed her closely and questioned, "Are you sure you aren't hurt, Cal?"

"Just my pride and seat. Somebody loosened that

saddle, Lynx," she informed him unexpectedly, thinking it wise to air her suspicion.

He stared at her. "Come on, Cal. Who would do that?"

"I don't know, but someone did. I checked that girth and tightened it. You were standing there watching me, remember?"

"I saw you lift the stirrup and work with it. Are you sure you tightened it, not loosened it?" he asked, fretting over her charge.

"I get thrown and you don't care. I tightened the damn girth! Forget it!" Cal snapped, heading for the water with a limp.

He surged forward and halted her progress. "If you're certain, Cal, I'll check into it. I'll ask Manuel if he saw anything."

Her face brightened, then glared coldly. "He's Salina's cousin, isn't he?" she asked suddenly, her mind spinning with that idea.

"Yes, why?" he inquired curiously.

"Nothing. Let's go swimming. I'm hot and achy."

"Just a minute, woman. What were you hinting at?"

"If I didn't know any better, I'd accuse that little witch of pulling this trick," she heatedly announced, lightly rubbing the sensitive area. "She has been nice lately, but . . ." she halted pensively.

"You're wrong, Cal. Manuel's been with us for years. Why would he let Salina get him fired? Or worse, beaten by me!"

"Salina's been here for years, too," she responded irritably. "Maybe her truce isn't so peaceful and sincere. She did flip sides very easily."

"I'll question Manuel tonight," Lynx told her, dismayed.

"No, let it ride. But I'll be watching both of them from now on," she decided aloud. If Manuel and Salina weren't behind this accident, that left only Lynx. For certain, it wasn't her oversight! Why was she always in trouble when he came around?

As Cal removed her boots and socks, Lynx observed her. If he didn't know any better, he might think she suspected him. She could have been injured badly. She wouldn't risk death or broken bones to gain his attention, not when she already had it. Surely it was a freak accident. Then again, maybe he should check out this curious event. Hopefully she hadn't deceived him yesterday with her revelations of the letters. Hopefully she hadn't learned of Salina's mischief and sought revenge by implicating her.

As he removed his own boots, he scolded himself. What was wrong with him? Too many years of loneliness, cynicism, and wariness. If he couldn't trust his wife, he couldn't trust anyone. Clearly, someone was trying to harm her, and he would discover who and why.

Her right side throbbing, Calinda merely played in the water for a time. She left the refreshing liquid to lie on a blanket in the sun, turning to her stomach to allow the sun's warmth to dry her clothes and to relax the stiffening in her right buttock. She wanted to dismiss her suspicions, but she couldn't. Too many past perils added to this one to alarm her. Who was behind them? Why? It was possible for Salina to be involved in this one, but not the others. Perhaps she was jumping the gun by accusing Salina and Manuel . . .

Lynx came over to join her, lying down beside her prone body. He moved her lengthy hair aside and nuzzled her neck. She squirmed and giggled. "I hope your

420

passions aren't as fiery as the sun's heat, my love. I refuse to place this hip against the hard ground," she teased.

"Maybe I can think of something," he playfully hinted.

Without lifting her head, Calinda peeked through curls fallen over her face. She smiled in amusement. "Always hungry, aren't we?"

He pushed aside the flaming locks which blocked a clear view of her lovely face and compelling eyes. His left arm went across her shoulders as he laid his face near hers. "Yep," he cheerfully agreed.

She shifted to her left side and curled against him, kissing the tip of his nose, then gingerly bit the strong chin. "You know, you're delicious," she said provocatively.

He turned to his right side and drew her closer to his stalwart frame. As she snuggled into his possessive embrace, the furry mat on his chest pillowed her damp head. Her fingers wandered through it as if passing through golden dried grass upon firm soil. Her hand roamed over his broad shoulder and slipped under his arm to fall over his side. She listened and thrilled as his heart-rate increased. She was intoxicated by her effect on him. How could her contact and simple actions stir his passions so fiercely? The same way his affected her! When she was in his arms, she felt so loved and protected, so barren of any thought but him. In his close proximity, no haunting enigmas existed, no riddles haunted her mind, no uncertainties harassed her heart. Was it safe and wise to love so strongly, gullibly, and deeply?

When she moved and groaned, he asked tenderly, "Hurt much?"

"Yep," she insouciantly answered. "It's only a bad bruise; it should be better by tomorrow or Monday."

"I was afraid you'd say that," he wailed humorously.

"If I can wait around for weeks to be with you, my love, surely you can manage a day or two for me," she taunted his disappointment.

"Right now, I'm having a helluva time, but tonight will be easy."

"How so?" she mocked his alleged control later.

"I promised Rankin I'd set a trap for those fence cutters. We're losing too many cattle to them. If I get home tonight, it'll be late."

"Lynx!" she shrieked in annoyance. "You were gone all day yesterday, and you just got home."

"In your condition, it might be wise to sleep out," he jested.

"What happened to friend, as well as lover?" she taunted.

"You think I could hang around you for that long without touching you?" he murmured skeptically. "Besides, it'll be our ranch one day, Cal. We have to protect our property. Who knows, perhaps one of those rustlers sneaked up and tampered with your saddle, hoping to send my thoughts in your direction instead of theirs. I don't like having bandits this close to my woman and home; I want them gone before I am."

She smiled and caressed his cheek. "Then you'd best hang around and protect both," she sweetly suggested.

"I plan to," he said. "Ready to eat?"

"I don't think I can sit up yet."

"Then I'll feed you lying down," he solved her problem.

They rested on their stomachs with elbows propped,

eating the sumptuous fare and drinking wine. "Who's the thoughtful one?" she inquired, nodding at the wine and glasses.

"Me, naturally," he stated proudly. "While you were upstairs."

They enjoyed the romantic setting another two hours before heading home. After a lengthy span in a tub of hot water, Lynx asked, "Think I should rub some liniment on that lovely backside?"

"Don't you dare touch it," she declared fearfully.

"Let me have a look," he insisted, removing the bath sheet from her slender body. He walked behind her and gazed at the large area of blackish blue. "Lie down on the bed, Cal. This needs to be checked. You sure nothing's broken?"

She followed his gentle order, stretching out on the soft mattress. "This might be touchy, love; bear with me," he coaxed.

She clenched her teeth as he probed her hip-bone. He shifted down to her upper thigh and examined it, then up to check her ribs. "Move to your left side, then wiggle it back and forth," he instructed.

She did so, but muttered how foolish she felt. "Any sharp pains when you move it around?" he inquired.

"Just soreness," she replied through gritted teeth.

"It doesn't seem broken, but there could be a crack. I think it's best if you stay in bed for a while," he concluded cautiously.

"That's the craziest trick to wrangle me into bed," she teased.

He frowned at her, then chuckled. "Since you're new at this set-up, I should tell you that a wife always obeys her husband."

"Is that a fact? Where is that marital law written?"

They both laughed. "You just want me out of everyone's hair. Think I'll be irritable and obnoxious?" she murmured coyly.

"I hope you'll be frustrated as hell," he sassily stated.

"Then, you're wasting your time, love; I already know that uncomfortable feeling. And you're to blame."

"Me?" he hinted beguilingly.

"You probably loosened that girth to keep me confined while you work all night," she speculated, her hand covering her giggling mouth. "If you want to trap me in bed, you shouldn't do it with a hindering injury."

"Not a bad idea, but too rash. I want you in bed, but not disabled. Think a hot, wet cloth will help ease the aching?"

"I can picture me lying here naked with a bandage on my rear."

They burst into shared laughter again. "Sounds appealing to me."

"You, Lynx Cardone, are a brute," she charged as she gingerly rolled to her back, the bed cushioning the injury.

He leaned over and kissed her, stealing her breath. "But a nice one," he debated, trailing his fingertips over her breasts.

She captured his enticing hand and playfully bit the area between his thumb and forefinger. "Ouch," he shrieked as if hurt.

"With an injury like that, you should be put straight to bed."

"You dangerous and wily vixen. I'd spank you if that lovely rump could take the earned punishment." His eyes glowed with deviltry.

"Do I get served dinner in bed?" she inquired, smiling at him.

"Food only," he mocked her double entendre.

"Yes, master dear," she pouted.

Lynx set a small table near the bed and placed her dinner on it. When she asked why he couldn't eat with her, she learned he was leaving to set his rustler trap. He kissed her and asked if she needed anything else. She sighed and shook her head. He kissed her again, this time a lengthy and sensual span. When Calinda wildly responded, he drew back and inhaled with a shudder. "You're a tormenting hussy."

"I know," she flippantly responded. "But you love me anyway."

"Damn right, I do. I best git while I can." He flashed her a woeful grin and left.

Calinda picked over her meal, then read. When Salina came for the table and dishes, the Mexican girl inquired about the fall. Guarded, Calinda astutely claimed it was a silly accident. From now on, she would keep her eyes and ears open.

Most of the night, Cal varied between quick naps and restless tossings. Once she awoke in a cold sweat, a nightmare torturing her: she could see those flaying hooves descending toward her helpless body, crushing her time and time again. Twice she got up and walked around to loosen taut muscles. When she returned to bed the second time, the door opened and Lynx slipped inside. It was five in the morning.

"Can't sleep, love?" he inquired worriedly.

"Now I can," she decided aloud, cuddling up to him on her left side, her arm lying over his iron-muscled chest. "Any success?"

"Nope. It's like they were warned off tonight. We'll try it again tomorrow night after we check around for a scout."

"Must you?" she asked.

"I've already explained, Cal. Don't make me go through it again. It's late and I'm exhausted. Can you slide over? It's too hot to snuggle," he growled, feeling frustrated and tense.

"It wouldn't be too hot if I weren't injured," she snapped, hurt.

"Why the hell do you think I'm so hot and miserable? I've been at boiling level all day. It's got me edgy. Woman, I need you," he confessed in a hoarse voice. "Do you know how you get to me?"

She smiled to herself. Her hand played over his flesh as it drifted downward to comprehend his aroused state. "Please, Callie, don't," he pleaded huskily, tremors passing over his body.

"You said you would think of something," she reminded him.

"You're hurt, love," he argued at his raging passion.

"Some pains are worse than others," she rebutted.

"I don't want to hurt you, Cal," he reasoned, his body aflame.

Abruptly Calinda recalled their sensuous adventure in the watershed. She threw the sheet aside and walked to the armless rocking chair. "Come over here, Lynx," she requested warmly, feeling wonderfully wanton and brazen.

"Please, Callie," he entreated.

"Shut up, my love, and come here," she commanded sternly.

When he reluctantly indulged her, she told him to sit down. "What are you doing, woman?" he asked, taking his seat.

"Remember that day in the tub?" she hinted, then sat in his lap, each of her legs crossing one of his. She boldly and bravely grasped his manhood and slipped it within her eager womanhood. She eased forward to lock their bodies together, her feet pressing against the backs of the rockers. "Now, Lynx, the rest is up to you."

He groaned in blissful torment. "You sure this won't hurt you?" he asked, praying for a negative reply.

"Not enough to make me want to stop," she said, leaning forward to seal her lips to his.

His arms encircled her waist as he carefully worked his pulsing shaft deeper into that inviting recess. As her lips tantalized his and her breasts threatened to burn his chest, he feared his manhood would explode instantly at the sheer ecstasy of her contact. As he began to move gently, the rocker swayed back and forth to match his steady rhythm. When her lips strewed kisses over his face and nibbled at his ears, his head fell back against the chair. He thought he would go wild with rapture when she seductively writhed her hips against his flaming torch. When her mouth returned to his, she seemingly devoured it with feverish savagery, her tongue outlining his lips several times.

"Merciful heavens, Callie, you're killing me," he moaned.

"Can you think of a better way to die, my love?" she reasoned, her breath warm in his ear as she nipped gently at his lobe.

"Never," he agreed, laboring to sate this desire before her position became unbearable to her. Soon, love's fiery heat was washing over him as the potent spasms staggered his control.

Exhausted and appeased, his hands rested on her thighs, his head leaning back against the chair as he sought to master his rapid breathing and pounding heart. She drew a chuckle from him when she nonchalantly said, "You owe me one, love. I won't let you forget it."

"Nothing could repay such generosity, love," he debated.

"Your love can and does, Lynx," she freely admitted.

"Then you have no debt against me, for I love you, Calinda Cardone." He pulled her tightly against him, holding her for a long time. Such love and tenderness filled him, warmed him.

"Now, can I snuggle?" she teased, laughing softly.

"Now, you can do anything you please."

He lifted her and carried her to bed. For the next seven hours, they were lost to reality and fate's demands.

After rising and dressing quietly, Lynx stood by the bed gazing down at his serene wife. He had never experienced such love and contentment. Calinda Braxton Cardone belonged to him of her own will.

Monday passed tranquilly for both. Lynx went riding with his father to make plans for tonight's snare. Calinda rested for most of the day. When Rankin and Lynx returned by mid-afternoon, they chatted and snacked together. Later, Rankin pored over the ranchbooks in his office while Calinda nestled in Lynx's arms as he read aloud the local paper. When he tossed it aside and pulled her closer to him, he related the events of a large round-up and cattle drive to market.

Salina entered the enormous room and asked if they needed anything before she prepared dinner. Lynx and

Calinda gazed longingly into each other's eyes and told her "nothing." Salina raged inwardly as Lynx stroked Calinda's cheek and murmured unknowingly, "I have everything I need right here."

Calinda's eyes softened and glowed. "Me, too," she replied.

Neither noticed Salina's hasty retreat from the infuriating sight, nor her glare of hatred and jealousy. She went into the kitchen, warning herself not to slam pots around in her irate condition. "When he sates his lust for you, *bruja,* your day is coming," she whispered balefully.

At dinner, Lynx brought a soft-bottomed chair to the table so Calinda could join them for the evening meal. The two men exposed their new plans to Calinda as they dined. Afterward, Lynx assisted Calinda to their room and into bed. "Think you can sleep better tonight?"

She grinned and nodded. "I have some dreams to create."

He bent to kiss her before leaving, to spend another useless night lying in wait for rustlers who had been warned of their concealed presence in three logical locations. It would be lunchtime on Tuesday before Rankin and Lynx learned where they'd struck.

In spite of Calinda's annoying torment, she slept fitfully all night. She hardly stirred when Lynx came to bed near dawn.

When she went downstairs past lunch the following day, Lynx and Rankin had left to check on Steve's report of a cut fence on the northern border of the ranch. Beside the number of steers taken, many had escaped through the opening and compelled the hired hands to search for them. The two owners realized it was time to do serious thinking about who was tipping off the rustlers. They rode to a private spot to discuss this unsettling mystery, wondering who couldn't be trusted.

Before they could dismount, someone opened gunfire on them. Lynx was off Star's back with one agile leap, concealing himself behind a slender live-oak. Rankin's startled horse reared and threw him. For three minutes, they were pinned down by the ominous gunshots. When Lynx heard the assailant's horse galloping off, he couldn't pursue him; Rankin was injured and bleeding.

He went to his father's side. Rankin sat up, cradling his left arm. "Broken?" Lynx hinted.

"Don't know," his father answered, grimacing.

"Let's get you to the house. I'll send Charlie for Doc."

"What about that bushwacker?" Rankin inquired angrily.

"He's long gone. Here, let me help you to mount."

When they reached the stable, Lynx told Charlie to fetch the doctor. Charlie took control of their animals before saddling another horse. Lynx assisted Rankin to the house. He asked the fretting Salina to tell Calinda they were home and his father was hurt. To his amazement, Salina told him Calinda had gone riding.

Rankin sank into a chair, then hastily told Lynx to go find Calinda. He could see how distressed his son was over Calinda's absence. What if she confronted that dangerous villain? Rankin had never seen his son so panicky.

Lynx remarked tensely, "I'll be right back, Father. Don't move. I've got to locate her before . . ."

When he didn't complete his anxious thought,

Rankin encouraged, "I'll be fine. Go get her."

Lynx went to question Charlie as he was just leaving. Charlie told him he had saddled a horse for her an hour ago. She had headed up the lengthy road toward the gate, walking unsteadily beside the animal. Lynx thanked him and accepted a double-back ride in that direction, if that was the one she had truly taken . . .

When they met her returning to the ranch, she was strolling cautiously, the horse trailing behind. Lynx slid off Charlie's horse, then waved him on to town. Charlie took off at a swift pace, kicking up dust behind him. Calinda turned and watched the rider, then focused her curious attention on Lynx as he inexplicably and verbally assailed her.

"Where in tarnation have you been!" he thundered at her. "I told you not to go riding alone. I thought you were injured!"

"What's chewing at you, Lynx?" she asked in bewilderment. "I went walking to loosen up my stiff backside. I'm tired of lazing around. Why are you shouting at me?"

"You shouldn't ride in your condition," he snarled in tension.

"I didn't!" she snapped back. "And stop ordering me around like a child or dim-wit! I've got to do something to ease my nerves."

"Then why did you take a horse?" he demanded.

"In case I couldn't get back on my own two feet. If a problem came up, I thought I could throw myself over the saddle and let him bring me home. I don't require your permission to leave the house. Shut up and leave me alone!" she warned frostily, her fanny aching.

"Damnit, Cal! We were attacked by a gunman on the range. Rankin is hurt. Charlie's gone for the doc-

431

tor. If you ever ride out alone again, I'll spank you, sore tail or not!" he shouted.

When his stormy gaze shifted to the gunbelt and weapon at her waist, she trembled at the horrifying gleam in his tawny eyes. "If you're wondering if it's been fired, Lynx, the answer is yes. If you care to wander up the road a piece, you'll find a very dead rattler with several bullets in him."

"Don't be ridiculous, Callie!" he stated sarcastically. "Why would you shoot at us?" he asked, revealing his line of thought.

"To gain ownership of this illustrious ranch?" she sneered, angered by his unnerving mood and harsh words.

"It's partly yours now!" he yelled, perturbed. "Why be greedy?"

Forgetting about Rankin during their implausible quarrel, she scoffed, "If I got rid of you two, I could be a wealthy and powerful widow. I could own everything in sight," she stressed, waving her hand.

He grabbed her by the shoulders and roughly shook her. "But you wouldn't have me around to give you pleasure and excitement!"

The argument silly, she still continued it. "Which times have been rare since we met! When you're like this, I'd just as soon be alone! Sometimes I wonder why I stay here to take such abuse!"

"Why do you?" he snarled coldly as she rashly provoked him.

"Because I love you, you bastard!" she shrieked in frustration. "Why, I don't know myself!" she added, jerking free of his grip.

"Let's get you home. Doc can check you over, too," he stated, berating his stupid words and actions which fear had borne.

"No, thank you. I don't care to have some strange man eyeing my naked derriere. Once was sufficient," she purred cattily.

"I'm being an ass, Callie. I'm sorry. I was worried about you, and I'm upset over Rankin," he suddenly apologized, leashing his temper and tongue. "I'm used to being shot at, but he isn't. This whole rustler affair has me edgy and fatigued. I shouldn't take my fury out on you. You just have a way of provoking me at the wrong time."

He looped the bridle reins over the saddle horn, then slapped the horse's rump to send him racing for the stable. He scooped her up into his arms and headed for the house.

"Put me down this instant, Lynx!" she demanded, wildly thrashing her legs to show her vexation.

"Stop that, or I'll drop you on your sore bottom. You've had enough exercise for today. Enjoy the free ride."

"Nothing's free around you, Lynx. Afraid I'll antagonize my injury and inconvenience you?" she taunted helplessly, still piqued.

He infuriatingly ignored her barb and kept walking. When they entered the house, he carried her into the den and set her down beside his father. She ruefully asked, "How are you, Rankin?"

"I haven't decided," he replied with a strained laugh.

She looked at his gradually swelling wrist. "Lynx, get a wide strip of cloth. We need to bandage this tightly to halt the swelling. Rip up an old sheet," she suggested, taking charge of the situation.

"We best wait for the doctor, Cal," he argued softly.

"We can't. He'll be too long arriving. I've seen injuries like this. I know what to do," she informed him. "And get Salina to bring me some salty water to clean this cut on his forehead."

When Lynx left to follow her instructions, she muttered, "He should have taken care of you rather than stalking me down."

"He went wild when you weren't here, Cal. I've never seen my son so panicky. He was afraid you had run into that cutthroat. He set me down and dashed out to rescue you again. I suspect my son has a bad case of love fever," he explained Lynx's behavior to a stunned wife.

Calinda was plagued by guilt over her conduct. Why did Lynx refuse to expose his great concern? Why was he so defensive and secretive about his emotions? He was so unacquainted with love, sharing, and fear that he didn't know how to deal with them!

When her sullen mate returned with the torn sheet, she smiled at him and thanked him. "Hold this, love," she told him, pointing to the cloth ends on Rankin's lower arm. Lynx placed his fingertips where she indicated. She carefully and snugly rolled the strip around the injured area. She informed Rankin it would be tight and uncomfortable, but it would prevent more swelling. When the bandage was secured in place, she cleansed the small cut on his temple where his head had struck a jagged rock. "That should do it until the doctor arrives, unless you want a brandy to ease the pain and settle your nerves." she hinted.

When she appeared to have trouble arising from her kneeling position, Lynx took her hands and helped her to her feet. She smiled into his wary expression. "You could use a stiff drink, too, my love."

"Did you see any strangers while you were out?" Lynx asked.

"No, I wish I had. But I wouldn't have known enough to shoot at him."

"Please don't go out alone, Callie," he gravely entreated.

"I know I'm a bad girl at times, too willful and impulsive," she confessed. "I'll do my best to correct those terrible traits."

"That sounds like excellent advice for both of us, including curbing these sharp tongues," he whispered softly, tapping her lips and his. "You scared the pants off me, woman," he admitted shamefully.

She didn't care if Rankin was in the room, she hugged him tightly. "What's this?" Lynx asked mockingly.

Her eyes said, "I love you; thanks," as did her radiant smile.

They sat together on the couch waiting for the doctor. She heard about the alarming episode on the range and their mutual suspicions about the thefts. The doctor was on another emergency, and it was several hours before he arrived.

After examining Rankin, the elderly doctor glanced at Calinda and smiled warmly. "You didn't need me, Rankin; she did everything possible in such a case. I would have treated you the same way. Rest easy, you're in good hands." He gave Calinda an approving nod and instructions for Rankin's care. "If you ever decide to become a nurse, let me know. I could use a smart and alert helper."

"Thank you, Doctor Weaver, but I can't stand the sight of blood. I get nauseous and faint," she told the amused man.

"Too bad," he murmured.

After the doctor was gone and Rankin was resting comfortably in the den, Lynx and Calinda went to their room to freshen up for dinner and talk privately. Lynx noticed a letter on the bed the moment he entered the room. He swaggered over and retrieved it; it was addressed to his wife. He turned and asked, "What's this, Cal?"

She glanced over at the item in his grasp, her eyes widening in puzzlement. "I don't know. Why?"

"It's a letter for you," Lynx casually announced.

"From where?" she inquired, coming toward him. "I hope not another one from the Simpsons," she fretted.

"It didn't come by mail," he stated, holding up the envelope with her name scrawled across the front.

Her face went pale and she trembled. "That's the same handwriting as the first one. How did it get here?" Cal asked fearfully.

"I'll ask Salina; you wait here." He left the room as she sank down on the edge of the bed, oblivious to her aching hip.

When he returned, he told her Salina hadn't seen anyone around, that she and Charlie had been cleaning the supply shed and checking the stock there. "You didn't see anyone come around?" he pressed. "How long were you out earlier?"

"I don't know; I didn't notice the time. I guess about an hour. But I didn't see anyone," she told him. "What does it say?"

"There's very little to block the view, Cal. How could someone ride up and away without you seeing him?" he probed.

"The same way no one else noticed a stranger! The

same way one attacked you two and got away without revealing his identity! There are plenty of things to block the view: the house, stables, and sheds! Are you accusing me of lying?" she demanded breathlessly.

"I just don't understand how these mysterious messages keep appearing from nowhere. I don't like the idea that someone can sneak in and out of my home at will. I think we had better keep the doors and windows locked, and maybe post a guard for a while."

"What if I hadn't taken that walk? I could have been in worse danger than you two. Clearly this mystery man doesn't want to be recognized. But how does he get close enough to watch the house for an opportunity to make a stealthy visit and then carry it out?" she reasoned in alarm.

"Let's see what our villain has to say this time. I wonder why he would leave it while I was home," he deliberated aloud.

"Burn it," Cal pleaded, a foreboding sensation washing over her.

"After he went to such trouble and peril to deliver it?" he teased.

"Who's doing this to me, Lynx? Who's trying to be rid of me? I bet it's just another lure. It won't work this time. I don't care what it says; I'll never leave this ranch again."

Lynx opened the envelope and silently read the message:

My dearest daughter,
    Forgive this manner of contacting you, but do not be afraid. The others will be distracted to give you time to find and read this message in secret. You have grown into a very beautiful young

lady and I am proud of you. I saw you in Lampasas, but could not risk coming to your side. I watched you for two days. My enemy was lurking in the shadows waiting to spring on me and slay me. We must meet and talk. There is much you should know about the Cardones. You have trusted them too soon, my child, and I fear for your life and happiness. They have used you and tricked you. It is urgent you come to Dallas. Let no one see you leave. I will contact you there and explain. Please trust me, daughter. Leave the ranch today. I will take steps to protect you from them.

A tic formed along his clenched jawline and he went rigid. His eyes narrowed and hardened. "I'm riding over to Dallas to check out this invitation," he coldly announced from his pensive study.

Cal jumped up and seized his arm. "No! You can't! Don't you see, Lynx? That note isn't for me; it's to lure you away. Please don't leave," she urged him frantically, eyes wide with terror.

"How do you know? You haven't read it," he remarked oddly.

"If it was for me, idiot, he wouldn't have left it where you were certain to see it. Besides, why wouldn't I give it to you? I have this awful feeling that letter means trouble."

"You burned the first one, then took off in secret," he said.

"That was before we had an understanding. I told you I wouldn't leave again. I've related the contents of all my messages."

"Read it, Calinda," he said firmly, holding out the

438

paper, curiously calling her by her first name.

"No, I don't want to," she refused, turning her back. "If he can't be open with me, I don't trust him. It must be a trick."

"Him, who?" Lynx inquired casually, as if trying to entrap her.

"How should I know? I just assumed it was a he."

Lynx insisted, "I'll read it to you. My dearest daughter," Lynx began icily. He looked over at her and sneered, "From Brax."

She slowly turned and stared at him, her body trembling and her face draining of natural color. Her lips parted as if to silence him, her tormented gaze wide and beseeching. Tears glistened in her sad eyes. She looked at him as if he had plunged a hot knife into her heart. As her chin and lips began to quiver, she looked on the verge of racking sobs. She sat on the edge of the bed and stared at him.

Lynx observed this strange reaction, holding silent until she composed herself. Her head remained lowered for a time as she was lost in deep thought. Finally she lifted it and met his searching gaze. "Shall I read the contents?" he asked when she didn't speak.

Her eyes and voice were dulled as she murmured faintly, "I don't care who it claims to be from, Lynx; I don't want to hear it. Why are you being so persistent and cruel? You recently told me to forget him and the past," she painfully reasoned. "Why must you torment me this way? My father has been lost to me for years. Don't bring him back to life."

"The past can't be over, Cal, not as long as he's trying to reach you. He was waiting for you in Lampasas. He didn't show his miserable face because of me. He's trying to set up another meeting."

"I was there long enough for him to come forward before you suddenly appeared. You're not saying you were there all along while that gunslinger Deavers was terrifying me?" she inquired in dread.

"No, Cal, I arrived that night. But your father thought I was lurking around," he concluded. "This note isn't a trick, Cal. From what it says, only Brax could have written it."

"He's never been a father to me, so stop shoving him down my throat! I don't want to see him! I don't want to speak with him! There's nothing he can say to justify his actions! I hate him! Is that clear enough, Lynx?" she panted in anguish.

"If you hear him out, Calinda, we could both learn the truth and be free of the past," he suggested to her astonishment.

The letter intrigued her, but pained her deeply. Reading the hatred and coldness in his eyes and tone, she accused angrily, "You mean, set a trap for him so you can gun him down!"

"Do you care?" he asked indifferently.

"He's a person, Lynx; I don't want you killing anyone. No matter how wicked he's been in the past, he's my father. If you slay him, we could never be happy together. Please, I'm begging you; don't chase this vengeful dream. Rankin and I need you here. Have you forgotten about the rustlers and that man who tried to gun down you two? Are you forgetting someone can slip in and out of this house?"

"Your messenger takes the blame for that incident, to stall us out there until you found this note," he frigidly informed her.

"You mean he's that dangerous, and you want me to walk into his den? I don't believe what I'm hearing.

440

My God, you westerners are all crazy and violent! I won't go!" she stated defiantly. "And if you do, don't expect to find me here when you return!" she added. Suddenly she was furious with him. He was acting as if she were conspiring with her father. "If my father is so evil and yellow that he can't come to me here, then he doesn't deserve to see me again. He made his decisions long ago; he'll have to abide by them. It's over."

Lynx began to chuckle. "Excellent, my love," he murmured happily, winking at her. Shocked by his genial mood, she gaped at him. "I just wanted to be certain you wouldn't feel drawn to him again. I was afraid his letter would compel you to Dallas. Now, I know I'm more important to you than he is. You're right, love; it's finally over."

Calinda glared at him, breathing heavily. She balled her fists and pounded on his chest until he seized them and stared at her in confusion. "Damn you, Lynx Cardone! How dare you pull a trick like that! It's unforgiveable! Your little note scared the wits out of me! Do you know how you frightened me, to think someone could sneak into our bedroom unnoticed! If you don't trust me by now, I don't belong here. How could you be so cruel and spiteful! Get your lousy hands off me!" she shrieked.

"Hold on a minute, love," he demanded, tightening his grip to keep her from pulling free. "I didn't have anything to do with the note! I was just trying to make sure it wouldn't entice you to follow its urgent summons. That's why I was picking at you. I had to know what you were feeling. I didn't write it, Cal; I swear."

Their gaze fused. Each was speechless as the other's words and actions settled in. "You didn't write it?" she inquired shakily.

441

"No, love, I didn't. I was just as shocked as you were."

She ceased her struggles. "Then who did?" she agonized.

"I hate to say it, Cal, but Brax. Read it and you'll see why," he coaxed, his gaze unreadable, as was his tone of voice.

Calinda glanced at the letter still clutched in her love's tight grip. She longed for the truth. But could she seek it at any price? Could she allow her father to keep torturing them in this cruel manner? Even if she followed the letter's instructions, it might be another wild-goose-chase. To go to her father might appear a betrayal of the Cardones. Besides, she had plenty of clues about her father's actions. There was nothing he could say to justify his evil deeds.

It was a difficult decision, but she made it. She shook her head, tears welling on her lower lids and threatening to spill over their narrow banks. "You know what that other letter did to me; I can't punish myself like that again. He killed himself to me, and I must let him remain buried in the past. I want him out of our lives, to stop causing a breach between us. Don't you see, Lynx? No matter what he says, he can't ever be a part of my life again, not after what he did to you and Rankin. Swear you won't go to Dallas. I could never forgive either of you for hurting the other. If I must choose between you two, I want my husband, the man I love more than life itself. If you truly love me, swear it."

Lynx pulled her into his arms and hugged her fiercely. How could he ever love her more than he did at this very moment. Yet, if he didn't do something about Brax, her father might continue to interfere in their lives. Brax held certain weapons which he could use against the Cardones, weapons to possibly destroy his life with Cal. Still, he had to handle this matter in such a way as to remain honest with her. "I won't go to Dallas, love," he vowed, mentally adding, *but I will go to town tomorrow and send a telegram for a friend to check out this riddle . . .*

Chapter Nineteen

Wednesday and Thursday were relatively calm days on the ranch. For some unknown reason, the rustling and fence-cutting abruptly halted. Lynx insisted on running the ranch while Rankin nursed his injured arm for a few days. Between Calinda's healing bruise and Rankin's disabled arm, they spent more time together. They played cards and took short walks. They even planned a large barbecue for early September when Lynx should be home to stay.

Lynx was out most of both days, giving orders or checking on various chores. This time of year hinted at the approaching fall when all ranches were active with round-ups, solitary ones if the ranch size allowed it or a joint one when several smaller ranches banded together for protection along the trail to the stockyards near the train depot.

At night, Rankin and Calinda would join Lynx and other cowboys as they played or listened to music, tossed horseshoes, or re-lived olden days when life was

444

perilous and challenging. Some of the men would sit around the table in the bunk houses drinking coffee and playing poker. It was the rule that hard drinking could be done only on Saturday night or Sunday, when the men were off, except for the few selected for that weekend's chores.

Friday was an exciting day. To practice for the fall round-up and to provide tension-breaking entertainment, the ranch-hands were involved in a mock-rodeo. Volunteers took turns breaking-in captured broncos, wild stallions and obstinate mustangs. There was a stirring bout of calf-roping, then a delightful session of trick roping. Rankin told Cal the men weren't permitted to ride bulls to prevent injuries. They rode horses, instead.

After observing the dangerous bronco-busting for a while, Calinda was relieved her husband didn't attempt such sport. But she could see the gleam of desire in his eyes; she could sense the eagerness to be on the back of one of those bucking stallions. When the hands encouraged Lynx to try it, he laughed and told them, "Next time," saying he couldn't risk an injury today. Knowing Lynx Cardone was exceptionally brave and daring, they accepted his explanation.

When Steve suggested they have target practice and a shooting contest, Calinda was given a first-hand observation of how fast and accurate Lynx was with his Colts. He could draw and fire in the flicker of an eye. She shook her head several times during the contest, wondering how the target could explode before she saw Lynx react to the "fire" shout. His movements were so fluid and swift, one moment he was poised ready and in a flash he was limber and the action was over! It almost seemed as if Lynx hadn't moved a muscle, as if he had wished the target shattered. It looked a greased reflex, so easy and natural, as if man and weapon were briefly one. Lynx never missed a target or failed to be first. In each instant, the gun was back in his holster before the others had drawn and fired. Cal was amazed.

At dinner, Cal kept staring at Lynx in astonishment. When he grinned and asked why she was watching him so strangely, she said, "You're so fast; if I blinked, I missed your shot. You hit every one, Lynx. No wonder you've never been beaten; I doubt any man could."

Laughter spilled forth into the room. Lynx winked at her and teased, "I thought you said there was always a better challenger."

"That was before I saw how perfect you are. I suppose I should relax now, but it frightens me even more," Cal confessed.

"Why?" Lynx asked, bemused and flattered.

"Too many gunslingers will demand to take your place. Don't you get tired of the killing and fighting? It's like one endless nightmare of death and violence. What if eager men pursue the colorful legend here?" Cal sadly expressed her fears.

"I don't kill or fight unless there's no other way out, Cal. Once I retire from the scene, they'll forget about me, be glad I'm gone."

"I recall reading about Wesley Hardin. Did the Rangers forget him when he fled Texas? No, they relentlessly pursued and captured him. Legends don't retire so easily, my love," she asserted warily.

Calinda wondered why both Rankin and Lynx had tensed at her mention of the Rangers, but she didn't question their reactions. If Lynx was in trouble, she would have heard about it. "Wes killed for the fun of it, love; I don't. Besides, he was an outlaw; I'm not."

"If you weren't rich, would you use your expert talents in that line?" Calinda stunned Lynx with a curious and serious question.

He threw back his head and laughed heartily. "No way, love."

To alter the topic, Lynx dropped his dismaying news on her. "I'll be leaving tomorrow for the last time, so you best get prepared to lose your privacy. I got a telegram today, and I'm needed."

Calinda's head jerked up as she protested, "Leaving? Tomorrow? But you can't. What about the problems and dangers at home? We need you, don't we, Rankin?" she sought Rankin's assistance.

Rankin sighed heavily, knowing the details of his son's trip. "I'm fine, Cal. The sooner Lynx leaves and gets this matter settled, the sooner he'll be home for good. I can't complain; this was his longest visit in years. I think you're responsible for the change in him."

"You can't be serious," she refuted Rankin's words.

"This wrist is nearly healed. I can manage things now. Those rustlers have moved on to other pastures. We'll be all right until he gets home," the man reasoned, smiling at his son. "I've been on my own a lot longer than Lynx. I can defend my land and family."

Calinda's stupefied gaze shifted from one man to the other. How could Lynx leave his home and family at a time like this? Why would his father encourage it? Witnessing their determination, she knew further debate was useless. "Where are you heading?" she asked.

"To Waco, then San Antonio," Lynx reluctantly deceived her. The telegram from Jones had said Dallas, then Austin. If he told her where he was heading, Cal would think he was breaking his promise. He would explain later when he returned from the state capitol.

"For how long?" she asked distantly.

"Anywhere from one to six weeks," he confessed uneasily, watching her reaction to that displeasing information.

"Six weeks would put it at mid-September. What about the round-up and barbecue?" she pressed dejectedly.

"I'll try to make it home before then," Lynx subtly promised.

"The barbecue can be cancelled, but not he round-up. We won't do social planning until we hear when you'll be home," Cal wisely yielded to this vexing situation. At least he had added eight more days to their time together. But if this didn't turn out to be his last time-consuming adventure, they would need to have a very serious discussion about their marriage and his feelings . . .

After dinner, Lynx and Calinda went to their room to spend time together before his imminent departure. Most of the soreness was gone from her hip, but it still boasted loudly of a purplish-blue reminder. On the surface Lynx was in a mellow and romantic mood, but inwardly he was dreading and resenting this new separation. He knew how it must appear to her at this trying time. He had no choice but to stall an explanation until his return. On this journey he would send frequent messages home to keep himself alive in her mind.

Calinda was exceedingly quiet and almost unresponsive tonight. Each time Lynx sought to draw her out of her remote shell, she would sigh heavily and make some nonsensical comment. She determined she wouldn't quarrel with him tonight, or plead for him to remain with her. But she was dismayed by how easily and readily he could pick up and leave after what they had shared recently and the new dangers around them. Her confidence in their closeness was slowly vanishing.

"You planning to pout and rub that icy shoulder against me all night?" he playfully ventured to bring an end to her distance.

"Surely you don't expect me to be cheerfully resigned to your leaving? You haven't even left and I miss you terribly," she said.

He laughed softly as he pulled her into his entreating arms. "If you were glad to see me leave, I'd be worried sick, woman."

Cal was so tempted to break her promise to herself, to cry and beg him not to go. What hurt most was knowing she couldn't do anything to alter his plans. She wanted to scream and argue with him; she couldn't. But neither could she behave as if all was wonderful.

Following two hours of blissful lovemaking, Lynx lay awake for a long time. He fretted over the way Calinda had struggled to control her responses to him, how she had tried to accept their lovemaking dutifully and not give passionately. He could almost read a resentful glitter in her eyes at his power to sway her masked resistance to mindless surrender. Lynx sensed she rebelled inwardly against her greedy body's power over her warring senses. Finally Cal had dismissed her futile guard and given herself over to his prowess and will, submitting wildly to tantalizing ecstasy. He worried over the way she had turned her back to him and wept softly after she thought he'd fallen asleep. Was it merely his departure which was affecting her this way? Was she doubting his love and commitment? What more could he say or do?

At seven on Saturday morning, Lynx nudged his wife and called her name to awaken her. He dared not slip off again. Besides, leaving her was the last thing he wanted to do. He craved a warm send-off.

Calinda yawned and stretched, opening her eyes. Lynx smiled down at her, fluffing her hair. "You want to sleep longer or eat breakfast with me before I ride out?" he inquired.

"What time is it?" she asked, trying to clear her hazy mind.

"Seven. I need to eat and pack a few things. I'd like to get going before that sun's too high and hot. I know you're tired, Cal, but I needed to spend time with you this morning," he revealed.

"Give me a few minutes to dress, then I'll prepare our breakfast."

"Salina should be up; she can do it," her husband suggested, wanting her with him every minute.

"If you don't mind, I would prefer to cook my husband's last meal home. In case you aren't aware of the fact, I'm a good cook."

He smiled roguishly. "You're good at many things, love. If Salina enters the kitchen, tell her we want to be alone this morning."

"She'll love that," Calinda scoffed under her breath.

"Who cares what she thinks, love?" he asked breezily.

"I did, but no longer. I'm tired of going beyond half way for peace with her. It's time you and Rankin accept the fact, she will never like me or my presence. I've never been a quitter, but I give up on her. I have other matters to consume my concentration."

"Cal, are you feeling all right this morning? You look a bit pale. I think you're working too hard," he noted.

"The harder I work, the better I sleep when you're gone."

"How can I debate that stirring excuse?" he murmured.

"I shouldn't have told you; now, you'll never get your hat on the enlarged head," she jested, deciding to play it lightly this morning.

"Zat a fact, Mrs. Cardone? You adding conceit to my long list of bad traits?" he teased.

"I think you're so self-assured that it comes across as enormous ego and arrogance. I think you're too accustomed to getting your way and wishes. No doubt I'm the first problem you can't settle with those blazing Colts and your great prowess," she remarked saucily.

His chest rumbled with laughter. "You're right, Cal. You're the most exasperating, challenging, and refreshing task I've confronted. Sometimes I can't decide if I'm coming or going with you."

"I can tell; it's usually going, too much and too long," she quipped as she brushed her tangled hair, her gaze flickering over him.

"I'll remind you of your demands when you grow weary of having me underfoot," he said, trying to sound stern.

"Save your breath, love, because I won't," she retorted coyly.

"We'll see," he mused aloud, passing his tongue over his lips.

"Yes, we will," she concurred. "See you downstairs."

451

"I'm coming with you. I'd like to see my wife in action."

"Afraid I'll poison you? Make you sick so you can't leave?"

"I wouldn't put any trick past you, woman," he told Cal.

"Why, Lynx Cardone, how wicked of you."

Lynx sat at the table sipping coffee and watching Cal as she prepared their breakfast. Salina had left in a huff when Lynx dismissed her from her duties. When all was ready, Cal served him with a bright smile. "See, I'm not utterly helpless."

They ate in near silence, the weight of his remaining time sinking down on them. Afterward, Lynx told Cal to leave the dishes for Salina and to keep him company while he packed his saddle-bags. She didn't argue or refuse, but followed his lead upstairs.

Cal stood at the end of the bed, clutching the tall post as if she required its support. Suddenly, she couldn't think of anything to say. She simply watched Lynx, her eyes easing over his arresting face and virile body. How was it possible to love and need another person so much that it hurt to be separated from him. With his departures, he seemed to take the air and sunshine from her life. Unlike a morning glory with the blazing sun, she folded her petals when his heat vanished.

Lynx walked past her several times as he retrieved and stuffed several shirts, pants, underwear, and pairs of socks into his bulging saddlebags. He added a sharp razor and shaving soap. His camping gear and supplies were packed and waiting in the stable with Star, along with a rain-slicker, his rifle, and extra ammo. He grabbed an extra vest and crammed it into the leather bag. Occasionally he would glance over at her and smile. Her gaze never left him.

Lynx read such loneliness in her eyes that he could hardly bear to look at her; Cal was so subdued now. He mentally begged her not to cry or debate this necessary last trip, which she didn't. He lifted his gunbelt and checked his pistols, then laid them beside his bags. He drew the large Bowie knife from its sheath and tested its sharpness with his finger, then replaced it. His keen gaze drifted along his holster belt, checking to make sure each hole contained an extra bullet.

Lynx went to his closet one last time, seeking some papers he wished he had packed earlier. He withdrew them from a hidden pocket in a winter jacket. Calinda turned to speak to him as he approached the bed, bumping into him and sending the loosely held papers in his hand fluttering to the floor. She was about to help him gather them when he grinned and distracted her with, "I've got 'em, love. Grab me a few bandannas; I sweat heavily on the trail."

As Cal responded to his request, Lynx retrieved the papers. He folded them and stuffed them into the bag, to read later. He walked to the coat-rack near his door to get his silver spurs and black hat, adding them to the items on his bed. He glanced around the room in deep thought. "That's about it, love. I wish I had your picture in a locket to carry with me," he surprisingly told her.

"I wish I had yours here," she agreed with his touching words. "Perhaps we can have a painting done when you come home."

Cal's gaze trailed Lynx as he prepared to leave. His stance and movements always suggested immense self-assurance and pride. She wondered what it was like to

453

fear nothing and no one. Lynx was so valiant and intelligent in most areas, so why couldn't he understand
how she felt about his absences and halt them? Why
weren't she and the ranch enough for him? If he loved
and needed her as vowed, how could he endure so
many separations? Even now, Lynx remained a
golden stranger who was as impenetrable as his black
attire.

Lynx dropped his saddlebags by the locked door
and placed his hat on them. He returned to the bed to
fasten on his spurs and gunbelt. Calinda went to him
and murmured, "How about my farewell kiss and hug
before you get all loaded down?"

Lynx tossed the gunbelt back to the bed and reached
for her. His mouth came down on hers as his arms
went around her as a steely band. Her hands slipped
up his back and held him tightly, dreading to release
him. At first his kisses were gentle and exploratory,
but soon they became forceful and demanding. Placing his palms near her shoulder blades, he crushed her
to his hard frame. Silky curls danced over his hands as
her head twisted to hungrily grind her mouth against
his.

He kissed the corners of her mouth, then tugged on
each lip in turn. He dropped kisses on her nose, chin,
and each brow before travelling to her ear. His voice
was thick with emotion when he muttered, "Your lips
are softer than moonlight. God, Callie, I need you
. . . I'm hotter than a hunk of beef spit over a roasting
fire."

"Love me before you go, Lynx," she entreated passionately.

He was dressed and packed, but it didn't matter at
that moment. Last night she had been restrained; pres-

ently, her need for him was urgent. He knew it wasn't a stalling tactic; he could feel the tension and desire within her, feelings which matched his own. He pulled away and picked up his gunbelt and spurs.

"Please, Lynx, just for a short time, let me be first in your life and thoughts," she pleaded, thinking he was about to leave her in this highly agitated state. What if she demanded he remain home?

"You are, Callie," he confessed, pulling the covers aside and gingerly dropping his possessions on the floor beside the bed. He held out his inviting hand to her, tawny eyes glistening with unleashed desire.

Tears of joy glimmered in her eyes as she placed her hand in his. He drew her forward and slowly undressed her. His smoldering gaze wandered over her body from head to foot. His hands pinned her jawline between them as he fused his eyes with hers. "Your skin is as silky and soft as a gentle rain. I can't even glance at you without wanting you. Do you know how beautiful and bewitching you are?" he asked proudly, his embrace and gaze possessive.

As her trembling fingers unbuttoned his ebony shirt, she replied, "Do you know how staggering you are to my senses?"

He yanked his shirt off, dropping it to the floor, his boots and dark pants quickly following it. He lifted her and lay her down, then joined her. His tongue flicked over her breasts and she quivered. His mouth captured one peak and tantalized it, then stimulated the other one. His hands caressed her body, fondling each curve and mound it encountered. It wasn't necessary to arouse her, but he savored his stirring effect on her. He played and tempted her until she was breathless and pleading. Her body was as thirsty as a desert; her skin as smooth as a serene pond. Her mood was as fiery as her hair when the blazing sun caressed it. His manhood entered into her gently. He charged and retreated leisurely until their passions demanded he hasten his feverish task. Tingles and warmth covered her body as the delightful series of sensations attacked her senses.

Cal arched to meet his entries, wanting nothing more than his total love and commitment to her. For a time, he was her entire world and being as their joined bodies strove for mutual completion. When tormented desires were appeased, they lay locked in each other's arms. Neither spoke for a time, relishing this special sharing.

When she shifted her head to look into his face, he smiled and said, "I love you, Callie; don't ever doubt it or forget it."

She wondered if he had been about to add, no matter what happens. She smiled tenderly and caressed his cheek. "I love you, too."

Lynx rolled to his back and placed one hand beneath his head. "Whew, now I need a bath and a nap. I'm drenched and exhausted."

"I could wash your back; I'm very good in the tub," she hinted seductively, her gaze exposing mischief and contentment.

"Oh, no, you won't," he wailed humorously. "If I let you join me, I'd never get going today."

"Perhaps next time?" Cal speculated mockingly.

"I'll hold you to that promise. Right now, I'd best get busy."

When she started to rise, Lynx pushed her into the mattress and pinned her beneath his body. "You stay here and rest, woman; I don't trust that gleam in those green eyes." He kissed the tip of her nose.

When he moved to get out of bed, she caught his arm and chided, "What's this, Lynx? No farewell kiss?"

He eyed her suspiciously. "That's why I'm in bed rather than on the trail. I don't dare risk taking one."

"How about accepting one?" she teased, undaunted.

"The next kiss you get from me, woman, will be a greeting. You rest; you're pale and you've got dark smudges beneath your eyes. And this time, don't drive yourself into the ground," he cautioned.

"Yes sir," she stated gaily at his pleasing perceptions.

Lynx stood up and pulled on his clothes. When he glanced down at her, Cal was grinning at him. "Don't you dare cast those bewitching eyes on me," he playfully warned. "I'm getting a bath and leaving while I can. Keep the bed warm; I'll be home soon. And I'll send you a telegram every few days," he added, winking at her.

She snuggled into her pillow. "Good. That might help me remember I have a carefree husband somewhere."

"Forget it one minute, and I'll thrash you soundly," he jested, trying to glare sternly at her, but laughing instead.

As he reached the door to gather his things, she called out, "Lynx, please be careful. I love you."

Lynx threw the saddlebag over his shoulder and put his hat on his tawny head. With the gunbelt swinging over one arm, he came over to the bed. He bent over and kissed her lightly. "I love you, Callie."

When the brief kiss ended, Lynx studied her face once more, then left. After a quick rinse in the watershed, he headed for the stable to complete his preparations. Rankin joined him. Lynx asked his father to watch after Calinda, telling him she seemed overly tired and pale. Rankin credited her appearance to her recent fall and emotional upheavals.

"Keep a guard posted around the house. I don't want her getting any more of those strange notes; they frighten her. If she gets any mail, hold it until I come home. I don't want her upset while I'm away. And make certain she never goes riding alone," Lynx requested.

"Not to worry, son; she'll be fine," Rankin assured him.

Calinda decided she would dress and wave goodbye to her husband. She stood up and swayed precariously, grabbing the post to steady herself. Her head was swimming. She sat down, then reclined. Maybe it was just the heat or excitement. Or maybe she was pushing herself too hard with unfamiliar strenuous chores. She had been feeling slightly weak and very sleepy lately. As she heard the pounding hooves of a departing horse, she realized it was too late to see him. She sighed wearily and curled into bed, falling asleep within minutes.

Lynx and Star boarded the Texas & Pacific Railroad to get to Dallas late that night. While Star rode comfortably in a cattle car, the undercover Ranger relaxed in the passenger section. When the train halted in Dallas, Lynx hurried to his stealthy rendezvous with Major Jones at the Windsor Hotel. With perseverance and courage, he might have that ruthless and wily Burrow in custody before the week was out.

After placing Star in the livery-stable, Lynx strolled

down the street, his perceptive gaze and keen senses engulfing sights and sounds. He had confronted many perils and criminals, but none which sent sparks of apprehension through him as this gaunt villain with an iron nerve, a lack of feelings, and a hair-trigger. That truculent character had been known to terrorize whole areas. The one thing about Rube Burrow that worried Lynx was that the killer had no fear of dying. Normally, even the worst criminals feared capture and death, but not Rube. That made him deadly and unpredictable.

Lynx slipped in the back door to the hotel and made his way to Jones' room. Once inside, Lynx was given a pleasant surprise. He sat down to listen to his commanding officer's words.

"You don't need to hang around Dallas, Lynx. After hitting the T & P five times, Rube made off for Mississippi and Alabama. Guess he's getting nervous about having Rangers chasing his tail."

"Who's going after him?" Lynx asked, perceiving that Jones wasn't going to hand him that assignment.

"He's got the Pinkerton men and several railroad detectives in hot pursuit. We'll let them harry Rube awhile. If he shows his guns here again, we'll be ready and waiting."

"Has Tom learned anything about the telegram I sent earlier?" Lynx inquired reluctantly.

"He's done plenty of checking around, but nothing so far. He's got the descriptions of the man and woman you mentioned, but they aren't here. He's been keeping an eye on the train depot to see if anyone seems to be waiting around for your wife."

"Is Deavers in town?" Lynx questioned, his eyes and voice cold.

"I did some checking on him; he's in San Antonio. Whatever the plot and whoever the instigator, I can't figure them yet. It sounds to me as if someone just wants her off the ranch, or in trouble with you. Anyone come to mind with that speculation?"

Lynx frowned. "Salina," he concluded. When Jones questioned his assumption, Lynx explained the Mexican girl's rivalry for him.

Jones chuckled. "You know the old saying about a spurned woman, Lynx. That could explain the mysterious notes. Living there, she's probably overheard enough to make them sound convincing. I think you'd best be careful with jealous ears around," he warned astutely.

"When I get home, I'll settle this matter once and for all. I should have reasoned this out before," he reprimanded himself.

"Something tells me you have other things on your mind when you're home," Jones teased his good friend.

"If Burrows is gone, does that mean I'm finished?" Lynx stated hopefully, grinning entreatingly at Jones.

Jones thoughtfully twirled his thick mustache. "Since you've already set aside the time, how about handling another matter for us? You can have your choice: Jim Miller or Kid Curry. Miller's operating around Abilene, and the Kid's trying to take on every gunslinger near Kerrville. Since you need to finish your work in Austin, Kerrville is the nearest. We've decided to reveal your identity as you retire. Knowing you're a past Ranger should make most outlaws leery of following you home to challenge that gun of yours. We want you to keep your badge just in case you need it to prevent trouble; we owe you some peace and protection after what you've done for us."

Lynx anxiously inquired, "What if Curry's left by the time I get to Kerrville? You want me to dog him and arrest him?"

"That won't be necessary. I know you're eager to get home and settle down. Just send any word you can get on him. I'll put another Ranger on his backside. Don't get too eager and head home before you visit the capital; you've got to testify for us," Jones reminded him.

"I'll take care of the Kid, my court session, and retiring before I head home," he agreed. "If you can spare him, I would appreciate it if Tom can make sure Braxton isn't around these parts. I don't want him interfering in Cal's and my lives anymore. When I leave Austin, I want my next stop to be home, permanently."

"Consider it done. After all, Braxton is wanted for assault and robbery."

"If you locate him, send the message to me, not home," Lynx cautioned. Jones nodded, then they discussed Kid Curry.

Calinda lazed around most of Saturday and Sunday. She couldn't seem to shake this sluggishness which was plaguing her. Between nightly slumber and naps, she was getting plenty of sleep; so why was she so tired and drowsy all the time?

On Monday, she decided to deny her annoying weakness by cleaning her room. As she was sweeping, she heard a rustle under the bed. She sat on the floor and peered beneath it. Sighting a paper, she used the broom to retrieve it. Evidently Lynx had dropped it while packing. She lifted it and glanced at the tele-

gram. Dismay filled her. He wouldn't break his word
to her; besides, he had sent her a telegram this morning from Waco. He couldn't be in Dallas!

Lynx,
     Urgent. Waiting in Dallas. Windsor Hotel.
Come Saturday. B running. Must pursue. News
in Austin after Dallas. J.B.J.

That last mysterious message had summoned Cal to
Dallas. Kyle Yancey was in Austin. Was Lynx chasing
the unexpected clue to her father? Had he sent someone a telegram to investigate matters in Dallas for
him? Was that why he hadn't taken off last Monday?
Was he waiting for a reply and allowing time to mislead her? Who was this "B"? Brax? This "J.B.J."?
How could she discover if Lynx was in Dallas? How
could she reveal mistrust in him? Yet, her suspicions
were overwhelming.

There was only one way to end her doubts and as-
suage her fears; send a telegram to the sheriff in Dallas. She could say it was urgent to locate her husband.
She could wait at the telegraph office for a reply. Yes,
she would do just that tomorrow . . .

Tuesday morning in the telegraph office, Calinda
paced the floor while she awaited an answer from Dallas. Each time the keys clicked noisily, she became excited and frightened. One hour later, the agent smiled
ruefully and handed her the sheriff's reply: he was
sorry he couldn't help her, but Lynx Cardone had left
Dallas on Monday, and his location was unknown.

Calinda was crushed by this staggering news. Lynx
had lied to her. She wanted to send another telegram
to ask if there had been trouble or a shooting there,

but she couldn't. Lynx couldn't kill her father in revenge; Laura was just as guilty! Cal had to face an indisputable reality; if Lynx had deceived her about Dallas, what else had he lied about or secretly done? She reflected on their days together.

Austin! The word rifled through her mind. Was Lynx heading for Austin? Had Lynx learned about Kyle Yancey? Was her disloyal husband stalking her father at this very minute?

Cal unsteadily approached the agent once more, to send another telegram. She wrote out the message and handed it to him?

Mr. Kyle Yancey, Lawyer, Austin.
Told to contact you by Elliott Braxton. Please send his address. Urgent I locate father. Waiting your reply in Fort Worth station. Calinda Braxton.

This time, Calinda was given a curious response within forty-five minutes:

Calinda Braxton. Have important papers for you. Will deliver. Explain. Meet where, Thursday. Awaiting response. Kyle Yancey.

Without hesitation or remorse, Calinda instantly fired a telegram back to the lawyer, requesting they meet in Fort Worth at the Canton Hotel. There was only one way to solve this weighty enigma and to halt its power over them; she must meet with this Kyle Yancey. If her love couldn't or wouldn't be honest with her, she would find someone else to do so! Perhaps then she might understand Lynx's deceptions and reluctance. God, how she despised and dreaded this furtive path of action, but Lynx was making it necessary.

As Charlie drove Cal home in the buggy, a flood of emotions and thoughts saturated her body and mind. *What papers? What explanation? Why a lawyer? Why in person? Why was she being so secretive?* There was an answer only to the last question . . .

Chapter Twenty

When Calinda received a telegram on Wednesday from Lynx, she realized how beguiling he was; clearly someone was helping him send messages from where he was supposed to be, not where he actually was. The first one had said Waco, when Lynx was in Dallas. This one alleged San Antonio, when she suspected he was in Austin. Cal agonized over her mistrust and her furtive actions. She fumed at Lynx and Rankin for compelling her to investigate like this. But this destructive mystery must be conquered and dismissed promptly. She and Lynx could never be happy as long as the dark past continued to assail them, and Lynx willfully created new mysteries. She prayed Kyle Yancey had left Austin before Lynx's arrival. When her husband came home, she wouldn't be so gullible and lenient. This time, she would demand frank answers.

Calinda had planned her strategy well. Tuesday she had hired a local seamstress to make her a new gown for Lynx's homecoming; she used this excuse to return to town on Thursday. She sat in the eating area of the hotel, nervously sipping coffee and squirming in her seat. The train from Austin was late; she prayed nothing had gone wrong, yet she dreaded to hear Yancey's words.

Cal was ensnared by pensive study when a man tapped her on the shoulder and asked if she was Calinda Braxton. Since she was the only lady present, it was a natural assumption. She turned and looked up into his face, a pleasant one with sharply defined features. His eyes were like warm chocolate. His hair was nearly gray, hinting at his advancing age. His manner and expression implied he was of a gentle nature. She gradually relaxed and nodded.

"You cannot imagine how glad I was to hear from you, Miss Braxton. I have been deliberating what to do with this packet. It has been in my safe for years," Kyle hastily began as he took a seat near her.

"I don't understand, Mr. Yancey. Where is my father?" Cal asked softly, her voice laced with a noticeable quiver as she stared at the ominous packet.

Kyle eagerly explained, "When Elliott Braxton gave me these papers for safe-keeping, he said he was leaving Texas. He instructed me to turn them over to you if he didn't reclaim them within six years, which is next month. He paid me handsomely to safeguard them, to deliver them to you if necessary."

"You mean you haven't seen my father or heard from him since then?" Cal murmured in dread.

"I'm afraid not. I was wondering how I was supposed to locate you, since you didn't respond to my letter two months past. I see you decided to come to America rather than write to me."

"What letter, Mr. Yancey? I've never received any messages from you. I've been living at the Cardone Ranch since May. I'm married to Lynx Cardone. I came to America to locate my father, but it's been impossible. He's been missing for years. A lost letter was recently delivered to me which told me to contact you. Why, I do not know. I was hoping you had news of him. I find this matter confusing. Is my father still alive?" she asked uncontrollably.

"I have no way of knowing, Mrs. Cardone. I was retained to hold this packet. If he didn't recover it within six years, it was to go to you. As you can see from the date, the deadline is near. Perhaps I am pre-shooting the assigned schedule, but I hardly feel he will return at the last moment. Since I have fortunately located you, surely your father will forgive my eagerness in settling this matter. Its contents are unknown to me, other than letters and a legal document. I was paid well to make certain this packet fell into no hands other than his or yours; that's why I personally delivered it," Kyle expounded.

"May I see the packet?" she asked apprehensively.

Calinda couldn't halt her hands from trembling as she accepted the time-yellowed packet. She inhaled deeply and slowly released it before breaking the wax-seal. She withdrew four papers. The largest one captured her attention first, the missing deed to the ranch. Why would her father place a stolen deed in her possession, making her an unbidden accomplice to his crime? She placed the other papers beneath it, to focus her concentration on the legal document. She paled as she read over it; the deed was for the Cardone . . . Braxton Ranch! She read it several times, then asked the lawyer to explain it to her.

Kyle glanced over the document, then informed her, "In essence, the ranch is jointly owned by Rankin Cardone and Elliott Braxton. In the event of the death of either or both men, their halves will be inherited by Lynx Cardone and Calinda Braxton. In case of mutual deaths in either family, the other family inherits everything."

"Are you telling me my father owned half of the Cardone Ranch?" Cal inquired dubiously, gaping at him. Surely Yancey was mistaken.

"Not owned, owns, unless he's deceased. In such case, you own half of the ranch and all entailed," he casually clarified, unaware of the shock of his devastating news, intrigued by her astonishment.

"That isn't possible, Mr. Yancey," Cal debated. "My father never owned any part of that ranch; he only worked there. He and Mister Cardone were close friends, never partners," she refuted.

Kyle Yancey peered over his spectacles to study the befuddled lady. To prevent any error, he closely examined the document again. "This deed is legal and binding, Mrs. Cardone," he evidenced, confused by her ignorance of this matter in light of her marriage.

"Then my father must have sold his half to the Cardones," Cal reasoned earnestly, dreading the implications of this new riddle. Had the proclaimed stolen money actually been for a sale? Had they lied about the theft because of her father's adulterous betrayal?

"See if there's a record of the sale in the packet," he suggested.

Calinda sought the next paper; it was a will. She handed the paper to the lawyer, who studied it. "According to this deed and will, Braxton transferred his half-ownership to you at his demise. I suppose it's safe to assume he's no longer alive, since he never returned. What did the Cardones tell you? You are married to this . . . Lynx Cardone?" he questioned, glancing at the deed for her husband's name. He mused, was her husband the famed gunslinger and insolent rebel?

Calinda flushed, then confessed they had told her nothing of this matter. "These papers are of little consequence at this date; your husband owns half of the ranch with his father. In the event of Rankin Cardone's death, Lynx Cardone will be the sole owner. Are you aware, a wife's property falls under her husband's control after marriage?"

"You're saying, they actually own the entire ranch now because of my marriage?" the dismayed girl asked for total clarity.

"That's the size of it," Kyle reluctantly concurred.

"And that's legal? No recourse?" she asked cautiously.

"None. Why would you ask?" he quizzed curiously.

Calinda didn't want to ask her next question, but forced herself. "If Lynx and I weren't married, where would I stand now?"

"You would own half and the Cardones would own half. By marrying one of them, it legally passed into their hands and control."

"Are you positive my father didn't sell it to them?" Cal probed desperately, consternation biting viciously at her heart and mind.

"Impossible, Mrs. Cardone. He left these documents with me before leaving Texas. To sell his portion, he would need to reclaim the deed as proof of half-ownership. He hasn't," Kyle stated simply.

"Then this deed is vital to prove his claim?" she pressed.

"Yes, or your claim," he gave the answer she feared, the answer which told why they were so intent on locating it and her father.

"If my father took $45,000 of the ranch's money with him when he left, would that constitute a verbal sale of

his portion? Would it be viewed as theft, a criminal offense?" she probed anxiously.

"Both partners should agree to such financial matters,
but it could hardly be called criminal to take money
from your own ranch. No matter, unless sale papers
were signed, witnessed, and filed, it doesn't change anything. As you see, the deed has not been altered or
stamped," he further expounded, holding out the un-
marked deed.

"I see," Cal murmured pensively. She owned half of
the ranch? Why hadn't they told her? Why had they
treated her as if she were penniless and dependent? She
could have claimed and taken half of that cattle empire,
a spread worth a fortune? Owned, that was the key
word. Through her hasty marriage, the Cardones possessed everything . . . In exchange for Laura, they had
stolen her inheritance.

Calinda didn't like what she was thinking and feeling.
Yet, she couldn't explain why they had withheld many
critical facts. Didn't they know her by now? Didn't they
realize she would have signed her half over to them because of her father's theft and betrayal? Her father had
lost all rights to the ranch; she would never have demanded anything.

It was apparent why they had been suspicious of her in
the beginning. It was evident why they suspected Brax
might return one day. It was obvious they wanted revenge, and it was noxiously clear how they had obtained
it. That final missing piece to the pernicious puzzle fell
rapidly and agonizingly into place, forming a picture
which she didn't want to view. She had been ignorant
and trusting; why had they used her for such a wicked
plot? After knowing her, why did they continue their
malicious tricks? They had gained possession of the

ranch; what more could they want? To lure her father and Laura back . . .

Calinda lifted her tormented gaze to ask a question. "Mr. Yancey, where would I stand if I left Lynx and the ranch?"

Surprise and bewilderment registered on the elderly lawyer's face. "Even if you abandoned both, the ranch will remain in your husband's control. That's the law, Mrs. Cardone."

"You mean, I wouldn't get anything? I've lost all rights by marrying Lynx? I couldn't even demand payment for my share?" she persisted painfully. "If they wished, could they force me to leave?"

"I take it you're asking me these questions in confidence as a lawyer?" he astutely hinted before responding.

"Yes, Mr. Yancey. Whatever your fee, I want this conversation to remain private between us. I must clarify this matter in my mind."

"Do you feel you've been duped, Mrs. Cardone?" he probed.

"I don't know. They never told me anything." Calinda slowly related relevant facts and how she had been treated since her arrival. She revealed the story of her father's disappearance and her attempt to locate him. "I'm confused by this secrecy and deception. If Lynx married me just to gain control of my half, it doesn't appear that way. Surely their affections and acceptance can't be false?"

Kyle realized the young woman was on the verge of tears. He saw how vulnerable and distressed she was. "I'm well-acquainted with your husband's reputation, Mrs. Cardone. I'm sorry to say, but I feel some miscarriage of justice has taken place. The fact they withheld this information from you suggests dishonesty. However, legally our hands are tied. We're dealing with two powerful, cunning, and wealthy men. Even if you vowed deception, we couldn't prove it. Unless the Cardones forced you to marry Lynx and are holding you prisoner, there's nothing we can do. I'm afraid you've given up any claim to the ranch. Evidently your father suspected something might happen to him, so he entrusted the papers to me for your protection. I doubt he envisioned a complication like this. But I do find it strange and hopeful that they are keeping you at the ranch. Perhaps they care more for you than you realize. Perhaps their desire for revenge has been sated. You're a beautiful and charming woman; any man would be pleased to have you as his wife. Why don't you ask your husband about this situation?"

"I can't decide how they would react to my knowledge of this matter. I know this might sound unfair, but I pray they aren't using this trick on me to lure my father out of hiding. Perhaps I'm safe only as long as I'm in the dark," Cal stated uncontrollably.

The moment that statement left her lips, memories of past dangers and mysteries attacked her mind. If anything happened to her . . .

"Aren't there other papers?" Kyle inquired gently, hoping there was an explanation to this injurious scheme.

"A letter and a note. I'm not sure I want to read them," she confessed, her whole world seeming to come apart.

"Would you like me to read them to you?" Kyle offered.

"I'd better do it myself," she refused softly, since the affair with Laura might be mentioned, the one point she hadn't revealed.

Calinda struggled to restrain her tears as her bleary gaze took in the note, then the heart-racking and revealing letter. Her shaky hand covered her dry lips; she feared she would be ill right there on the floor. Her face was extremely pale; her once lively gaze was now empty and moist. She rested her arms on the table, crushing the two letters in her tight grasp, staring unseeingly at them. Her shoulders were slumped in despair, as if the burdens of the world had been placed on them. Her head was lowered; she appeared to hardly breathe. Sensing a traumatic shock in those letters, the sensitive lawyer remained silent while she mastered her emotions.

At last, Cal understood the motive behind Laura and Brax's actions. Each time she was positive every incisive axe had fallen, another obscure blade hovered over her head before slashing down to sever a vital part of her. God, how this gradual evisceration racked her body and soul. She didn't know if she should be bitter, understanding, or furious. Right now, she was too distraught to think about anything. Later at home . . . Home? She could never call the Cardone Ranch home again. Yet, she had to return there, at least for a while.

She thanked Kyle Yancey for his kindness and assistance. When she tried to pay him, he smiled and refused. "I'm sorry if I've been the bearer of dire news. If you need my services again, please don't fail to contact me," he urged, touched by this suffering child.

"Promise me you won't breathe a word of this to anyone?"

"I promise, Mrs. Cardone. I truly hope things work out for you."

She smiled faintly and said, "They will; I'll make certain."

Calinda left him to spend the night in the hotel room

and return to Austin tomorrow. As Charlie drove her home, she was remote and sad. In response to Charlie's concern, she told him she was merely exhausted. At the ranch, Rankin was out riding and Salina was busy with chores. Calinda reluctantly mounted the stairs to the room shared with Lynx when he was home. She went inside, locked the door, and flung herself on the bed to sob in anguish.

Cal didn't want to ponder the insinuations in her discovery of the ranch deed and the joint betrayal of their parents. Was she a naive pawn in a monstrous game of revenge? She and Lynx had known each other for three months and had been married for nearly two. Yet, she knew so little about him and his existence, and too much about their interlocked pasts. She could justify his secrecy about Laura and Brax, but not about the ranch. His continued silence painted him guilty.

One suspicion bred with another to produce a litter of rapidly growing doubts. So beguiling and irresistible, Lynx had used his prowess to disarm and enchant her, to fool her completely. How could he do such terrible things to her, if he truly loved her? Was it possible he had set a trap for her, then carelessly ensnared himself by falling in love with his prey? Had she unknowingly managed to alter Rankin's resentment and hatred into trust and affection? Did they feel it was harmful to reveal their deceptions and initial motives? Was Lynx afraid of losing her if the truth was exposed at this late date?

So many previously unnoticed clues entered her mind. Cal remembered that night in bed when they had joked about brands. She knew his feelings toward his traitorous mother were more than lingering grief. So many of his past words and expressions assailed her groping mind, especially their discussion of that lost letter when he had refused to be candid. What had Lynx blurted out after Rankin was shot: "It's half yours now!" Other slips from the two men filtered into her crowded mind, to swim around in her mental ocean of turbulence.

Cal recalled the many times Lynx had alluded to a fear of losing her. Had Lynx left home to destroy all clues to the past, to protect their love? What would he say if she confronted him with these newly discovered facts? How would this letter and note affect him? Would they ease his lingering anguish and sever any remaining ties to the past? Or would it serve to breed more trouble and bitterness? She read the heart-stabbing letter again:

My dearest daughter Calinda,

Since this packet has been given to you as prearranged, it means I am permanently out of your life. Please do not grieve for me, but accept me as dead. I do not deserve your respect. I pray you will try to understand and forgive me. If you will read further, I will attempt to explain events which changed many lives, including your own.

I know grave mistakes which I have made. One was in not sending for you and your mother. If you two had been with me, such dire events might never have happened. You were too young to realize the lack of love between me and your mother. We both married for selfish reasons. I, for her social rank and family wealth; she, because I was the best of her suitors and an escape from her father's family.

As I lived and worked in this exciting and challenging territory, I met a beautiful and unique woman whom I came to love beyond all reason or caution. She consumed my thoughts and feelings. I forgot all responsibilities and morals. I tried to fight my hunger for her, but I failed. I knew it was wrong to desire her, but I was helpless to resist. Once I even planned to leave Texas to halt this powerful temptation.

You see, my daughter, the woman is Laura Cardone, the wife of my closest friend and mother to a boy I love as a son. I could go for pages telling you about her and our fated love, but it would justify nothing in your eyes. When I forced myself to see what our love would do to Rankin and Lynx, I tried to desert her and the ranch. I could not.

There was a complication, my daughter. Laura discovered she was carrying a child. There was no doubt that the child was mine, and not her husband's. We were forced to make a costly decision. I had to take money and betray my friends to get my true love and our unborn child away. Once this decision was made, we could never look back or return. When Rankin discovered our affair and plans, we fought bitterly. I dared not leave Laura behind, so the money was vital for our safety and survival. How I wish you could have met the flame of my heart and known her.

If you ever meet the Cardones, please give them patience and respect. I know they must hate me and desire revenge. To prevent them from locating us, we must flee far from Texas. Laura and I are grieved over the loss of our two children, but we must protect ourselves and our new child. I know your resentment must be great, but please forward this letter to Lynx, as he also deserves an explanation. You and Lynx must forget us. We have brought much pain into your lives. A total break is best for all of us.

In time, I pray you will find understanding in your heart for us. If you wonder if we regret our costly love and harsh decision, we cannot say this early. Believe me, Calinda, when I swear our love was uncontrollable. We will do our best to find happiness and peace together with our new child. If you ever meet Rankin and Lynx, I'm certain you will realize what special men they are, if they allow you the chance to get to know them.

By now, you are a young woman. I hope you are strong enough to accept these stunning facts and deal justly with them. Please don't hold the Cardones responsible for my actions and weaknesses; please don't make them suffer more for what I have done in the past.

If I am rambling in this letter, it is because I hardly know what to say in our final communication. Be happy and find true love, my child.

Your father, Elliott

Calinda lifted the note which had been attached to the deed and forced its reality into her warring thoughts.

For your many sacrifices, I give you all I have left to offer, my undying love and half of a prosperous ranch which I helped carve from a wilderness with my own sweat and blood, at the side of my closest friend Rankin Cardone and his beloved son Lynx, who were like my brother and son.

If you are living in England, please do not come to America with hopes of finding me. If you are in Texas as you read this letter, I regret any vengeful battle you might face to claim your inheritance. Kyle Yancey is an honest and talented lawyer; use him to gain what is rightfully yours. I do request you find the means to repay a debt of $45,000 to Rankin, ranch money which I took to begin my new life elsewhere. Possibly you can sell him a portion or all of your claim, or repay him from monies earned from the ranch and cattle if you decide to retain possession.

I used the money from the sale of our Georgia home to buy land and cattle in Texas with Rankin, except for the $10,000 which I sent to Thomas for your support. With time and work, the Cardone/ Braxton Ranch became one of the most successful spreads in the West. God, how I love this land and agonize over leaving it forever. I know this is not a fair exchange for a father, but I want you to have my share. I pondered selling my half to Rankin for ruining his life, but I owed you something more. I beg you to give Rankin first choice at any sale. If you want no part of the ranch, please sign the deed over to Rankin. I owe him this and far more. Forgive me.

Calinda put the papers inside the packet and went into her old room. She opened the closet door and pinned the packet beneath one of the billowing gowns which had belonged to Laura Cardone. Some other less painful time, she would decide what to do with it. She returned to her room and locked the door.

All she could do was wait and observe. She couldn't make any plans, for there was too much she didn't know, too much to consider. Her reactions depended upon the feelings of Rankin and Lynx, feelings she must discover soon. Until Lynx returned, she must wait. Maybe there was a logical and reasonable explanation . . .

For now, Cal was mentally, physically, and emotionally drained. An idea came to mind; from this day forward, she would lock her room to prevent any more mysterious letters from appearing on her bed. She would observe and listen to everything which surrounded her. She was positive those furtive messages were not from her father. Someone was trying to lead her away from the ranch or to cause dissension with the Cardones. Maybe she should study Salina more closely. If her life was in jeopardy from some evil force, she must be more careful and alert. She must avoid anything which hinted of a perilous trap. The most difficult and expensive task would be to uncover the motives of the Cardones . . .

One piece of this obscure puzzle kept returning to unnerve her; Lynx was always around when one of these dangers or mysteries occurred. But if he wanted her harmed, why did he always rescue her? Since the Lampasas episode had resulted in their marriage and her loss of the ranch—why the kidnapping, her dangerous fall, his declarations of love, and the inexplicable letters? If a marriage hadn't lured her father back, why would a series of accidents? Surely they realized Brax and Laura wouldn't remain anywhere near Texas? Even so, how could Brax learn Cal was in danger? Could the return of the ranch deed satisfy the Cardones? Cal shuddered as if chilled. What if her father or Laura had lied? What if the child was Rankin's? The money, his child, the ranch, and his wife would certainly supply Rankin with plenty of hatred, an obsession for vengeance. It was so complicated.

All Cal wanted was Lynx and the truth. They could

have the ranch; she didn't care. But if Lynx didn't confess when he returned, she must consider leaving. She couldn't live under this shadow of delusion and mistrust. It was settled; everything hinged on Lynx and his love. Cal would do as her father had asked, consider him dead.

Cal wished it wasn't so, but she understood mindless and irresistible love. She had met a handsome and unique man whom she had come "to love beyond all reason and caution," as with Brax to Laura. Her father's words pained her deeply — "consumed my thoughts and feelings . . . forgot all morals . . . helpless to resist . . ." — it was as if Brax were describing her relationship with Lynx . . .

By Friday, much of Calinda's anguish and disappointments had altered to smoldering anger and fierce determination. She wasn't a child or a simpleton to be protected; she wasn't a stranger to this affair, one who didn't deserve any facts. This situation had become wearisome and intolerable, it was time to end it.

A telegram had been delivered late yesterday, one from Brownwood which informed them Lynx was on his way home. Rankin had told her that town was only a day's travel from the ranch. Any time now, her husband should come riding up to his home. Was she ready to face him? How should she behave? What was there to say?

Cal was moody and cool today. Rankin asked, "Is something wrong, Cal? You don't seem yourself today. Eager to see Lynx?"

"Would you please stop fretting over me? I'm fine," she declared peevishly. "I'll be convinced he's home to stay when I see it. How's everything going on your ranch?" she inquired innocently.

"Never better, Cal," he replied, smiling proudly.

"You really love this place, don't you? I imagine it was awfully expensive to buy; it's so large. Did your family have money to loan you?"

Assuming Cal was opening a simple talk, Rankin calmly replied, "No. I earned the money and staked out the land. Some of it I fought Indians and Mexicans to hold. It was dangerous back in those early days. A man held his possessions by his gun, courage, and determination. I've worked hard to make this ranch what it is today."

Cal wouldn't dispute that Rankin had made this empire what it was at present. Infuriatingly, she could understand why the Cardones must feel that her father didn't deserve any portion of it or the increased profits. She could comprehend their desire to protect their home and labors, their fear of her walking in and demanding an enormous share of everything. But she was a Cardone now, and none of that mattered anymore. "How long did my father work here?" Cal boldly and unexpectedly asked. "If you don't mind answering," she slyly added.

Rankin stiffened and frowned. "Would you understand if I said I preferred not to discuss your father or those days? You know we parted on bad terms." He waited tensely for her reaction, having been told of the arrival of Brax's misplaced letter.

"I won't press you, Rankin. I just wanted to know something about him. If I didn't have his picture, I doubt I could recall him. It just troubles me sometimes to know so little about my own father. This place is so beautiful and so special; I can't understand why he would leave."

"I know it must be confusing and painful, Cal. Maybe

481

one day we can discuss him in detail," he relented slightly.

If Cal was mistaken about Rankin, she could hurt him deeply by probing into Laura's memory. She decided against any questions or mention of her. "Could I ask one last question, Rankin?"

He nodded, but his face was lined with worry.

"Do you ever resent me because Brax is my father? Does it make you uncomfortable for me to live here?" She kept her gaze locked on his face.

"That's two questions," he teased to calm his frayed nerves. "To be honest, at first I was leery of you. But you got under my tough skin and won my heart. If there's one thing I've learned in life, each man stands on his own. Another can't take his punishment or rewards. To answer your last question, not in the least. In fact, I love having you around. You're about the most delightful creature I've met. I'm proud and pleased you're a part of the Cardone family."

If Cal was any judge of character, he was being honest. But then again, she was too naive and trusting; she wanted and needed to believe him. She had misjudged the Simpsons. Too, the Cardone men hadn't been frank with her. "Thank you," she said, smiling faintly.

"Think we should plan a special dinner for Lynx? You can wear that lovely new gown," he hinted, fretting over her strange mood.

She sighed heavily, then blithely answered, "I'll wear the gown, but Salina can handle dinner. Our truce is too nice to spoil at this special time. I think I'll take a short ride before I bathe and dress."

Rankin reminded her, "Lynx doesn't want you riding alone. Take Manuel with you. Charlie's probably working on the hands' chow."

"That won't be necessary. I'll stay within sight of the house."

"I would go with you, but I need to work on the books. I've got to do some figuring on expenses until we make our fall sale."

His statement opened the door for her to probe, "I wish there was some way to replace what my father stole from you and Lynx."

Rankin's smile faded instantly. "What did you say?" he asked warily, alerting Calinda to her reckless slip.

She quickly covered it by explaining, "I wish I could replace the joy and trust my father stole from you and Lynx. Why?" she queried.

"Forget about it, Cal," he said sternly. "You've more than repaid us. Be happy here; that's all we need. Besides, you're part of this family now."

"You know something? You've been more of a father to me than Brax. I truly appreciate what you've done for me, Rankin," she tested his reaction to those statements.

To her astonishment, he hugged her fondly. "One day, my grandson will own all of this. I look forward to you and Lynx having a child. You've brought sunshine back to the ranch, Cal."

Cal smiled through misty eyes. If they had a son and he inherited the ranch, she will have lost nothing. Horror filled her as a wicked thought flashed through her warring mind; what if they took her child to replace the one stolen by her father? Both men frequently mentioned a baby. Their revenge would be complete: the ranch and a child, compliments of the enemy who had stolen both long ago.

Cal shook her head to vanquish her wild imagination. What was the matter with her? She was going crazy! No one could be that evil! She must get away from this haunting house for a time and clear her wits. Cal felt she was going around in a vicious and tormenting circle. If only she weren't so fretful and jittery these days. If she could just shake this sluggishness and this urge to burst into tears at every turn. She needed privacy and a good self-scolding to get rid of this pressure and despair. She was a grown woman, a resilient and smart one. Why couldn't she think and act like one? She had to put a bridle on her wild imagination! She had to pull herself together before Lynx arrived and questioned her irrational behavior.

How long could she wait for Lynx to reveal the truth? It was imperative that Lynx confess everything to her willingly, not from compulsion. She silently and desperately prayed that love, not vengeance, was the true flame in his heart. After reading her father's letter, that endearment was no longer special or beautiful . . .

Chapter Twenty-one

Once mounted, Calinda rode straight for the hillside where Laura Cardone was alleged to be buried. She halted the snowy animal and dismounted, trying his reins to a bush. She scanned the tranquil setting where several trees and many wildflowers seemed to offer beauty in the face of dark treachery. She walked to the headstone and read. So timely and so false: September 15, the day her marriage would be three months old and Laura was claimed dead six years past.

Cal was an adult, a Cardone. Why couldn't she know the truth? She tried to envision Brax and Laura together, then Rankin and Laura. Were Brax and Laura happy now? How could they be after the trail of pain left behind? How ironic that she should love Lynx as wildly and uncontrollably as Brax had loved Laura, as if cruel fate were determined to mingle the two family lines. In similar circumstances, could she sacrifice all to have Lynx? What if Lynx had been married when she arrived here? Would she have fallen in love with him? If so, could she have destroyed lives to have him for her own? Could true love be so malicious and costly?

Suddenly a rifle-shot thundered across the landscape, startling the forlorn girl. A searing pain racked Cal's body as a bullet hurled through her left shoulder. At the stunning invasion of hot metal, Cal was jolted forward and thrown to the ground, across Laura's make-believe grave. Despite dazed senses, she had enough wits to play dead.

As Cal lay there, she heard pounding hooves as an unseen rider fled this evil deed. She fearfully realized she would be dead now if she hadn't flinched at the lethal sound. As her head had jerked upwards and shifted her body, the death-intended bullet had missed its mark.

Cal moaned as she attempted to move; pain and nausea washed over her as she glanced down at her torn shirt above her left breast where blood was flowing rapidly to soak it. She drew her gun and placed it on the ground beside her for defense if her assailant returned. She accepted the knifing pains as she tested her shoulder and arm for a break; they moved, but produced immense agony and each movement increased the flow of fiery liquid.

Her fingers touched the wound, her blurring vision staring at their crimson tips. Shot, someone had actually shot her! Why? Who? Cal pressed her shaky hand against the wound to staunch the heavy flow of blood, her action tormenting the injury. She struggled to rise; she knew she must reach her horse and get home. She swayed precariously, her senses whirling in ominous warning.

If she passed out and no one found her soon, she would die. She crawled to the nervous animal and used her quickly vanishing strength to yank the reins free of the bush. If she could manage his back before losing consciousness . . . She commanded her head to clear and her body to function. Cal gripped his foreleg and attempted to pull herself up to the saddle, smearing scarlet fluid over his white hide. She grabbed the horn, but blackness challenged her. Slowly she sank to the ground, leaving a bloody trail down the saddle and animal.

Cal was too weak and fuzzy-headed to mount. In desperation, she lifted a fallen branch and thrashed the animal's legs, startling him and sending him racing off. She prayed he would run for home and not halt to graze. His solo return should entreat someone to come looking for her. She rolled to her back, her right arm falling over the earthly mound beside her. Cal tried to resist the threatening blackness, but it was too powerful. The last thought she remembered was watching the leaves gently over her head and thinking, if I die . . .

"Don't tell me you let her go riding alone," Lynx chided his father on his return to discover their nettling disobedience.

"She'll be fine, son. She said she'd stay close by. You're just annoyed she isn't here to greet you," Rankin teased his son.

"I didn't see her when I rode up," he argued, an uneasy feeling coming over his lithe frame. For some inexplicable reason, he recalled her jest about a mental link with him, especially in times of peril. He implausibly shuddered. "You know how stubborn and impulsive she is. She could be anywhere. I'll go find her."

Rankin chuckled at his son's displeasure. "Think you'll return in time for dinner?" he jested, recalling their tardiness on his last visit.

"Maybe. Maybe not," Lynx quipped, grinning mischievously.

"You just missed her; she left about thirty minutes ago," Rankin informed him. "I'll walk you to the stable. I need to ask Steve a question. You and I can talk later."

As they approached the corral, a noise drew their attention to the east; it was a riderless horse coming in. Rankin hastily shouted, "That's the horse Cal was riding when she left!"

Lynx ran toward it, then seized his reins. The bright red blood stood out alarmingly against the horse's ivory hide. "It's blood!" Rankin shrieked as he joined his son, who was gaping at the stains and tensing in panic. For a moment, Lynx thought his heart had stopped.

"He came from the east slope. I'll go after her," Lynx stated in a deceptively calm voice, his insides turning as he re-saddled Star. He tested the blood smears. "They're fresh. She must have been thrown and injured," he concluded as he swung into his saddle. "Damn her!" he snarled angrily in mounting apprehension. "Get some of the men to help search for her. Fire three shots when she's located."

"I'll come with you," Rankin called out.

"No time to wait," Lynx shouted over his shoulder.

Lynx headed in the direction from which the horse had arrived, his eagle eyes scanning the terrain as he galloped along. On the crest of the first hill, he halted and looked around, seeing nothing. He raced wildly to the pond, finding nothing there. Dread filled him. She could be bleeding to death in some hidden location! The one thing which gave him hope was the realization she had attempted to mount.

As Lynx guided Star one way, then another, he noticed hired men had joined his frantic search. Lynx kept recalling the appearance of mysterious letters, Cal's previous kidnapping, her peril in Lampasas, the day he and his father were bushwacked, that tampering with her saddle girth . . . Why had he ignored so many warnings?

Suddenly, three gunshots pierced the silence. Lynx's head jerked in that direction, then he encouraged Star to a swift pace. Before he reached the location, a coldness attacked his senses as he became aware of where he was heading.

Jed and Seth were bending over a prone body near his mother's grave. He jumped off Star's back before the animal halted. Taut with suspense, he ran to Calinda's limp body and dropped to his knees. The front of her shirt was saturated with blood; even her sleeve was soaked as the ominous red stream flowed to the ground. She was very pale and motionless. Never had Lynx experienced such anguish and terror.

"Is she . . ." Lynx didn't finished the unacceptable thought.

"Still breathing, but bad off, Lynx," Seth replied first.

"Get the doctor, Jed! I'll carry her home," Lynx ordered.

"Best patch her first, boss; she's bleeding fierce. She was back-shot. Looks like the bullet passed clear through," Seth told him.

Lynx yanked off his shirt and wrapped it tightly

around her shoulder. He carefully lifted her into his arms. Seth held the precious burden as Lynx mounted and reached for her. Jed raced off for town. Lynx gently kneed Star and headed for home, praying all the way.

Rankin caught up with him and rode along, fearing to ask any questions. Without accepting any help with her, Lynx slipped off his horse and carried her to their room. Rankin rushed into the kitchen for water and bandages, telling Salina what the commotion was about.

As he left Salina, a merry twinkle danced in her eyes. *Too bad, Calinda, but I said you'd never survive here.* She wondered who she should thank for this thrilling assistance . . .

Lynx ripped off Calinda's shirt and studied the wound. He rolled her to her side; thankfully the bullet had indeed passed clear through. He placed a thick bandage beneath her shoulder and laid her down. He pressed another one to the jagged tear on her chest. She was spilling too much blood, he fretted. He couldn't lose her; he couldn't . . .

Lynx had seen plenty of gun-wounds, but he was too overwrought to assess the severity of this one. Likewise, he was too worried to analyze this shooting astutely. Fury chewed at him. He exploded, "By God, I'll kill whoever did this!"

"You want me to wash the blood off her arm and hands?" Rankin offered, needing to do something to ease his own anxiety.

"Not yet. I want to keep her as still as possible. Cal?" he called to her, but she was beyond hearing him. "Who would do this?"

"Maybe those rustlers are back, or whoever's been

sending those notes," Rankin suggested with a shaky voice.

"But she's never hurt anyone," Lynx debated.

"I'll go tell Steve and the boys to scout around. Maybe they can find a clue," Rankin suggested, then left.

Lynx sat down beside Calinda. Tears moistened his eyes, and his voice exposed his pain as he whispered, "Don't you go and die on me, woman. It took me too long to find you. I love you, Callie; I need you. Please don't leave me. I promise you, I'll find whoever did this and make them pay," he swore furiously.

Lynx was near a frenzy by the time the doctor arrived. Rankin had to force him to move aside to allow the doctor to examine her. Lynx hovered on the other side of the bed, his gaze never leaving her ashen face and limp body. Normally cool-headed and durable, he absently twisted his hands over and over as he watched the dire scene and realized what it could cost him.

The doctor dabbed at the rebellious wound and frowned. "What is it?" Lynx fiercely demanded, his self-control strained.

The doctor glanced up at the towering man with his darkly tanned bare chest and agitated expression. The older man's forehead wrinkled in concern and concentration. "There's a lot of bleeding, and I can't tell what the bullet struck. It's a crazy angle."

"But it passed clear through," Lynx argued, tensing in consternation, awaiting news he didn't want to learn.

"I wish it hadn't. Now we have two places for infection to attack. But it isn't as bad as it looks, son. I'm going to doctor and patch the hole in her back first, then stitch that front wound. That exit injury is the worst of our worries. When I sew it shut, I'll put some medicine on it. You best settle yourself, son; I'll need you to help me, just in case she comes to," he explained, doubting she would this soon. How horrible that such a charming creature had to face such violence and pain.

A moanful noise left her dry lips. "Can't you give her something?" Lynx insisted, caressing her creamy cheek.

"Don't want to rush things, son. The sooner she wakes up, the better her chances for licking this battle."

"What do you want me to do?" Lynx inquired hoarsely.

"We'll do the back first. I'll need you to hold her still."

Calinda was shifted to lie crossways, her head near the edge. Lynx was instructed to hold her still. "When we start on that front, even if she wakes up or screams, don't let her move an inch. Understand?" the doctor expounded.

Lynx took his assigned position. He had witnessed lots of bleeding and pain, but none had affected him as hers was doing. She moved slightly as the doctor cleaned it and placed a medicinal salve there. He washed away the surrounding blood and dried the area to bandage it.

"Now, let's do the front," the doctor stated. "Turn her over gently, Lynx. This is the tricky one. Appears a rifle shot."

Lynx carefully rolled her to her back and straddled her waist, confining her body between his legs, positioning himself to prevent any movements from her. He locked his fingers around her wrists and imprisoned her hands near his bent knees. "I'm ready, Doc."

"This is gonna hurt, Lynx. Even if she stays out cold, she's gonna struggle instinctively. I'm gonna try it without drugging her. I need to ask her some questions. Don't let go of her hands," he cautioned.

The doctor worked several minutes trying to see through the flow of blood from the torn flesh. Finally, he pinched the two sides together and took his first stitch. Calinda jerked and groaned. When he took the second stitch, she tried to twist away from the excruciating pain. Lynx tightened his grip on her wrists and increased the pressure on her body with his knees.

On the next stitch, she cried out in agony and thrashed her head from side to side. Cal attempted to fight the forces which were inflicting more pain on her and preventing her escape, but Lynx refused to allow her body any damaging movement. The doctor waited a few minutes to let her settle down. When he began anew, she screamed into the imprisoning blackness, "No . . . Stop . . ."

"It's all right, love," Lynx tried to comfort her. "We'll be finished soon. I'm here with you, Callie."

The doctor took another stitch as her eyes flew open wide. Calinda shuddered and screamed. Perspiration glistened on her face, as well as on Lynx's. He couldn't bear to see her suffering like this, but he couldn't prevent it. Damn, he felt so helpless, a new and distressing emotion. "How much more? She's coming around."

"Just one, Lynx. Ready?"

Lynx nodded. Calinda tried to uncloud her vision, her feet pounding the bed as she screamed, "Stop! No . . ."

"Please, doc, give her something. Anything," he

urged.

"Not yet, Lynx. I can't stop now. In a moment. I know best," the struggling man explained hurriedly, resolved to hasty completion.

Calinda didn't arouse fully, but she didn't settle down. Amidst her frantic exertions, her cheeks stood out like red patches on a snowbank. Her body quivered spasmodically as if she were freezing. Her respiration was erratic. Drops of blood seeped between the tight stitches. The wounded area was fiery red and puffy, but for the whitened spots around the stitches. Tears were rolling into her tousled hair.

"You want me to release her, doc?" Lynx asked, watching his wife in shared anguish.

"Not yet. She might claw at the stitches. Let me bandage her first. She should settle down soon. Don't worry, son; she's dazed."

As the doctor cleansed the wound, she cried out, "Lynx!"

"I'm here, love," he responded, carelessly loosening his grip.

Cal's hand flew upwards to rub the throbbing area. Lynx grabbed it before it made contact. She yanked to free herself, crying.

"I'm sorry, love," he murmured sadly, cursing his inability to help her.

When the wound was bandaged and the blood washed away from her upper body, the doctor suggested Lynx put her in a gown. "You'll need to sit with her. Don't let her tamper with that wound. She appears to be breathing fine; I hope that means the bullet missed her lungs. I can't feel any breaks. I'll give her something for pain and rest. When she comes to, try to get some soup into her. If she starts to run a fever or get delirious, send for me immediately."

"I'll take care of her, doc," Lynx vowed. "She'll be all right?" he was compelled to ask, eyes tenderly roaming her grimacing features.

"I think so. She might sleep all night. Her body's had quite a shock. But if she comes to in pain, give her one teaspoon of this," he instructed, handing Lynx a small bottle from his scuffed bag. "No matter how much pain she has, no more than one spoonful every six hours. Make sure you keep it out of her reach; people in agony get desperate," he cautioned, forcing the drug between her lips.

"Right, doc. What if the bleeding doesn't stop?"

"I don't expect it to halt for hours. It'll take time for those cuts to settle down. Those stitches are gonna be sore; she'll want to pick at them when she's asleep. If you get tired, tie her hands to her sides before you fall asleep. If she tears open that wound again, won't be nothing I can do. And don't let her get out of bed," he added.

Rankin saw the doctor out and came upstairs. Lynx related the action and the doctor's advice. "I can watch over her while you sleep, son. We'll take care of our girl."

"Thanks, Father, but I'll take care of her myself. If anything happens to Cal, I'll never forgive myself. I shouldn't have left her alone. She's been in danger since she arrived. Who's doing this to her?"

"I think we best find out soon," Rankin suggested.

It was an hour later when Rankin returned to the somber room. He told Lynx he would watch over Calinda while his son bathed and ate. For the first time since this drama began, Lynx realized he wasn't wearing a shirt and had dried blood on his hands and chest.

He nodded and left reluctantly, too weary and anxious to talk.

As Lynx ate quickly in the kitchen, Salina asked, "Is she all right, Lynx? Nobody will tell me anything," she stated as if worried.

Lynx's haunted gaze lifted to stare at Salina. "I doubt you give a damn, Salina, but we don't know yet. When I discover who's behind those mysterious letters and this shooting, I'll kill the bastard, or bitch," he added, sending his intimidating and crafty point home.

"You mean she might . . . die?" Salina probed incredulously.

"Not if I can stop it. And by God, I'm doing all I can. If she does, this land isn't big enough for her killer to escape me," he snarled.

"Who would shoot her?" Salina murmured.

"Just as soon as she's out of danger, I'll find out," he vowed.

"Is there anything I can do?" Salina offered guilefully.

"Stay clear of her," Lynx demanded harshly in surprise.

"What is into you, Lynx?" she asked petulantly

"The devil, Salina, and he's battling to break free."

She watched him closely. "Are you accusing me of having something to do with this accident?" Salina questioned his surly mood.

"Accident?" Lynx growled skeptically. "You could hardly label cold-blooded murder an accident. I've been doing some thinking, and I've decided someone is trying to use any method to get her away from the ranch and me. You wouldn't have any idea who might try something reckless and deadly like that, would you?" Although he continued to eat with his head lowered, Lynx was furtively observing Salina.

"*Como!* Are you *demente* with grief?" she panted in alarm.

"The fires of hatred and revenge burn brightly and fatally, Salina. You were eager to spy and tattle on her before. Is there anything new you think I should know?" he quizzed the nervous girl.

"She has been acting very strange since you left, if that is your meaning. I saw her restless and sad. She went into town Tuesday and Thursday. Both times she returned in crazy moods. She spends much time alone in your room. Does that help any?"

"What else?" Lynx pressed, glaring coldly at her.

Salina thought for a time, then added, "Maybe she is not well. She has been pale and tired lately. She cries a lot in her room."

"How would you know that?" Lynx demanded tersely, engulfing her with that burning gaze which seared off even a brave man's courage.

"The signs, Lynx. Puffy and red eyes?" she hinted, unable to battle that forceful gaze which was glacially intimidating.

"Why would she cry so much?"

"Maybe she was missing you or upset with you," she replied flippantly . "How should I know? You ordered me to steer clear of your wife." Salina realized it was time to cease her dangerous game; it was getting out of control.

"Who went into town with her?" Lynx persisted with resolve.

"I think Charlie," she replied, ready to end this conversation.

Since it was too late to speak with Charlie tonight,

Lynx returned to his room. "Anything, Father?" he asked instantly.

"Not a peep or move, son. She'll make it, won't she?"

"She must," Lynx replied wistfully, plagued by Salina's words.

Lynx stretched out beside Cal and waited for her resilience to take command of her weakened body and to strengthen it. Several times, she stirred and moaned, but didn't arouse. When she attempted to reach for the injury, he would capture her hands and hold them until she settled down once more. When she became so restive that he dreaded further injury, he forced more medicine between her lips. Gradually she quieted. Off and on, he tested her forehead for a fever, finding none and saying a grateful prayer. But by dawn, the front bandage exposed signs of fresh crimson stains.

Lynx had slept little that night, each muffled utterance or movement catching his attention. His father entered the room around seven to check on both of them. He stayed with Calinda while Lynx flexed his stiff muscles and went for coffee. Lynx was back in the room within minutes. Lynx felt like a splotch on a cowhide, providing nothing but its decorative presence.

Around eight o'clock, Calinda began to squirm in distress and send forth muffled whimpers. As her hand went upward to rub her groggy eyes, Lynx surged forward and seized it, cautioning, "Don't aggravate it, love. Lie still."

There was a terrible aching on her chest and back; she shifted in discomfort, sending sharp pains through her body. She cried out, fighting to reach the level of awareness. "Callie, can you hear me?" Lynx's voice probed the encasing shadows.

Cal struggled to open her eyes. She moistened her dry lips, breathing raggedly. She couldn't understand why she was in such agony and why she couldn't awaken. She could hear Lynx talking to her, but she couldn't respond. Her head rolled from side to side as she resisted the encompassing blackness. "Help me, Lynx," she murmured, before slipping beyond communication.

"I'm here, love," he told her, but he knew it was too late for her to catch his words. She was having a terrible time seeking, and yet resisting, consciousness. Lynx couldn't endure her anguish. After checking the time, he forced more medicine between her lips.

Hours passed and the doctor arrived. He questioned Lynx about her condition. They talked for a few minutes, then he removed her bandages to examine the wounds and change the dressings. He glanced at Lynx and smiled. "So far so good, son."

As Calinda yanked to free her hands, she screamed, "Let go!" Her lids fluttered and her slumberous eyes touched on Lynx who was confining her. Pain racked her body as she hazily recalled the shooting. Why was he being so cruel to her? Why couldn't she think clearly? "Why . . . do you want me . . . dead?" she asked unknowingly, stunningly. "I've . . . given you . . . every . . . thing," she sobbed. "Don't . . . kill me," she pleaded groggily, senses deluded by medicine and pain.

Lynx was shocked into speechless disbelief. He stared at his ailing wife. The doctor noted his incredulous expression. She thrashed on the bed, crying and begging. "Callie?" Lynx finally brought an entreating word from his tormented body. "What are you saying, love?"

In a brief flash of awareness, she shrieked, "Don't touch me! You won't deceive me again," she whispered, slipping beneath that cloak of protective darkness once more where breathing didn't hurt.

Lynx's palm flew to her face to test for fiery warmth. "Is she delirious? Did you hear what she said?" he yelled in dismay.

"She's just confused and in pain, Lynx. She doesn't know what she's saying. There's no fever or infection yet. She's out of her head."

"But she called my name," he debated anxiously.

"That's natural, son," the doctor tried to calm him.

"Natural to think I did this?" Lynx stormed in bewilderment, for that was how it had sounded to him.

"It's the pain and drug talking, Lynx, nothing more," he tried again to quiet the distraught man.

"You sure, doc?" Lynx challenged skeptically, worriedly.

"Yep. Is there any truth to her wild rantings?" he teased.

"Hell, no!" Lynx thundered from rising tension and fatigue.

"Then forget it. We can't have her upset over saying something she won't even remember. She recognized you standing over her when she's tortured with pain; that's why her dazed mind held you to blame."

Lynx nodded, but wasn't totally convinced. For a brief instant, there had been full awareness in her expression, one of inexplicable fear and accusation! Unable to question her actions and words, he was compelled to let them pass. He observed her lovely, unblemished face. Some natural color had returned and her cheeks weren't bright red anymore. She was weak, but alluded to inner strength. All of which the doctor pointed out to him as encouraging signs.

"Unless you need me, son, I'll check on her tomorrow afternoon. She's doing just fine. Keep her quiet and still," he reminded.

Off and on for hours, she briefly came to wakefulness, then quickly sank back into her plaguing darkness without speaking. As she battled unseen foes, she mumbled incoherently. It was nearing the dinner hour when Calinda regained full consciousness. Lynx jumped up from his chair near the bed the moment she sighed in misery and wiggled slightly. She forced her drowsy senses to clear and her heavy lids to open. As Lynx sat down beside her and smiled, her baffled gaze shifted to him. "What . . . happened, Lynx? Merciful Heavens, I hurt."

"You tell me, love," he coaxed gently, moving damp curls from her face. "I've been crazy with worry and fear since yesterday."

"Yesterday?" Cal echoed as she fought to recall the memory.

Lynx explained how he had arrived home and found her missing, how her horse had returned with blood on him and the saddle, how they had searched for her, and how he had found her wounded near his mother's grave. Lynx observed her closely for all reactions.

"Laura's grave?" Cal repeated, simultaneously trying to recall and to forget the pernicious episode.

"What were you doing out there alone, Cal? Who shot you?"

"Shot me?" she continued her repetitious confusion. "I . . . You . . . found me? I . . . remember a shot. I saw blood . . . on my fingers. I couldn't . . .

mount. There was a horse . . . galloping off. I passed out. It hurts," she said, grimacing and reaching to soothe the pain.

"Don't touch it, Cal. The doctor said you were to stay quiet and still. We don't want that wound opening or those stitches breaking. You didn't see anyone? Think hard, Callie."

"The doctor was here?" she asked, blinking her eyes to stay alert and awake. "It's throbbing, Lynx." Tears rolled down her cheeks.

"I know, love, but you can't touch it. You didn't see who fired the shot?" he pressed cautiously, tenderly dabbing the moisture.

"No. It happened too quickly. I didn't die?" she murmured suddenly, as if astonished she was alive. Was she suppose to survive?

Lynx smiled. "No way would I lose you, woman. You sorely tried to desert me, but I wouldn't allow it. I stayed with you all night and today. I even helped Doc stitch you up. You were determined to fight us; I had to sit on you and hold you down," he stated merrily, joy and relief coursing through his body and mind.

"How long was I out?" she asked, her lids drooping.

"Since yesterday when it happened. It's nearly dinner time. Think you can drink or eat something if I help you?" he coaxed.

She yawned, groaning as the reflex enticed needling torment. "I'm so sleepy and weak," she whispered faintly. She closed her eyes, surrendering to sleep before answering. But she didn't rest long before she began tossing and crying.

Lynx came to her side, entreating, "Relax, love."

Cal looked up at him. Slowly her mind cleared. "How about a stiff brandy to dull this agony, Lynx?"

She gritted her teeth.

Lynx chuckled at her attempt at humor. "Afraid not, love. But you can have soup and some medicine," he counter-offered.

"I'm not hungry. I'll take some water and the medicine."

"You need some food in that tummy, Cal. It's been over twenty-four hours since you were . . . injured. You lost a lot of blood, and you're very weak. Please take just a little soup," he beseeched her.

"I'm not hungry, Lynx, just in pain," she argued sullenly.

"I'm sorry I wasn't here to protect you, Cal. I promise it won't happen again. Please, let me take care of you and get you well. Do you know how I felt when I found you lying on the ground, bleeding to death? If my heart didn't stop, it skipped many beats. It tore out my guts to w ch you suffer yesterday while we were working to save you. For a time, Cal, we didn't think we could, I've been sitting her all night, afraid to leave you, praying for your survival. For the first time in my life, Cal, I was petrified. I felt useless. You cried and screamed and begged me to help you, but I couldn't do anything. When I find out who did this, I'll kill him!" he declared forcefully, a glimmer of fierce rage and ominous resolve in his stormy expression.

Calinda gazed at him, witnessing the tenderness and anguish in his expression. But were they real? How could she doubt him? How could she think clearly and calmly. Her thoughts were controlled by pain, drugs, and weakness. "When you search for him, be careful; he's a crack-shot, as you call it. If I hadn't been startled by the gunfire, the bullet would have been accurate, right in the heart."

503

"Thank Heavens he didn't check on his accuracy. Why did you go riding alone, Cal; you promised you wouldn't," he softly scolded her. "If your horse hadn't raced home with blood on him, you might have died out there."

"Is that how you knew I was hurt?" she asked, shifting gingerly.

Lynx related the few untold events of yesterday, unaware of how they settled in her warring mind. Another timely arrival and rescue? The bloody horse had alerted others, besides him, to her peril? If the animal hadn't returned to the stable, how long would Lynx have waited before seeking her, long enough for her to die? "You didn't see anyone?" Cal inquired; he shook his head ruefully. "I guess I was lucky," she murmured, looking down at her bandaged body.

"Damn lucky, woman," Lynx corrected her, wondering at her piercing and unreadable gaze. What was she thinking? "Can I play doctor, Mrs. Cardone?" he asked, trying to lift some curious burden.

She focused on him, then remarked, "You look terrible. You need a shave and some sleep. I'll be fine." She forced all thoughts from her mind, except getting well and easing the pain.

"I've had something, rather someone, more important on my mind." He bent forward and kissed the tip of her nose. "Soup?"

She stifled a yawn and winced, tears coming to her eyes as she trembled. "I'll try, after the medicine," she reasoned desperately.

"Fine," Lynx promptly agreed. "Don't move until I return."

After he left the room, she clenched her teeth as she tried to check the extent of her injuries. Cal fought to keep from crying and screaming as she shifted on the bed. There was a bandage on her back and front, and she could detect the stitches beneath the front binding. She noticed the crimson traces on the front bandage; it was still bleeding a little. Her nerves were tight and tense; the stitches nerve-racking. Her weakness was most noticeable, and hindering.

Cal glanced at her surroundings; the room was messy. Clearly her husband had been at her side since the shooting, but why? To see if she survived? Or died? Playing the concerned husband? For whom? Salina and Rankin couldn't care less about her! Who had tried to murder her? Why? They had possession of the ranch; they didn't need her dead. If they wished her gone, all they had to do was force her off the ranch. It was senseless!

Cal told herself she was foolishly mistaken. Lynx would never do such a vile thing. He might be capable of vengefully taking the ranch or wanting to hurt her emotionally, but never murder her. She had to figure out who was fatally pursuing her . . .

How she wished she could change her recent past. She wouldn't look at Laura's portrait or hear Salina's words. She wouldn't go to Lampasas. She wouldn't send word to Kyle Yancey or converse with him. There was so much she wished she didn't know; but she did, so many haunting coincidences and complexities.

When Lynx returned, she was sobbing. "Please don't cry, love," he entreated, coming over to her. "You might injure yourself." How he wanted to pull her into his arms, but he dared not risk her movements.

"It hurts so much, Lynx," she wailed, meaning the combination of physical and emotional pains. Yet, she needed his solace.

JANELLE TAYLOR

He took the bottle of medicine and poured out one spoonful. He said, "Take this, love. It'll ease the pain."

Without thinking or hesitating, she swallowed the nasty-tasting liquid. As she choked and coughed, she shrieked in pain and twitched. "Be still, Cal," he advised sternly. "You'll rip open that wound."

"That's easy for you to say! You're not the one in agony!" she shouted, ordering herself to lie motionless after paying for her outburst.

Lynx captured her face between his hands and shouted, "Like hell, I'm not! Damn you, Cal, if you break those stitches, I'll hold you down and replace them myself," he threatened harshly to calm her.

"I'm sure you love torturing me, you beast! Do something!" she hoarsely pleaded, shuddering with torment, clenching her teeth.

"What?" he asked in frustration, wringing his hands.

"Kiss me!" she replied angrily, knowing the power of his lips to blind her to reality. "Just hold me and kiss me."

"But you're hurt!" he debated. "You've got a fever!" he fretted.

"Use that potent magic on me; give me something else to think about until that medicine works," she frantically reasoned.

His lips covered hers as he concentrated on keeping his hands off her body. For what seemed hours, but was only minutes, the feverish kissing and throbbing pain continued. Gradually, both softened. Lynx felt her still body begin to relax. He leaned back and looked down at her. "Well? Did I help any?" he murmured huskily.

The drug alleviating her distress, she smiled.

"You're the best treatment I know, Cardone. Thanks."

"For what, love?" he asked, watching her mood mellow.

"For saving my life again, and for easing the pain."

"That's the medication," he refuted happily.

"Perhaps," she stated skeptically. "If you want any of that soup in me, you best hurry. I'm getting awfully sleepy."

He sat on the edge of the bed and carefully spooned the soup into her mouth. "If it wouldn't hurt so much, I would laugh at this ridiculous scene," she murmured, forgetting all but him.

"I think it's fun," he remarked mischievously.

"Then perhaps I'll shoot you and become your amused nurse."

Minutes later, Cal's lids were very heavy. Each time he went for her mouth with the spoon, he had to tap her lower lip and say, "Open up, lovely mouth."

Finally her eyes closed and she didn't respond. She was sleeping peacefully for a change. He set the bowl and spoon on the dresser and headed for bed, relatively calm for the first time in two days. Suddenly he realized he might roll over on her and inflict more damage or pain. He fetched his sleeping roll and reclined on the floor, his senses alive and alert to her every sound even in slumber.

Chapter Twenty-two

When Calinda awoke around six the next morning, she lay very still as she summoned the courage to assess her strength. Her entire shoulder area ached and complained, but she felt stronger and more alert this morning. The tight stitches nagged at the sensitive wound, especially with movement. She felt her cheeks for any warmth, relieved to find no exceptional heat residing there. She stalled her impending action as her mind swept away all lingering cobwebs.

Using her right arm, Cal tried to shove herself to a sitting position. The strain on her disabled left side harassed her immediately. She panted, "Ouch!", then gently eased back to the mattress. She attempted to hold her breath until the throbbing lessened.

Lynx bounded up from the floor and approached her. "What's wrong?" he asked in alarm.

Her startled gaze flew to his worried frown, unshaven face, and mussed hair. He stood there barefoot and bare-chested, attired in snug-fitting jeans. He reeked of masculinity. "Where did you come from?" Cal asked in amazement. Her gaze was a loving brush and his virile frame a receptive canvas, as her eyes moved over him.

"I was sleeping on the floor," Lynx answered quickly, inflamed by her appreciative study of him.

"On the floor? Why?" she quizzed, meeting his warm gaze.

"I was afraid I might hurt you during the night. I do have a habit of snuggling up to you," he merrily ventured.

"Why didn't you sleep in the other room?" she reasoned curiously.

"And leave a willful and impulsive vixen alone all night?" he jested. "Doc says you can't leave that bed, so I stayed here to make certain you followed his orders. I do have a stake in you, love."

"Surely you didn't think I would hop up and dance around?" she played along with his insouciant mood.

"From what I've seen, Mrs. Cardone, you have a defiant streak which I don't trust. Am I wrong, or were you trying to get up?" he challenged, making his point. "Looking for me, afraid I'd deserted you in your hour of need?" he roguishly hinted.

"If there's one thing I've learned, husband dear, it's knowing you'll always show up in the nick of time. How do you manage such cunning?" she asked saucily, veiling her seriousness with a smile.

"Fate," he nonchalantly replied. "Somebody's keeping an eye on us, giving us guidance and protection."

Cal motioned to her condition and speculated, "You call this protection? Our guardian angel was snoozing this time," she charged.

"Not for long. You were found quickly, and you're

better this morning. Right?" Lynx gingerly sat down on the bed near her waist.

"I'll decide later. Any clues on my would-be assassin?"

"None yet, but don't worry," he advised, smiling broadly.

"Why should I? I have my fearless and powerful husband here with me," she murmured, her gaze fathomless. "To answer your earlier question, I wasn't trying to get up, just determine my damage."

Lynx seized a trace of a curious resentment in her tone. "Do you blame me for this, Cal?"

She tensed, then forcefully relaxed. A flush sped over her face; her gaze lowered briefly. "Why should I blame you, except for being absent when I obviously needed your protection?" she asked in a tone which was perplexing and alarming. "You didn't shoot me, did you?" she tried to jest lightly, but failed to deceive him.

"If you have even the slightest reservation about me, Cal, then we're in deep trouble, love. I wouldn't do anything to harm you."

"Wouldn't you?" she debated gravely. "You keep secrets from me; that hurts me. You stay away from home for ages; that hurts me. You can't protect me from danger because you're too busy defending your unknown friends; that hurts me. I can't make you happy or content; and that hurts most. You can halt one stab of pain by ceasing this distressing conversation. May I have my medicine now?"

"You need to eat first, Cal. That drug makes you pass out," Lynx entreated, following her request for a truce for the time being.

"I'd rather be out, Cardone; that way no pains attack me."

"You've got me worried, Callie. Do you honestly think I had something to do with the shooting?" he pressed earnestly.

"No, Lynx, I don't believe you shot me," she replied.

"From the look on that lovely face, you think I'm capable of doing it, don't you?" he demanded, piqued.

"Please don't do this, Lynx. I'm just tired, and confused, and miserable. It was a joke. If I recall, you made the same jest when you and Rankin were attacked. Don't pay any attention to my irritable mood and stupid rantings. I just want everyone to leave me alone."

"Including me?" he speculated in dread.

"Right now, my nerves are tight, I'm in terrible pain, and I need to rest and think. My heavens, Lynx, someone tried to murder me! It's hard to accept the fact someone hates me that much. After that last mysterious note appeared, I told you I sensed danger or evil lurking nearby, but you assumed I was trying to trick you into staying home. You listen to your own instincts, but deny feminine intuition."

"Since we don't know who did it, we also don't know the motive. Some outlaws think nothing of gunning down anybody in their path. It could have been one of those rustler scouts who thought you saw him or the same person who ambushed father and me. Or it could have been our mystery man trying to deliver another letter. Maybe whoever did it didn't realize you were a woman," Lynx speculated.

"I don't pass for a man, Lynx. If it was that sneaky villain, why kill the person he's trying to contact?" she rebutted.

"If those letters were meant to lure you away into

danger, he didn't need to deliver it after he caught you alone and helpless! I told you to stay home or ride with someone, not alone!" he snarled.

"Stop being so bossy! In spite of that marriage certificate, you don't own me! I'm weary of your terse orders and defensive attitude!" she snapped at him. "I'm also damn tired of your secretive conduct!"

"I'm just trying to protect you, wife," he growled sullenly.

"From another town?" she scoffed sarcastically.

"That's really what's chewing your tail, isn't it? My private trips and long absences?" he challenged to unmask her resentful anger.

"Where did you go, if that's not too nosey?" she asked frostily.

Perceptive, Lynx noticed the alerting hint in her voice. "Why? I told you before I left where I was heading; I sent messages home."

"I didn't ask where those messages came from or where you were suppose to go. I asked where you went after you left the ranch."

"If you already know, why the question?" Lynx fenced warily.

"Would you hand me that box of writing paper?" Cal asked, more than ready to begin a journey toward the truth.

"You can't work like that. You've got to take care of yourself."

"Hand it to me, or I'll fetch it myself," she said stubbornly.

Cal opened the box which he placed in her lap. "This might explain my irrational and unreasonable annoyance, my devoted husband."

Lynx unfolded the paper, recognizing it immediately. A tremor washed over him. "Where did you get this? You searched my things?"

"When you were packing that morning, you dropped some papers; remember? Evidently this one went under the bed; I found it Monday when I was sweeping. What logical excuse do I receive this time for deceiving me? I suppose you're going to deny you went to Dallas?"

"No. I went to meet Major Jones, at his request, as you know from reading my mail. I didn't tell you because I was afraid you'd think I was breaking my word. I didn't look for your father, Cal; I swear it."

"Being dishonest is easier than explaining? Am I so dense or untrustworthy that you must constantly deceive me?" she sneered icily.

"Before you ask, woman, the 'B' stands for Burrow, a man Jones wanted me to locate for him. I had my reasons for keeping quiet."

"You always do, Lynx, about many things," she stated coldly.

"What's that supposed to mean?" he inquired, eyeing her warily.

"Nothing, Lynx, it doesn't matter anymore. I'll follow that old adage, ask me no questions and I'll tell you no lies . . ."

"Why did you go to town twice this week?" he asked unexpectedly to catch her off guard. He had a bad feeling about her trips.

She paled, then stammered, "To . . . get a new dress for your homecoming. I selected the material and hired a seamstress Tuesday, then picked up the dress Thursday. Looks as if I'll wear it later."

"Why the rush job for a husband who has you infuriated?"

"You were expected home Friday, remember? As you know, I'm impulsive; I decided at the last minute to wear something special."

"But you found the telegram Monday, *Llama de mi corazon*. You had me painted black by Tuesday," he debated her half-lies.

Briefly Calinda went rigid as she stared at him. "All the more need to look ravishing when I'm trying to bewitch my own husband into sharing his life with me, to explain why he can't be content and honest with me," she sought to mislead him. "And please don't call me that."

"I told you I'd clear up any problems between us when I got home. Couldn't you wait to hear me out before judging me guilty?"

"That was my exact intention, but a nasty bullet got in my way. Tell me, Lynx, does someone want me dead or just off this ranch? Even a fool can decipher this many hazardous clues. I want to know who's declared himself my enemy and why," she stated bluntly.

"It isn't me, love; but I aim to discover who it is. Nothing suspicious happened while I was gone?" he probed.

"Can you interrogate me later? I'm hungry and hurting," she avoided the subject with truthful excuses. "Didn't you return too quickly?" she questioned, realizing this contradiction in his plans.

"You sound disappointed I rushed to finish and hurry back. I'll get you some breakfast and medicine, if you promise to stay put until you're well." He refused to move until she gave her word.

"Yes, boss," she replied, smiling tightly.

When Lynx attempted to kiss her, she turned her head and pleaded, "Not now, Lynx. I feel terrible."

"Llama de mi corazon isn't an insult, Callie," he told her, wondering at her glacial reaction to the endearment. "It means . . ."

"I know what it means; I asked Salina to translate," she injected.

"What did she say?" he questioned, assuming the worst.

"Flame of my heart. I simply dislike words I can't understand."

That morning birthed three days of fencing and probing on both sides. Calinda wasn't allowed out of bed. She depended on the medicine to keep her out of his verbal reach during those first few days after the shooting. She ate, slept, and rested. When Lynx would enter the room, Cal would often pretend to be asleep, unaware that she didn't have him fooled at all. When he tried to entertain her, she would politely ask him not to be so amusing, that laughter aggravated her wounds. When he tried to help her with meals, she would tell him that was her only means of diversion and feed herself. She refused to allow Salina to visit her, and Lynx agreed with that decision. Rankin would come by for a few moments, but she would feign fatigue to keep his trips to her room brief.

Lynx slept in the other room, but checked on her frequently. He realized she was very guarded and remote, but couldn't decide why. Cal remained pensive and moody, quick to deny his assistance and company. Lynx fretted over her lack of warmth and her resistance to him. She watched him strangely when he was in the room. She permitted his kisses, but hers lacked honesty. After that first morning, she hadn't questioned him again; it almost seemed she didn't want to converse with him on any topic.

When the doctor came around, they would chat genially and she would exchange smiles with the elderly man. He told her the stitches could be removed in a week. Both were delighted that no infection set in on either injury. He jovially commented on Lynx's excellent care of her while Calinda stared at her lap. The doctor said he wouldn't need to drop by for several days unless there was a problem. He showed Lynx how to change her dressings, then said she could begin sitting up for short periods each day. "A while in the morning and afternoon. Nothing strenuous, my girl. Lots of rest and good food. No lifting anything," he issued his orders cheerfully.

"I'll make sure she obeys, doc," Lynx said firmly.

"Just be patient, Calinda, don't rush this," he added.

She smiled and nodded. "I'll be up and around before long."

"Not before I give the word, girl," he reminded her.

Four more days passed. Lynx would prop her up on pillows each morning and afternoon so she could read. When she tried to lengthen her schedule, Lynx refused to allow it. He would bring his meals to the room to eat with her, finding it difficult to draw her out. When he insisted, Cal would play a game of cards with him. He continued to sleep in the other room, becoming restless and moody himself. To relax her, he persisted in sponging her off each night before bedtime, to her arguments and rebellion. When she demanded a real bath, he denied it until the doctor said she could exert that much energy.

Being close to her and unable to touch her was sheer torment. At least she could grant him some affectionate kisses and bright smiles! At least she could talk to him, tell him what was troubling her! This chilling silence was gnawing at him, reeking pain and injury. Why couldn't he reach her, soften her? It was frustrating.

By the tenth day, a storm was brewing in Lynx. He had been working hard to drive himself into exhausted slumber, recalling her past confession of a similar desperation. He had reached his limit of patience and understanding. It was time to clear the tainted air between them. Cal had punished and tormented him enough! It was time for her self-pity and reserve to end. He left the range early to confront her.

When Lynx arrived home, she was in no condition to settle anything with him. The doctor had been there to remove the stitches, and she was nervous and uncomfortable. She constantly wiggled her foot to get rid of some of her anxiety. Her cheeks were flushed a bright red, and she was pale around her mouth. He strolled over to the bed and sat down. Her gaze darted around the room like a busy insect.

"I saw Doc leaving. How does it feel?" he asked solicitously.

"Like hell, Cardone," she unnaturally snapped at him.

"Need something for the pain?" he tried to help her again.

"Doc says I can't have anymore of his magic fluid. Sometimes he's as mean as you are. I want some sherry," Cal declared.

"Did Doc say you could have any?" he inquired, trying to keep his composure. She was as squirmy as a captive on an Apache antbed.

Cal glared at him. "I didn't ask. But if I don't get some relief, I'm going to scream my head off. It's easy for you and Doc to give orders; you two aren't injured or upset," she panted breathlessly.

When Lynx continued to observe her, she added, "Please."

"Let me see your chest and back," he said unflinchingly.

"After the sherry," she informed him crisply.

"Before the sherry," he called her bluff, their gazes meeting and silently battling. "I'm serious, Calinda Cardone."

Lynx comprehended her distress when she readily agreed when he knew she wanted to scream a refusal at him. "Doc just put on new dressings," she tried to prevent his touch and nearness.

"I'll re-do them," he dismissed her excuse, grinning. "You shouldn't be embarrassed, love; I'm well-acquainted with what's beneath that gown," he hinted provocatively.

"It's ugly and sickening," she taunted him.

"Is that why you're shutting me out of your life, afraid a tiny scar will repulse me? Isn't that cold-shoulder getting heavy by now?" he probed.

"If you've come here to start another quarrel, Lynx, I'm not in the mood. What's unbearably heavy is this bed and room. I want some fresh air, sunshine, and exercise before I go mad. How would you be feeling if you'd been laid up for over a week with no end in sight?"

"Ornery as a trapped badger," he roguishly replied, then chuckled. "I know it's hard to laze around in pain and boredom. One sherry coming up," he stated, bowing at the waist before leaving.

When Lynx returned and Cal reached for the glass, he held it away from her and reminded, "My inspection first, Callie."

She spread her arms on the bed and invited, "Proceed, tyrant."

He carefully lifted the front patch and studied the fiery area with its sealed white line. The surrounding flesh exposed yellowish purple bruising. He gingerly replaced the bandage, then checked the back injury where a fairly healed hole greeted his vision. When he was satisfied, he handed her the glass. "Looks marvelous to me."

She smiled indulgently and sipped the golden liquid. Lynx remained silent, his body rigid. A haunted expression filled his tawny eyes. Mentally he seemed to be far away from her, so sad, so miserable. "Lynx, why are you staring at me like that?" she asked.

He straightened and shrugged. "I was just thinking how close I came to losing you. Now that I have you, Callie, I can't imagine my life without you. For the first time, I realize what my father went through years ago when Mother . . . I don't know which is worse, the agony or the fear of facing life alone. I'll see you later," he murmured hoarsely, then turned to leave, berating his show of vulnerability.

"Lynx," she called to him, drawn to that sensitive facet.

Expecting an apology for her treatment of him lately, he slowly turned and waited. "Tell me about your mother,"she entreated instead.

"I can't, Callie," he said, shaking his head.

"It's been nearly six years according to the date on her tombstone. How long will you suffer like this?" she asked quietly.

"I wish I knew. Sometimes it seems like yesterday. Sometimes, as if she never existed. If only I knew . . .

Why were you at her grave?" he asked, twisting the conversation around to her.

Cal was prepared for a reply. "I saw her portrait in the attic. She's very beautiful. I was wondering what she was like; you two favor so much."

"That's why it was so hard on Rankin back then. Every time he looked at me, he saw glimmers of her. It was tearing him apart. I thought if I left for a while, those painful memories would end. I discovered something terrible; you can't leave problems behind when they're inside your head."

"You can't grieve forever, Lynx. Why can't you let her go? You expect me to do that with my father," she reminded him softly.

"There's a big difference between us, Callie. I had my mother until I was seventeen; you were a small child, too young to recall Brax. If it was as simple as speaking words, I could," he murmured softly.

"Words aren't simple, Lynx, not from you."

"When you're better, we'll talk, love, not tonight." He smiled at her, then headed for the door again.

Before she realized what words were forming in her mouth they had spilled forth to halt and stun him. "She isn't dead, is she?"

Lynx whirled and faced her, then stalked forward to the bed. "What did you say?" he demanded fiercely, all tenderness gone.

Bright and quick, she cunningly deceived him, "In your heart, she isn't dead yet. She's like a ghost haunting you."

"You're wrong, Callie; as far as I'm concerned, she's dead."

Calinda's heart screamed, *why can't you confide in me?* Not that it mattered, but he hadn't lied to her, just misled her, again. "So we're just supposed to forget our parents?" she inquired sadly.

"We have no choice, Callie; they're gone forever. Do you want me to join you for dinner tonight?" he asked for the first time since her perilous battle with death.

"Need you ask?" Cal parried as if honestly surprised.

For a brief moment he looked like a vulnerable boy as he said, "Something tells me I do. I won't ask why; you'll tell me when you're ready to discuss it. Until then, know this, woman; I need you."

Tears glistened in her eyes. "I need you, too. But we have some problems to work out before things can be right between us."

"Yes, I know. But this isn't the time. See you later," he told her, then left. As he walked down the steps, Lynx was curiously exhausted. Not once since his return had she said, I love you . . .

He headed for the stable. It was past time to speak with Charlie and to investigate her depressing trips into town. Maybe some vital clues or an answer could be located . . .

When dinner came and went without her husband's appearance, Calinda wondered why Rankin had brought her meal and why Lynx had ridden into town and stayed so late. While she ate, she deliberated this situation. Had she carelessly tipped her hand? She admitted she had been acting suspicious. Just in case that cunning rogue discovered something, she must prepare her defense. Mastering her weakness and pain, Cal retrieved Brax's will and letter and placed them where Lynx could find them, if he made a search. It was too soon to let him see the note and deed, for they revealed things which Lynx should confess willingly, mainly the ranch ownership. After conning another sherry from Rankin later that evening, she was entrapped by slumber when Lynx arrived near midnight.

Lynx walked into the room and stood beside the bed, staring down at his wife. Why would Cal meet with a lawyer from Austin? Why keep it a secret? Why send that phony telegram about him to the sheriff in Dallas? What papers had the man brought to her?

Lynx possessed a calculating and crafty mind. He was well-versed on intense investigation. These clues tumbled over in his keen mind like a colorful kaleidoscope until a devastating picture formed before his mind's eye. She had learned things he wished she hadn't, but what was the extent of her knowledge?

Tomorrow he would unravel this entwined mystery. He cautioned himself as he gingerly searched the room, fearing to awaken her. When he located two papers hidden beneath her underwear, he seized them to read in the other room, immediately recognizing the handwriting on those pages, alarmingly noting the dates. Lynx dreaded confronting her, knowing he couldn't avoid it. This discovery explained her interest in the portrait and Laura's grave. It explained her distance and mistrust. If she knew everything, it was frightfully clear why her imagination was running wild about the shooting . . .

In the other room, Lynx unfolded a paper which turned out to be a will. He quickly scanned it, finding no mention of the ranch. He was shocked and confused to learn he was Brax's heir if anything happened to Calinda. He tossed the will aside to devour the contents of the lengthy letter. Lynx couldn't believe his eyes; Brax had confessed to the affair with his mother. Calinda knew Brax was guilty of theft and adultery!

Did she understand why he and his father had kept silent about that painful betrayal? That knowledge explained why she had given up her search. But the reason for the hasty departure of Laura and Brax staggered him; somewhere he had a half-brother or half-sister . . . But so did his suffering wife! No wonder she was so confused, frightened, and saddened!

Chapter Twenty-three

In spite of his late and restless night, Lynx was up early the next morning. He wanted his chores done by mid-afternoon so he could have plenty of privacy and time with Calinda. With Brax's will and plaguing letter, his wife had just enough misleading evidence against him to damage their relationship, but hopefully not enough to destroy it. Lynx tried to force the words in Brax's letter from his mind, but he couldn't. At last, he had some answers, but not the ones expected or imagined. Oddly, he felt unshackled from the past; yet, he was still fettered by unbroken links in that fateful chain.

Lynx planned his strategy all morning. He would discuss Brax and Laura with Cal, fill in the gaps about what happened long ago. He would beg her forgiveness for keeping that affair and betrayal a secret. When Cal was well enough to be left alone a few days, he would place her under Steve's guard, then head for Austin to question this Kyle Yancey. Before Lynx revealed the truth about his connection with the Rangers and her ranch partnership, he must know everything she and Yancey had discussed. When he returned to her side, there would be no more secrets between them. Somehow he would make her understand his deceptions and accept his love. He had been a fool to keep such facts from her this long! If she accidentally discovered the truth about the ranch, there was no telling how she would interpret it. Telling his love everything wasn't as risky as keeping silent. Whatever it took, Lynx must force her to understand.

When he arrived home, he carefully prepared himself with a bath and fresh shave. He pulled on snug jeans and a baby blue shirt, hoping to cast a boyishly innocent facade. He left his tawny hair fluffy and his shirt opened beneath his heart level. He left off his spurs and gunbelt. Lynx was aware of how he affected her, he must use that to sway her.

When he swaggered into their room, he halted and gaped at her. Cal was sitting on the floor beside a tub, her naked body glistening with beads of water, her freshly washed hair dripping into the tub over which her chin was resting on her folded arms. Her daring offense was blatantly evident, as was its exhausting effect on her. Lynx hurried over to Cal and lifted her limp body, heading for the bed. "What the hell are you doing, woman?" he thundered angrily. "You're supposed to be taking it easy. Doc said no lifting or exerting."

"Taking a bath, idiot," the disobedient girl weakly panted. "Take me to the balcony to dry my hair; I'll soak the bed."

"Don't you know you're too weak to bathe alone, much less wash your hair?" he scolded as he wrapped a sheet around her nude body.

"I couldn't stand this greasy hair and filthy body a day longer. I thought I could make it if I hurried," Cal said softly, battling to control her nausea and woozy head.

"You thought wrong!" he declared in annoyance.

"Please don't fuss at me, Lynx. I feel awful; I think I'm going to faint," she told him, hoping he would cease his tirade.

He carried her outside into the warm sunlight and sat down with her in his lap. "I'm soaking your shirt," she whispered.

"It doesn't matter, love. Just relax," he coaxed her tenderly, his fury vanishing as he realized how helpless she was.

"I need my brush. If my hair dries like this, it'll be in a thousand tangles. Please," she entreated.

"Serves you right, woman. As punishment, I'll enjoy removing each one. Whatever possessed you to push yourself like that? Couldn't you wait until I was home to help?" he scolded in frustration.

"I was miserable, Lynx. I didn't know I was that weak. Besides, I've been enough trouble for you." Cal began to weep softly from tension and fatigue. As she sniffed, she murmured, "I'm sorry."

Trying not to hurt her, he snuggled her against him. "I know you've had it rough lately. Things will be better soon; be patient."

When part of her trembling and weakness passed, he sat her in the chair to fetch a towel and her brush. He lifted her and placed her in his lap again. Lynx gently dried her hair, then worked to unmat the curls with her brush. When Cal told him she could do it, he chuckled and vowed he would handle the stimulating problem. Lying in his arms with nothing but a sheet around her, Calinda was intensely aware of his sensual body and manly appeal.

"Lean your head over my arm," Lynx instructed.

She did as told, her cascading tresses falling over it. With sweeping stokes, he soon had her wavy curls silky and shiny. Sunlight danced over her hair and slowly dried it, bringing its fiery glow to life. She closed her leafy green eyes and relaxed completely. The sun was warm; the breeze was refreshing; his embrace was intoxicating; and she was fatigued from her exertions.

As her respiration became slow and even, Lynx smiled. His admiring gaze shifted over her delicate and striking features. She had the cutest nose and most inviting lips. Her neck was long and slender, her shoulders creamy, but for the darkened area which exposed her recent brush with death. He quietly dropped the brush to the floor to allow his fingers to trail over her satiny flesh; they travelled as if mapping her slender arms, her softly rounded shoulders, and exquisite features. Not even the smallest blemish marred her compelling face. How could a woman be so beautiful and enchanting without recognizing the power and extent of her magic? His artless wife accepted her ravishing looks as easily and unnoticeably as her breathing. The fact that Cal never used her beauty and power over him as weapons touched Lynx deeply.

It had been so long since their last passionate union that his body ached for hers, his heart yearned for her loving responses. He had hurt her deeply by deceiving her, regardless of his motives. Did she doubt his love, too? He had destroyed what faith she had in him. He had disappointed her and confused her. As he watched her sleep peacefully, he silently prayed for her forgiveness and understanding. She appeared so fragile, yet she was strong in many ways. Her traits reminded him of the yucca, also white and lovely, so stubborn and resilient, so vulnerable to destructive forces. He sighed heavily.

His confessions must be postponed until tomorrow. Cal wasn't strong enough in mind or body to delve into such a weighty matter. Since her father's letter hadn't mentioned his partnership with Rankin, Lynx assumed Cal didn't know that injurious fact. Lynx was relieved Brax's will had stated nothing more than Calinda was his sole heir. But Lynx was bewildered and disturbed by the last line in the bequest which granted all of Brax's possessions to Lynx Cardone, in the event of the death of Calinda Braxton . . . For love or retribution?

Lynx was intimidated by the evidence against him, but what difference could one more day make? Her face nestled closer to his shoulder as Cal snuggled up to him. Careful of her left shoulder, his arms embraced her possessively. With her in his arms, Lynx didn't care how long she slept. His heart was bursting with pride and love; he could never lose her, no matter what.

Salina observed the tender and infuriating scene on the balcony as she came to discard the bathwater and remove the tub. She soundlessly made her way to the door and peered outside. Sensing her presence, Lynx glanced over at Salina, placing his finger to his lips. Salina eased onto the porch and looked down at the sleeping Calinda. Her gaze lingered on the remains of Calinda's misfortune, one Salina wished had been fatal. As her eyes slipped up to Lynx's partially concealed face as he also stared at his wife, the truth was never clearer to her: Lynx was actually in love with Calinda.

Lynx motioned and mouthed for Salina to complete her task, to leave them alone. Salina nodded and left, masking her new defeat. There was no one to thank, not the powers of heaven or hell. How she hoped Calinda would be terrified into fleeing the ranch and Lynx.

Lynx watched the blazing sunset to the west, calmly allowing her to sleep until she was fully recovered. When she sighed heavily and moaned in discomfort, he concluded her position was bothering her. He carried her to bed, gently tucking her beneath a light cover. He would change clothes before dinner. Perhaps that black outfit which always glued her eyes to him . . . Or that red silk shirt . . .

When Cal awoke in the bed and saw she was alone, she quickly checked the drawer to test her unsettling theory; the papers were there, but not as she purposely left them. A stand-off was certain as each would wait for the other to approach the dismaying subject. She had piqued him into seeking an answer, but how had the clues affected him? Would Lynx ignore them or confess? She would follow his lead.

"Feeling better now?" he asked tenderly when he returned to find her supposedly stirring for the first time. He took a seat at her side.

Cal lifted her head and looked around, aware of the passage of time and their enticing solitude. If Lynx was a black-hearted villain, how could he be so tender and gentle? As his right palm moved up and down her arm, she smiled and thanked him for his concern and care.

"Any pain, love?" he inquired, his tone lacking any anger.

"Just a dull ache with little twinges every so often. It seems to be healing nicely. Now, all I have to do is regain my strength. You make a comfortable bed, Cardone," she teased, recalling his embrace, needing this brief sharing of tenderness.

"Speaking of bed, that's where you're staying, woman. No more defiance until you're well. Agreed?" he whispered against her forehead, then kissed it, thrilled when she didn't retreat from him.

"That's the best rest I've had in weeks. I think I'll keep you around as my doctor," she teased playfully, feeling better than she had since his last visit home. She looked up into his arresting face and asked, "Still mad at me?"

"A little. I was planning to take you outside to the swing, but you've had too much activity for one day." He smiled raffishly.

"Tomorrow?" Cal wheedled. "If I'm good?"

He grinned and nodded. "Otherwise, I'll tie you to the bed," he jested. "Ready for dinner?"

"Starved, for a change," she hastily accepted.

As they dined in the room, Lynx waited for her invitation to return to their bed, but Cal didn't extend one. He wouldn't press her tonight; she needed another few days to fully recover. To avoid upsetting her, he let their talk slide until another day. She was still insecure and leery tonight, but he knew why. He turned on the charm to beguile her. Instead of creating a serene mood, his romantic overtures made her uneasy. His assumption was accurate; she doubted his love and sincerity. It shouldn't surprise him, but it did trouble him. Winning her over would be a stirring and difficult task.

They made light conversation for an hour, then he cleared the small table. Following a heady kiss, he tucked her in and said goodnight.

During the next few days, Lynx watched her get stronger each hour. Cal was permitted to sit up and to be assisted outside for short periods. Between generous nature and his constant attentions, her improvements increased and the wounds gradually healed. With the continued schedule of nourishing food, lots of rest and sleep, light exercise, fresh air and warm sunshine, and his assistance, she was managing nicely by the fifteenth day after the shooting. Her spirits enlivened and her tensions lessened. She was irresistibly drawn to his agreeable mood.

By the twentieth day, Calinda could get around by herself. She would take her meals with the two men in the dining room. She would sit downstairs for a couple of hours each afternoon and evening, listening to the men's conversations, joining in when they persisted. When they tried to discuss the barbecue, she persuaded them to wait until she was as good as new.

Salina stayed out of Calinda's sight as much as possible. She performed her chores as usual, but spent most evenings away from the ranch. She had become evasive and remote lately. Calinda wondered if Salina was thinking about a new life away from them. Salina made no attempts to converse with Calinda, but politely responded when addressed. Perhaps Salina now realized nothing and no one would drive Cal from the ranch and Lynx. Although the Mexican girl wasn't hateful, neither was she cheerful. Something had changed Salina's resentful and sarcastic manner, but Calinda didn't know what. In fact, the girl almost seemed frightened of something, displaying a subtle wariness and reluctant resignation. But Calinda had problems of her own to solve. Tomorrow would be three weeks since her attack. Yet, Lynx had said nothing about the letters he had secretly read. He was being so damn carefree and jovial! There was a smugness and confidence in him which vexed her. Why wouldn't he talk about the papers? He was behaving as if nothing uncommon had transpired, as if he intended to ignore and forget the entire matter. Why was he being so loving and charming? Yet, he put no pressure on her to share his bed again. He appeared content with their present arrangements, too patient and genial to suit her. She was cognizant of his piercing gaze and proximity. He guarded her so closely that she almost felt a prisoner.

Cal prayed her enemy would soon be captured, and that he would be exposed as a callous stranger. What foe was smart as to leave no clues, so skilled as to be an excellent marksman? The assailant had to be an expert shot, so Cal did not suspect Salina. Salina was malicious and conniving, but surely no killer. Brax's will presented another suspicion—if Lynx had known about the bequest, which would have come first: marriage or . . .

Calinda received a startling jolt that next afternoon. As she gingerly strolled outside with his strong arm supporting her, Lynx nonchalantly told her he would be away at the state capital for two or three days. Although she had enough strength to walk alone, he still insisted on aiding her. He was in a blithe mood today, joking and smiling.

When Lynx made his unexpected announcement, Cal halted abruptly and turned to stare at him. He swiftly expounded, "I was planning to take you with me, Cal, but it's too soon for you to make a tiring trip. I've put it off too long as it is. I couldn't leave until you were better. I've asked Steve to guard the house until I get back. Will you promise not to over-do and stay inside the fence?"

"Why do you have to go to the capital?" she inquired, acting as if she didn't know Austin was his impending destination . . .

"You recall that story in the newspaper from Round Rock about the Bass gang?" When she nodded, he went on, "Major Jones, you recall him, asked me to help him locate two members. You see, I can get in places and speak with men the Rangers can't. J.B. Jones and I have been friends for years, so I agreed to keep an eye out for Sam Pipes and Frank Jackson, two of Sam's men. They passed through Waco when I was there, so I followed them. I have to testify at their trials because I witnessed a bank robbery. Jones had the cases put off while you were so ill. The trial is set for Monday; I'll take the train from Fort Worth tomorrow. As soon as I tell the court my side, I'll come straight home. No more than four days, I promise," he informed her, truthfully preparing her for his impending confession.

Cal wondered why he hadn't mentioned his close friendship with Jones when she met the imposing Ranger. How convenient that the trial would be in Austin where Kyle Yancey resided. How convenient that the Ranger who had discouraged her search was his close friend, a friend linked to the peril in Lampasas. Even if Lynx hadn't learned about her meeting with Yancey in town, the letter had revealed his name to Lynx. Was he planning to question the lawyer before confronting her, to see just how much she knew before telling her too much? That explained why he hadn't said anything to her yet.

"I want to go with you," Cal told him. "Lynx, you promised no more solitary trips. I can relax on the train, then wait in our hotel room while you're in court. If I take it easy, I'll be fine. Besides, I'll have my doctor with me," she reasoned evocatively.

Lynx shook his head. "I swear you can go next time. It's too soon for such a strenuous journey. This isn't a new promise, love. It's an unfinished part of our last separation; I came home early because they weren't ready for the trial. I had planned to take you with me. If I can testify early, I'll catch the train home that same day. You get well, woman; you and I have some serious talking to do."

"All right, boss," she relented, knowing they could both use some privacy to think and plan. He couldn't be lying about the trial for it would be too easy to check out his reason. She prayed Yancey would hold her confidence about the ranch deed until she decided how to handle that distressing matter. But Lynx was an intimidating, powerful, wealthy, and relentless man; he might be able to persuade Yancey to talk.

"You understand? You don't mind?" he probed at her silence.

Cal responded light-heartedly, "I know you have to go and do your duty for law and order. I don't have to like it, but I won't interfere. Too bad you never joined the awesome Rangers; they could use a man with your skills and courage."

He chuckled roguishly. "What man could make a proper Ranger with a wife like you waiting at home?" he murmured playfully.

534

"Texas's loss is my gain?" she ventured coquettishly.

"I hope so," he mirthfully replied. "Is it?"

"A lack of self-assurance has never been one of your weak points, Lynx. I would say you're a man who's never heard the word no or accepted defeat. Have a nice time and a safe trip."

"You don't have to sound so eager for my departure," he mischievously chided her when she smiled saucily.

"I thought I was being very lenient and bright this time by not pestering you with childish tears and quarrels. Are husbands so hard to please? Which do you prefer, futile hysterics or mature resignation? A word of caution, don't let Jones fill your head with new adventures and challenges. I'll expect you home by Tuesday. You don't want me coaxed out of bed to come seeking my errant husband, or to be enticed to seek a more devoted and appreciative *esposo*."

"You leave that bed or this house, woman, and you'll answer to me. Savvy?" he demanded seriously.

"Don't return by Tuesday, and you'll answer to me. Savvy?" she captured his taunt and flung it back at him, then laughed.

"You're a mighty demanding vixen," he stated with a chuckle.

"On the contrary, I'm not demanding at all," she corrected him. "In fact, I'm the best thing that's ever happened to you."

"I can't argue that point," he promptly concurred.

"I'd better go inside now; I'm a little shaky. What time is your train?" she inquired as they made their way into the house.

"Eight, so I'll say farewell tonight. I'll need to ride out at dawn."

They ate a quiet dinner downstairs, then chatted with Rankin for a short time. Since Lynx had to get up early, they headed upstairs. He kissed her goodnight after packing, then headed for the borrowed room, resolved this would be his last night to sleep alone.

Calinda tossed on the bed for hours. Perhaps she should go and see if Lynx was still awake. Wouldn't it be better to settle one topic before he left, rather than battle over several when he returned? For surely he would pull the devastating information from Yancey. She needed to know just how much he would confess before he learned she knew everything. If she could take him unprepared, she might learn more. If she gave him time to come up with some plausible explanation . . .

That was the best solution, to get Laura and Brax out of the way before the ranch issue must be dealt with later. If he didn't contact Yancey, she would reveal everything on his return. The stress of remaining silent and uncertain was intolerable.

Cal threw the covers aside and headed for the door. Even though Salina's room was downstairs, it was beneath this one. Cal didn't want that nosey witch to hear her trip to the guestroom at the other end of the hallway. Cal tiptoed to the door and stealthily eased it open a small amount. She listened to make certain there was no noise from downstairs. Before Cal fully opened the door to step into the hallway, she froze and witnessed a stunning sight: Salina was slipping into Cal's old room, dressed in a transparent nightgown!

Mesmerized, Calinda stayed there for a few minutes. If Salina was merely delivering a message, why was it taking so long? If she needed to speak with Lynx about something, why wait so late? Why be so

sneaky? Why dressed in that sexy nightgown? A lus-
cious Mexican beauty had no business in her husband's room this time of night and hardly attired! It
had been four weeks since they had made love, but
was Lynx this desperate for a woman? Like mother,
like son?

Cal paced the room as her fury mounted. How dare
those two commit such an unforgiveable betrayal!
Were they having an affair right under her nose? A
new one? An old one? Was Lynx punishing her for the
letters? For the past? My God, was he using Brax's
type of treachery to destroy her? Make her fall in love
with him, then betray her with another woman, in
their own home? How could he be so cruel and vindictive?

Salina had stolen into the room where she knew
Lynx was sleeping alone, had been sleeping alone for
weeks. A man of his virility must need a woman by
now. Her decision to leave the ranch had been made;
she would join Clint Deavers in a few days. Before she
left, she would have Lynx Cardone one time. He owed
her for all the years she had waited for him, craved
him, endured his teasings and rejections. Once Lynx
departed, she would make certain Cal learned about
tonight and the ranch! She would devastate them with
one blissful night.

Salina walked to the bed, gazing down at the sleeping figure. He was magnificent, lying naked on the
covers. His natural instincts were dulled at home
where he must feel safe and content. She removed her
gown, running her hands over her sultry body, envisioning a passionate night with this bronze god. Before he could clear his head, she would have him
writhing in need! Maybe he would mistake her for Ca-

linda if she kept silent. Before Lynx became aware of who she was and what was taking place, they would be making savage love. If there was one thing Salina knew, it was how to use her hands and lips to drive a man wild with desire, to entice him beyond reality or wisdom.

Salina gingerly lay down beside Lynx. His body was so perfect and appealing, she didn't know where to start or which temptation to use. She had waited for this night too long. As her deft hand reached for his manhood, the door flew open and lantern light flooded the room.

When Salina shrieked in alarm at untimely discovery, Lynx stirred and jerked upwards. Simultaneously his keen senses took in many facets of this baffling situation: he and Salina were in bed together naked; and Calinda was standing in the doorway with a lantern, glaring at them. "What the hell's going on here?" he snarled.

"It's obvious, my adulterous mate," Calinda sneered coldly. "You animals deserve each other! I hate you!" She whirled and slammed the door. She rushed to her room and bolted the lock.

"You lousy *puta!*" Lynx shouted at the shrinking Salina. "How dare you sneak in here and cause trouble! Get the hell out of my room! Better still, you malicious whore, get out of my home!"

Salina cowered beneath Lynx's full-blown rage. She begged to explain, but Lynx wouldn't listen. He cursed and berated her, threatened to beat her if she didn't leave instantly. When she groveled and cried, he grabbed her and shoved her toward the door. Still she resisted and pleaded. Lynx forcefully yanked her fingers from the door and pushed her into the hallway.

"Get out of my sight before I forget you're a female! If you ever step foot on this ranch again, I'll strangle you!" he thundered at her, flinging her gown into her furious face.

Rankin came rushing to the bottom of the steps. "What's happening, son?" he asked, then his eyes widened as they observed the naked Salina, clutching a gown and swearing at his son.

"Throw her out, father, or I won't be responsible for controlling my temper! She sneaked into my room and tried to seduce me, right in front of Cal! Take care of her; I've got to speak with my wife."

Lynx pounded on the sturdy oak bedroom door, but Calinda refused to open it. He tried to reason with her, explain his innocence. When she kept silent with the door locked, his anger increased. He beat on the door, demanding she let him inside to talk. "Damnit, Cal! I was asleep, dreaming. I didn't know she was there. Honestly, I didn't. I swear I haven't touched another woman since we met. Please let me in."

As Calinda sat on the bed listening to his quarrel with Salina and hearing his shouts of innocence, she knew what must be done. Guilty or not, she must leave the ranch before he returned from Austin. If he loved her, they would work something out after both had been given time alone. She needed to get away from him, the ranch, and these demands for a while. If she couldn't trust him, she shouldn't be married to him. Lynx had been given ample chances to be honest with her; he had rejected each of them. After he departed tomorrow, she would leave for Georgia and get her head and nerves together. She hadn't been herself in weeks, too jittery, too weepy, and too listless. With all this added trouble of the past and the recent shooting, she needed time and solitude, away from Lynx and these continual dangers.

When Lynx circled to the balcony doors, he thundered, "Open up, Callie, or I'll kick them down! We're gonna talk right now!"

Calinda walked to the doors and unlocked them. Tonight, she would say goodbye to him, for a short time or forever. Either way, Lynx Cardone would know what he was missing, or losing. When he stormed inside, she closed the door and bolted it.

He seized her shoulders and shouted. "I'm not guilty, Cal!"

"You're hurting me, Lynx," she murmured softly. "You don't have to explain. It's over."

He loosened his grip. "Please believe me, Callie," he urged, fearing the addition of this spiteful ruse to her stack of misconceptions.

"Make love to me," Cal astonishingly commanded.

"What?" he quizzed in bewilderment. They were quarreling over another woman and Cal wanted to make love?

"Make love to me right now," she repeated distinctly.

"But you're still mending. If you think I need a woman that badly, love, you're wrong, Callie. I don't want Salina or any other woman. I need you. When I return, I'll prove it," he mysteriously vowed.

"I need you now, tonight," she stubbornly insisted.

"You're hurt, Callie," he reasoned, noticing how pale she was in the moonlight. "I didn't mean to squeeze your shoulder. I was just frightened by what you must be thinking. Is it all right?" he fretted.

"There are different kinds of pain, Lynx. Right now, I want you so much it hurts deeply. How can I think about anything else when you're around? You've become the only reality for me. You block out everything and everyone. I need that. Please."

"Do you believe me about Salina?" he pressed.

"Even if it were true, it doesn't matter tonight," she parried.

"You love me that much?" he questioned incredulously.

For one last attempt to elicit a truthful explanation before she carried out her desperate plan, she said evocatively, "I could forgive you anything, just once."

"I swear there's nothing to forgive tonight, Callie," he responded. "I didn't invite her to my room and I didn't touch her."

"Then love me before you leave," she enticed sadly.

Lynx was enchanted by her urgency. He lifted the gown over her head. Before he could lift her and carry her to the bed, she turned and went to it, reclining there, holding out her hand in sweet invitation, her liquid green eyes beckoning, her seductive aura overwhelming. He came forward and joined her.

Her desire was as tangible as a physical caress. He sat on the edge of the bed, filling his greedy senses with her stirring nuance. Her hand reached out and caressed his golden chest, playing over the lean muscles of his stomach and rippling bulges on his shoulders. A bittersweet aching surged through him, plaguing him until she became his one thought. His gaze drifted over her full, taut breasts with their darkened peaks. His tawny eyes glowed with fiery passion as they travelled down her sensual curves and graceful limbs.

Weeks of starved senses ignited his body to smoldering flames, fires which licked dangerously at his resolve to take her leisurely. His molten passion engulfed her, sharing his seething warmth. He was almost afraid to touch her, lest his control be quickly vanquished and he took her swiftly and urgently. She was an overpowering force.

When Calinda's hand moved over his ribs and passed his narrow waist to draw little circles around his groin, he shuddered and moaned. "Your hesitation reeks of distraction and disinterest, my love, but he does not agree," she boldly taunted, trailing the backs of her fingers over the stiffened shaft. "He shouts of an appetite to match mine."

Lynx leaned over and tantalized her breasts with his lips, his hand moved downward to stimulate her as was he. He labored lovingly and deliberately, tearing away her reason. When his mouth sealed upon her parted lips, the kiss fused into a savage and feverish blend. Their need so compelling, he slid within her body, halting instantly to master his wavering control. Never had he know a female who enticed his manhood to seek bliss the moment he invaded her womanhood.

Calinda arched to meet his hips each time he withdrew and entered again. Her body took his instinctively, as her heart absorbed his tenderness. The sensations were so pleasurable and intense that she feared she would faint from their rapturous torment. Like a morning glory, her release burst forth into full bloom, bearing its beauty to the blazing sun above her, enticing him to feed her with his power. When her love's day was past, she gradually folded her exquisite petals.

Lynx pressed fleeting kisses upon her brow, her nose, and her lips. As his own sated passions brought a covering of contentment, his kisses softened on her lips. "Surely you know you are the only woman for me?" he murmured huskily against the silky flesh of her shoulder.

"And you, the only man for me, my love," she replied, her tears hidden in the darkness of the room.

"Sleep, my love, when I return, all will be right between us."

"How can I sleep when I crave you again and you stay so near?" she whispered raggedly. "There is so much I need from you."

Lynx wondered at the anguish and desperation in her voice. How he longed to speak his heart to her, but not when he was leaving for days. What must be said between them would take more time than he had left. He had done everything to prove his love and need with actions during these last weeks. How could she deny what she witnessed and perceived? It seemed as if she compelled his touch as proof of his feelings, a way of entreating reassurance from him.

"As I said, a demanding and greedy vixen," he teased, his tongue flickering over her breasts.

"Oh, Lynx," she cried out as if in torment. "Why must love be so complicated and painful?"

"Only when you resist it or question it, *mi amor,*" he told her.

Her arms tightened around him as she sought appeasement for a yearning deeper than her sexual desire. They loved until exhaustion claimed them, to take them far away to a land where only peace and love reigned . . .

Far into the night, Calinda awoke. She watched her love sleeping so peacefully at her side while she agonized over the dark span between them. If after tonight he still couldn't come to her fully, there was no way for her to reach him. Some evil monster was standing between them, and her husband was refusing to slay the destructive beast. Was her love for him so blind that she refused to see the truth? If he truly loved her and needed her beyond all else, he would prove it. He would not; therefore she must leave this traitorous haven. He knew how deeply she was troubled, how frightened and confused. Yet, some dark secret was more powerful than her love. Until that secret came to light, she could not live here with him.

He was heading out at first light to learn just how much she knew. She could not be here when he returned to confront her, too late to matter. If it must end between them, then let it be so before more damaging evidence was brought to light. If somehow there was hope for them, he would locate her and convince her. If not . . .

Silent tears washed down her cheeks until merciful slumber ended her anguish for the present.

Chapter Twenty-four

As Lynx tiptoed out of their bedroom at dawn, Calinda awoke. She hesitated but a few minutes before slipping into her robe and heading downstairs, her barefeet treading inaudibly on the floor. At first, she told herself she was going to have breakfast with Lynx, to send him off properly; then, she warned herself to honesty, as there was so little of it in this house. Cal was intensely aware that Lynx realized that she knew many things about the past. She was worried and frightened by his silence. Why wouldn't he confess the truth? Was there more she didn't know? This ceaseless mystery was tearing her apart. Unanswered questions loomed darkly and suspiciously in her mind.

She made her way near the kitchen to learn if Salina was present, to see if there was something she should know about them before he left. She pressed herself tightly against the wall, ears alert, breath held in suspense as she prayed for a clue to change her plans.

Rankin was sipping coffee at the table while Lynx

prepared their breakfast. For a time, the two men were silent. Rankin broke it when he asked, "Did you tell her anything, son?"

"No. I'm waiting to see what this Kyle Yancey revealed first. I'll go to his office after I finish in court," Lynx responded thoughtfully.

"You think he told her about the ranch?" Rankin worried aloud, dreading explaining their deception to Cal.

"If he did, she hasn't let on. From that letter, all she knows about is Brax and mother. Can I ask you a personal question, Father?" he inquired seriously, daring to state his curiosity for the first time since reading that provoking letter.

"About the child?" Rankin guessed astutely. When Lynx nodded ruefully, Rankin sighed heavily. "If there is a child, it could be mine. Either Brax lied in the letter to Cal, or your mother lied to Brax. As if they didn't hurt me enough with their betrayals, now they add more anguish and doubts; I might have another son or a daughter out there somewhere. I thought it was over, son, but it isn't. *Demonio!* I was willing to let the past die until Cal showed up in May. We've got to locate them, Lynx. I can't allow them to steal anything more from me. No son of mine will grow up without his rightful name and heritage."

"How could we be certain whose child Mother carried away with her?" Lynx questioned, musing on this unknown relative.

"Since she was sleeping with both of us, I suppose we can't. This new child might favor her as you do. Only if the child resembles Brax or Cal would we know the truth. But I'm confused, son. If

Cal has the deed, why is she keeping it a secret from us? She is your wife."

"For the same reason she kept all those mysterious letters and her visit with Yancey a secret," Lynx reasoned. Having discussed this matter before, they didn't relate their assumptions again, leaving Calinda's curiosity unsated. But Cal was alerted to the fact the Cardone men hadn't known about the child.

"What will you do if Yancey told her everything?" Rankin asked.

"There's only one thing I can do, use my charm and cunning to convince her it was a terrible mistake," he said, winking at his father and grinning broadly, feeling renewed confidence in their future after their night of love. "I doubt she knows where Brax is."

"I doubt you'll need to woo her; you have her dazzled as it is."

"Cal's a bright girl, Father," Lynx stated playfully.

"I always heard that love was blinding," Rankin retorted.

"Maybe before the shooting, but she's too wary and skittish now. We'll have to be very careful what we say and do for a while. She's faced lots of dangers and gathered plenty of evidence; we don't want her spooked into running away. Cal's seen me in action. You know she's got to think it's awfully strange I haven't captured her attacker. Make sure you or Steve guard her until I return. Once she realizes I'll never let her leave the ranch, she'll settle down and accept it. Besides, she doesn't have any money or a place to go." He proclaimed smugly, "Calinda Braxton is mine."

"Does she know the truth about you and Jones? Does she have any idea where you go and what you do?" Rankin inquired to make sure he didn't expose anything Lynx hadn't told Cal.

"None. She'll be shocked when I enlighten her," Lynx jested.

As Lynx spooned up the scrambled eggs, Calinda stealthily returned to her room, false impressions storming her senses. When Lynx returned, they would hold her captive to prevent trouble and embarrassment. She must escape while he was gone!

All day, Cal prepared to seek her freedom. When she discovered Salina's absence, she asked herself if Salina had taken off alone or with Lynx. Perhaps his little tirade had been for his wife's benefit. Damn him for using her, for hurting her! She had fallen into his clutches so readily and willingly. She was a fool! Now, she had lost everything. If only she'd learned about the ranch and treachery sooner; she might have prevented this tragedy.

All morning she had battled nausea to pack lightly and to conserve her energy. That afternoon, she took a long nap, having decided to slip out during the night. Even if she wanted to flee the moment Lynx rode off, she couldn't because of a sturdy guard named Steve. When she awoke later, she felt much better; the curious sluggishness and queasy feeling had passed. She decided it must have been her nerves or a lingering result of her wounds. Thankfully they had healed to the point of mild discomfort. But there was no time to spare.

To prevent any suspicion, Cal cooked dinner for Rankin and herself. But he chided her for her exertions, saying Charlie would cook for them. Calinda brushed aside his soft scolding and forced a disarming smile to her lips. After the meal, Rankin helped her clear the table and do the dishes. When he invited her to play cards or to read together, she told him she needed to lie down and rest.

"See, I told you not to work so hard," he taunted her gently.

"I'm fine, Rankin, just taking it easy like my husband ordered. Perhaps we should have invited Steve to eat with us; I'm sure he's tired of sentry duty by now. Is this caution really necessary?"

"Yep. He's only around during the day; at night, I'm here if you need anything. I'll make sure the doors and windows are bolted before I turn in. Give a shout if there's a problem. Goodnight, Cal."

"Goodnight, Rankin," she replied, knowing this was the last time she would see this traitorous man she had come to love more than her own father. But how critically she had misjudged him.

"Is something wrong, Cal?" he inquired at her somber gaze.

"I was just thinking, you've been more of a father to me than Brax. I hope you realize how much I appreciate all you've done for me."

He shifted nervously, remorseful over his past actions. Soon, everything would be settled, there would be no more guarding secrets or stepping lightly. He smiled. "I couldn't be more fond of you, Cal, if you were my own child. You're a very special young woman."

She thanked him, grimacing inwardly at his deceit. She went to her room to lie down, to wait for the proper moment to slip out. Since tomorrow began a new week, the hired hands should be asleep soon. She dozed for a while, checking the clock each time she looked that way. At one o'clock, she stood up, summoning the courage to head for safety and peace of mind. She would carry out some plans here first, then take a horse and ride northward to the train depot in Wichita Falls. When they started a frantic search for her, surely it would be eastward toward Fort Worth.

Barefoot for silence, Cal made her way to Rankin's work-room, gratified to find the door between his office and bedroom shut. Inside, she closed the other door and cautiously placed a Spanish shawl on the floor to prevent any light from sneaking under it to alarm him. Cal lit the desk lantern, but wisely kept the wick low. She jimmied a drawer and withdrew the cash-box. She shivered in suspense, fearing discovery before she could make her escape. There was no time left to deliberate whether she was right or wrong; she only knew she had to get away for a while. When she had regained her stamina and confidence, she would contemplate a message to Lynx. She counted out three hundred dollars and stuffed it into her shirt pocket. She retrieved two sheets of paper and sat down to write on them.

To whom it may concern:
  I, Calinda Braxton Cardone, do willingly surrender all legal and moral claims to my half of the Cardone Ranch to Lynx Cardone on this date September 1, 1878, in exchange for my marital freedom and the sum of $45,300 in said debts to Rankin and Lynx Cardone. Neither I, nor any of my heirs or relatives, will have future claims against this land from this date forward. Nor will Elliott Braxton, proclaimed deceased last month, nullify this agreement should he ever return and lay claim against it.

Cal signed the statement and placed it with the official deed which her father had stolen years ago. On the other paper, she wrote a letter to Lynx. She sighed painfully before ending their stormy affair. What did one say in light of such treacherous betrayal? How did one say goodbye forever to the love of her life? What words could halt this vicious circle of despicable vengeance?

Lynx,

As you have doubtlessly learned by now from Kyle Yancey and the letters which you found in our room, I know the dark secrets which you and your father withheld from me about our parents and the ranch. The letters were placed there intentionally for your discovery. Many times I have opened the door for your admissions, but you refused to enter and banish your deceptions to the past where they rightfully belong. Your secrecy speaks loudly and painfully. I can understand your mistrust and silence in the beginning, but not after our marriage and your vows of love. I have no knowledge of the whereabouts of Laura and Brax, nor will I make any attempt to locate them. To avoid more suffering on everyone's part, I'm leaving the ranch and yielding its deed and ownership to you. I know this is unnecessary as the unjust law states our marriage relinquished my claim to you. Even with the truth and the deed, I would never have placed any claim on your ranch. I also give you everything which I leave behind to dispose of as you wish.

With the deed in your possession, you have what you desired from me. Surely your hatred and revenge can be sated with this substitute victory over Brax? Please don't come after me, but allow this tragic matter to end; bury the past and find peace and happiness.

I must apologize for taking money as my treacherous father did, but surely half of this ranch is worth $45,300? I will consider all debts and obligations fulfilled from both parties. I shall never understand your cruel deceits. How I wish we could have discovered the trust and happiness which my father prevented. Don't concern yourself over my safety and health. Perhaps one day you will regret all you have sacrificed for an earthly mistress without warmth or feelings, as your dirt vixen is far more demanding than I.

I don't know how many of my troubles and dangers were at your hands, and I hope I never learn that final secret. I give you back your freedom, as I retrieve mine. Knowing everything, how I loved you and needed you . . .

Calinda

She folded the letter and placed it inside an envelope, dropping her wedding band inside, then sealing it and writing his name on the front. In a neat row, Cal placed the deed with her relinquishing statement, her father's will and letter for proof of her past ownership, and the heart-rending letter to Lynx. She stared at the line of multiple betrayals, then went upstairs.

Cal gathered the small bag with the few things she would need for her journey. She didn't know what she would do when she reached Georgia, but she would find a way to survive. If she had learned anything since coming here, it was how resilient and bright she was. She slipped out of the house and to the stable. She saddled a horse and walked him far from the yard before mounting, denying the twitches in her shoulder. She sat on the animal's back and gazed at the hacienda style home she had shared with two unknown foes for many months. It was over, this cycle of tragedy which her own father had initiated.

She clicked the reins and rode off without glancing back. Cal knew which road headed off from this one toward the north. She shifted her gunbelt to be ready for any trouble ahead. She was wearing a light jacket to conceal her feminine figure, her flaming curls tucked beneath her hat. She had separated the money, hiding some inside her hatband, some inside her right boot, and some inside her jeans pocket. If she were robbed, chances were they wouldn't find all of it.

She chose a steady pace and rode for hours, halting to rest the animal as the sun peeked over the distant horizon. She travelled within sight of the dirt road, but a safe distance away from anyone who might come along. She would eat and rest later, once she was assured of her success. Besides, she was too queasy to eat so early. Usually that lingering annoyance faded by lunchtime.

As the sun rose higher in the pale blue sky on this humid September Monday, Cal became warm and damp. She headed for a cluster of trees to rest and cool herself and the horse. She slowly consumed the cold ham and biscuits which she had prepared yesterday. She watched the horse as he grazed peacefully at the thirsty covering at his hooves. She was so weary and sleepy, but she dared not doze this soon. She needed to travel most of today and tonight, then sleep around daybreak. After her initial caution, she would ride at night and sleep in some hidden place during the day to prevent being seen or accosted. As she looked over the rugged landscape, pangs of loneliness and trepidation assailed her. Was she mistaken, impulsive, rash?

When she came to an area which was fenced off on both sides, she had no choice but to ride along the dusty road. When Cal noticed a single rider approaching her, she tensed, checking her pistol for readiness. The man passed her and nodded in greeting. Calinda noticed how well-armed he was, but his expression was genial and his gaze friendly. Calinda rode on, unaware of the way he twisted in his saddle to stare at the retreating back of a beautiful woman with blazing hair sneaking from beneath her tan hat. Intrigued, he shrugged and rode on toward Fort Worth, assuming she lived nearby.

Mid-afternoon, Calinda reached a large stream. She reined in her horse and slid off his back, allowing both of them to drink. She refilled her canteen and splashed her face with tepid water. When she heard the mournful sounds of cattle nearby, she panicked; for cattle meant cowboys, witnesses to her passing. She mounted up and headed off again, her attention northward. Cal refused to think about what she was leaving behind or what she was facing. She tried to defensively block-out all realities, but for her arduous trek.

Calinda had planned on Rankin's normal schedule to aid her flight. But the concerned man returned home early since Salina was gone. Near three in the afternoon, Rankin headed toward the house from the stable. He greeted Steve and went inside, dismissing him from his watch since early that morning. He glanced around curiously as he entered the quiet house. He called Calinda's name, but there wasn't any response. He went into the empty kitchen, then the den.

Rankin decided Cal must be napping, so he headed for his office to do bookwork. As his eyes touched on the neat line of papers, an ominous chill walked over his body. He snatched up the ranch deed to scan it and her attached paper, freezing in consternation. He noticed the letter and will which he had read another night. He lifted the envelope with his son's name on the outside. He cast aside any reservations and ripped it open, shocked and alarmed by the words which greeted his eyes. He tossed the papers aside and rushed upstairs. She wasn't in her room. He looked in every room, checking beside and behind furniture to see if she had passed out somewhere. He looked on balconies and finally realized the astonishing truth.

A hopeful thought tugged at his mind. How could she leave with Steve on guard? Surely Cal was outside somewhere, perhaps hiding and waiting to sneak off tonight. He rushed to the stone fence and called Steve back to the house. Rankin questioned the guard about her absence. Steve told him he hadn't left the porch all day, even to eat. He said Charlie had brought his food and had tried to offer some to Mrs. Cardone, but she didn't answer their knock. They assumed she was resting upstairs. Steve hadn't seen Cal all day.

"That's strange; I can't find her," Rankin worried aloud.

Steve said he would search around the house and ask at the stable. If she left, it was by the kitchen door. Steve checked the water-shed, the supply sheds, the stable, and the surrounding yard. He questioned

Charlie and several other men, to no avail.

When Steve returned with his unsettling news, Rankin was panicked by her incredible departure. How could she run away? What should he do? How long ago had she left? To go where?

Rankin chose his words carefully when he spoke with Steve. "She hasn't been herself since that shooting, Steve. She's scared and sick. Get some of the men to search the ranch. Bring her back whatever she says. I'm heading into town to warn Lynx. I'm putting you in charge of getting her home."

Steve nodded and went to issue those orders to the men who had returned from the range. The desperate search for Calinda was on within minutes. Rankin and Seth headed for town at a swift pace. It was five o'clock when he sent his telegram to the Texas Timbers Hotel in Austin. He paid the agent to remain open until he received an answer from his son, offering the agent on the other end the same amount from his son to pass their urgent messages along.

At six-thirty, Lynx returned to the hotel from his tormenting meeting with Kyle Yancey. It had taken heavy persuasion to pull the facts from that elderly man. As Lynx had feared, Calinda had the ranch deed and her version of the truth. He cursed his distance from her and the train which didn't leave until morning. As certain as the changing seasons, his love had been subtly probing for his confessions. He understood how his refusals must have appeared to his confused wife. He raged at what she must be enduring at this very moment.

The clerk called Lynx over, handing him an urgent telegram. He told the puzzled Lynx that the sender was awaiting a response at any hour. Lynx unfolded the paper and shuddered in terror:

Lynx, Have ranch deed. Cal knows truth. Said nothing. Ran off. Can't locate. Send advice. Hurry home.
                              Rankin.

Lynx rushed to the telegraph office and pounded on the door. The man let him inside after he gave his name. He composed his response:

Rankin. Search everywhere. Ask sheriff for help. Horse too slow. No train until morning. Home at two. Meet me. Must find. Saw Yancey. Looks bad. Wire Dallas sheriff. Check trains. Stages.
Lynx.

Lynx paid the man for his delay and assistance. He rushed to Major Jones' room at the hotel and poured his troubles and fears out to his friend. Jones said he would send messages to all his men to be on the look-out for her. Jones felt great sympathy for his friend, but gently scolded Lynx's actions. "There's no fair swap for truth, son, not even with good intentions," he finished sadly as they parted.

The violence and dangers of this wild frontier having been forced upon her, Calinda stubbornly drove herself onward until her head and shoulder throbbed and tears threatened to choke her as she tried to govern her pain and emotions. She had been riding since two this morning, and the moon's angle indicated it was nearly midnight. But for rest and water stops, she had been on this deserted trail for over eighteen hours. Surely it was safe to slow her flight.

Cal had made a wide detour around one small town and concealed herself when a stagecoach thundered past her. Fortunately, there had been cedar brakes and live oak stands or arroyos to offer her protection from wary eyes. She had continually observed all directions to prevent anyone from approaching her unseen, a time-consuming measure, but a vital one. She had controlled the reins with her right hand, but the jolting motion of her pace was plaguing her sensitive injuries. Each time the horse's hooves touched the ground, pains shot through her chest and back. The muscles around the wound had grown stiff and angry; her head was pounding. Her body ached all over; Cal was exhausted. She was forced to give in to her body's demands.

Lynx couldn't sleep all night; he paced his room until it was time to catch the train to Fort Worth. Along the journey the clicky-clack of the rails seemed to chant, "She won't come back. She won't come back. She won't come back . . ." Lynx heard that ominous message until he was tensed and haunted. For someone alleged to be cunning and fearless, he had been a cowardly fool.

Whatever it took, he would locate her and force her to listen. He didn't care about the ranch if he lost her. Even from an unknown distance, Brax was hurting him; the traitor was stealing another love from his life, one more precious than his devious mother.

When the train slowed, Lynx bolted off and ran

toward his father before it halted. Rankin's forlorn expression said everything; no news. Lynx accepted her letter and read it, quivers passing over his towering frame. Could he blame her? But she was wrong. She was still mending. There was no telling what kind of perils she was confronting along the trail. But what trail?

He listened to Rankin's revelations of yesterday, tormented by her desertion and desperation. Lynx tried to think as she would. Where would she go? She had nearly two days on him. But she was a woman, and she wasn't fully healed. He had to make certain he chose the same direction to overtake her. He grimaced at the thought of his beautiful and vulnerable wife out there alone somewhere, a temptation to any man who saw her, too weak or untrained to defend herself.

"You checked the stagelines and trains?" Lynx asked.

"Everything I could imagine, son. She took a horse," he hinted.

"She could catch either anywhere along the line," Lynx fretted.

"They've been told to watch for her and alert us if she's spotted," Rankin tried to encourage his distraught son and himself.

A tall, lanky man ambled toward them. He smiled genially and spoke to Lynx. "You look like a puma with a thorn in his paw, Lynx."

"I've got a terrible problem, N.O.," Lynx began, then explained it to Lieutenant N.O. Reynolds of the Texas Rangers, one who had been at Round Rock and knew of Lynx's secret identity.

"What does she look like?" Reynolds inquired

sympathetically.

When Lynx described Calinda, Reynolds beamed in pleasure. "Sounds to me like the lady I saw on the road to Wichita Falls yesterday," he casually informed Lynx, then gave his impression of her and the horse.

"She was alone?" Lynx fearfully inquired.

"Yep. Thought it strange, but didn't question it. Figured she lived around there. Too pretty to be out riding alone."

"When? Where?" Lynx asked, his hopes building by the minute.

"About forty miles south of Jacksboro, that's where I was coming from, around threeish." Reynolds flexed his aching muscles.

Lynx quickly tallied how far ahead she must be by today. Even riding all day and night, she couldn't make Jacksboro by now. He had to reach her before she entered that rowdy and hazardous town. "Why don't you hop that train to Taylorsville, then head southwest to intercept her?" Reynolds offered the same solution Lynx was planning.

"You hold the train while I rent a horse and get some supplies," Lynx entreated Reynolds' help.

"I brought Star and supplies, son. I figured you would head out quickly as you arrived," Rankin informed the optimistic man.

While Rankin went for Star at the livery-stable, Reynolds and Lynx made arrangements with the conductor to take Lynx to Taylorsville. By six Tuesday evening, Lynx was heading northwest on the AT&SF Railroad. Within two hours, he would be riding Star to reach the Jacksboro road about ten miles south of town. He would follow the road southward with the hopes she hadn't reached that far yet. In her weakened state, Cal must be travelling slowly and cautiously.

Lynx guided Star off the train at the water-stop and leaped on his strong back. As if sensing his beloved master's urgency, the mettlesome and nimble beast galloped off in the assigned direction. Possessing great stamina and intelligence, the animal raced swiftly, his keen ears pricked for any hint of danger.

Steadfast and unrelenting, the two travelled as one to rescue the love of Lynx Cardone. Besieged with panic, Lynx wondered where his wife was beneath this same full moon which hopefully lit his path toward her. What if she had altered her course? What if she were battling some villain this very moment? What if she had fallen ill beneath her reckless pressures? Somewhere in this vast and precarious territory, his woman was defenseless and suffering.

He urged Star to an even faster pace. With at least a twenty-hour headstart, she could be anywhere and in any danger . . . Lynx recognized he had several advantages over Calinda: he and Star were fresh and anxious after their train ride; and they could make better time than she could since she would be compelled to ride cautiously to appease her disabled body. He was around thirty miles from the Jacksboro road; considering where Reynolds had seen her, she had to be around forty miles to the south. If Cal made fifteen to twenty miles tomorrow, he should intercept her at least that many miles below that turbulent settlement, if she held true to course and didn't collapse. If Fort Richardson hadn't been abandoned in May, he could have telegraphed there for assistance. He glanced at the moon, assessing the time as ten o'clock. If he travelled all night, he could make up for her lead.

Lynx tried to focus his attention on another subject to distract his troubled mind. He recalled his last talk with Jones when he had refused to continue with the Rangers. Someone else could battle the aggressive Apaches who were stirring up again in the Pecos area, and someone else could struggle against the forces of Mexican *banditos* and American desperadoes.

Calinda had slept restlessly for several hours last night, then urged herself to halt this murderous pace and yield to short naps. Her fatigue was increasing, as were her morning bouts with nausea. Preoccupied, her symptoms failed to register accurately in her muddled thoughts. She continued to believe the squeamish feeling was connected to her injured condition and physical distress. The mixture of blazing sun, hard riding, and painful agony took its toll as the day passed from ice blue skies, to a brilliant sunset, to deepening shadows of impending night. Planned as the moment to switch from day riding to night riding, she was coerced by inflexible and merciless nature to suspend her trek until morning or until sufficiently rested.

Just before eleven, Cal walked the animal into a dry gulch and gingerly dismounted. She tied his reins to a small mesquite bush, then denied her fatigue and anguish to remove his saddle. She drank from the canteen and sighed listlessly. Too lacking in spirit and strength to consume the unappealing nourishment, Cal spread a blanket on the sandy ground and was quickly devoured by sleep.

Lynx journeyed all night, halting as streaks of pinkish gray dawn filtered across the landscape. While Star caught his wind, grazed, and watered, Lynx quickly prepared a small fire for enlivening coffee. He tossed down three cups of the black liquid and some dried beef with biscuits. He rinsed the dishes and pot in the river, then stripped and dove in. He splashed himself and ducked many times to refresh his lagging spirits and depleted energy. If he came upon trouble, he must be revived and alert. He packed up his gear and headed off again.

When Calinda awoke around eight she felt terrible, she wanted to cry like a baby. She was sore and miserable. After sleeping so long, she was still drained. She choked and heaved several times, but her stomach was too empty to eject anything. She felt dizzy and wobbly. She wondered how she could saddle the horse or ride in this weak state. But she realized Lynx must be aware of her escape by now. Was he tracing her flight this very moment? Did she even care?

She reclined on her back to settle her whirling head and agitated stomach. She sipped water, dabbing at the fluid which dribbled down her chin from her shaky hands on the canteen. She poured some into her cupped hand and rubbed it over her ashen face. She lay down again. Nothing seemed to help. How she longed for a bath and soft bed.

Cal had to lie there in misery until mid-morning

before nature showed her any sympathy and assuaged the unfamiliar harassment. She forced one biscuit down with water, but feared it wouldn't remain inside very long. Placing most of the weight of the saddle on her right arm, she tossed it over the horse and fastened the girth beneath his belly. She tied the blanket behind the saddle and pulled herself up on his back. She wanted to sob hysterically when she realized she hadn't untied the reins from the bush and they were refusing to be yanked free. Was everything and everyone against her?

Cal dismounted and untangled the leather strip, gritting her teeth in vexation. She leaned forward as the horse climbed out of the coulee and follow her command. Ignorant of what menacing threats lay ahead, the quest for unwanted freedom was underway again . . .

Chapter Twenty-five

The first two hours were hellish for Calinda. Her stomach was still churning feebly. Her head was aching; her shoulder was screaming for relief. How she craved some of Doc's magical elixir. Two fiery patches flamed on her cheeks against her milky complexion. She was colorless around her pale lips, which were dry from her erratic respiration. Dark smudges lingered beneath her somber green eyes.

Calinda swayed precariously in the saddle, leaning forward countless times and gripping the horn to keep from tumbling to the hard ground. Her appetite had vanished; all she desired was soothing water, liquid which her tummy battled to accept. At that moment, she would have given all of her money for a sip of medication and a soft bed. By now, she didn't care if Lynx overtook her; in fact, she found herself praying he would, reflecting on his tender and loving care after her injury. Never had she felt worse in her life, not even during or after the shooting. Oddly, his supposed betrayal didn't pain her as much as her own body did at this time.

Calinda feared she was going to faint soon. She weaved to and fro on the horse, struggling to retain her senses and balance. Her jumbled thoughts told her Lynx had had a logical explanation for his actions. She shouldn't have fled so recklessly. No matter what she assumed Lynx had done, he had always rescued her from peril and taken care of her. Why had she run away before giving him the chance to explain?

Cal felt so alone and wretched. She was afraid, afraid of life without Lynx, afraid of her worsening illness, afraid of the path ahead. She even feared she might die out here alone. She was swiftly becoming too hazy and weak to fend for herself. A hysterical sob came forth as she realized the seriousness of her predicament.

What was her love thinking and feeling? Was Lynx glad to be rid of her? Would he honor her request not to pursue her? Or was he alarmed and worried about her? Had her desertion cut him deeply? Was he furious with her? What if he did come after her? How would he know where to look? She cursed herself and the burdensome past, hoping she hadn't been too cunning for his tracking skills.

Her dazed vision noticed a thick cluster of trees ahead. Knowing she couldn't stay alert or in the saddle much longer, Cal headed the horse in that direction. To conceal them from dangerous eyes, she guided him into the center of the leafy copse.

Suddenly a man bolted forward and seized her reins. She wavered dizzily. She vaguely took in a tousled blond head and steely eyes. Between rapid blinks, her blurry vision momentarily settled on the pistol in his grip. Her stupefied mind couldn't analyze her danger. She could hear his voice, but couldn't make out his words as her ears buzzed precariously. Her eyes closed and she fell over into the arms of the astonished outlaw.

He stared at the beautiful bundle in his grasp, then smiled. He deposited her on the spot which he had hastily deserted. He holstered his sixgun and secured the reins of her horse to a tree beside his stallion. He swaggered over to kneel beside her, taking in her unique beauty and sorry condition. He removed her hat, allowing the fiery curls to spread around her head, dabbing her face with his handkerchief.

He shoved one eye open, enchanted by the rich greenness of it. He ran his rough fingers over flesh which was creamy and smooth. Clearly she was real sick. He removed her light jacket to allow her body to cool. Unfastening the top three buttons on her shirt to assist her breathing, he tingled as his fingers made contact with silky skin. She certainly was a looker. Probably around his age.

Why was she out here alone? He removed her gunbelt and put it out of reach, should she awake soon. He slipped off her boots, knowing how refreshing that was to a warm body. When the money fell to the ground, he chuckled and stuffed it into his pocket. He searched her, finding the other two hidden sums. He grinned; she was a bright gal.

Where was she heading? What was wrong with her? She was ravishing, but in sore shape. Running away from some vicious father or a horrible husband? How vulnerable and childish she looked. Yet, her face and body declared her very much a woman. His loins flamed, tugging against the restraint of his jeans. He threw back his yellowy blond hair and laughed coldly; what Billy Bounet wanted, Billy took. Billy lazed against his saddle, observing her as she slept. The famed outlaw glanced at the sun and smiled salaciously; it was early, around two. This fragile filly was no match for him . . .

Even at eighteen, Billy was fearless and deadly, with a string of murders and robberies to his credit. He was a dreaded legend who terrorized the areas of Santa Fe, Brazos Forks, the Panhandle, and Plains. Some knew him as William Bonnet, Henry McCarthy, or Kid Antrim. Most knew him as Billy the Kid. With his Winchester rifle, Smith & Wesson pistol, Mexican blade, and his steely eyes Billy could frighten most men into backing down. This girl would be no trouble at all.

Lynx had connected with the southern road from Jacksboro, but he still had at least twenty miles to ride before catching up to his wife. He halted everyone he passed to question them. When he could find no one who had seen Calinda along the trail, Lynx prayed it was her bright mind which allowed her to elude discovery and not some other force which had taken her off the trail: illness or peril.

As Lynx rounded a bend in the road, he came face to face with no other than Salina Mendoza and Clint Deavers! His heart lurched to find these two on the same trail as his missing wife. Clint reined up instantly, glaring at the golden image clad in black. Salina whitened and had difficulty controlling her horse.

"Well, well, who do we have here, Salina?" Clint muttered, his gaze lethal and frosty. Clint hadn't forgotten how this man had tricked him and called his bluff, acts which still riled the gunslinger.

"Lynx, why do you ride this way?" Salina asked weakly.

"I might ask the same of you, Salina," Lynx snarled. "That's bad company you're keeping. I wondered where you'd flown to."

"Were you looking for me?" she asked wishfully, her eyes and face brightening, much to Clint's annoyance.

Lynx laughed sarcastically and shook his head slowly. Lynx appeared utterly relaxed and unruffled, but he was tense and alert. "Did you notice Callie along the trail?" he casually inquired, observing their reactions for clues he dreaded. "Seems your malicious trick worked after you left. Any idea where she went?"

"You mean Cal ran off again?" Salina asked in amusement.

"You've been scheming to run her off ever since her arrival. What did you expect after she caught you naked in my bed?" Lynx ventured, pleased with the effect of his enlightening words on Clint. "If I hadn't been so busy trying to calm her down the other night, I would have beaten the daylights out of you for that malicious prank," he sneered scornfully.

Salina flustered. She glanced over at the nettled man beside her. "He lies, Clint. I have never slept with you," she charged hotly.

"Only because I kicked you out on your lustful ass. I've been telling you for over two years that I'm not interested in a slut like you. And don't go looking insulted! Only a cheap *puta* would sneak into a married man's room while he's sleeping! It takes a daring, heartless bitch to crawl naked into his bed with his injured wife in the next room. Ask Deavers, who would look at you even once with Cal around?" Lynx added harshly, noticing the gleam of agreement in Clint's eyes.

"If Cal had not been wounded and an invalid for weeks, you would not have needed a woman so badly," she shot back at him.

"Wounded?" Clint echoed in surprise. "That pretty little thing got shot? Who did it?" he demanded as if he deserved to know the identity of anyone who would dare such an outrage. He hadn't been able to forget her since their meeting in Lampasas.

"I'd bet my boots Salina knows. I learned how cruel and devious she is when she tried to pin an adultery charge on me," Lynx announced.

Stressed, Salina exposed a look of guilt before she could control her expression. She stammered, "Don't be . . . absurd! Why would . . . I shoot Calinda? She is a pain in the rump, but that's *loco*."

Clint stared at Salina. Lynx drilled his intimidating glare into her frightened face. "You little bitch!" Clint thundered at her. So much for their plans of kidnapping that spicy redhead for her revenge and his pleasure! Salina had promised him money and Calinda if he aided her plot. All along, she had wanted to kill the sweet lady!

"He just tries to anger you, *mi amanta*. Do not listen to him," she pleaded, her nerves jittery between two powerful males.

"Where is she, Salina?" Lynx demanded suspiciously, capturing a curious interaction between them. "What have you done to her now?"

"Que se yo, diablo!" she screamed at Lynx in rising panic.

"The hell you don't know!" he stormed back, eyes blazing in fury.

"We haven't seen her, Cardone, but I'll gladly help

570

you search. This ain't no safe area for a lady like that," Clint merrily offered.

"Caramba!" Salina cursed at the grinning outlaw.

"Shut up, Salina," Clint warned in mounting repulsion.

"You two were behind those mysterious notes, weren't you?" Lynx questioned, but didn't expect any answer. He was astonished when Clint responded almost immediately.

"This *chica* planned the whole thing. I should have known she was up to no good. If you'll recall, she wasn't your wife at the time. I knew you were lying, but I had a soft spot for her. Can't blame me for falling under her spell. Must be powerful to snare you. If she's run off from home, I take it she's available again?" he baited Lynx.

"Vete al infierno!" Salina heatedly damned them to hades.

Lynx was too aware of the passage of time. But before he rode off, he had to make certain these two weren't involved in Calinda's disappearance. What if they forced her to write those notes and leave? What if Cal assumed he would pull clues from the letter? What had it said? Lynx tried to envision it, but he was distracted by Clint's cold blue gaze and palm resting on the butt of his pistol. It was rash to think of other things in the face of death . . .

Stalling for time, Lynx exposed Salina's plot the other night. He icily added, "No Deavers, she ain't available and never will be."

"Well?" Clint hinted guilefully. "Need my help? If Calinda's finished with you, I'm ready and willing to marry her."

"Damn you, bastard!" Salina screamed at Lynx,

watching him thwart her final plan. Once Clint had taken his fill of Calinda and she had driven her small dagger into that witch's heart, Salina had planned to return to the ranch and offer herself to the grieving Lynx. "I wish Manuel's aim had been accurate; she would be dead! Too bad that horse did not trample her! I should have told Clint to rape her that first night in Lampasas! You are a fool, *diablo!* Manuel should have killed you that day on the range! She is a *puta!* A *feo gata!* A *sucio bruja!*" she shouted rashly, going for the gun at her waist. If she couldn't have this irresistible devil who haunted her, no woman would!

Lynx was about to lurch forward to slap her vulgar mouth, pushed beyond reason and control as that bitch spouted crude insults about his beloved. But Clint viciously slapped Salina's face three times as he growled satanically, "No, you don't, you slut! He's mine! Trick me, will you!"

Salina couldn't recoil swiftly enough to avoid those bruising blows. Tears rolled down her face. Her dark eyes were wide with terror and disbelief. She begged for Lynx's protection. Deavers clearly wasn't done with her yet.

Clint laughed wickedly. "Let me see you use that ugly face to fool any more men! Get out of here before I break your arms!"

Again the Mexican girl appealed for Lynx's help. "Sorry, Salina, but I have to be going." Right now, Cal could be in more trouble than Salina was. Lynx despised such brutality, but he didn't have the time to help this girl who had maliciously played havoc with his life and his wife's. He chilled his heart and conscience to her sufferings. Salina had chosen this path and must ride it to the end. Besides, Deavers was too edgy to suit him.

"Not so fast, Cardone. It's time you and I settle our differences, here and now."

The puissant Texan leveled his potent gaze on Clint. "We have no quarrel, Deavers. Don't force me to kill you," he stated clearly, unshaken by the outlaw's threat. But it was his way to avoid death if possible. He would reason first, bluff second, and shoot last.

"You're wrong, Cardone. You made a fool of me in Lampasas; I don't take that insult lying down. Let's dismount and see who's the fastest," Clint suggested stubbornly, wishing he hadn't shot off his mouth so quickly. Now, he couldn't back down.

"I don't have time to argue with you, Deavers. Cal's out there lost somewhere, maybe in danger. Let it pass for today," he entreated.

"How long does it take to die, Cardone?" Clint scoffed. "If you survive, you go after her. If I survive, then I'll take your place. It's very quick and simple, the winner gets her."

"I'd kill you before I let you near her again," Lynx snarled.

"You'll have to," Deavers replied, grinning at his rigid foe.

"No, I won't," Lynx said lightly. "I'm a Texas Ranger; you're under arrest." He gingerly withdrew the badge from his pocket and flashed it before Clint's infuriated eyes.

Abruptly Clint burst into taunting laughter. "You're a Ranger about as much as you were Calinda's husband in Lampasas. No more sneaky tricks, Cardone. Get off your horse," he demanded.

"I'm a Ranger, Deavers, and you're a bloody fool."

Clint and Lynx challenged each other with their

combative gazes. Clint wavered in doubt, then scoffed, "You're married. You wouldn't join the Rangers with a wife like that at home. You're lying."

"Will you relax a minute while I prove it?" Lynx asked.

"How?" Clint skeptically queried.

"Like this," Lynx replied negligently, lifting his boot and swiftly digging his spur into the leather of Clint's saddle. "Recognize that?"

Clint gaped at the tiny depression in the shape of a star, then lifted his apprehensive gaze to the impassive face of Lynx Cardone. "You?" Clint hinted incredulously.

"Me," Lynx answered nonchalantly, not a tiny trace of dishonesty or fear on his face. "What's it to be, Deavers?"

Clint glanced from the imprint of the star to the confident look on Lynx's face. He hesitated in doubt. Lynx was fast and accurate, and the Unknown Ranger was untouchable in courage and daring.

"You've got ten seconds to dismount or ride off," Lynx stated.

Clint wiped the moisture from the corners of his mouth as he assessed the situation. Salina was bending over her saddle, weeping. Her gun was on the ground; no help to him. Could he take this man who was two daring men in one? His irrational pride mocked him.

"I don't want no trouble with Rangers. Another day?"

"Another day," Lynx calmly accepted, wary of this man.

Clint reached over and took Salina's reins. He glared at Lynx, then headed past him. "Count on it, Cardone," he sneered.

Lynx didn't move a muscle, but watched the man closely. Clint spurred his horse and rode off, pulling Salina's along with him. Lynx nudged Star in the ribs to move out, his keen instincts alive.

The moment Clint halted and yanked his Winchester from his saddle to backshoot Lynx, the intrepid Ranger went into lightning action. In one graceful movement, Lynx had whirled and drawn his Colt and fired at Clint's left shoulder. The rifle flew to the ground as Clint yelped in pain, the bullet lodging beneath his shoulder blade. Even at that distance, Lynx was accurate.

"Another day, Deavers!" he shouted, then prodded Star into a fast run. Wounded, Deavers would be forced to head for Jacksboro. When Lynx had time, he would wire the Ranger there to arrest him and Salina for their crimes. In their condition, they wouldn't get far. When he returned home, Lynx would deal with Manuel. Besides being Calinda's attacker, he was doubtlessly the rustlers' informant.

Lynx's eyes flickered to the sun's angle. He ranted at the loss of time; it was nearing five o'clock and he had a lengthy distance to cover before darkness. Soon, he would be forced to slow his pace to search the sides of the trail. Lynx didn't want to ride past her!

Ten miles southward, Calinda was stirring for the first time since early afternoon. Her hand went to her forehead as she mechanically mopped the beads of perspiration from it. She inhaled and exhaled deeply as she tried to clear her senses. When her eyes opened, there was a roughly dressed man hunkered down beside her. She caught her breath in panic and surprise. Her eyes darted around, assessing her location and situation. Her hand eased down to her waist, finding her

575

gunbelt missing. She tensed in panic.

Billy noted each of her actions and expressions. She was a feisty little beauty. "Good morning. Or is it good afternoon?" he playfully murmured, caressing his knobby chin with his left hand.

"Who are you? What happened?" Cal asked shakily.

"Don't know what happened, little lady, but I'm called Billy," he smugly announced, sitting down beside her.

Calinda struggled to sit up, but her head swam. "Best lie down a while, Ma'am. You don't look so good," Billy advised.

"May I have some water?" she asked politely, amusing him.

He handed her the canteen and helped her rise to drink. As she relaxed with her head against his saddle, she asked, "Where am I?"

"Just south of Jacksboro. Where you heading alone and in this sorry shape?" he asked, intrigued and stimulated.

"I was meeting my husband there, but I became ill. I guess I'm lost," she responded cautiously, slyly.

"No ring on your finger," Billy informed her.

"I lost it. He's buying me another one. May I have some more water? I must have a fever. I'm so thirsty," she told him to stall for time to think and plan.

"A good shot of Irish whiskey will do more for you," he offered.

"No thank you. I don't partake of strong spirits," she alleged.

"What do you partake of, Ma'am?" he asked alarmingly.

"I beg your pardon?" Cal replied, trying to disarm

576

him with manners and innocence.

"Got me a real lady on my hands," he congratulated himself aloud. "What about that? Billy the Kid with a lady, imagine that."

Billy was slightly miffed when she failed to recognize his notorious name and the reputation that went along with it. He had expected to strike terror into her heart with it. "What should I do with you?" he asked absently, running his fingers through his shaggy hair.

"Do you live around here? Will your family help me get home?"

Chilling laughter came forth from this belligerent man. "Nope!"

"You don't live around here, or they won't help me?" she asked softly, as if for clarity, but actually for time.

"I don't live anywhere, and I ain't got no family," he declared.

"Then I must head for Jacksboro before night comes," she stated, glancing at the enclosing shadows. "If my husband isn't there or searching for me, I'll stay in the hotel."

"That ain't a good idea, Ma'am," Billy murmured.

"Why not?" Cal asked, focusing trusting eyes on him.

"Lots of reasons," Billy replied, eyeing her strangely.

"Such as?" she continued this desperate talk which prevented any actions for the present. *What to do?* she fretted mentally. She had to get away from this leering man, but how? She wisely realized she musn't offend him. She must portray the distressed lady perfectly, and hopefully play on any chords of decency at the same time. Cal noticed her missing boots and jacket;

worse, she was aware her shirt was opened to the cleft between her breasts. Obviously, Billy had discovered the money in her boot and shirt pocket, but what more did he want from her?

"Such as, that's a dangerous town for a lady alone. Such as, you ain't strong enough to ride that far. Such as, I don't want you to leave," he added the reason which struck terror into her heart.

"You needn't worry, Mister Billy, I'll be fine," Cal tried to sound light and brave. "My husband taught me how to shoot. I appreciate what you did for me. If you'll give me your address, I'll see you're paid for your trouble and kindness. Where's my gun?"

"Over there," he told her, pointing to where it lay near her saddle. "But you won't be needing it. I'll take care of you."

"That's nice of you, sir, but I'm feeling some better now. I should be heading out," she remarked, attempting to rise.

Billy warned, "Stay put," then placed his hand against her injured shoulder to push her down. Cal screamed in pain and went white. Billy came to full alert as she cradled her left arm and tears spilled forth. He confined her wrists in one hand and pulled the shirt aside to check her baffling action. She was inhaling raggedly; her eyes squeezed tightly as she endured the agony which knifed her body.

He stared at the astonishing area, then gaped at her tormented expression. "That's a gunshot," he stated in wonder.

"Get your hands off me," she commanded faintly, grimacing.

"People don't order Billy Bonnet around," he snapped at her. "What's you name?" he demanded forcefully.

"You arrogant brute! Leave me alone. Can't you see I'm hurt and sick?" she panted breathlessly.

"Don't pain me none," Billy retorted as if utterly insensitive.

"Please, Mister Bonnet," Cal entreated softly.

"Please, what?" Billy taunted, his mood becoming larkish.

"Please take your filthy hands off my wife before I put a slug in your miserable hide," Lynx warned icily from behind him. Billy the Kid! His blood ran cold. He'd need all his skill to get Cal safe this time.

Billy flung himself to his back, ready to snatch his gun from its holster. He halted that reflex as he eyed the barrels of two ivory-handled Colts pointing down at him. On the shirt pocket of this audacious man was a shiny Ranger star. On the towering man's face was an expression of coldness and determination.

"Lynx," the name slipped from Cal's dry lips as her astonished gaze glued to his stern face. Lynx didn't look at her, keeping his gaze glued on the pugnacious outlaw. She sensed the gravity of this moment and fell silent to avoid distracting him. Her heart surged with relief and love. Again, Lynx was at her side when danger struck; and this time, Cal knew positively he wasn't behind this new peril. But how did he get that Ranger star? Had his friend Jones let him borrow it to help him out in just this kind of situation? No, she thought, he probably stole it and if it'll scare Billy I'm glad he did!

Billy insouciantly reclined on his back, propping up his lean torso with his flexed elbows. He grinned conceitedly. "Surely there's only one man with a crazy name like that," Billy murmured. "Didn't know you were a Ranger, Cardone. I ain't committed no crimes in Texas. What's your beef with me?"

"None today, Billy, if you release my wife," Lynx played along with Billy's deceptively genial mood.

Both men appeared to be complaisant and even-tempered, but were cunningly ready to spring into action. It was a ploy of the best gunmen; throw your opponent off with a slack body and placid manner. Each man was aware of the latent force behind the other.

Billy didn't fear any man, not even one behind a badge. Neither was afraid to die; but it was a part of life somewhere down the trail. He was acquainted with the reputation and might behind the man called Lynx Cardone. Billy never doubted he was faster than Lynx, but he pondered if this situation was worth the trouble. Having incompetent sheriffs after you was one thing, but enticing the Rangers to hotly and rashly pursue you was another. But who would know what happened out here? Unless he boasted of having Cardone's notch on his gun. But why kill a famous man if you couldn't take credit for it?

"How's the shoulder, love?" Lynx inquired, cunningly lacing his words with tenderness, revealing an emotion which was lethal to challenge. Yet, his pleasant gaze remained on the smiling Billy.

"Terrible. What took you so long to find me?" Cal asked, taking his unspoken clue and using it. "I fainted on the trail and Billy found me. Up to now he's been a perfect gentleman." She wondered if Lynx would use the same ploy on Billy which had worked on Clint, or was he planning to use that stolen Ranger badge to win this battle?

"You do have an infuriating way of getting into mischief, woman. When I get you home, I plan to tan the seat of your britches. Father's out of his mind with worry. We've got Rangers everywhere looking for you," Lynx gently scolded her. "You sure you're alright?"

Calinda played along with his deceit, amazed by the realization that they often communicated without words or with sly ones. Acting the contrite wife, she lowered her head and murmured, "I'm sorry, Lynx. If you'd stay home, I wouldn't get crazy and come looking for you."

"Is that a promise or a threat?" Lynx teased her, using their playful banter to mellow the wary outlaw.

"Both," she stated petulantly. Now that he was here with her, she wasn't afraid of anything, even confronting the past with him. She wondered if Lynx would get into legal trouble for posing as a Ranger.

"Well, Billy, do we call a truce and go our separate ways; or do we battle over my wife? You and I have no quarrel. I just want Cal."

Well aware of Lynx's reputation for fairness and extreme prowess, Billy mused on his decision. His gaze flickered over to the injured beauty. She was too pretty and spunky to die. And she would die if he killed her husband, for she would fight him to the death. Perhaps another day he would challenge this man to a duel. This wasn't the time or place, for his mind wasn't into killing either of them. The spark of love between them tugged strangely at his heart.

Calinda cringed in fear as she awaited the outlaw's choice of behavior. "Please, Billy, don't fight him. I don't want him to kill you any more than I want you to slay him. I love him and need him."

Lynx was moved by her words. "Can you ride,

Cal?" he asked.

"I'm feeling better; I think so," she answered him.

"Take Star and ride out," Lynx commanded tenderly.

"What about you?" she worried anxiously.

"If Billy insists, we'll handle our business after you go. Leave now," he ordered again. "I'll bring your horse."

Calinda didn't move. She merely stared at her husband. He wanted her away safely, even at the cost of his own life. How could he make such a sacrifice if he didn't truly love her? She wanted to run into his arms and beg for his forgiveness. The dire circumstances prevented it. What if Lynx was killed or wounded?

"Move, Cal," he warned sternly. "I've had enough of your defiance. We wouldn't be here if you had stayed home where you belong."

"That won't be necessary, Cardone. You have my word you two can ride out together," Billy suddenly announced, grinning.

Lynx eyed him intently. His guns remained where they were and his gaze continued to study this imposing rival. Years of training and experience took command of his senses. Lynx had played similar scenes many times. Rarely had he misread a man's intentions or honesty. He smiled and nodded, slipping his Colts into their holsters, to her shock.

Calinda was frozen in mid-step. She couldn't believe what Lynx was doing. He was actually putting away his weapons and turning his back on this truculent man. He calmly saddled her horse and called her over. She couldn't budge, her lips parted and her eyes wide.

"Callie, let's go home," Lynx coaxed indulgently.

Calinda shook her head, then gaped at both men. "Billy gave his word; that's good enough for me. Let's ride, woman. I'm hot and tired and mean-spirited right now. I've been dogging you for days. If you ever pull another stunt like this, I'll thrash you soundly."

Lynx trusted this outlaw? What kind of western code of honor was this?

"Cal!" Lynx stormed, breaking her trancy state and propelling her forward with his potent tone.

Lynx helped her to her mount, then told her to head out before him. Confused and alarmed, Cal did as told and waited near the edge of the worn trail. Though it seemed hours, it was only minutes before he joined her. Unaware of holding her breath in tension, she slowly released it when he was beside her. She wondered what the two men had said to each other after her departure. She looked over at the thicket. Billy was leaning against a slender tree watching them, a wide grin on his nicely featured face. Billy waved to her, then chuckled before disappearing into the thicket.

"Lynx," she began softly, but was cut off instantly.

"Shut up and ride, woman, before Billy changes his mind. We'll talk later. Right now, I'm not in the mood to hear anything but hooves."

Stunned, she stared at him. Lynx slapped her horse's rump to send him running forward. Cal lurched in the saddle and caught her balance. She promptly reined up and snapped at him, "Don't you dare order me about! I don't care to talk to you now or later! You go your way and I'll go mine. But thanks for another of your timely rescues."

Lynx's attempt to give her strength through anger and fear backfired on him. "Woman, if you don't get moving, I'll spank you right here. I want some distance between us and Billy. Do you know who that man was?" he asked. He hastily enlightened her on the lethal and infamous Billy the Kid. "I trust him to keep his word for the moment. But I don't plan to give him time to change his mind. You damn fool, don't you realize how weak you are? We'll be doing good to make five miles without stopping. Not that it matters to you, but he's probably faster and better with a gun than I am. If you don't want to be returned to him, stop stalling with this foolishness or you just might find Billy again," he warned.

"You think he'll come after us?" she asked fearfully.

"Wouldn't surprise me none. Now, get moving before I lose my temper. Anything else you want to know can wait until later."

"Have you been home yet?" she asked in dread.

Lynx drilled his volatile gaze into her nervous one, suddenly and irrationally furious and impatient with her, harsh emotions born of tension and relief. "No, I didn't have time. Rankin met me at the train Tuesday. I've been after you since then."

"I see," she murmured, pondering his radical change in mood.

"No, Callie, you don't see anything yet. But you will," he vowed sullenly. Lynx seized her bridle and headed off at a gallop.

Calinda had no choice but to hang on tightly and to weather the storm before her.

Chapter Twenty-six

Except for the incessant pounding of the horses' hooves, Lynx and Cal rode in strained silence for a lengthy time, each trying to master their warring emotions. Following their initial brisk run to put distance between them and the notorious outlaw, Lynx set their rate of movement at a steadfast pace: inflexible, resolute, and indisputable. He rode slightly ahead of her, never glancing backwards.

Peeved by his harshness, Cal followed in rigid disquiet. A flurry of conflicting thoughts and emotions filled her. She knew he was serious about that criminal behind them. Yet, her fears had dissipated, allowing resentment and puzzlement to flood her mind. Lynx was behaving as if she were at terrible fault! He knew the truth, both sides, but was holding his tongue for now. *What will he say later when we stop? He's returning me to the ranch, but why? What don't I see?* She eagerly anticipated, yet dreaded, their imminent discussion.

Cal observed the assertive and moody man before her. In Billy's camp, Lynx had evinced a courage and cunning which amazed her. Did the man lack all traces of fear and hesitation? He was so dashing, intelligent, and daring. When he had joined her afterwards, she had absently noticed a quivering tic in his darkly stubbled jawline, the unnatural anxiety in his gaze, and the glacial edge to his stirring voice. Mingling with that novel tension, fury had danced wildly and brightly in his tawny eyes. Even now, his tightly leashed anger could be detected in his taut body as it swayed rhythmically with the motion of his mottled steed. His vexation was like a tangible object.

Lynx was dressed in that pitch-black again: snug shirt, pants, shiny boots, and felt hat. He wore a fiery red bandanna around his throat, a startling contrast to the inky attire. The color of it seemed to match his now leashed rage; it fluttered capriciously in the breeze which he was creating. His corded muscles were strained against the tight material of his shirt and pants. His skin was so bronzed by the sun that only his wheatish hair and red bandanna denied a satanic facade. Was that the intention of his ebony outfit, to intimidate, to charm?

Her gaze drifted down to the gunbelt around his firm waist, displaying a row of coppery colored bullets in small loops and flashing two weapons with creamy butts. From her angle, Cal noted the way the tooled leather holsters were securely strapped to his sinewy thighs to prevent interference when he needed to extract his guns quickly. What a mesmerizing vision of imposing looks and immense prowess.

Lynx rode as if a temporary appendage of his stallion, their traits seeming to blend and match. The splendid beast was eye-catching with its ebony mane, tail, and legs. Star's belly was a dull white, with small sooty splotches here and there; his rump was like midnight. His majestic head was charcoal, but for a large white patch beneath his dark mane. She assumed that marking had labeled him Star. He was sleek and fast, intelligent and loyal to his master. Uncannily, Star almost seemed human.

Cal wondered when they would cease this tiring journey and delve into his suspicious chicanery. If Billy wasn't trailing them, they must be two hours ahead of him. Dusk was gradually closing in on them with the disappearance of the sun. It must be around eight or nine o'clock by now. She had rested late this morning and napped this afternoon, but her energy and stamina were vanishing as the light.

Lynx had remarked on her weakness this afternoon, so he was aware of it. Why did he keep pushing her in this unfeeling and relentless matter? Was he trying to punish her, to lower her guard, to lessen his anger, to drain her fighting spirit? What pretext would he claim for his trickery? He was responsible for her problems and misconceptions, if they were misconceptions. He was responsible for alienating her and driving her away. The first move should be his, but she was reaching the point where she couldn't wait for it. She was exhausted; her injury pained her; she was hungry and thirsty; she needed some privacy.

When Cal observed a grove of trees to their right, she headed for it, shouting over her shoulder, "I'm stopping whether you do or not."

She nudged her horse to go in that direction. Astonishingly, he didn't argue, but trailed her. When she reached the stand of trees, she alighted and tied her reins to one. She headed for a deep ravine not far away and disappeared over the side. After she excused herself, she reluctantly and sluggishly rejoined him, sitting down beside a tree and leaning against it with her eyes closed.

Lynx noted the way she cradled her left arm and breathed deeply. She was pale, but rosy-cheeked. He heard her tummy growl softly. How did one open the type of conversation they needed to share? There was so much explanatory ground to cover, and she was in a sorry state to begin such a vital and taxing journey toward honesty and love.

Lynx retrieved his canteen and walked over to hunker down beside her. "Water?" he offered, holding the container out to her.

Cal opened her eyes and accepted it, drinking slowly, then moistening her lips. Returning it, she thanked him and relaxed against the tree trunk again. She had kept her gaze on the canteen, then lifted it to stare at the hovering tree above her. As if wary with him, she didn't speak. Her tummy signaled its craving once more. Her right hand caressed it lightly, as if trying to comfort it.

"I'll start a fire and get us something to eat. You rest," he stated matter-of-factly, standing to carry out his task.

Her leafy eyes shifted to his chest, settling on the silver star pinned to his pocket, a vivid contrast to the ebony shirt. "What are you doing with that Ranger badge?" she asked in a muffled tone. "Did you steal it or did Jones persuade you to join up with them? You won't be staying home?"

Lynx sank to one knee and propped his elbow on it, cupping his chin and fusing his fathomless gaze to her uneasy one. This was the perfect moment to correct one misconception. "I've been an undercover Ranger since I was twenty-two. Jones has been my commanding officer for two years; he's one of the few men who knows my secret identity. Before the Rangers, I was a detective for the railroad and a covert agent for the government. My little trips that riled you so much were missions for Jones and the Rangers. To protect lives and carry out critical assignments, I couldn't expose myself to anyone, not even the Rangers I worked with. Most thought I was a paid gunslinger, or I was helping out Ranger friends as favors. That's why I couldn't explain myself before now. I told Father the last time I was home, but I wanted to wait and tell you everything when my stay was permanent. I didn't want you worrying over my safety or accidentally dropping any clues which might endanger your life and mine or hinder my missions. I asked you to trust me, Cal, until I could explain things. After I testified against those two men I arrested, I resigned in Austin on Monday. They let me keep this badge for protection. With each mission, more people were learning or suspecting my position. It was hard to keep silent, love. I had to or lose any chance of success. That's why I was so upset about my pictures in the paper. I'm not an effective secret anymore."

"You've been a Ranger all this time?" she probed incredulously.

He brought her saddle over and dropped it on the ground. "Ever hear of the Unknown Ranger who leaves a star as his mark after each secret mission?" he inquired, watching her carefully.

Cal nodded. As with Clint, he demonstrated his enlightening point by forcefully striking his spur against the smooth leather of her saddle, leaving a star indention there. "Does that tell you anything, my mistrustful wife?" he ventured playfully. He withdrew a small and shiny star from his pants pocket and placed it in her palm. "That night I rescued you from Cole Stevens and his gang, I left one of those on the window sill. It was a rash move; that's why I was so antsy to get out of there. Getting the picture, Cal?"

She leaned forward, her trembling fingertip touching the tiny depression. She looked at the matching size in her damp palm, then stared at the silver spurs attached to his ebony boots. She let these clues and his words filter into her mind and settle there. As he hunkered down beside her and met her astonished gaze, she murmured, "You?"

"That's right, love, me. In case you've been wondering, I'm not a gunslinger or an outlaw. I've been on a mission every time I left home, not pursuing your father or crazy adventures, and certainly not luring my wife into danger just to play hero. That's also why I was always around or not far behind where there was trouble. To carry out my assignments, I had to get to know outlaws and suspicious characters and mingle with them to gain clues about past and future crimes. As long as no one knew who or what I was, I could come and go as I pleased; that made me valuable to the Rangers and the law. With my colorful reputation and secret identity, it was exciting and simple. At least it was until you walked on the scene. Since that night at the Red Satin Saloon, my life and guts have been turned inside-out by one infuriating and rebellious young lady."

"Your life?" she scoffed. "What about mine?"

"What about yours, Cal?" he probed in a mellow voice.

"Since the day I arrived out here, I've endured one violent episode after another. If anyone had told me what Texas was like, I would never have come. I would have wed one of those fops the Simsons shoved on me. I hate this place and these evil people!"

"Including me and the ranch?" he inquired lazily.

Her face grew scarlet and warm. She lowered her fiery gaze and squirmed nervously. "No," she bravely replied, her tummy pleading audibly as she made the stirring admission.

"Good," he casually remarked. "After we've eaten and rested, we'll settle our differences. It's past time you and I reach an understanding," he informed her mysteriously. "Relax, Callie. Believe it or not, but you're perfectly safe with me. Before I start the coffee and supper, I want you to know one thing which might expel some of that mistrust and fear. I know who's responsible for those strange letters and the shooting: it was Salina. She'll be arrested tomorrow."

"Salina?" she murmured pensively.

"I'll explain it all later, but I swear it was her. Neither Rankin nor I had anything to do with it. Why don't you lie down a while? How's the shoulder feeling?" he altered the subject for now.

"I ache all over, but it's not the worst aggravation at present. If I lie down, I'll probably fall asleep, and I'm starved."

"I can tell," he muttered in amusement. "When did you last eat?"

"Just a biscuit and water this morning," she confessed ruefully.

Lynx shook his tawny head and chided her, "If you're planning any future travel, you best learn how to prepare for it. I hope you've learned a valuable lesson with this dangerous mischief."

"I've learned quite a few valuable lessons lately," she purred cattily, frowning at him.

"School isn't over yet, Cal; it hasn't even begun," he hinted.

"It's about time to be educated on certain matters, don't you agree my devious husband?" she sullenly inquired.

His expression waxed serious. "All the time I've been dogging you, I've been praying it wasn't too late for that education. Is it?" he challenged, tensed in dread of her reply.

Following a pensive moment, she repiled guardedly, "That depends on you, Lynx, and how you explain those matters."

She was bemused when he admitted freely, "I won't say it wasn't intentional, Cal. But I did have reasons."

"I'm sure you did. When I hear them, then I'll decide my course."

"Agreed," Lynx acquiesced. "Now, rest until supper's ready."

He spread out his sleeping roll and motioned for her to lie down. His tenderness and concern chewed at her irritation and bitterness, devouring them bite by bite. Cal stretched out and sighed in relief as her body thanked her for being kind to it. She yawned, then curled to her right side to watch him as he worked.

Every so often, Lynx would glance over at her and smile, as if making certain she was still there. When the coffee was ready, he poured a cup and brought it to her. Cal sat up, accepted it, thanked him, and began to sip it gingerly. Soon, fragrant odors wafted on the breezy currents of warm air.

Lynx had set a tin plate of fried bacon and steaming beans on the grass before her, cautioning, "Careful, they're hot." He took her cup and refilled it, adding sugar. He brought the cups over and set them on the ground, dropping a hunk of bread on her plate. Retrieving his own plate, he asked, "Mind if I sit this close?"

"After this service, of course not," she murmured merrily.

He took a seat beside her and worked on his supper. The beans and bread were easy to get down. But her sensitive stomach rebelled against the greasy bacon; even its smell repulsed her. As her tummy churned unexpectedly, Cal swallowed hard several times to combat her sudden nausea. She took a few sips of the coffee and inhaled in suspense, relieved when the sensation passed.

"You all right, Cal?" he asked, noticing her curious behavior.

"Just a little queasy. I guess because my stomach's so empty." She sat down the plate and cup, resting her face between her hands.

"You don't look too good, woman. What's the problem?"

Her voice and hands were trembly. Her face had lost most of its color, leaving it chalky. "I'm just exhausted. My head's spinning and my ears are ringing."

He gently seized her shoulders and pressed her to the bedroll. He grabbed the canteen and yanked off

593

his bandanna, wetting it and wiping the beads of moisture from her face. He examined the wound above her left breast, relieved it wasn't inflamed or infected. It appeared to be healing properly. He fretted over this curious state.

"Does it still hurt, Callie?" he asked apprehensively.

"A dull ache most of the time, but it rarely throbs anymore. I feel so awful, Lynx. So weak and shaky. How long will this last?"

Unless there was some internal problem, her condition had nothing to do with the gunshot. She had no fever. Was she merely worn out from lingering misery or assailed by intense stress?

"Why did you run off in this shape, woman?" he muttered.

"Because I was frightened and confused and miserable. I don't want your damned old ranch! After all this time, Lynx, didn't you two know me better than that?" she asked sadly, tears of tension escaping. Cal snuffed and wiped at the embarrassing droplets. "I hate cry babies! And I seem to be crying so much lately," she berated herself.

"I know, Salina told me," he unthinkingly remarked.

"I bet she told you lots of things which were none of her damn business!"

"I'm sorry she hurt you so many times, love. I didn't realize things were that bad between you two," he apologized.

"How could you know? You were never home! When I found your mother's portrait, she was delighted to tell me all about the treacherous Laura Cardone and my despicable father. I hate them both!" she cried, some of her spirit and strength returning as she reclined. "I hope I never lay eyes on either of them as long as I live."

"Which won't be long, Callie, if you don't take better care of yourself. When did Salina tell you about them? I wasn't aware she knew anything about the past."

"She was always spying on all of us. I tried to warn you two about her. But I was viewed as the outsider, the troublemaker. She told me a week or so after you rescued me from Stevens. Then she relished pointing out your pictures at Round Rock. No doubt she knew everything and was savoring the slow release of her facts."

"Why didn't you tell us what she was doing to you?"

"Ha!" she sneered sarcastically. "Do you recall how you acted when I accused her of being behind that fall I took? I know that girth was secure. Either she did it or Manuel did at her request."

"But why would she do such things?" he entreated craftily as the truth of her torments came to light, wanting her to solve the riddle.

"She told me when I arrived that you were hers. I told you she threatened me with a knife if I got near you. If she isn't in love with you, she wants you desperately. She's dangerous and wicked."

"Not anymore," he informed her, relating the confrontation with Clint and Salina.

"My God, Lynx," she said softly. "I wouldn't wish a man like Deavers on anyone, even her."

Lynx went on to explain his knowledge and theories about Lampasas and the letters. He told her how he had discovered where Cole was imprisoning her. He revealed who the "B" was in that telegram which she found beneath the bed. He repeated how he had come into possession of her stolen locket and why he had concealed it from her. He expounded on his Ranger career and last few missions.

"I never lied to you, Callie. But I'll confess I allowed you to misread certain events and people. I worded sentences to keep you in the dark. I didn't clarify misconceptions you had. I disarmed you with love. But I did it so you wouldn't be hurt anymore. I loved and respected your father deeply. You can't imagine how he hurt me. As for my mother, I'll never accept or understand what she did to me and father," he vowed bitterly.

He was seated beside her, his left hip touching hers as he gazed down at her, his palms flat on the ground on either side of her body. "Don't you see why I couldn't reveal their treachery and betrayal? God, Callie, it knifed me up every time I heard or spoke their names. We didn't even know about the baby until we saw that letter you concealed. I don't know who lied, but Rankin assures me it's my half sister or brother."

"It's been so many torturous years, Lynx. They're gone for good, no matter whose child it is. Why can't their malicious hold over all of us be broken?" she sobbed.

"For us, Callie, it can, if we're willing to allow it. But for my father, is isn't that simple. He loved Mother and trusted her. He would have given his life for your father. If it were your child, could you forget about it? If it was the person you loved more than life itself, could you accept the betrayal and loss?" he reasoned sadly.

"I wish Brax had never written that letter," she murmured.

"At least we know why they ran," he debated her words.

"How could something like that happen? To betray and sacrifice your husband and child for a man like my father?" she scoffed.

"You never knew him, Callie. One day soon, I'll tell you about Brax and those early days when we were all a happy family."

"Why did you marry me, Lynx?" she asked helplessly.

"We've talked enough tonight, Callie. You need to sleep and recover. I promise we'll discuss the rest tomorrow. I can't let you walk out of my life. If you force me to hold you a prisoner at the ranch, I will," he told her gravely.

"But you have full control of the ranch now. What more do you want from me?" she panted in exasperation and anguish.

"Damn the ranch and that blasted deed! I love you and need you, woman. If you don't believe that, we don't stand a chance."

"You don't have to shout at me," she reprimanded him.

"Don't I? You take off and nearly get yourself raped and killed, and I shouldn't be furious with you? When I met up with Deavers and Salina on the Jacksboro Road, I nearly went crazy with fear. I swear to you, Callie Cardone; if you ever step foot off that ranch again without my permission or knowledge, I'll hunt you down and lock you in your room! As to the ranch, I'll sign half of it over to you the first chance I get. That should prove I didn't marry you to take control."

"But why didn't you say anything about it?" she pressed.

"At first, we didn't trust you. Now that you know the truth, can you blame us? I was pressed for time when I found you in Lampasas. I married you because I love you and wanted to keep you home safe. I told you I would reveal everything soon. I guess I was waiting for us to get to know each other better. When I realized you were truly in love with me, I panicked. I couldn't risk exposing my deceit until I was home to deal with your reaction. Then when you were shot and suspecting me, I tried to prove how much I loved you and wanted you. When that matter came up in Dallas, I knew how you would take that news. Then word came about the trial in Austin. I figured you needed time to fully recover. And I needed to learn everything Yancey had told you, in case some of it was lies. I swear I was going to spill everything the moment I got home. I saw those letters from Brax, and they had me plenty worried. I caught your little clues and enticements to confess, but I didn't know you had the deed. I felt you weren't in any condition to be jolted with the past. I'm sorry, love; I honestly didn't mean to hurt you or deceive you. I can't lose you, Callie; I love you with all my heart and soul." He waited anxiously for those words to sink into her mind.

In her gut and heart, Calinda knew he was being totally honest. In a way, her own deceptions had blocked the truth. As these revelations settled in, she remained quiet and thoughtful.

"Callie? Do you believe me?" he asked hoarsely.

She looked him in the eye and murmured, "Yes."

A whoop of joy and relief rent the air. A broad smile claimed his lips. "You'll come home with me? You won't leave again?"

"Yes. No," she cheerfully replied, smiling up at him.

He fell to his back on the grass, sighing loudly. She rolled to her side and asked, "May I go to sleep now? I'm beat."

"Sleep as long as you wish, love. I'll be right here," he stated, patting the ground as his gaze caressed her.

"How about if you be right here?" she retorted, patting the bedroll, eyes heaped with smoldering embers of desire.

"In your condition, just for protection and sleep," he teased, warming to the fires in her green eyes.

She laughed and pouted, "For tonight."

"Think I can move back into our room when we get home?"

"If you don't, I'll hunt you down and hold you prisoner," she jested, laughing happily and honestly for the first time lately.

"I'm already your prisoner, Callie," he told her huskily.

"And I, yours, my love," she seductively responded.

"No more secrets, Callie; I swear it," he promised sincerely.

Cal leaned over and kissed him, provocatively and sweetly. Lynx gingerly pulled her into his embrace. They snuggled together on the bedroll as she relented to the strong callings of slumber. He watched her for a time, then closed his eyes.

They rode for two days, halting frequently to relent to her need for rest and to master her dizziness and nausea during the mornings. When they camped that second night near a river, she bathed and splashed joyfully as she refreshed her body and spirits. When she grew queasy at dinner, Lynx studied her closely. He hadn't noticed any change in her figure when they made love, but he suddenly recalled how sensitive her breasts had been.

Striking as swiftly and unexpectedly as a lightning bolt, a suspicion jolted him. Lynx eyed her intensely. She was relaxing on the bedroll in a lively mood. He sat down beside her and asked, "Cal, is there something you haven't told me?"

Baffled, she met his piercing gaze. "Such as?" she hinted.

"This illness of yours, tell me about it," he coaxed.

Naive, Cal related all of the symptoms which had been plaguing her of late, excluding one which she had failed to notice. "When's the last time you . . . you . . ." he faltered as he tried to select the appropriate word to use in her presence.

"When I what, Lynx?" she pressed in bewilderment.

"When you did what all women do every month?" he stated, actually blushing in modesty. "Are you pregnant?" he asked abruptly.

"Pre . . . pregnant?" Cal stammered in astonishment. Her mind went to whirling with that added clue. "Am I?" she asked him.

Lynx chuckled. "You do have all the signs. Right?" he teased as she reasoned on his assessment. "When was the last time, Cal?"

"Before I was kidnapped," she told him shyly.

"That doesn't pin down any date, love. Since we were married?" Lynx aided her deliberation.

"I didn't marry you because I was carrying your child," she informed him, if that was his implication.

"It doesn't matter. If you were, it was my doing," he jested.

"The last time was three days after our wedding. Since then, I haven't . . . I suppose it happened after you rescued me from Stevens."

"From your symptoms and our timing, that should make it about two months into blooming," he concluded, patting her flat abdomen.

"Are you angry?" she fretted anxiously.

"To be expecting a son or a daughter from my beautiful wife? Never, love. Our first baby, imagine that?" he stated at the pleasing wonder of it. Chills suddenly washed over him. "Are you sure you're all right?" he queried.

"I suppose I'm normal, if your judgment is accurate."

"I mean about the shooting and all the pressures you've been through lately? You were pregnant during that fall. I could kick myself for endangering you and our baby like that," he criticized himself.

With this discovery, she felt better immediately. She wasn't sick or dying; she was carrying her love's child, their child. She lovingly caressed the area which would soon expand and tell everyone. "Our baby," she murmured in ecstasy.

He looked at her, fierce love and pride storming his body. He captured her face between his hands to engulf the radiance there. "I love you, Callie. I promise everything will be fine now."

"I know, my love," she quickly and joyously agreed. "Our baby," she stated again, giggling softly. "There's so much I'll need to learn. Heavens, Lynx, I don't know anything about babies or having them," she vowed, suddenly apprehensive and insecure.

"That makes two of us, but we'll learn together."

A bright and serene smile greeted him as she said, "Yes, we'll learn together. I love you, you arrogant and mysterious rogue. You with your sneaky silver spurs," she jested, playfully striking one with her finger and watching the tiny stars fly round and round, glittering in the moonlight. "A golden stranger in magical black," she teased.

"Never would I have believed I would marry a girl I met in the Red Satin Saloon, lying seductively in my bed in that sleazy red and black gown. You can't imagine the contrast in my first thoughts and feelings compared to them right this minute."

"Knowing you, Lynx Cardone, I can well imagine," she stated.

"Good thing I didn't toss you out of my room that night. Then some other man would be experiencing this special moment."

"Fate, my love, that guardian angel you mentioned. After I met you, mean and lecherous though you were, I could think of no man but Cody Richards," she murmured dreamily.

"What?" he shrieked.

"As you recall, that's the name I was given for my late caller, that mysterious drifter in devilish black with hair and eyes of gold."

"I owe fate a large debt for withholding my identity until we could meet again. Hearing it at the ranch, you would have surely fled."

"Maybe not," she whispered softly, revealing her ruse that night.

They both laughed as they reflected on their first meeting at the ranch. "You think you can stay home and take care of your greedy husband and child? Or should I use this spur to place my mark of warning and ownership on a lady who carelessly wears red satin?"

They exchanged playful looks and laughed. Calinda softly parried, "I'll make you a bargain, my love; you hang up those silver spurs and I'll promise to never wear red satin or visit another saloon. Besides, my fierce and cunning Lynx, your ownership is much too vivid as it is, or soon will be," she insinuated, tapping her abdomen.

Impassioned, he murmured seductively into her ear, "I love you, *Llama de mi corazon, mi alma, mi mente, mi vida . . .*" Catching his slip and knowing why she had once rebelled at that endearment from her father's letter, he leaned back and apologized, "I'm sorry, love; I forgot. But I never knew Brax called Mother that."

She smiled provocatively and replied, "Honestly, it doesn't matter anymore. But I would like to know what you're saying. Perhaps I should have lessons in Spanish? When my other education is completed, if ever," she speculated mirthfully.

Lynx tenderly grasped her face between his strong and gentle hands, whispering huskily, "I love you, flame of my heart, my soul, my mind, my life . . ."

Her rapturous gaze devoured his compelling features. *"Yo te quiero, mi amante;* that's all the Spanish you taught me."

"That's more than enough, Callie Cardone." His lips covered hers as they sank entwined on his bedroll, the musical sounds of a lovely September night offering serenity to their passionate lovemaking beneath the Texas moonlight.

Epilogue

On the prosperous Cardone Ranch, it was late spring of 1881. In March of '79, Calinda Braxton Cardone had given birth to a son. The child had been named Travis Cardone, in memory of Colonel William Barrett Travis who had commanded the ill-fated and heroic stand by the Texas Rangers at the Alamo. Except for Lynx's silver spurs and badge in a drawer, the name Travis was his only link to past days with that dauntless force. Also keeping her promise, Calinda had never worn Laura's red satin gown again.

Following Lynx's last rescue of his wife and their return home, the ensuing months had been peaceful for the Cardones. Manuel, Salina, and Clint Deavers had been arrested for their crimes. Their names were never mentioned again on the ranch.

To Calinda's relief and joy, not once since his retirement from the Rangers had Lynx appeared restive or discontent. He seemed too busy with the ranch, his adoring wife, and growing son to have time or energy to desire anything other than what he proudly possessed. Neither had thought it possible, but their love and passion had increased with time. Even Rankin had been snared by love; he had been seeing Eliza Adams, a lovely widow from a nearby ranch, for over eleven months.

At two, Travis was a happy and active child. He was bright, daring, and confident. Mischievous and determined, Calinda was constantly chasing after her small son to keep him out of danger. Travis was frequently seen riding with his parents or keenly witnessing the exciting facets of ranch-life. Even though he was so young and small, Travis Cardone thought nothing of climbing the ladder into the stable loft, or sneaking under the corral fence to get closer to the horses, or unwisely testing the heat of a branding iron out of curiosity, or showing his strength by "helping" with chores.

Often when Travis attempted something too difficult or perilous, Calinda would sigh and shake her head, playfully warning her husband, "Merciful Heavens, Lynx, he's as daring and stubborn as you. But he's also as handsome and smart. His skin's as bronze as yours and his hair is just as tawny. I hate to imagine how many hearts he'll break."

Lynx would chuckle and retort, "But he had your mysterious and expressive green eyes, *mi corazon*. I must confess, he is a handsome and roguish devil already."

"I do wish you'd stop filling his head with all those tales of Rangers and their colorful exploits. If not, he'll join up the moment he's of age. Do you regret leaving the force? Do you miss it?"

Lynx would gaze into her lovely and entreating face

to declare honestly, "Never, *llama de mi corazon*."

Only once, three months ago, had Lynx left home without Calinda. As the dark secrets of the past had unfolded, they had been conquered by their love and serenity. Unexpectedly, a letter had arrived from California, a stunning letter which demanded attention and action. Both Rankin and Lynx had journeyed to San Francisco to sever the last remaining tie to their turbulent past.

In California, a startling tale had awaited the two Cardone men on a windy and chilly March day in '81. Upon arrival, the two men learned that Laura Cardone had died in childbirth in February, alone and probably terrified. As merciful fate would have it, the ailing child had not survived. According to local authorities, Elliott Braxton had vanished six months earlier, proclaimed dead at the hands of hostile Indians in Colorado where he was supposedly checking out a silver claim he'd purchased.

Letters found in Laura's and Elliott's possessions had exposed their ties to the Cardone family in Texas; thus, Rankin and Lynx had been notified of the three deaths and a lingering problem: Carlotta Braxton, eight years old . . .

Laura's body was returned to the Cardone Ranch, to finally and perhaps fatefully occupy that grave on the hillside. While Rankin was discovering and claiming his lost daughter and Lynx was meeting and seeing his sister for the first time, Travis Cardone was celebrating his second birthday, without his father or grandfather . . .

There was no doubt Carlotta "Lottie" Braxton was the daughter of Laura and Rankin. Lottie's hair was as black and shiny as coal; her large eyes were as dark as midnight. An undeniable resemblance to Rankin was stamped on the girl's face. Almost immediately upon returning, Lottie had been officially declared Carlotta Cardone, another heir to this vast and opulent empire.

It hadn't taken long for Calinda to notice several dismaying and saddening facets to this curious child. For the tender age of eight, Lottie was exceptionally mature and disturbingly withdrawn. Calinda realized the girl was slightly spoiled and willful. Lottie had given both Calinda and Travis a difficult time after her arrival. To make matters worse, Rankin overly indulged and excused the audacious child, seeking to make up for her suffering.

Calinda decided she would become just as beguiling as Lottie, to win her affections and trust. Only then could she effect any changes in Lottie. Surely a grown woman could outwit a defiant child? Perhaps Lottie's behavior was defensive. Perhaps Lottie needed correction and instructions. Perhaps Lottie wasn't to blame for her offensive traits and actions.

With time, effort, affection, and patience, Calinda made tremendous progress with the little minx. As time passed, Lottie began viewing Calinda as her big sister. Before summer ended, peace and love ruled on the Cardone Ranch, and the past was dead forever.

When Eliza Adams finally won Lottie's affection and trust, the romance between her and Rankin flourished, The timing was perfect for Calinda to encourage Lynx to build that dream-house on the bluff not far away, the one they had discussed and planned for so long.

With Eliza and Lottie in Rankin's heart and future, perhaps that was a perfect solution for all. They would be close, but not too close.

When Calinda seriously broached the subject of the new house, Lynx was very receptive to the idea. Rankin had been hinting strongly at a new family of his own. Plus, Lynx was noticing some changes in his beloved's body which boldly hinted at another child, and Lynx was eager to point them out to her. Another child with his only love, his first love, his wild and wonderful love . . .